OUTMATCHED

What happens when a boxer finds chemistry with a geek?

Parker Brown can't believe she needs to hire a fake boyfriend. When she landed her dream job in renewable energy, she thought she'd be entering a world at the forefront of progressive thinking. But the head boss prefers to promote employees who are "settled." Thankfully, she's found the perfect candidate, a fellow intellectual looking for some quick cash. What Parker gets is his protective big brother—Rhys Morgan. The tall, muscled ex-boxer with a foul mouth shows up just as her boss does, and now she's stuck with the manipulative jerk.

Responsibility weighs heavily on Rhys. Now permanently out of the ring, he's trying to hold together his late father's gym and keep his younger brother, Dean, on the straight and narrow. To save Dean from himself, Rhys takes his place, ready to give this society girl a piece of his mind. Instead, he finds an opportunity. Even though they can hardly stand each other, posing as

Parker's boyfriend is a win-win deal. She gets to keep her job, and he'll charm her star-struck boss into sponsoring his gym.

Problem is, they can barely keep their hands off each other. And what started as an easy deal isn't so easy anymore. Because what future can a rough ex-boxer, afraid to open his heart, and a polished society geek, who has sworn off real relationships, possibly have?

They say opposites attract. These opposites are about to combust on impact.

Outmatched

A Novel

By Kristen Callihan and Samantha Young

Copyright © 2019 Kristen Callihan and Samantha Young

Edited by Jennifer Sommersby Young
Cover Design By Hang Le

ALSO BY KRISTEN CALLIHAN

Other Adult Contemporary titles by Kristen Callihan

The Game On Series:
The Hook Up
The Friend Zone
The Game Plan
The Hot Shot

VIP Series:
Idol
Managed
Fall

Adult Paranormal Romance titles by Kristen Callihan
Darkest London Series:
Firelight
Ember
Moonglow
Winterblaze

Entwined
Shadowdance
Evernight
Soulbound
Forevermore

ALSO BY SAMANTHA YOUNG

OUTMATCHED

A NOVEL

KRISTEN CALLIHAN

SAMANTHA YOUNG

ONE

Rhys

My DAD once told me that most people didn't intend to ruin their lives; they simply made a series of stupid choices. He'd been in his battered leather chair, wide shoulders hunched over the executive rosewood desk that had been the pride of his office. The same chair I slumped in now, facing the same expansive desk.

Idly, I traced a finger along the edge, the once-gleaming wood now dull and nicked. As a kid, it seemed odd to me that Dad wanted this ornate desk, more suited to a law firm, as the centerpiece of a bare-bones boxing and martial arts gym office. When I'd asked him about it, he'd smiled in that faint way of his.

"Lights Out is my pride and joy, boyo." He'd spread his big, scarred hands over the shining desktop. "Here is where I represent it. Like it or not, appearances matter."

Actions and words counted equal measure in his world. Act decisively, speak your piece with truth, and make good choices.

What would he think of my choices?

"Nothing good," I muttered, then pressed the pads of my fingers to my aching eyes. At the moment, I wasn't thinking much of my dad's choices either.

Dad's been gone for four years. The pain had dulled a little around the edges, but the emptiness remained. It was the fine, hot rage I felt toward him that freaked me out. Dad was never perfect. I'd known that for a long time. After Mom died, he'd fallen down a rabbit hole of his own making. But this shitshow he left on my hands was another story and made it hard to forgive and forget.

Shit, I wasn't allowed to forget. The bank wouldn't let that happen.

I was clueless that my finances and the gym were in so much trouble until the day I found my dad hunched over his desk. The day Dad told me he'd mismanaged my money—a toxic mixture of bad investments and gambling—and that he'd remortgaged the gym to try to cover it.

A month later, Dad was dead. Heart attack, the stress and shame of what he'd done catching up to him in the worst of ways. And I became the new owner of Lights Out, and a mountain of debt.

My jaw locked tight, the rage hitting me again. I wanted to get up, walk away, and never look back. From outside the glass walls of the office came the sound of juvenile laughter. The junior group was practicing capoeira, one of the gym's newest offerings. The classes were all full, but only half of the boys could afford to pay. And while it was my prerogative to turn them away, I knew I'd never do that. This gym was their lifeline in a world that would easily drain their joy and leave them empty shells of their former selves.

"That's a pretty nasty expression you got going." Carlos stood by the door I'd made the mistake of leaving open. A grin split his face. "You find a rash or something?"

"Yeah, right under my balls," I replied without heat. "You want to take a look?"

"I'll leave that to your lady friends."

Carlos knew I hadn't been with any lady friends, as he put it, in a while. Don't get me wrong—the opportunities were there, I just hadn't wanted to take them. I didn't have the stomach for... well, anything lately. First with Dad's fucking debts, then with Jake—I didn't want to think about Jake.

Carlos pushed away from the door and dropped his ass in the chair opposite my desk. "So," he prompted, "what's with the face?"

I rubbed the back of my aching neck. "The usual. Money."

Carlos leaned forward, bracing his arms on his knees, his easy smile gone. Most people never saw Carlos without a smile. Between us, Carlos was considered the happy one, those big brown puppy eyes of his drawing ladies in like honey to bees. He'd played up the role with ease, hiding a darker interior almost no one knew about. That he trusted me enough to show his true self now and then was something I'd never take for granted.

"No change?" he asked.

"Not enough. I'm behind on the mortgage payments by a few months. Bank is breathing down my neck."

"What about this Kyle Garret?"

Six months ago, a guy named Kyle Garret approached me about buying the gym. After looking into him, Carlos and I found out he was a big real estate mogul, buying up property all over Boston and the East Coast and turning it into swank condos and housing developments.

"I'm not that desperate." Okay, I was. But this place had

been everything to me growing up. It was filled with ghosts of my past, and while some of them were painful, others kept me going. All I had to do was walk through the gym, and I'd remember: the juice bar in the lobby where mom would greet Jake, Carlos, and me after school with banana shakes and a big smile. Studio B where Jake and I took our first punches and truly learned why boxing was the Sweet Science.

My brother Dean and I used to hide under Dad's desk and play "spy." Which was to say, Dean would play spy and I'd humor him. That was until the day my parents slipped into the office for a quickie and didn't know we were under there. Some memories aren't pretty, but they were mine and they were all I had left. I wasn't about to lose that too.

Carlos sighed. "You know if you got back into the game, I could set up a match—"

"No." It wasn't a shout but it damn near felt like one in my head. A cold sweat broke out on my lower back as I glared at Carlos. He damn well knew I was out of boxing. For good.

His expression was empathetic. "Look, man, I know. But I don't think Jake would want—"

"I said no."

Just thinking about Jake opened a hole in my chest. Best friends from the cradle, closer to me than my own meathead brother, we'd had each other's backs. Both fighters. Both headed for greatness. Hell, we had greatness in our palms. Until an unlucky hit to the temple ended his life.

A greasy lump of horror and shame slid down my throat. Losing him was hard enough; knowing that Dad lost a crap ton of money because he'd bet on Jake and lost tainted every memory I had of both of them, of boxing.

Jake had left behind his wife Marcy and their baby girl, Rose. Hell, I'd grown up with Marcy, and I hadn't seen her and

Rose in months. Every time I did, guilt and grief crippled me for days.

"I'm done with that game," I told Carlos, though I shouldn't have to. He knew I was done.

The urge to scrub my skin rode me. I showered two hours ago, but I felt unclean, sticky with regret and rage. Dad's shame had somehow transferred onto me and I couldn't rid myself of it.

His smile was weary. "Yeah, I know. But this gym is all I have too. It goes and we all lose our home."

I couldn't sit there anymore. Lurching up, I paced the small space. "We need to bring in more business. No, what we need is a sponsor." And a fucking miracle.

Carlos rubbed his chin and watched me pace. "That could work, but what would the draw be?"

"Fuck if I know." My chest sagged with a sigh. "Tax write-off? The joys of helping inner-city youths?"

Dark humor lit Carlos's eyes. "Your lack of enthusiasm isn't exactly selling me here."

"Because I'm no good at bullshitting. I'm a shit salesman."

"That you are, bro," said a voice from the door.

Dean, my baby brother and expert bullshitter, lounged in the doorway. I honestly didn't know how the fuck we were related. First off, instead of wearing jeans and a shirt like any other guy here, he was dressed in a three-piece suit that I knew cost more than his rent—rent that I paid. The little pissant.

Secondly, he was too fucking pretty. From grade school on, girls cooed over his blue eyes and sandy hair. Prince fucking Charming. I pushed away the thought that he looked like my ma. I missed her daily.

That was the hell of it. I missed too many people.

"What's wrong with you?" Dean asked, ambling into my

office. He stopped short and gave me a wide, fake-ass smile. "Today, I mean."

I shot Carlos a quick, *do not say a damn word* glare. He blinked, and I knew he understood. I kept Dean away from the business troubles. He had potential to be something great—if he ever got his head out of his own ass and got a job.

Carlos stood up and rolled a kink out of his neck. "Rhys has a case of limp dick."

I elbowed Carlos hard enough to knock him sideways. "Get the fuck outta here with that shit. You want to jinx me or something?"

Carlos snorted and looked to Dean. "Got any advice for that, college boy?"

"Thoughts and prayers?"

"You're both hilarious." But our ploy had worked. Dean was distracted.

As soon as Carlos left, I leaned against the edge of my desk and looked Dean over. "What's with the suit? You going on an interview?"

Please let it be that. The boy had a degree in computer science from BU, had aced his MCATS, and had multiple offers from grad schools across the country, but he was floundering, working as a waiter and spending his free time dicking around with women.

He grinned liked it was Christmas morning. "Something like that."

This kid. "It either is an interview or it isn't."

"Oh, I got the job." His grin wouldn't die. "Tonight's more like a trial run."

Fighters rely on instinct, and mine kicked into high gear. "Trial run? What the fuck are you talking about, Deanie?"

His smile fell flat. He hated when I called him Deanie.

"What kind of shifty-ass, suit-wearing job has trial runs?" I pressed when he turned mulish. "Or starts at... six in the evening?"

"Look, I was really excited to tell you about this because it's fucking brilliant. But if you're going to give me shit..."

"Talk. Now."

"Fine." Dean pulled out his phone and headed my way. "I found this wicked cool app where you put in your photo and skill set and it finds you people who are looking to hire."

"That's... good." And yet my hackles stayed up. There was something fishy about his manner.

"So I figure, what the hell, no one is hiring for what I have a degree in now. But I'm good at other things."

"What other things?" This *fucking* kid. Only nine years younger than me and I swore he'd aged me a decade every frickin' year I had to deal with him.

He shrugged. "Like charming women, making them feel good."

Slowly, I stood at full height. "Making women feel good."

"Yeah," he said like I was dense. "I'm brilliant with women."

"What's the job, Dean?"

Oblivious, he tapped on his phone. "So, this app put me in touch with this cute honey, Parker, who... get this... will pay me to be her escort." His eyes lit up. "Isn't that a pissah? I can't believe it. The amount she's willing to pay me is crazy. Easy money and all for doing what comes natural to me. Best part? It's an open-ended deal."

All the blood in my head rushed to my toes before flooding back up in a surge of black heat. "You're prostituting yourself? Is that what I'm hearing?"

Where did I go wrong?

"What?" His blond brows snapped together. "No! I'm an escort. I take Parker out on dates, go with her to functions and parties. Shit like that. I mean, I'm not going to say no if she asks—"

"No. No fucking way." A snarl tore out of me and I clenched my fists. "I did not drop eighty thousand dollars on your education so you could become a rent boy for some snobby rich chick..."

"Oh, right, bring up the fact that you paid my way. Again." He glared at me with hurt in his eyes.

"Because I did!" I ran a hand through my hair and grabbed the short ends. I was liable to tear it out at this point. "I put every cent I had left into this gym and you. I was happy to do it. Thrilled." It had been the least I could do; Dean needed direction, an education, a way out. "I'll be damned if my efforts are flushed down the toilet because of the whims of some vapid, brainless..."

"Hey, Parker is wicked smart. Look at this." He shoved his phone in my face. "She went to MIT..."

I snorted. "Figures."

"And her family is on dozens of different charity boards."

"Which means dick all to me." I took the phone—it was that or have it pushed up my nose—and studied the article he had open. A sweetly pretty girl, about the size of my thumb, with big brown eyes under severely straight brows smiled back at me. It was a strained smile, nothing like the beaming, happy grins the older couple next to her wore. The couple were obviously her parents, and they were all standing on a rolling lawn overlooking the ocean, a massive Cape Cod-style mansion in the background.

"Jesus," I muttered. "They're New Yorkers, Dean."

"So?" He laughed. "What do you have against New Yorkers?"

"The rich ones are assholes."

The article said something about how Mr. and Mrs.

Charles Brown were "summering" on the Cape and fundraising for a children's literacy campaign. Which was nice, but it didn't mean *they* were nice people.

"Didn't peg you for a snob, brother."

I curled my hand around the phone. "Do you know how many of these types I met when I was on the circuit? They're all about wanting to give back to the little people, wanting to be your friend. In reality, they view people like us as fresh meat. We're amusing at best. And when we fail to entertain them any longer, we're gone."

Just ask all the so-called friends who disappeared when Jake died and I'd quit the business.

"Parker isn't like that. She's sweet. Shy, really." Dean's chin kicked up. "And if she wants to use me as her personal pretty-boy puppet in exchange for a boatload of money, I'm going to let her."

"Dean..."

"I told you because I thought... never mind what I thought. Point is, this is my life and my business. I'm going to pay you back my way."

Finally, my baby brother was growing some claws. I'd been more of a father to him than our own for years. With that responsibility came a certain amount of telling him what to do. But I wanted him to fight back, take charge of his life. Just not this way. He was too smart for this. I was the one who rolled around in the muck. Dean needed to stay clean.

I knew that look he wore. He was serious. Nothing would persuade him otherwise. Out of all our differences, in that way we were alike—both of us stubborn to the core.

He turned to go but I held out a hand. "Hold up."

Dean stiffened but waited.

I pocketed his phone, the move so casual he didn't see it. "If you insist on doing this..."

"I *am* doing this."

My back teeth met with a click. *Relax. Take it easy.* "Then you should probably meet her without gunk in between your teeth."

Dean's look of horror would have been funny if I wasn't so pissed. "There's something between my teeth?" He ran his tongue over them.

His teeth were clean, but Dean snacked constantly. The threat was real enough.

"Yep. You didn't get it." I inclined my head toward the private office bathroom. "Go clean yourself up."

He didn't wait to be told twice but hurried toward the small room.

I followed at his heels, grabbing one of the wooden visiting chairs from the side of the desk as I went. He was too distracted to notice. "So, where you meeting this girl?"

"Yvonne's."

"Swank." I'd walked by it once. The place looked like a social club for the ultrarich.

Dean chuckled. "Not like I'm paying."

I rolled my eyes.

"We're having dinner drinks in thirty so I'll have to hustle." At the mirror, he made a grimace, inspecting his commercial-worthy teeth. "I don't see anything..."

I didn't hear the rest. Swiftly, I pulled the door shut, turned the handle down, and wedged the chair under it. Just in time too. The door rattled fiercely.

"Rhys! What the fuck? Open the fucking door!"

Yeah, not likely. It would hold until someone let him out. I'd let Carlos know... In an hour.

"Rhys!" Dean's muffled shout followed me out of the office. "This isn't funny. Are you kidding me?" A hard thud rang out. "You fucking bastard!"

I was. But I didn't feel an ounce of remorse. Dean was too good for this. He could hate me all he wanted. But I would make it crystal clear to this Parker Brown that she wasn't going to go anywhere near my brother again.

A fine fury worked its way through my system as I got on my bike. Parker Brown. She wasn't going to know what hit her.

TWO

Parker

It wasn't my first time dining at Yvonne's. However, it would be my first time dining at Yvonne's with the guy I'd paid to pretend to be my date. My stomach roiled as I sat on the plush bar stool closest to the entrance. Opposite the bar ran a long, marble-topped, low divider wall between the bar area and the restaurant, where chatter and laughter from the diners had become white noise.

I was so short my feet dangled off the bar stool, and I impatiently kicked against a bar that probably cost more than my annual salary.

Speaking of which... I glanced nervously at my watch. Dean was supposed to be here already. We'd arranged for him to come ten minutes earlier than my boss and his boss so we could go over our game plan again.

Throwing back the cocktail the harassed bartender had put

down in front of me, I tried to quell the aggressive flutter of butterflies in my belly. Seriously, it felt like they'd escaped my gut, swarmed all over my lungs, and were now intent on suffocating me. I wiped a clammy hand across my forehead. "Get it together, Parker," I muttered, probably looking and sounding like I was about to commit a felony.

Was lying to your boss a felony?

No, definitely not.

Immoral?

Yes, definitely yes.

But really it just proved how much I loved my job and just how far I was willing to go to get a permanent contract with Horus Renewable Energy. I'd joined the fledgling three-year-old company after I'd earned my PhD in "Dynamic Modeling of Generation Capacity Investment in Electricity Markets with High Wind Penetration." Say that five times fast.

I was ecstatic to find a job as a data analyst with a company that had developed a market dispatch model that forecast future power prices and the impact of renewable power generation of market dynamics.

It was everything I'd ever wanted out of a job and I was feeling good about it until Pete in payroll told me with a smug smirk that I was only hired to meet the diversity quota and I'd probably be let go after my six-month contract was up.

And why?

Because the big boss with all the money, the main investor, Mr. Franklin Fairchild, was only interested in hiring employees who had proven their commitment in their personal lives. It was some 1950s retro bullcrap. Unless an employee was in a serious relationship/married, a parent and/or living in their own home and not a rental, Fairchild considered them a bad investment. Where was the commitment? If we couldn't commit in our personal lives, surely we'd up and run from the company at the first sign of a sweeter deal elsewhere.

I'd also verified with more reliable sources than Pete that it was correct.

Being the only single, childless female analyst who sharing a rented apartment with a roommate, I freaked out. Said roommate, Zoe, offered me the solution in the form of an app. I found Dean on the app, the perfect fake boyfriend. He was educated, from Chelsea, down-to-earth, charming, good-looking, and he'd agreed to pretend to be my boyfriend for an indefinite period. *Indefinite.*

Seriously, what was I worried about?

No one would ever find out.

"You." A deep voice said at my side. The tone was accusatory.

I turned my head and blinked rapidly against the sight in front of me. A very tall man glowered at me, nostrils flared, like a bull getting ready to charge. My eyes dipped down his body and back up again, thinking I'd never seen a specimen like him up close before. The guy was at least three inches over six feet, dressed in jeans that had seen better days and a long thermal shirt that showed a very defined muscular build. Very defined. His shirtsleeves were rolled up, showing off thickly veined forearms. Didn't Yvonne's have a dress code?

I looked into what would have been beautiful green eyes if they hadn't been glaring at me. At me?

What the heck? I didn't have time for miscreants right now. "Can I help you?"

"Parker Brown?"

Oh crap.

"Yes?"

His eyes narrowed. "I'm Rhys Morgan. Dean's big brother. He's not coming."

For a moment, I could only stare. How could this guy be Dean's big brother? Dean was fair-haired and blue eyed, clean-cut and handsome in a pretty way. This guy had close-cropped dark hair, the aforementioned gorgeous green eyes, needed to shave a few days ago, and with his rugged, angular features and broken nose, definitely not a pretty boy. I guess some women might find him appealing but he was too big and rough for me.

I liked my guys nerdy and cute.

Anyhoo, back to my point... I snapped my attention away from the impressive definition in his biceps. "You don't look anything alike."

His nostrils flared again. "Yeah, we're nothing alike. I wouldn't let some uptown Masshole prostitute me."

My cheeks burned as I glanced around in horror. Loud! Wow, he was loud! I hopped off the stool and pressed my hands to his chest to push him toward the exit but stopped. He had *pecs*. "Oh, those are well developed." I dropped my hands like they'd been burned.

Dean's supposed brother grit his teeth in obvious agitation.

"Let's talk a little away from the bar." I led him around the corner to the hallway between the entrance and the restaurant, giving a tight "All is okay here" smile to a passing host. Turning around to face Rhys, I almost smacked right into his chest.

He took hold of my biceps and gently pushed me away from him. Off the stool, I had to tilt my head back to meet his gaze, and as he towered over me, I suddenly wondered if it was a bad idea to engage in any kind of conversation with an angry man who could crush me like a bug between his two big paws. However, I would not be easily intimidated. Okay, sure, this guy was intimidating, but I'd studied in a male-dominated field for years. Now I was the only woman in the company I worked for. I'd learned quickly to not let any guy, no matter how smart or physically impressive he was, *see* that I was intimidated.

Or discombobulated by him.

Even if I was.

"First, I'm not from Massachusetts." I didn't know why that was important, but I really hated the term "Masshole," which referred to the rich blue bloods around here who weren't very nice.

Rhys sneered. "You're a New Yorker who summers." He pronounced *summers* like "summahs" with a thick Boston accent I normally found adorable. There was nothing adorable about this guy. "Same fucking difference, Tinker Bell."

Ugh. There was so much to hate in that last sentence. "Please don't curse." My mother nagged swear words out of my vocabulary before I even got the chance to fully explore their usage. Consequently, discomfort was a knee-jerk reaction to unwarranted curse words. "And mocking my height is extremely rude."

"You know what's extremely rude?" He stepped right into my personal space, forcing me to crane my neck to keep eye contact. "Hiring a desperate kid to service your needs."

I was certain my whole body turned as red as a bull flag. For a moment, I could only splutter. "That-that-that is so not what I did," I hissed. "For a start, he's not a kid. He's twenty-five years old. Moreover, I am not paying him to 'service my needs.' I'll thank you to not insult me by assuming that I need to pay for *that*."

He dragged his gaze over my body and grunted.

"I'm going to ignore whatever that noise meant since *I've* evolved beyond the Tertiary Period. Back to my point: Dean is a grown-up and I hired him to escort me to dates and events that involved my colleagues and my boss. Without going into the details, I need my bosses to think I'm in a committed relationship so they'll consider hiring me for a permanent position. Mr. Fairchild is a little old-fashioned that way." There. That was very diplomatic. I beamed at myself. It was the first time I'd described the situation without calling Mr. Fairchild a plague on women's rights.

Rhys scowled. "Wipe the smile off your face, Tinker Bell. I could give two New York-sized shits why you hired Dean. It was fucking wrong and you know it."

Anxiety and hurt mingled as I glared up at my accuser. Had hiring Dean been wrong? I'd thought it was mutually beneficial. At no point had I felt like I was taking advantage of or using him, but his brother was making it seem that way. Like I was a privileged princess who thought I could do whatever I liked because I had money.

I crossed my arms over my chest. "I refuse to stand here and be made to feel like I did something wrong. If you're upset by your brother's choices, that's your problem, because he did have a choice and he was being well compensated. Two thousand dollars a week to go on a few dates throughout said month is more than fair." It was ludicrous. I'd had to dip into my trust fund for it. But no guy was willing to be my fake boyfriend for an indefinite amount of time without excellent compensation.

Not that I was tragically unattractive or had an awful personality. It's just that most people needed an end date because they had other commitments. I couldn't give them an end date just yet.

Rocking back on his heels at the sum, Rhys seemed momentarily struck dumb.

Good, because I needed him gone! "Look, Mr. Morgan, my bosses will be here any minute so I would really appreciate you leaving. Now. Now would be good." I indicated the door behind me. "Bye-bye." He didn't move. "Adios?" Still staring at me. "Vámonos. Ciao. Au revoir." I sighed heavily. "*Shoo.*"

He scowled. "Did you just shoo me?"

"Only if it worked."

"Darlin', you're cracked in the head. Anyone ever tell you that?"

"Look—"

"Parker, there you are!"

I squeezed my eyes shut, wishing a door to a multidimensional would open so I could shove Rhys Morgan into its dark depths and hope he ended up in a world of giant sand snakes.

My boss had arrived.

Opening my eyes, I turned, pasting on a bright smile as Jackson Sánchez, my boss, strolled toward me with Mr. Fairchild on one side and Jackson's fiancée, Camille, on the other.

My stomach lurched.

When Jackson said Mr. Fairchild wanted to meet the newest member of the team (that would be me), I'd promised him I was bringing my boyfriend, knowing I needed to impress Fairchild. Not only did I feel bad about lying to Jackson, whom I genuinely liked and admired, I now was without said boyfriend. Because of the caveman at my side. A caveman who was quite possibly going to blurt out what I'd done and ruin any chance I had of extending my contract with Horus. In fact, I'd probably get fired.

Where was a sand snake dimension when you needed one?

The three of them crowded in around us and I swear those butterflies returned with a fury, definitely intent on suffocating the life out of me.

I was so doomed.

"Mr. Fairchild, this is our newest and most impressive recruit, Parker Brown." Jackson grinned at me.

I held out my hand to Mr. Fairchild.

Franklin Fairchild was from Boston's old money. He'd taken what he'd inherited as a young man and quadrupled it by investing it wisely. By his own admission, he was surrounded by a great team of advisors. It was those same advisors that told him renewable energy was a smart place to invest.

He wasn't particularly green, which chafed a little, as he had way more input in the company than I'd thought a guy like him would have time for.

Fairchild shook my hand, an aggressive, energetic pump up and down. "Tiny woman, big brain, huh?" He laughed.

Oh yeah, like I'd never heard that one before. My smile was pained. When Jackson turned to Rhys, my smile was paralyzed with agony.

"And this must be the boyfriend." Jackson couldn't hide the surprise on his face. Of course he was surprised! Rhys was not at all what anyone would expect of me and I certainly knew I wasn't Rhys Morgan's type. A guy like him probably dated women with massive breasts and asses honed to defy gravity from daily squat thrusts.

My mouth was opening, the word *no* about to spill out in great vehemence when—

"Yeah." Rhys held out a hand to shake Jackson's. "I'm Parker's boyfriend. Rhys. How's it going?"

I think my brain was having a signaling issue because I thought I just heard him say he was my boyfriend.

Rhys smirked at me, the devil dancing in those disarming eyes.

He did!

He most assuredly did!

What the heck was he up to?

I was going to vomit. I was going to vomit all over Mr. Fairchild's Prada loafers.

"Rhys?" Mr. Fairchild practically bulldozed past Jackson to get to my tormentor. "Rhys Morgan, I'll be damned."

Wait, what?

I watched Fairchild pump Rhys's hand, grinning at him like

he was the second coming, and then felt the floor disappear beneath me when he turned to Jackson and said, "You didn't tell me Parker was dating Rhys Morgan."

At our blank expressions, Fairchild guffawed. "He's only the best goddamn heavyweight boxer this country has seen in a generation." He clamped a hand down on Rhys's shoulder. "You're sitting with me, son."

What?

As Mr. Fairchild led Dean's brother into the restaurant, Rhys looked over his shoulder at me and winked.

Actually winked.

Ugh, he *was* the devil.

In all my sand-snake dimension wishing, had I inadvertently wished open a gate to another dimension where an angry boxer just lied to my bosses about dating me?

Jackson and Camille grinned. "Guess who just became teacher's pet," Jackson teased. At my frown, he laughed. "I'm kidding. But it's always great to keep Fairchild interested at these dinners. This is good, Parker."

No.

This was a disaster.

THREE

Rhys

WHAT THE HELL was I doing? Though I ambled at apparent ease by Fairchild's side, it felt like I was hurtling downhill on a runaway cart. I didn't want to be here. I sure as hell didn't want to be arm candy for an entitled—albeit cute—rich chick. Yet here I was, walking through a restaurant that looked more like an exclusive gentlemen's club library.

Patrons watched us pass, more than one set of eyes lingering on my ripped jeans and scuffed work boots. This was a place for suits and silks, not rough and scruff.

The responsible side of me was saying get out, turn around and get the hell out now, that this was a disaster in the making. Unfortunately, I lived my life listening to the hothead inside who said let it ride. Plus, there was the bonus of Parker Brown glaring a hole through my back with each step I took.

She was a piece of work with her outraged protestations of

innocence. That she somehow managed to look down her cute nose at me even though the top of her head barely reached my shoulder was a true talent. Little Miss Priss had actually shooed me. It would have been adorable if she hadn't been trying to buy my brother's services.

Even though I was laughing it up with Fairchild, pretending to listen to him ramble on about boxing stats, my awareness was attuned to Parker the same way it would have been if we were opponents about to enter the ring. Yeah, you worked the audience into a frenzy by talking yourself up, but what you were really doing was psyching out the competition.

And Parker Brown was rattled. I swore I heard her mutter something about sand snakes, whatever that meant. Her ire amused me.

When I saw her picture, I thought she'd crumble as quickly as dry toast when I told her off. I thought she was mildly pretty. I'd been wrong on both counts. Sure, she'd been flustered and blushed a nice deep pink, but she hadn't folded. And her picture hadn't done her justice.

A pixie with delicate bones and fine features, her skin was porcelain smooth, glowing with good health, her dark brown eyes too big for her heart-shaped face. I didn't go for women like her. I liked a good, sweaty fuck to take the edge off. I'd be afraid I'd break Parker. Hell, I could probably span the woman's waist with my hands.

I shook off thoughts of holding that slim waist steady as I... No. No. No. *Discipline, Morgan. Use your fucking discipline.*

"Rhys Morgan, I'll be damned," Fairchild said for the tenth time, his level of enthusiasm never waning. "Could have knocked me over with a feather when I saw you standing there."

A simple uppercut would have knocked him over. Though he was fairly tall and appeared to be in reasonable shape, he had a glass jaw look about him—surface tough guy who'd talk a good game, then fold under the first sign of any real physical threat. That said, he obviously thought he was the man.

He strode through the space as though he owned it. Maybe he did. The guy oozed wealth, from his gray bespoke Savile Row suit to his fine Italian leather loafers. I once had the means to buy those things and strut around like an overpuffed peacock. But those days were best forgotten.

Unfortunately, I was in for a walk down memory lane with Fairchild. He clasped my shoulder and gave it a shake and a squeeze. "Where have you been, son?"

Only one person had the right to call me son, and he was dead. I gritted my teeth and shrugged lightly, dislodging his grip. "Here and there."

The pretty hostess stopped at a table in a secluded corner. She pulled out a chair and Fairchild smoothly sat down before Parker could. All class, this guy.

I turned and gave my "date" a smile with teeth before pulling out another chair. "Sweetheart?"

Glossy dark eyes shot sparks of pure rage at me as she returned my smile—it was more of a grimace, honestly—and took the proffered seat with the easy grace of someone born to money.

"Thank you."

Butter wouldn't melt in that mouth.

Like that, I imagined her mouth slick and soft and melting on my... *Discipline, damn it!* No way in hell was I going to allow myself to be attracted to Ms. Parker Brown, Fifth Avenue princess.

She was nothing more than a possible solution to my current problems. Because, as much as I hated to agree with Dean, a couple thousand dollars a week for pretending to be her boyfriend was easy, much-needed money. And, in a stroke of rare but brilliant insight, it occurred to me that I could kill two birds with one stone here. Fairchild was a fan and fucking loaded, which made him a potential sponsor for the gym. I only had to convince him of it.

Otherwise, I'd chalk the night up as an opportunity to rattle Parker Brown's chain as payback for attempting to buy my brother. Then I was out of here and out of her life.

Clearing my throat, I sat in the chair next to hers. But Fairchild scowled with all the petulance of a spoiled kid. "I thought I said you were sitting with me, Rhys. Ms. Brown, change seats."

Parker paled, her pink lips parting and working like a confused fish, and I already knew, from the fire she spit at me earlier, she was battling between telling him to piss off and doing the thing that would earn her greater job security.

I was almost willing to let her suffer, but my mom didn't raise me that way. Besides, Fairchild was an asshole. I might have needed his money, but if I lay down like a mat for him to walk on, he'd have zero respect for me.

Leaning forward, I pinned him with a stare even though my smile was easy. "I can converse with you just fine where I am, Fairchild. Besides, I like having my honey close to me."

I slung my arm over Parker's slim shoulders and gave her a loving squeeze. A gurgle escaped her. She covered it up by smiling wide and pained as she leaned into my embrace, the picture of a loving girlfriend. But under the table, a spiked heel pressed down on the toe of my boot. Hard.

When I didn't wince or move away, her brown gaze flicked to mine.

I grinned at her. *Steeled-toed boots, honey. That's what you get for tussling with a blue collar.* Her sidelong glare promised retribution later. I was looking forward to it. Far too much. She was fun to rile. But it was a mistake touching her; the scent of roses and something richly smoky floated from silky soft skin. Some twisted part of me wanted to lean closer and take a deep breath, fill my lungs with that strange mix of innocence and sin.

What the hell was I going on about? Innocence and sin? Who the fuck said that? God, this chick was messing with my mind. I dropped my arm and sat back in my seat. Jackson took the chair opposite.

The waitress arrived to take drink orders—I was the only one who asked for a beer, something that had Parker's lips compressing. It wasn't as though I was dipping into the hard stuff like Fairchild, who had asked for a Macallan 25, neat. I might not know much, but I knew a glass of that would set him back at least two hundred dollars here. She should have been happy I'd stuck to my five-dollar draft beer.

As soon as the waitress left, Franklin was at it again. "Still can't believe you quit, Morgan. Oh, I understand about losing your father." He waved a hand as if to bat that inconvenience away. "But you could have simply taken a mourning break."

The official story I'd given the world—and Dean—was that when Dad died, I'd lost heart and had decided to focus on my family. It was true for the most part, and it seemed like the best reason to give, because I would be damned if I brought Jake into the mix. No one would get anymore of him at my expense.

Now, Fairchild was in my face, demanding more. I grinned with teeth that wanted to take a bite. "I don't regret my decision. I've moved on to better things."

"Better things?" He scoffed. "Nothing could beat stepping into the ring and annihilating your opponent."

I was pretty sure punching this guy in the mouth would beat that. But I gave him an idle shrug in response and said nothing more.

Thankfully, Jackson became Mr. Manners—probably

trying to cover for my refusal to bend to Fairchild's will—and changed the subject.

"Franklin," he said, "I'm so glad you're finally meeting Parker. Her suggestions for our forecast model have made significant improvements to it, which has led to interest from a *huge* client in the European market—"

Fairchild made a derisive noise and waved a hand, cutting Jackson off. "In my day, you played the field based on your gut, not fancy computer software."

Parker recoiled at his verbal hit. And I had the impulse to throw a punch for her. But like any good fighter, she took the strike, then pushed back, tensing and straightening her spine.

Her smile was cool water. "I agree, Mr. Fairchild. Nothing tops the power of well-honed instincts." She kept her voice carefully modulated, totally unrattled. "The true purpose of my job is to provide information to back up that instinctual drive by taking numerous factors—hourly energy demands, wholesale power prices, generation mix,"—she waved an elegant hand as if to say this was all elementary shit—"and factoring in such variables as the proportion of power generated from renewable sources, and cross-border power flows for several European markets, and condensing that information into reports and data tools."

We were all staring at her now, enthralled by her ice cream voice and gentle confidence. And she knew it.

"With that," she said, "our clients have a clearer picture on how to proceed in various avenues."

It was obvious she could go on and on but she stopped then, resting her hands on the table, and stared back at Fairchild with those brown doe eyes.

I wanted to laugh or maybe clap. This wasn't the flustered harpy I'd been arguing with, or even the nervous Nelly I'd seen at the bar, tapping her toe in an agitated rhythm as she waited for Dean. This Parker knew her shit and wasn't going to be cowed.

Unfortunately, Fairchild blinked as though he was coming out of a fog and gave her a bland look before turning to Jackson. "Well, she can talk, that's for sure."

Jackson looked like he wanted to kick Fairchild. Parker just looked kicked.

Fairchild's watery gazed settled on me and a smile lit his weathered face. "Whatever gets the job done, eh?"

Like I was supposed to chuckle in agreement? Fuck, I was supposed to charm this dickhead. I'd have to walk a fine line between agreeing and pushing back.

I shrugged. "I've never underestimated the importance of having the best on my team."

Fairchild chuckled and gave me a broad wink. "You're being modest. Rhys 'Widowmaker' Morgan doesn't need anything but a good one-two punch to knock out his opponents."

Widowmaker. Inside, I recoiled, feeling slightly sick. When I was in the circuit, I'd assumed the title the press gave me with pride. It was a mark of distinction to be given a nickname. Then Jake died. Jake, who left behind Marcy and their infant daughter, Rose. I hadn't been responsible for Jake's death, but I sure as hell didn't want to be called a widowmaker now.

My shoulders felt too tight. I rolled them and took a sip of water. "There's nothing like a good knockout hit..." *Let me demonstrate. Pretty please?* "But I wouldn't have had the skills without my trainers." I leaned toward Parker until our shoulders touched. A sizzle of heat licked along my arm. *Damn it. Focus.* "And lately, I've come to realize the love of a good woman makes everything better."

I was going to gag on my own words. And if the sound Parker made under her breath was any indication, she was already gagging. But I gazed down at her anyway, the very picture of a smitten fool. "Parker here is the best."

Fuck, I sounded like a tool. I wanted to kick my own ass.

But I knew guys like Fairchild. He admired me for my boxing. But part of him would also hate himself for that admiration because he saw it as a weakness. I had to show him a little weakness in return. A small feint to reel him in, make him feel superior, followed by a little jab to keep him on his toes. Fairchild's ilk liked a challenge, but not one that was too hard.

It was a dance I hated playing. But I'd do it for the gym. For Dean, even though he'd never appreciate it. But most importantly, to pay the mortgage on the gym and not have to resort to selling the place to someone who'd tear it down and slap up gentrified condos. Besides, Parker Brown—despite the enormity of her gorgeous brain—was in over her head here. She didn't need Dean. He'd have fucked this up already by irritating the hell out of Fairchild. She needed me.

"Isn't that right, sweetheart?" I asked, wrapping an arm around her once again, and giving into the urge to nuzzle her hair. God, she smelled good. I'd have to get used to that. And the way touching her made my dick immediately perk up.

Down, boy.

She smiled so tight and fake, I wanted to laugh. Her hand came down on my thigh—way too close to said dick. Pale pink nails sank into my flesh, her grip hard enough to feel even through my jeans.

That's a bite I'll be feeling later. She really was cute in an angry pixie sort of way.

"You're too sweet, lumpy," she gritted out.

Lumpy? I huffed a small laugh.

"You two been together long?" Fairchild asked as the waitress set down our drinks.

"Feels like forever," Parker said lightly.

"I admit, I'm surprised to see you here," Fairchild went on, taking a sip of his Scotch. "The whole time you were fighting, you always had a new lady on your arm." He chuckled. "I remember one fight, Morgan showed up with three women," he said to Jackson. "One on each arm and one leading the way to the ring."

This fucking guy.

I wanted to meet Parker's gaze and give her a commiserating look. Not that I thought she'd appreciate it right now; the woman was tight as a drum and nearly vibrating with irritation. "Eh, well... when you know, you know."

I saluted Parker with my beer before taking a deep pull. I didn't know shit about romantic love. But for a chance to save everything I *did* love, I'd fake it. With that, I leaned forward, bracing my forearms on the table—much to Miss Priss's evident dismay.

"Forget the women," I told Fairchild. "Did you ever hear the story about the time I met Donny Douglas for an underground fight?"

As expected, Fairchild's eyes lit up. "I didn't. When was this?"

Hook, line, and sinker. I launched into the story, knowing it would keep Fairchild entertained, that with each word, he'd want me around more—and Parker by extension. Yeah, she needed me. She just didn't know it yet. But she would.

FOUR

Parker

I SHIVERED in the chilly late spring night, my heart thumping in my chest as I watched Rhys talk in undertones with Mr. Fairchild. Jackson and Camille had already left. Finally, Fairchild got into his Town Car, and I narrowed my gaze on Rhys as he sauntered back over to me.

He walked with the swagger of a man who'd just won a boxing bout.

The big jerk.

"So, I just saved your ass." He had the audacity to grin.

The anger that had been slow-cooking in my gut since we'd all sat down to dinner threatened to boil over. If I stayed here one more second, I would eviscerate him with the power of my mind.

I was sure of it.

There was no way a person could be *this* angry with

someone without that energy manifesting itself. I abruptly turned away from Yvonne's and began walking south toward the apartment I shared with my best friend Zoe. It was thirty minutes by foot, which should give me some time to walk off my uncharacteristic rage.

"I'll walk you home and we can discuss terms." Rhys fell into step beside me.

Bafflement overtook the fury. "Excuse me?"

He shrugged. "You still need someone to pretend to be your boyfriend, right? And I think I can say with certainty that Fairchild thinks I'm the shit."

Yes, Fairchild definitely thought Rhys was the poo. Of course he would. They were both Neanderthals. I gritted my teeth, frustrated that my short legs could never out-stride the tall boxer beside me. A boxer, for goodness' sake!

Not that I didn't appreciate boxing. Any competitive sport demonstrated discipline, determination, and skill. Those were all good qualities.

No, the boxing didn't bother me.

It explained the muscles and the broken nose.

What bothered me was the sycophantic bromance that had developed between Rhys and Fairchild. He never outright agreed with any of the backward, bordering-on-misogynistic bull-twaddle that came out of my boss's mouth, but Rhys also hadn't outright disagreed.

For most of the evening, Jackson, Camille, and I had to listen to Rhys entertain Fairchild with stories of his glory days as a boxer. It wasn't that the stories weren't somewhat interesting; it was just that they opened the door for Fairchild's commentary. And his toxic masculinity.

The whole point of the dinner was to show Fairchild I was an important addition to the team. All he cared about was Rhys.

"You derailed my dinner," I seethed.

"Derailed it?" Rhys huffed. "Anytime Jackson brought up the subject of renewable energy, Fairchild's eyes glazed over. You should thank me for keeping the guy interested enough to stay through the entire meal."

"Yes, I so enjoyed him constantly grilling you about how much blood you've spilled and how many women you've bedded. That's what I always look for in my dinner conversation."

"Hey, it's not my fault your boss has no manners. The point is, I kept his interest. The guy loves me."

Ugh, unfortunately true.

"It seems to me if you want this guy to keep you around, then the way to do that is to pay me the two thousand dollars a week to be your fake boyfriend. He wants me around and where you go, I go, right?"

I stumbled to a halt, the anger mixing with frustration because I knew there was logic in his proposal. He was absolutely correct. And I hated it. "I don't know you from Adam."

The muscle in his jaw ticked. "Like you know my brother from Adam? Or is the difference that he has a degree and I'm an uneducated meathead who runs a gym?"

Why did he deliberately try to see the worst in me? "You are very prejudiced."

Rhys's expression darkened. "Tinker Bell, like you said, you don't fucking know me."

"Don't curse at me." I crossed my arms over my chest, refusing to be intimidated by him even though my legs were shaking a little at the idea of agreeing to his proposal. "I'm hardly going to hire a guy who hates me because I grew up with money."

He exhaled heavily, his earlier tension seeming to dissolve.

"Tinker Bell," he said, his tone softer, "I don't fucking know you either. How can I hate you?"

Tinker Bell. Is that how he saw me? Tiny, spoiled, and ill-tempered? Ouch. Wrinkling my nose, I began walking again. "Don't call me Tinker Bell."

"Do we have a deal?" Rhys persisted as he fell into step beside me again.

I cut him a look. "Why do you want to do this?"

There went that muscle in his jaw again. Tick, tick, ticking. "I need the money," he bit out.

As if that was something to be ashamed of?

Still, Dean needed the money because he was unemployed. Why did an ex-professional boxer who owned a gym need money? I wouldn't be involved in anything nefarious. I said as much to him.

He grimaced. "It's nothing criminal. Jesus Christ. All the money I earned boxing went to my family, to Dean's education, and other shit they needed. Now the gym isn't doing great and the extra cash could help inject some new life into it."

"You paid for your brother's college education?"

He grunted; I took that as confirmation.

The anger inside me simmered a little. A guy who spent his earnings on his little brother's education couldn't be all bad, right? It was actually kind of sweet.

I considered him. "If we do this, I'll need you to be flexible with your schedule. You must be able to attend events and dinners at the drop of a hat. That was the deal with Dean."

Rhys looked down at me with those too-beautiful eyes and nodded. "Deal."

I bit my lip, hesitating over making it official. Dean was so easy-going and charming, I'd been instantly relaxed in his company. The thought of playacting a romantic relationship with him hadn't bothered me in the least.

I surreptitiously looked over his big brother as he strolled down the street at my side, hands in his jeans' pockets, impatiently waiting for my answer. Butterflies fluttered to life in my belly and the slight tremble in my legs returned as I imagined pretending to be Rhys's girlfriend over the next few months.

The man was rough, obnoxious, cursed way too much, and he had the ability to piss me off, which was hard to do. That Fairchild liked him wasn't much of an endorsement either.

And yet it was the latter that would persuade me to say yes.

"Fine, but I want you to sign a contract."

"Did Dean have to sign a contract?"

"No. But then Dean never ambushed me for the job either."

"You tried to prostitute my kid brother. I'm not going to apologize for my behavior."

The flame of outrage smoldered to life once more. "For the hundredth time, I did not try to prostitute your brother!"

A bark of laughter from across the street made me tense, and I watched the couple who'd overheard me stare at us as they chuckled their way out of earshot.

I colored and glowered up at Rhys as if it were his fault.

The big jerk grinned. "Maybe you should learn to control that temper, Tinker Bell. It's going to get you in trouble one of these days."

There was a possibility I'd kill him before we ever signed a contract.

"I did not try to prostitute Dean," I said quietly. "And while we're on the subject, that's not what this is about. You realize there will be no actual sex happening between us?"

"Don't worry, small fry, you're not my type."

Indignation and hurt pride made me sneer. "As if you're mine."

Rhys flicked me a dirty look. "Yeah, I think we both know

I'm not your type. Now that that's sorted, do we have a deal or what?"

It occurred to me Rhys was something of a contradiction. "Why is it okay for you to 'prostitute' yourself and not Dean?"

His brow furrowed. "Didn't we just confirm this isn't prostitution?"

"Don't be obtuse."

"Look, my brother didn't go to college to piss that education down the toilet making easy money escorting you to an event every now and then. He needs to focus on finding a career. *I* have a career—I run a gym. I need money for that gym. Doing this brings in that money. End of story. Now, do we have a deal?"

"Contract first."

He sighed, scrubbing a hand over his unshaven jaw. "Fine."

Oh dear lord in heaven, was I going to do this?

"You all right?" He squinted at me. "You look a little pale."

"That occurs with hypotension caused by a drop in blood pressure and that happens when you go into shock, which is what I'm sure is happening to me right now." I flicked a weary hand at him. "Deal with the devil and all that."

"Anyone ever tell you you're cracked in the head?"

"Yes," I huffed. "You. This evening. Before you hijacked my life."

"Saved your ass, you mean." He winked at me.

"Morgan, I'm putting no winking in the contract. No winking, no calling me Tinker Bell, and no cursing." I drew to a halt, not far from my building, and narrowed my gaze. "Do you recycle?"

Rhys looked at me like I really *was* cracked. "Who doesn't?"

"Oh, you'd be surprised. So that's a yes?"

He shrugged impatiently. "Yeah, of course I recycle."

"Do you have a 'honk if you like' sticker on your car?"

His brow furrowed. "No..."

I sighed in relief. Okay, maybe we could do this. "Where's your gym? I'll bring the contract around this weekend."

"It's called Lights Out, just off Fourth in Chelsea. I'm usually free during lunchtime."

I nodded, wondering at the name. It sounded more like a nightclub than a gym. "All right. I'll drop by Saturday afternoon." I moved to walk around him.

"I'm still walking you home."

"You don't need to do that."

"And yet here I am doing it." He gave me another boyish grin that caused those butterflies to flutter again. I felt outmaneuvered, and I couldn't remember the last time someone had made me feel vulnerable, like I had little control over the situation.

Oh man. This guy was such a bad idea.

We walked the rest of the way to my building in silence, shooting each other wary looks (okay, mine were wary; his were deliberately provoking) as we strolled.

Finally, we turned onto Harrison Avenue, where Zoe, my college roommate and bestie, owned a modern, two-bedroom apartment bought for her by her wealthy absentee father. She let me stay there for less than half the actual rent the room would normally cost. It was great. I got to stay in a nice place, in pricey Back Bay, and the bonus? It had nothing to do with my parents.

If I'd gotten an apartment I could afford on my salary, I'd be living well outside the city in a place my parents would disapprove of. That would have caused me anxiety, they would have constantly plagued me to use my trust fund on a nicer place, and my stubborn refusal to do so would have caused a rift between us, thus leading to more anxiety on my part because I hated disappointing my parents as much as I hated relying on their money.

Thankfully, Zoe didn't want to live alone and begged me to take her second bedroom.

Win-win.

"This is me." I stopped outside the glass-fronted reception. Lights blazed inside, showcasing the marble floors and expensive furnishings of the huge reception space.

I glanced at Rhys. His expression had flattened. "Figures," he muttered.

I frowned, wondering why he was so prejudiced against people with money. He hadn't seemed that way with Fairchild, and he had more money than God. Shuddering at the thought, I huffed. "Well, good night, then."

There was no boyish grin this time. Instead he gave me a curt nod before walking away.

"Oh yeah, he's Prince Charming all right." I hauled open the reception door, wondering what the heck I'd just gotten myself into.

Rhys

"WAKEY, WAKEY, ASSHOLE!"

The shout barely broke through the fog of sleep when the slap of cold water hit. All over. A gasp of shock tore from my throat, and I lurched up, already swinging.

Dean, smart little fucker that he was, had made sure to stay out of striking range. He stood by the bedroom door, empty bucket in hand, smirking. "Sleeping naked, Rhys? I'd pegged you for a tighty-whitie type."

With a roar, I launched out of bed. He dropped the bucket and ran—saved by the fact that I wasn't about to chase my brother down buck-ass naked. Cursing, I wiped off my face and reached for a pair of sweats. The little fucker was going to get it.

My feet pounded the floorboards. I hadn't heard him leave my loft, so I knew he was somewhere. So, not as smart as I'd thought he was.

He stood in the kitchen, one of Mom's coffee mugs in hand, sipping as though he had all the time in the world to live.

"Asshole," I snarled, rubbing a hand through my hair, water droplets scattering. "You think holding on to Mom's mug is going to stop me from beating your ass?"

He shrugged. "I know you don't want to risk breaking it."

"Then you better hold onto it for the rest of your short life," I said as I strolled up. When he started to smile, I struck. A lightning-quick but light jab. Dean let out a grunt, the cup slipping as he touched his busted lip.

I caught the cup in my other hand before he could blink and took a much-needed sip of coffee. Unfortunately, it was loaded with sugar. Grimacing, I set it down on the counter and eyed my scowling brother.

"Asshole," he muttered. "Fucking *fast* asshole."

"At least I pulled the punch. I'm guessing that little show..." I nodded toward the bedroom, "was for last night?"

A flush of rage colored his cheeks. "You're damn right it was. I was stuck in there for over an hour, not to mention I missed my date with Parker, who won't answer my calls, by the way."

Interesting. The thought of Parker made me smile. For reasons I didn't want to dwell on.

Dean saw the smile and glared. "You're such a dick."

"I know." I shrugged. "But I warned you that plan of yours wasn't going to happen."

He gave me a pleasant look, the kind we used to give Great Uncle Morty when he'd do ventriloquist impressions with his false teeth in hand. "I'm not sure if you've realized this, but you're not actually my father. He's dead and I'm a goddamn adult."

"I'm as good as, and have been for years." Waving him off, I went to get my own coffee. "I'm not rehashing it, Dean. It's done. Your job opportunity is gone."

"You don't know that." He pressed his hands on the counter, bracing himself. "I'll explain to Parker—"

"It's done. Use that fancy-ass education your big brain earned and go get a true job. Make your life happen." I quirked a brow. "And then you can pay me all your back rent."

"If you cared so much about me paying rent, you'd have let me go on my date. No, this is about control. You can't stand not controlling everything around you."

He might have a point. I took another sip of coffee—black, thank you very much. "That may be, but believe it or not, it's more about me wanting more for my baby brother. Sappy but it's the truth."

Dean shifted his feet, not meeting my eyes. "Fine. I get it." His chin lifted high and stubborn. "But what you did was shitty and wrong."

"It was."

He shook his head in disgust. "I'm calling her—"

"I took the job."

The words landed between us like a stink bomb. Dean's nostrils flared as his eyes narrowed. "What job?"

I was pretty sure he knew, but I answered anyway. "I'm going to pose as Parker's boyfriend."

The kitchen clock ticked out a loud ten seconds before he responded. "You? You're telling me you went in my place last night?"

It was weird how much he sounded like my mother just then, the way she used to get when we'd done something really wrong, right before she totally lost it.

"Yes. I met up with her and we came to an agreement. It's a done deal," I told a silent Dean. "So, like I said, put on the suit and hunt down a job you're made for."

I felt like an asshole. How could I not? I was. But some things had to be done. You sucked it up, pushed away the guilt, the regret, and got on with it. I'd been doing that my whole adult life. And my adult life had started way before I'd been ready.

"I can't believe you," Dean rasped. "You fucking stole my gig with Parker." He laughed broadly and without humor. "You dickhead! You weren't worried about me. You just saw a good opportunity to make some cash yourself. You selfish, fucking—"

"Hey." I pointed at him in warning, guilt riding me hard. Because he was right. And he was wrong. "That's not what I had planned when I went over there. I planned to hand her her ass."

"And then you saw how cute her ass was," Dean said, nodding as though it all made sense to him now.

"No." *Yes. Maybe.* "I realized that she was hanging out with Franklin Fairchild."

He blinked. "Who the fuck is that?"

"Some big-shot billionaire with too much time on his hands and not enough ways to spend it. Parker works for one of his companies." I glanced around the sparse loft apartment before pinning Dean with a stare. "I didn't want to worry you, but we're in danger of losing the gym—"

"Good! It's not like I wanted you to buy this place anyway."

"This place," I ground out, "was Dad's dream, his legacy to us."

"Exactly. *His* dream. *His* legacy." Dean flung an arm up. "It was never about me. You were the golden boy, the star. I can see why you'd want it, but don't include me in this."

"Fine." I set my mug down with a sigh. "Regardless. If I hang around Parker, and therefore, Fairchild, I can try to convince him to sponsor the gym."

Dean paced, grabbing at the ends of his hair. "So instead of me being pimped out, you're going to pimp yourself out? Am I getting that right?" He laughed again. "Fucking unbelievable."

He stopped short and faced me. "You know what I don't get? Why the hell do you even need money? You were making bank when you were boxing. Where the hell did it all go? And don't tell me it went into the gym and my education again. You made way more than that."

What was I supposed to tell him? That a huge chunk of my early earnings had gone to paying for Mom's cancer bills? We lived in the supposed best country in the world, yet my middle-class family was quickly bankrupted because my mom had been dying and my dad, who owned his own business and didn't have good insurance, couldn't afford the hospital bills. I'd stepped up and paid them.

Maybe Dean knew that much. But he sure as hell didn't know that Dad, who had been my manager and was supposed to handle my money as well, lost almost all of it on shitty investments and gambling. That I hadn't known the extent of the damage until after I'd bought the gym and paid for Dean's tuition.

I could barely stomach that as it was. Dad had been my idol. Until he wasn't. And frankly, I felt like a damn fool for letting it happen. That's what you got when you trusted somebody, even the ones you loved. If you wanted to survive in this world, you didn't let anyone fully in.

"The money is gone," I said instead. "But the gym could turn a good profit if we updated it. We need new equipment, to redo the locker rooms... hell, the whole place needs a good coat of paint. In this market, we won't be able to pull in new members if Lights Out stays looking like a shithole."

I didn't mention the offer from Garret. Dean would tell me to take it and I wasn't hearing that. It was the last possible solution. "If the gym becomes profitable," I added, "you'll earn money too."

Because the place was half Dean's, whether he wanted it or not. I'd made certain to give him that safety net.

I expected him to scoff as he usually did when I spoke of the gym. But he nodded, tight and decisive.

"Okay, then. You got the job being Parker's fun boy."

"Believe me, there will be no fun involved."

"Please. I've seen her. She's hot. Audrey Hepburn hot, but nevertheless, hot."

I didn't want to agree. Not when I had to face the woman every day. But Dean was right. She was a total Hepburn. I'd bet my best leather jacket that she had a strand of perfectly matched pearls in her jewelry box—and that she'd look classy as fuck in them.

"Doesn't matter what she looks like," I told Dean. "We have a business agreement. Nothing more."

"Nothing?" Dean's blond brows lifted high. "Because I could have sworn there was a hint of maybe the arrangement leading to—"

I lifted a hand to stop him. I did not want to hear about Parker's apparent willingness to actually date Dean. It stirred up feelings in my gut that I wanted no part of.

"Trust me," I said. "It's all business."

He grinned wide and knowing. Smug bastard. "Interesting."

"Whatever." I grabbed my cup and poured the cold remnants of coffee into the sink.

At my back, Dean snickered. When I turned around, he still wore the smirk.

"So," he said expansively, "while you're Parker's neutered pet..." He just loved rubbing it in. "I'll take a nice, office job, just as you wanted."

"Well, okay, then," I said, pleased to hear him finally making sense.

"Thought you'd like that." He was far too happy. "So you won't object to taking your things out of the office. Because I'm going to need the space."

Wait. "What?"

Dean looked at me as though I was two years old. "As the one with the big math-type brain, I'm going to sit my ass down and manage the accounts of Lights Out."

When I simply stared, he tutted and shook his head slightly.

"You've been saying you're crap at account managing. Well, move over, bro. Because I'm the new office manager."

Shit. He'd go through the accounts. He'd find out about the second mortgage, and just how deep in the red we were. He'd find out about everything.

"Now, wait a minute," I began. But he cut me off by turning his back to leave.

"Forget it, Rhys," he said as he walked toward the door. "You got your way with Parker. I'm doing this and you can't stop me." He paused and grinned. But his eyes were cold and angry. "As you keep telling me, I own half the gym. It's time I start taking care of my end."

He was going to do his damnedest to make my life hell. The

promise was right there in his expression. He let me see it, made sure I understood. Then the door slammed, and I let out a bark of incredulous laughter. Damn if I wasn't proud. The other half of me was filled with dread because we'd eventually have some hard conversations, and I wasn't exactly good at communicating.

Didn't matter, though. I'd overslept and it was getting late. Parker would be coming by soon and frankly, I needed to prepare myself for dealing with her, let her know who was in charge here.

Dream on, Morgan. She'll have you by the balls before you know it.

Why did I look forward to that?

FIVE

Parker

A SELFISH BONUS TO BEING "GREEN" (other than the awesome eco-warrior status) was it kept me active and fit. To my parents' frustration, I refused to accept the Mercedes-Benz Cabriolet they'd bought me as a reward for earning my PhD. Maybe if it had been a Tesla I'd have been swayed, but, unfortunately, despite me yelling the word "green" from the rooftops since I was fourteen, my parents couldn't wrap their heads around what that meant.

As far as they were concerned, every young woman would love to drive around in a luxury convertible. Plus, the Mercedes had an "eco" stop/start button so why wasn't that green enough?

I gratefully declined the car and splashed out on an electric hybrid bike when I got the job at Horus. For journeys to the office I used the bike at full power, so I didn't arrive sweaty and

out of breath. Today, however, as I rode the six and a half miles
north to Chelsea, I reduced the power, meaning it took me the
normal forty minutes to get there.

The truth was I was dragging the ride out, reluctant to step
inside Lights Out. For the past few days, I'd lied to Jackson and
my colleagues, and it was not fun. Jackson had informed our
small team about the dinner date with Fairchild and how the
big boss waxed lyrical over Rhys Morgan. Thankfully, only one
guy on the team knew anything about boxing and recognized
Rhys's name, and even then, he wasn't a fanboy.

However, they all wanted to know how Rhys and I met, a
subject that didn't come up at dinner because Fairchild had
monopolized the conversation. Prepared for those kinds of
inevitable questions, first I'd googled Rhys and then I'd learned
as much as I could about his career.

He'd been a heavyweight fighter. A champion. From my
research I'd discovered there were four major professional
boxing organizations that held bouts. The International Boxing
Federation, the World Boxing Association, the World Boxing
Council, and the World Boxing Organization.

When Rhys was twenty-eight years old, he became the
WBC heavyweight champion. Some other guy was the heavyweight champion that year for all three other associations, so I
wasn't sure how that worked. Honestly, I wasn't sure how any
of it worked. However, I was smart enough to realize that Rhys
Morgan had been an awesome boxer. It was a mystery to me
why he'd retired at thirty-one, until I'd found an interview Rhys
had given explaining how he'd lost his passion for boxing after
his father died.

The boxing community seemed to mourn the loss of Rhys
and I came to understand why. There was a YouTube video of
the fight that garnered him his heavyweight title. It was brutal
but fascinating to watch. Rhys Morgan was built like Hercules,

all muscles and gleaming skin, and he was fast. As I watched him move around the ring, impressively light on his feet despite his size, I'd felt those butterflies in my belly again.

He was beautiful in a primal way.

I knew nothing of his sport, and we came from very different backgrounds.

Moreover, Rhys was determined (which was a polite way of saying he was a bit of a steamroller) and vibrated with this passionate energy I'd never experienced before.

He might not be my type, but he was a catch. Many women would want to be in his orbit, and I was sure he'd have his pick.

And *I* was going to pretend to date this guy.

Would anyone really buy it?

A car horn shook me out the memories of watching Rhys fight. Those images were currently playing in a loop in my head. Yet, it would be safer while cycling if I concentrated on getting to Lights Out in one piece.

Seriously, this whole debacle was distracting.

So far, I'd avoided telling Jackson about how I met Rhys. I hated lying about dating him and the more I embellished the deception, the guiltier I felt. Avoidance was my friend right now.

There was absolutely no way anyone could find out about Rhys beyond my work colleagues. God, if my parents or my sister Easton found out, I'd die.

Okay, so that was melodramatic... but I would certainly feel like I might combust with shame if I had to fib to my family about Rhys. Probably because they wanted so badly for me to meet someone and fall in love.

I was thirty years old and single, and my parents were worried because I'd been single a while now. Like, a *while*. A whole lotta **while**.

Thirteen years.

My stomach lurched at the number.

It sounded worse than it was. I mean, I *had* dated during those thirteen years. And had lots of sex. Okay, maybe not lots. But I'd had sex. In my quest to feel that spark of chemistry once again, I'd gotten myself a little something-something over the years. Some of it bad. Some of it good. All of it... just... meh.

There was no point in settling down with someone I didn't spark with. I'd rather be single forever than settle for less than I knew was possible. And I knew what was possible because for a brief, splendid moment in time I'd had something special.

So I kind of gave up, especially while working on my PhD. My career became my entire focus.

Ironic that a relationship was the one thing I needed to advance my career.

Twisty little universe.

Yes, my parents were definitely not going to find out about Rhys. I didn't want to get their hopes up. Mostly I just didn't want to lie to them. Not that it wasn't slightly tempting, considering my younger sister had just gotten engaged. My family wasn't putting any pressure on me, but I felt it anyway.

Ugh, societal pressures were the emotional equivalent of a black hole. No matter a person's obstinate refusal to bend to them, every single one of us got sucked in somehow. Boo to black holes!

Speaking of... I slowed to a stop outside the gym on Fourth. It was a red-brick, seventies-style building, three-stories with tinted brown glass windows and a flat roof. Well-maintained greenery, grass and hedges, grew along the edges. But there was something drab about the building; the signage above the door was peeling.

"Here goes nothing," I muttered to myself as I got off the bike and padlocked it to the railings by the entrance.

For the past few nights I'd spent my free time writing up a

contract for Rhys to sign. Every time I thought I'd finished it, I'd think of something new. Hopefully, he'd sign the thing with no arguments.

That wasn't entirely honest of me. The butterflies in my belly demonstrated there was a part of me that didn't want Rhys to sign the contract at all. Part of me wanted him to tell me he'd changed his mind.

There was no reception area, so I strolled across the glass-fronted atrium and through double doors that led into the ground-floor space. This was the gym. Considering it was a Saturday afternoon, it wasn't as busy as it should have been. Sure, there were people there, working out, but every machine in the room should have been in use and wasn't. As I took in the peeling paint on the walls, some aging workout equipment, worn workout mats, and a sad little water cooler on either side of the room in lieu of a fancy drink dispenser, I could see for myself why Rhys needed the money. There were no TVs for people to watch during their workouts. They were stuck with the music pumping out of the PA system unless they brought their own headphones to drown it out.

The gym was run-down. It needed sprucing up to be brought into the twenty-first century. Curiosity still lingered over where his earnings from boxing had disappeared to, but it was none of my business. All that mattered was that Fairchild liked Rhys and Rhys would keep me on the boss's radar long enough for me to get a permanent position.

The contract in my hand trembled a little as I tried to contain my nerves.

"Can I help you?"

I turned toward the masculine voice and found myself face-to-face with a beautiful man. The blood beneath my cheeks grew hot as I stared into dark chocolate eyes framed by the longest lashes I'd ever seen on a guy. He had warm, tawny skin and a head full of thick, jet-black hair. When he smiled, two incredible dimples popped in either cheek.

Dreamy bedroom eyes, ahoy there!

"Do you speak?"

I flushed and laughed at my ridiculousness. "Yes, I have been known to produce speech."

The man's eyes danced with laughter. "Good to know. I'm Carlos. Can I help?"

I glanced down at the contract in my hand before being compelled to look into Carlos's eyes again. Seriously, I thought Rhys had beautiful eyes, but this guy could give him a run for his money. "I'm here to see Rhys Morgan. He's expecting me."

Carlos grinned. "Are you Parker?"

"That's me."

He held out his hand. "Nice to meet you. I'm a trainer here."

Carlos's hand was calloused and strong. It was very nice to touch. I returned his smile. "You too."

"This way." He indicated with his head toward the left. Carlos led me out of the main gym into a small hall that housed an elevator and a stairwell. "He's on the second floor where the boxing gym is."

We took the stairs, and I followed the trainer into a space similar to downstairs except half of it was taken up by two boxing rings. There was a class being taught in the clear side of the space, and as we walked past, I recognized the martial art as capoeira. Interesting. I wondered if Rhys knew capoeira. That would be a sight to see.

At the sound of Rhys's familiar, booming voice, my eyes flew in his direction. He was standing outside one of the boxing rings, shouting instructions at two young men who wore nothing but long shorts and boxing gear.

My gaze drifted down Rhys's back. My lower belly fluttered.

It was just nerves.

The guy was an intimidating specimen. So tall. Much taller than Carlos who I put at around five foot ten. Even that was tall for me. I only stood at five foot two. Hence why I'd put a "No Tinker Bell" clause in the contract for Rhys.

Rude!

Unless I'd misread his reasons for calling me that. Tink *was* loyal and adorably feisty.

But that was beside the point.

My eyes glanced off the well-developed muscles revealed by the basketball tank Rhys wore and the way his joggers cupped his firm, high, and very muscular ass. There wasn't an inch of fat on the guy.

"Rhys. Company!" Carlos yelled as we approached.

The man himself turned around, and I felt the breath expel from my body as his intense gaze drank me in. As he took in my low-heeled T-bar shoes, pleated pale blue skirt, and black Ted Baker shirt with its little jeweled bow tie, a frown deepened between his brows. I didn't care what he thought of my appearance. I thought I looked cute. That's all that mattered. It's not as if I thought much of his appearance.

Okay, so I could admit that he was attractive in that caveman, overtly masculine, alpha-male kind of way that some women found appealing.

I wasn't one of them.

I was above that sort of primal need for power and strength in my chosen mate.

At least I was determined to be.

A guy had to be funny and thoughtful above anything else. Plus, I liked my men short and cute. Not intimidating and so tall they'd have to lift me up to kiss me.

An image of Rhys doing just that flashed through my mind and I expelled it with such force, I almost said the word "blech" out loud.

Sure enough, Rhys frowned as we drew to a halt in front of him. "You okay, Tinker Bell? Does boxing offend your fragile sensibilities?"

I scowled at his sarcasm. "Why would you say that?"

"Because you look like you just swallowed something nasty."

"Nope." I shrugged. "Although you should know that when I googled this place, hardly any information came up. You need a website. Or at least a Facebook page."

Rhys cut Carlos a look. "What did I tell you? She's already fucking dispensing business advice."

Carlos smirked. "She's not wrong, is she?"

I grinned at Carlos, and suddenly Rhys took hold of my biceps, his expression fierce. "We'll be in the office."

"You don't need to manhandle me," I grumbled as he led me across the gym. He opened a door to a narrow corridor, hurried us down it, and then pushed open another door that led into an office.

There was a beautiful and impressive rosewood desk in the center of the room, completely at odds with the chaos of the rest of the space. There were wall-to-wall shelves filled with folders and files spilling out here and there.

The urge to advise him to put in a proper filing system was real, but I considered his reaction to my earlier advice and replaced the words with, "Nice desk."

He grunted and moved around me to sit on it. The desk was expansive. Yet somehow, he dwarfed it.

My goodness, I forgot how big he was.

Rhys's eyes dipped to the papers in my hand. "I'm guessing that's the contract."

"Yes." I held it out. "Hopefully, everything within it is acceptable to you."

Without saying a word, or offering me a seat, he began to read through it. After a few minutes, he reached behind him for a pen and scored across the paper.

Irritation bloomed in my chest. I'd spent ages on the paperwork! "What are you doing?"

He flicked me an exasperated look before returning to scan the paper. "I already told you I recycle. You don't need to put a clause in the fucking contract demanding I do so because 'People won't believe we're dating otherwise.'"

Okay, so maybe that had been a little much.

His pen struck through another line. "I will not curb my language. 'Fuck' is a beautiful word. It has several meanings and can be used in almost any fucking sentence. You want reality?" Those green eyes bored into me, making it impossible to look away. "No one would believe I'd date the language police."

Grumbling under my breath, I fought to let that one go.

"What was that?"

"Nothing."

"You have something to say, say it."

Fine! "I just don't think it's necessary to use the F word every five seconds."

Rhys curled his upper lip. "F word. Really? You're thirty years old, Parker. It's well past time you started using your grown-up words."

I gave him the middle finger.

A smirk tickled his lips as he looked back down at the contract. "Well, that's something at least."

More time passed as Rhys slowly read. I didn't know if it was because he was a slow reader or if he was deliberately being aggravating. Just as I began to tap my foot, he ran the pen over another line. "What now?"

"I don't need you to buy me a wardrobe. I have handmade tailored suits in my closet from my boxing days. You need me in a suit, I have suits. And don't pass out from shock, but I even own a tux."

I considered that clause. I'd stated in the contract that he'd need to dress the part at dinners and events. I had presumed Rhys wouldn't have the kind of formal wear required. "I'm sorry for assuming otherwise. I didn't mean to insult you."

He raised an eyebrow at my apology but didn't respond beyond a muttered, "No problem."

"Jesus Christ," he huffed a few seconds later, running his pen across the paper again. His expression was incredulous. "As long as I'm not being an absolute prick or a derogatory asshole to you, I think you can let me call you Tinker Bell. It's not meant as an insult. And I should have a nickname for you. It projects an aura of intimacy." He smirked, that boyish wicked grin of his.

Ignoring my physical response to his smile, I crossed my arms over my chest. "Well, why can't you just call me sweet-heart? Sweetheart is nice. Not the way you've been saying it, in that sarcastic, condescending, *makes me want to punch you* way. But if you changed your tone, sweetheart would definitely work."

"Sweetheart," he said in that sarcastic, condescending, *made me want to punch him* way. "Don't ever try to punch me. You'd break your tiny little hand."

Before I could come up with a suitable response, he continued. "Everything else looks okay." He stood and placed the contract on the desk to sign. Then he held out the pen. "Your turn."

Oh my God. I was actually going to do this. I was going to engage in a ruse with Rhys Morgan, pretending I was his girlfriend. Glancing between us, my doubts resurfaced that anyone would believe it.

"What?" he asked.

I wrinkled my nose. "No one will believe this."

During my Rhys googling I'd come across photos of him with women. He had a definite type. Hair color, eye color, face —they all changed with every new woman but what didn't was the long legs, curvy hips, generous boobs, and overtly glamorous style.

They were sexy bombshells.

I was *so* not his type.

"You mean because I'm a low, rough boxer and you're a Fifth Avenue princess?" he said with a teasing smile.

"No." I squirmed, not sure how to say it without coming across like I was insecure. I was not an insecure person. "I'm just... people are used to seeing me with men like your brother. He has a computer science degree and definitely makes more sense on paper. You're more physical and you date women who are the absolute opposite of me."

If Rhys heard the last part, he didn't acknowledge it. "You think I'm a fucking moron because I don't have a fancy college degree?" He crossed his arms over his chest and frazzled me on the spot with the heat of his glare. "I'll tell you something, *princess*"—he said the word with such distaste, I longed for Tinker Bell to make a reappearance—"some of the smartest, most capable people I've ever met don't have a fancy college degree from MIT."

"I didn't mean that. I just meant... I'm worried that people won't buy the idea of you and me as a couple."

"Well, sweetheart, I can sell anything." He crossed the room to stop in front of me, forcing me to look up. His eyes smoldered so intensely, my breathing went bye-bye. Rhys trailed the back of his knuckles down my cheek and neck; a shiver skated down my spine. As if he'd felt it, his eyes danced.

His voice lowered, smoky and husky. "Don't you worry about me convincing people I want you." He bent his head to whisper in my ear, "I always put a hundred and ten percent into any job."

Skin burning hot, sensations tingling in places they had no business tingling, I stumbled back from his overwhelming presence.

What the heck was that?

Avoiding his gaze, I nodded. "Uh-huh. Okay. Well. That is comforting to hear." I pushed past him to the table where the contract sat and quickly signed. "I'll make copies and have one couriered over for you for your records and then I'll be in touch when I need you again, which might be soon because Jackson said Fairchild has been asking about—"

"Tinker Bell, you're rambling." Rhys cut me off.

He was grinning. *Huge.* Self-satisfied. Very, very pleased with himself for rattling me.

The big jerk. "If you're done crowing, I'll need your number." I pulled my cell out of the small backpack I had with me and waited.

Rhys gave me his number.

"Okay. I've sent you a text so you have my number now. Text me your bank details. I'll send the payment at the end of the first month." I slipped my cell back into my backpack along with the contract. "I'll be in touch."

"I'll be awaiting your call, *boss.*"

I sniffed haughtily and moved to stride past him. "That's an improvement on Tinker Bell."

Just as I cleared his personal space, I felt a tug on my pony-tail and let out a little squawk as my hair tumbled down around my shoulders. Whirling around, I glared at the sight of my ponytail holder dangling from his fingertips. "What the heck?"

He shrugged. "No one would believe I'd date a woman who wears a ponytail other than to work out. You have nice hair." His gaze looked over said hair. "Why hide it?"

"Because," I said, snatching the holder back, "I rode my bike here and I need to be able to see, not to be constantly shoving windblown locks out of my eyes. I'm sorry if that interferes with your caveman expectations of what constitutes feminine beauty, but if you get to say the F word, I get to wear my ponytail." I spun away, my strides furious and stompy.

"You got a lot of rage in you, Tinker Bell," he called at my back.

I pulled open his office door with one hand and threw up my middle finger with the other. His laughter followed me all the way down the hall.

If we made it through this ruse with me going to prison for assault instead of murder, I'd call it a win.

The guy really pushed my buttons.

And I hadn't even known I had any.

SIX

Rhys

ANGRYTINK: Hey. This is Parker. Parker Brown.

My phone dinged loudly. I fumbled around my bed, finally finding the damn thing under a pillow. Wiping the sleep off my face, I rolled onto my back and read the text that had pulled me out of a pleasant sleep. I smiled. It was just so ... Parker. Settling in, I answered her.

RhysThis: Don't have to tell me who you are. Your number is programmed on my phone. What do you want?

AngryTink: Well, good morning to you too, Happy Pants.

My smile turned into an evil grin. The girl was always going to punch back and make it count.

RhysThis: That's Mr. Happy Pants. Though,

TBH, my pants aren't too happy at the moment. Want to help me out with that?

AngryTink: Tempting. Truly. But, no.

RhysThis: RU sure? 'Cuz Happy Pants Rhys is much more agreeable than Sad That He Had to Self-Satisfy Rhys.

AngryTink: Would you please behave?

RhysThis: I'm not the one who mentioned the emotional state of my pants.

AngryTink: ARGH!

A chuckle rumbled in my chest as my thumbs tapped out a response I knew would piss her off more.

RhysThis: Was that even English? Honestly, Ms. Brown, I thought you were educated.

She took a moment to answer. I could picture her, phone in hand, grinding her teeth.

AngryTink: You're deliberately trying to annoy me, aren't you?

RhysThis: You're quick. I'll give you that.

AngryTink: Mr. Morgan, I'm about ten seconds away from finding an alternate fake boyfriend. A goat on a rope would be a better candidate at this point.

It was cute she thought that was threatening.

RhysThis: Yeah, probably. But the goat doesn't have a signed contract. I do, Tinker Bell.

AngryTink: ARGH@!!

RhysThis: You're kind of cute when you talk pirate.

She didn't answer. Rubbing my chest, I sat up in bed and tried again.

RhysThis: Parker? You there?

RhysThis: Parker?

Hell. Maybe I pushed too far. Or maybe she dropped her phone. Or threw it. She might have thrown it.

RhysThis: You really going to give up that easily?

The phone rang in my hand, startling me. Parker Brown. I guess we were through with texting.

"You missed the sound of my voice, didn't you?" I asked.

Hers was crisp with irritation. "My thumbs got tired. Would you please behave yourself for a moment, Morgan?"

"Misbehaving is much more fun."

"Be that as it may, I have business to discuss."

So fucking proper. It shouldn't have turned me on. But it did. Which was unfortunate. Scowling, I hauled myself out of bed and walked toward the kitchen. Coffee was in order. Coffee and a good dose of reality. Flirting with Parker Brown was a stupid idea.

"All right," I said, filling the carafe. "What's up?"

"We've been invited to a cocktail party tonight."

"Aw, look at us, already getting invited to places as a couple."

She let out a long-suffering sigh. "Honestly, the speed in which they accepted our fallacy as a reality surprised me as well."

"I bet." I snorted and flicked on the brewer. "Just chalk it up to the magic of my winning personality."

"More like your winning record," she muttered.

"Nice volley, sweetheart." I grabbed a cup off the shelf. "And a hard punch too. I didn't know you had it in you."

"There's a lot in me that you don't know about... wait... I don't know if that made sense. Never mind. The point is that you don't know me."

I smirked at her rambling. She was too cute.

Focus, Rhys. I poured myself a cup of coffee and took a much-needed sip. "So, where's this gig tonight? Some fancy hotel?"

"No. It's on Fairchild's boat."

"I'm not wearing boating shoes, Parker. I'm saying that right now."

"His boat is a two-hundred-foot yacht, Morgan. No boating shoes required."

Right. I should have known. Suffocating heat invaded my chest, and I set down my cup with a clink. Who was I kidding? I was a racehorse being pulled out and put on display so the guests could get a good look at the merchandise. It was my job here, and forgetting that was stupid.

Parker nervously filled the silence with more rambling. "No, I think a nice pair of trousers and a button-down shirt would work. If you'd like, I'd be happy to provide you with—"

"I told you I had proper clothes." I rolled my tense shoulders and glanced at my closet. The thought of putting them on made my skin tighten. "Don't you worry your pretty little head. I won't embarrass you."

"You are determined to be in a foul mood over this, aren't you?"

"Let's just say the only woman allowed to pick out my clothes was my mother, and that stopped when I was seven."

"Fine. Moving on, we need to get our stories straight about how we met. I was going to discuss this with you on Saturday, but ..."

She trailed off with a strangled sound. And I found myself smiling again.

"I distracted you, didn't I?"

She didn't say a thing. Because we both knew it was true.

"How did we meet?" she asked. "I can't quite figure out what to say that will be believable."

"Because the idea of us makes absolutely no sense?" I offered lightly. I mean, I could have been insulted, but she was right—we didn't make sense.

"Yes." She sighed. "I'm not very good at acting."

She sounded so forlorn, I was almost sorry for her.

"My mom once told me that love doesn't make sense." As soon as I said the words, I winced, feeling like a sentimental fool. I was never sentimental. But I pushed on. "Falling for someone isn't about logic. It's chemistry."

She was quiet for a second. When she answered, she sounded softer than before. "That's ... well, that's surprisingly romantic."

Don't go there, honey.

"Yeah, well, it's a good line of attack. I'll tell them ..." I rubbed my neck and stared out the grimy window where the sun shone down on the black tar rooftops. "I'll tell them I was on my way to meet my brother for a drink."

She snorted loudly.

I bit back a grin. "I was late and in a hurry so I wasn't watching where I was going. You were walking out of the door. I was going in. We collided. And there I was, my hands full of this irate little pixie with the prettiest brown eyes I'd ever seen. How could I resist? So I asked you to join me for a drink to make up for nearly plowing you down. But it was just an excuse because I knew I'd be a fool to let this gorgeous uptown girl walk out of my life without at least trying to get to know her first."

Utter silence met me on the other side of the line. It was so quiet, I could hear a morning news program playing on her end. An uncomfortable flush worked its way up my chest. This is why I didn't talk too much.

"Parker? You there?"

She made a noise in the back of her throat, as if she were

choking. "Yes. Yes. I'm here. Sorry."

"Well? What do you think? Will that pass muster?"

Silence greeted me again and I swore I heard her mutter "fiddlesticks." But then she answered crisp as new bed sheets. "Yes. That's ... good. Perfectly adequate."

Perfectly adequate? Well, hell. I thought I'd done all right. It had been kind of sappy, sure, but I couldn't see anyone not believing it.

She cleared her throat and charged on. "The party starts at seven thirty. Boston Harbor. We could meet—"

"I do not meet my women for dates. I pick them up. Always."

"Morgan," she said with asperity, "I am not your woman."

She couldn't see my grin, but it didn't stop me. "Tinker Bell, I have a contract that says otherwise. Better get used to it. I'll pick you up at seven."

"Sand snakes," she snarled under her breath.

Whatever that meant.

"Oh, and Tink?"

"What?" Another snarl. Such joy and light from my irate pixie.

"Prepare yourself for some physical contact. Because I touch my woman. Always."

"I KNOW what you're trying to do."

I paused, my hand hovering near the small of Parker's back as she halted on the sidewalk outside her apartment. "What am I trying to do?"

I honestly didn't have a frickin' clue what she was thinking. Hell, I was trying my best not to look too closely at her. If I did, I might not stop. Parker wasn't dressed like any of my usual dates. She was wearing a black halter-top dress that started at her collar and skimmed her slim form to a few inches below her knees. It wasn't tight and revealed nothing but her tanned shoulders and arms. It was incredibly sexy.

Maybe *because* it didn't show everything. Only hinted at it. I had to use my imagination. My imagination was vivid.

I itched to undo the clasp at the back of her long, graceful neck and see that top slide down to her waist. She didn't have large breasts. They were little cupcakes. Goddamn, but I wanted a bite.

I pushed the thought away and peered down at her big brown eyes. She'd put on makeup, some shimmery gold color that made her eyes the color of rich coffee. Her petal-pink lips pursed in annoyance.

"You think I'll balk at riding this stupid motorcycle and then you can play Mr. Superior about it."

I glanced at my Harley Fat Boy, and then at her dress. That fancy silk dress hugging her hips and slim legs. Hell. "You might not believe it, sweetheart, but I didn't actually think."

Her brow quirked. "Oh, I believe that."

Funny.

Grunting, I rubbed my jaw—which was now smooth and bare. Yes, I'd shaved for her. I'd put on fresh pressed gray slacks and a cream cashmere top. Both from my circuit days. They were a little loose on me; I'd lost about ten pounds of muscle since I'd stopped training. But I had them on. I'd done it for her. An effort lost to the blunder of picking her up with my Harley.

"I'll call us an Uber." I pulled out my phone but her slim hand on my wrist halted me. Why I felt that touch all the way to my balls was a mystery for the ages.

"This wasn't a trick?" She eyed me like a little human lie detector.

"Fucking hell, Tink. I'm not out to get you here. I'm getting something out of this arrangement too. I just didn't think. I have a bike. It's what I ride. But I'll get us an Uber, all right?"

My verbal spew ended in a ringing silence. The sun was sinking, shrinking golden rays that highlighted the red strands in her hair. She had it pulled back in one of those fancy updos that lay like a coiled snake at the back of her head. Delicate pearl earrings dangled from her small ears. Everything about Parker Brown was delicate and pretty.

An illusion. The woman had an iron core.

"You really shouldn't cuss so much," was all she said. "It shows a lack of imagination."

"Bullshit."

Her brows kicked up. "It's not bull ... bull-hockey."

Bull-hockey. Jesus. This woman.

"It is." I laughed at her scowl. "Cursing is a sign of intelligence and those who do it frequently are both happier and healthier than the poor repressed souls who keep it all in."

"Oh, bull-pucks."

"Hockey? Pucks? What's next? Bulls on skates?"

A flush worked over her cheeks, and she growled.

I laughed again. "Look it up if you don't believe me."

"I will." She stomped over to my bike. "Are we going, or should we stand here talking nonsense all night?"

If I had my choice, we'd talk nonsense.

"You really going to ride on this?" I handed her the spare helmet I'd brought along.

She sniffed, all polite irritation, and put it on. It was adorably huge on her head. "My mode of transportation is a bicycle. I think I can manage." And then she did something I knew was designed to kill me. She pulled the skirt of her dress high up her thighs, exposing some truly spectacular legs, and straddled the bike.

I stared at those beautiful, smooth legs, imagining my tongue tracing a path up the curve of her thigh, and my dick twitched. I got on my bike before I had a situation going on in my pants that would make driving uncomfortable.

It wasn't easy, though. Not with Parker's thighs bracketing mine and her hands gripping my sides. By the time we pulled up to the docks, I was practically sweating. It was a relief to park and get some much-needed distance from my tiny tormentor.

She handed me her helmet and smoothed her hair. "All right." She took a deep breath that did great things for her tits, and then let it out. "Let's do this."

We both looked up at the massive, sleek yacht hovering at the end of the private dock. People were already crowded on its multiple decks, the windows aglow in the setting sun. Laughter and chatter drifted out into the night.

I took hold of her elbow and guided her forward. "Act like you own the place and you will."

She glanced up at me with a bemused smile. "Is that how you do it?"

"What do you think?"

"That you just admitted you're full of hot air," she said lightly, and making me chuckle.

But despite my swagger, as soon as we stepped onto the pale wood mid deck, a sweat broke out on my lower back. The crowd was thick with bleached-toothed, rich assholes and gorgeous women. Everyone had a drink in hand and everyone was exposing those white-capped teeth with fake-ass smiles.

The yacht itself was stunning. Sleek, polished wood panels and brilliant white leather furniture, multiple decks, each with its own full bar. There was a sunning platform at the aft deck, and a big-ass hot tub on the middle deck where women in string bikinis frolicked.

I'd been on yachts like this. I could even appreciate the craftsmanship and beauty of the vessel. It was the human element that got under my skin and crawled around like ants. It was too familiar. Too much like that world I left behind. The world I never belonged in but was pulled into to provide entertainment.

I rolled my shoulders, and Parker glanced up at me.

"Are you all right?" she asked in a low voice.

"Of course. Piece of cake, babe."

I doubted she believed my bullshit. Whatever she might have said was lost as Fairchild glided up to us.

"Morgan!" He was all smiles and wearing a white linen suit with purple velvet slippers. Honest-to-God purple slippers— with his initials embroidered on them in gold thread. I choked back a snort as he reached for my hand and pumped it. "Good to see you."

He afforded Parker a glance. "And Ms. Brown."

"Parker, sir. Please call me Parker."

"Parker," he repeated blandly. "Fine, fine." His watery gaze landed back on me. "Let me show you around, Morgan. Ever been on a boat?"

"One or two." I took hold of Parker's elbow, feeling the tension humming through her arm. "We'd love a tour."

Actually, I'd love to toss him overboard, but hey, being in his company was what both Parker and I needed. So, I'd deal.

Like a king, Fairchild strutted through the crowd, slapping shoulders, shaking hands, and all the while introducing me. "Rhys Morgan. The Widowmaker. And his friend Parker."

Somewhere along the way, I grabbed a glass of champagne off a waiter's tray and handed it to Parker. She gave me a tight but grateful smile and took a healthy swallow. "None for you?" she asked, leaning in to be heard over the increasing chatter.

"Nah. The stuff gives me a shitty headache."

Her lips pursed again, and I knew she was fighting the urge to correct my language. I wouldn't be surprised if she eventually brought out a swear jar. But Fairchild had heard me and dropped his conversation with a loud older man wearing a palm tree-printed silk shirt.

"Let me get you a real man's drink," he said.

Parker muttered into her glass as he led us over to a bar.

"What'll you have, Rhys, my boy?"

"Ice water, if you have it," I said to the bartender.

"Would you like it in a glass with lemon?" she asked.

This place.

"I'll just take the bottle."

"Water?" Fairchild scowled. "Live a little, man."

I accepted the ice-cold blue glass bottle of water the bartender offered me. "I'm responsible for getting Parker home safely. And I don't drink and drive."

Wrong thing to say. His scowl turned on Parker as if it were her fault I wasn't chugging down a beer with him, and she visibly stiffened.

"Plus," I added, "I'm teaching a class early tomorrow and I like to stay in top form." Absolute bullshit. Not the class, but a beer wouldn't hurt. Fairchild didn't need to know that, though.

He perked up. "You're teaching classes? Boxing?"

"Tomorrow is kickboxing, but, yeah, we do boxing classes as well." I took a sip of the water. Jesus. It actually tasted better than usual water. "My gym, Lights Out, offers all sorts of classes. You should stop by. I could hook you up with a private instructor."

And then you can show your appreciation by becoming our sponsor.

He hummed. "Maybe I will. But you shouldn't be teaching classes. You should be in the ring. Would you consider fighting again?"

My gut turned to lead and my throat closed. I wasn't on some fancy yacht anymore. I was sitting on the hard-plastic chair that cut into my thighs and put a kink in my back. The same chair I sat in for three days straight, waiting in vain for Jake to wake up. Sitting there as the doctor told us Jake was brain-dead. Sitting there, watching as Marcy decided to pull the plug, that Jake wouldn't want to be left in a bed like that.

It was the day I found out my dad had lost almost all my savings on a bet that had Jake winning with a KO in the eighth round. He'd been knocked out in the seventh. Never to rise again.

Bile burned up my throat, and I swallowed convulsively. I was going to be sick. All over Fairchild's purple and gold slippers.

A smooth, slim hand slipped into my loose grasp and squeezed.

Parker.

I blinked down at her, confused, and she smiled up at me, all bright and sunny.

"Rhys once told me it was best to tap out on top," she told Fairchild.

Lies. But also true.

I licked my dry lips. "True. My time in the ring is over."

Fairchild frowned but nodded with clear reluctance. An awkward tension had settled over us and I couldn't find a way to cut it. Parker, on the other hand, glanced around the boat and then turned back to Fairchild. "This is a beautiful craft, Mr. Fairchild. Am I mistaken or are those solar panels you have there?"

He glanced at the area she pointed to. "It is. Now, Morgan. About this so-called retirement."

I held up a hand. "Sorry, Fairchild, but can you point me in the direction of the bathroom? Nature calls."

I barely listened to his directions before I got the hell out of there, unable to listen to another word about me going back to the sport. The bathroom was down a long hallway, near the bow. Connected to a stateroom, it was glossy and quiet. I ran cold water over my wrists and splashed my face. Bracing myself on the sink, I stared into the mirror, hardly recognizing myself.

Lines of strain bracketed my mouth and crept out from the corners of my eyes. I was thirty-four going on fifty-four, and I was hiding out in a bathroom like a chickenshit.

"Buck the fuck up, Morgan." Pushing off from the sink, I opened the door and came face-to-face with Parker.

From the compressed line of her lips and the raised schoolmarm brow, I knew I was going to have to talk. I just didn't know what the hell I was going to say.

Parker

AS SOON AS Rhys disappeared to use the bathroom, Mr. Fairchild lost all interest in me. A red-haired woman with impressive breasts was clearly far more intriguing. He walked away toward her without saying a word, demonstrating beyond a doubt that I needed Rhys by my side to stay on the jerk's radar.

It baffled me that a man wearing a white linen suit and purple slippers with gold embroidered initials held the fate of my future in his tiny little billionaire hands.

Rhys, and his not-so tiny hands, was currently off somewhere, freaking out.

He might be more stoic about it than most people, and

Fairchild was too self-involved to have noticed, but the subject of Rhys's retirement appeared to be a sore one. I was worried about his pallor when he strode away. Throwing out polite smiles to anyone who met my gaze, I hurried to follow in my fake boyfriend's wake.

My concern was disconcerting.

Rhys was a big boy. One who showed up on a Harley to take me to a formal event. Not that I was complaining. I mean, I'd have to research its emission levels, but aesthetically the bike was delicious. It *felt* sexy. Really pleasantly sexy with my inner thighs pressed against Rhys's hard thighs and the machine purring beneath me as the wind blew the tantalizing scent of Rhys's spicy cologne around me.

Yum.

Who knew?

I threw that thought away. I could not have sexy thoughts about a man who would never have those kinds of thoughts about me in return. And I could not be hot for a guy who required a swear jar.

It wasn't him, I reminded myself. It was the bike! The bike made everything hot.

I *really* hoped it had low emissions.

Still, I followed my curiosity to the bathroom Fairchild had directed Rhys to and waited outside for him. As soon as he opened the door, I blocked his path.

He sighed just before his expression shut down.

Uh-uh.

Answers were needed.

"The whole reason I agreed to this deception was because Fairchild was interested in Rhys *the Widowmaker*."

"Don't call me that," he snapped.

And not snapping in that playful, antagonistic banter thing way we had going. This time he meant it.

What had happened here?

Sympathy softened my tone. "Rhys, if there's a reason you find it difficult to talk about your boxing days, maybe we shouldn't do this. I don't want to put you in that position. Especially not with someone like Fairchild."

He lifted his chin, his features taut. "I'm fine. There's nothing to see here."

"I disagree." I gave his arm a squeeze, and he tensed at the gesture. Feeling awkward for touching him when he hadn't invited it, I took a step back. "Something is going on with you. Is it... about your dad? Does your retirement remind you of why... of him?"

With an exasperated sigh, he stepped out into the hall. "He's not the real reason I quit. Someone died. It wasn't one of my matches, but I knew the guy, and it was a wake-up call. No sport is worth leaving your little brother behind with no fucking family to speak of. My career didn't end the way I thought it would. That's it. But"—he pushed into my personal space and I felt warm tingles between my thighs—"I can do this. There's no getting out of this contract, Tinker Bell, so forget about it."

He was deflecting, and I was going to let him. There was more to his story, I knew it, but I was also aware that I didn't have his trust yet. That was fine. I could deal with that. It wasn't as though I trusted him completely. Or that we were even about sharing personal information. Rhys wanted to keep this all business—why should I argue?

"I wasn't attempting to get out of the contract. Unfortunately, I need you." I made a face. "As soon as you left, Fairchild spotted a pair of breasts across the yacht he fancied more."

Rhys snorted and slipped his hand into mine. "Then let's go find him and show him how wrong he is."

A spark of awareness shot up my arm. He had big, strong hands with calluses on his palms. I'd never dated a man with calluses before. They were surprisingly appealing.

Not that we were dating.

Needing to distract myself from whatever was happening to my body, I blurted out, "Did you know super yachts are bad for the environment?"

Rhys shot me an amused look. "There's a surprise."

"It's true. However, last year an eco super yacht was launched in the Netherlands called the Black Pearl. *The Black Pearl* – you know, like from Pirates of the Caribbean. It's got these big black DynaRig sails so it uses wind power. A true zero-emissions boat—"

"Is there a reason you're rambling, Tink?" Rhys asked, laughter in his voice as we walked onto the upper deck.

It was annoying to consider he might be perceptive enough to know the difference between one of my rambles and when I was merely being informative. "Of course you'd consider anything related to environmental awareness as 'rambling'"

He spun on me suddenly, forcing me back against the upper deck railing. Bracketing his hands on either side of the rails, he bent his head toward mine. Rhys frowned, as he seemed to search my face for something. "Let's get rid of whatever stuck-up idea you got in your head about me. I might not be marching through the streets with my fucking Greenpeace sign, but I watch wildlife documentaries and I care that our selfish shit is devastating the planet's ecosystems. Princess, I like animals more than I like people, so I definitely don't like what we're doing to *their* planet. Did you see the documentary with the walruses?" Rhys shook his head, genuine anger lighting his eyes. "I'm a grown fucking man, and I nearly bawled like a baby watching that shit."

Rhys's sincerity caused a tightening of attraction deep in

my gut. He watched wildlife documentaries? I *did* bawl like a baby at the walruses and was strangely turned on that he was compassionate enough to admit to *feelings* on the matter.

I might have emitted a moan.

His eyebrows rose toward his hairline, and then a wicked grin flashed across his face.

Yup, I definitely emitted a moan.

If I were Hermione Granger, I could make the railing behind me disappear, thus plunging me into the waters below. A far more efficient equivalent to praying for the floor to open beneath my feet.

His eyes danced with delight. "Did I just push one of your hot buttons?"

I flushed bright red, and Rhys threw his head back in laughter. The big jerk. Narrowing my eyes, I tried to shove his arm away from the railing to free myself, but he wrapped his arms around me instead.

"What are you doing?" I huffed, staring up into his smiling, cocky, too-handsome face. My hands were braced on his powerful chest, his were pressing deep into my spine, and the tingles I'd felt earlier were now progressing to pivotal erogenous zones.

It was disconcerting to say the least.

"Caring about wildlife gets you hot. Good to know."

I squirmed in his arms. "Does this conversation really require cuddling?"

His grip loosened, his hands coasting down my waist to my hips. "We're supposed to be a couple, remember. Couples touch. In fact—"

"Morgan!" Fairchild's voice cut through us, reminding me we were not alone.

Rhys turned toward the voice, dropping one hand but sliding his other arm around my waist. Mr. Fairchild crossed the upper deck with the tall, glamorous redhead from earlier. She wore a white dress that clung to every smooth curve of her body, of which there were plenty. Her huge breasts strained against the draped, low neckline of the dress, so much so even *I* stared.

Mine were bee stings in comparison.

"Morgan, this is Adriana Bellington. She attended one of your fights, immediately recognized you—"

"And forced Fairchild to introduce us." Adriana fluttered her lashes at him. If it were possible, I think even her boobs were fluttering at Rhys.

I was discomfited to find myself comparing assets as the redhead pulled Rhys away from me to kiss his cheeks and crush her humongous tatas against his chest.

I'd never felt insecure about my figure but then I'd never pretend dated a guy whose usual type was voluptuous women. That niggle of insecurity was accompanied by more than a hint of annoyance.

He was my fake boyfriend. Who cared if he preferred watermelons over my little peaches? He'd never get near them for it to be an issue.

"Nice to meet you," Rhys said to Adriana, moving back toward me and doing an admirable job of averting his gaze from her enviable frontage.

The redhead flicked a look and summarily dismissed me, and moved a little closer to Rhys. "I've just taken over owner-ship of Sportbox."

Rhys raised an eyebrow. "The sports network?"

"The very one."

A successful businesswoman, in sports, and she was ridicu-lously sexy.

Wonderful.

"We're making boxing a focus. It's a pity you're no longer

fighting. Perhaps we could grab a drink together and you can tell me what you've been up to?" Adriana nodded her head toward the bar.

"A sound idea," Fairchild agreed. "Perhaps you can let me convince the man to come out of retirement."

Adriana smiled at Rhys in a way there was no misinterpreting the come-on. "Oh, I'm very good at convincing a man to see things my way."

"Oh wow," I muttered before I could stop myself.

Seriously?

Rhys appeared to be struggling not to laugh as he wrapped his arm around my waist again and pulled me into his side. A minute ago, I'd felt feminine and fragile in his arms and with those feelings came unexpected sexy ones. Who knew overwhelming masculinity could be a turn-on?

Now, however, next to Adriana Bellington, I felt like a little girl.

It was upsetting that my fake date could provoke such feelings of self-doubt.

I did not like this revelation at all.

Rhys was unaware of my inner turmoil as he stroked a hand down my hip. "I'm here with my girlfriend, actually."

Adriana's features flattened with surprise and displeasure.

This was how it would always be, I realized. No one in Rhys's previous or current circle would ever believe he would date someone like me, and no one in mine would believe I'd date someone like him.

"Well, it was nice to see you." Adriana flicked a look at me. "And meet you." She turned to Fairchild. "We'll talk later about the Hamilton deal."

Fairchild nodded and watched her walk away. She was something to watch. He turned to us. "What a woman." He winked at Rhys. "You've got an 'in' there."

My jaw dropped.

It might have even made a sound hitting the floor.

Rhys's hold on me tightened. "Not meaning any disrespect, sir, but I'm not sure that's the kind of thing I like you saying in front of my girl."

Fairchild blinked and then stared at me as if he were seeing me for the first time. "Oh. Of course. I meant no harm by it. My apologies." My boss gave me the first genuine smile I'd ever received from him. "Very rude of me."

"It's quite alright," I lied because I'd been raised to accept an apology when it was given. And also because I was still trying to impress this man even if that made me feel like a sell-out.

"Yes, yes, Jackson has been very impressed by you, Parker. And if you managed to make this man settle down," he said, slapping Rhys on the shoulder, "then that's truly impressive."

Thankfully, he told us he'd be right back and disappeared so I could turn to Rhys and growl my frustration.

A real, honest-to-goodness growl.

My fake date snorted.

"It's not funny," I hissed, turning toward the water. "He's despicable. I'm suddenly worthy of his attention because I'm not just some girl you're taking 'for a ride' but someone *you* are serious about. He is everything that is male and white and privileged and *wrong* about this country."

Rhys leaned on the railing, his arm brushing mine. "Then why are you trying to impress the guy? You got money to tide you over while you find another job."

I looked at him, startled to find his face so close. His proximity afforded me the opportunity to study his eyes. There was a ring of light golden brown around the inner iris that I'd never noticed before. The vivid pale green of the outer iris swam into the golden brown, so startling you could never call them hazel.

Mossy green, I thought.

A beautiful mossy green.

And naturally soulful too. A woman could fall into those eyes if she wasn't careful.

With a sigh, I looked out at the water. "Because I love my job. It's an important job and it's everything I've worked for. My family wanted me to join their fancy law firm in New York and I refused because this is what I wanted to do. And I *hate* disappointing my family. That's how much I want this job."

"So we put up with him."

I wrinkled my nose. "He doesn't seem to bother you that much."

Rhys shrugged. "We're trying to impress the guy. I'm not going to be outright rude to him even when he's being a prick."

I jumped on that. "You think he's a p-r-i-c-k?"

He threw me that boyish grin as he gestured behind us. "I think they're all *pricks*—if you sound out your words, Tinker Bell, you'll get there eventually."

I rolled my eyes and decided to ignore that. "Well, that's not fair. About them being pri—*nkles*. You don't know them."

"Let's be clear." He turned toward me. "I didn't call them *prinkles*. That sounds like something you put on a fucking cupcake. And I know enough about these people to know most of them are pricks." A hint of bitterness laced his words.

"If you think these are 'my people,' you must think I'm a prinkle too."

Rhys smirked. "Do I think you'd taste nice on a cupcake? Yeah, I fucking do."

Determined not to laugh at his teasing in case it encouraged him, I fought a smile and shook my head at him like he was a naughty schoolboy. This just seemed to delight him more.

"Truthfully," he said, nudging me with his arm, "what's with the schoolmarm, no-cussing thing?"

My amusement died. "It's not a thing. I just don't like curse words."

"You're a grown woman, denying herself the right to a gratifying 'fuck' every now and then. That ain't right."

I blushed at the lurid images that suddenly filled my head.

"Dirty Tinker Bell," he tutted, grinning, "I wasn't talking about that kind of 'fuck' but —"

"Argh." I pressed a finger to his lips to stop him from saying anything that might make me want to punch him and melt all over him in equal measure. The man had way too much sexual charisma for it to be fair. "Stop."

His lips twitched against my finger, and I instantly dropped my arm.

"If you must know, my *mother* hates curse words." I smoothed my hands down my dress and turned back toward the party, thinking of how miserable events like this made me and always had. Much to my mother's chagrin. "She's a complicated woman. This is a woman who marched with over one hundred thousand men and women on Washington in 1977 in ninety-five-degree heat to demand an extension on ratifying the Equal Rights Amendment." I was extremely proud she did that. "But this is the same woman who has very specific ideas about men and women. She believes in our equal rights and she believes a woman can do anything a man can do, career-wise. She does not, however, have a problem with a man cursing but believes for a woman to do so is extremely unladylike."

Rhys shrugged. "Again, you're a grown woman. You can do whatever the hell you want."

That's what everyone said out loud, but I had to believe I wasn't the only one who could still be reduced to childlike status by my parents. I loved my mom and dad. They'd given me a lot of opportunities in life and they loved me. It was in my nature to people-please, especially my parents, so denying them anything was hard. And I'd denied them a lot over the years.

"I've disappointed them," I admitted. "My parents. In different ways." I flicked Rhys a look and found him watching me, curiosity in his gaze. I glanced away and gave the party a breezy smile. "The least I can do is keep my mouth clean for my mom." I chuckled but was desperately searching for a passing waiter with a tray of ten champagne flutes I could divest him of.

"If that's true, why do I need to keep *my* mouth clean?"

Thinking about it, I had no answer. Perhaps her distaste had become my distaste, but truthfully, I was growing used to Rhys's cursing. It was just who he was. And it wasn't as if I was ever going to introduce my cussing fake boyfriend to my mother. I didn't want my parents to know I'd stooped to lying to make my career happen, and I didn't want to lie to them and get their hopes up that I'd found someone I was serious about.

"I guess you don't," I conceded as I straightened my shoulders. "We should find Fairchild and remind him I exist."

Rhys decided to give me that, not pushing the subject of my parents, which I appreciated. We moved down to the middle deck where Fairchild conversed with a group of men while women in string bikinis lounged behind them in a hot tub.

It was a clichéd scene that belonged in the 1980s. This yacht was my worst nightmare.

"Ah, there he is!" Fairchild spotted Rhys. "Men, you have to meet Morgan. Morgan, come here."

Rhys tightened his grip on my hand and led me over.

Whatever he'd been feeling earlier, Rhys let go as he charmed Fairchild and the men around him. They asked about his days as a heavyweight champion, an existence that was such a far cry from their own, and Rhys indulged them. My boss, Jackson, appeared with Camille, along with a few colleagues and their partners. We spoke a little, a light relief at a party that made me uncomfortable, but they soon dispersed among the crowds. Except Jackson who stayed with Fairchild, listening to Rhys.

Other people joined and left the conversation, businessmen and women, members of Boston society, and Rhys handled them all with amazing aplomb. It occurred to me that, during his professional boxing days, he would have been surrounded by wealthy people. He was used to them.

He was better with them than I was, and I grew up in this world.

As the night wore on, I longed to be back in my apartment, curled up on my bed with the fantasy novel I was in the middle of. It was about faeries and war and romance and kick-ass heroines.

Or I'd prefer to be hanging out with the guys. "The guys" were my friends from MIT who hadn't left Boston. Every second week we found a quiz night to attend and took far too much pleasure in annihilating our competitors.

Rhys was in the middle of convincing Fairchild and a few of his friends to drop by the gym for boxing lessons when I felt a hand on the small of my back. I turned sharply and looked up into a smiling, familiar face.

Stephen Chancer.

An ex.

Ish.

We'd gone on three dates. I'd slept with him on the third and then told him it wasn't going to work out. Mostly because if I couldn't stop thinking about electricity markets with high wind penetration during *his* penetration then I was calling it a fail.

However, my concern wasn't over bumping into a man I'd rejected. He and I had been set up by his aunt, who knew my mother. For the most part I'd avoided mingling with East Coast society during my time at MIT, much to my mother's despair. Stephen was the one time I'd let myself slip into that world, and to be honest, it wasn't just his lack of industry in the bedroom that made me call it quits. He relied too much on his parents' money and was kind of a snob.

None of that mattered now.

What mattered was him telling his aunt I was dating ex-boxer Rhys Morgan.

"Stephen, hi." I flicked a wary look at Rhys who was too busy answering whatever question Fairchild had asked to notice who I was talking to.

"It's so good to see you." At five foot seven, Stephen didn't have to bend his head far to press a kiss to the corner of my mouth as I turned to him.

I frowned at the intimacy and shuffled a little away. Stephen followed me. He'd never really been aware of the whole personal space thing.

Oh boy.

"How have you been? What are you doing here?" he asked.

Go away, go away, go away.

"I'm well, thank you. Mr. Fairchild is the CEO of the company I work for. Horus Renewable Energy."

"That's great." He raised his champagne flute to me. "My father is in business with Fairchild. He couldn't be here tonight, so I came in his stead. My date"—he glanced around the deck—"is around here somewhere." Stephen turned back to me, eyeing me speculatively. "Did you come here alone?"

"No, she's with me." Rhys suddenly appeared at my side, his arm sliding around my back to rest possessively on my opposite hip. I felt his lips brush my forehead. "You okay, sweetheart?"

I glanced up at him. His appearance was not good. Now

Stephen would find out and possibly tell his aunt who would then tell my mother and the world would implode. So if that was true, why did I find myself relaxing against Rhys and wishing he'd take my hand and lead me out of the party to his sexy bike?

I nodded, struck mute by the thought.

"I'm Stephen." The aforementioned held out his hand to Rhys. "Parker's ex-boyfriend. You are?"

Rhys grabbed Stephen's hand and gave him a rough handshake that made Stephen, my so-not-ex-boyfriend, wince. "I'm Rhys. I'm Parker's."

His word choice was deliberate, and I found myself desperately trying not to snort with anxious hysteria.

Stephen raised an eyebrow as he glanced between us. "You don't sound like you're from around here?"

I tensed at the snootiness in his tone.

Rhys's hand flexed on my hip. "Funny," he said, his voice flat, "here I thought it was my accent they called Bostonian, not yours."

I smiled smugly at the answer.

Stephen wrinkled his nose and then cut me a superior look. "Everything makes so much sense now."

Ugh. Snob!

Watching him walk away, I grew tenser. What if he told his aunt about Rhys?

"Hey, you okay?"

I turned toward Rhys. "He's not my ex-boyfriend," I blurted out. "We went on three dates. Three not-very-memorable dates."

"Yeah." Rhys frowned down at me and lowered his voice. "You hate it here, Tinker Bell."

It wasn't a question.

"And no wonder."

Fairchild's party was not a great example of East Coast society. Not everyone was as superior as Stephen or as misogynistic as Fairchild. The billionaire just drew a bad crowd. Still, I'd never been at home at this kind of event and clearly it was showing.

"I think it's time to go." Rhys nudged me toward the exit.

"Why?"

"Because you're fucking miserable, and if Fairchild realizes that, he's not going to be impressed."

True.

"Argh," I half-growled under my breath.

Rhys shook his head, smirking. "Come on, Angry Tink, we need to say goodnight to our host."

Fairchild was disappointed to see us leave. Okay, he was disappointed to see Rhys leave. Jackson, on the other hand, looked envious of our departure. And everyone else... well, who cared about any of them.

"Freedom," I said melodramatically at the bottom of the boarding ramp.

My date snorted and then led me across the lot to where he'd parked his Harley. It really was a hot bike. As he handed over my helmet, Rhys held onto it a second.

His gaze was searching.

I squirmed. "What?"

He shook his head slightly. "You aren't what I expected."

Truthfully, Rhys wasn't what I'd expected either, but those thoughts were dangerous. "What?" I yanked on the helmet and straddled the bike. "Awesome?"

With a grunt of amusement, his gaze flickering over my legs, Rhys got on the bike. "That wasn't the adjective I was looking for, no."

"Boo!"

He glanced over his shoulder, his expression incredulous. "Did you just fucking boo me? First a shoo, now a boo?"

"Your lack of deference required a boo."

"You know what requires a boo? I forgot to kiss you in front of all those pricks."

I shivered at the thought. "There was no need."

Rhys huffed. "You might not have noticed but there were assholes eyeing you as soon as Fairchild told them you were my woman."

"Boo to that too. Misogyny at its finest. 'A woman is only as interesting as the man who dates her.' Where's a bucket to vomit in when you need it?"

"Don't you be vomiting anywhere near my baby." He patted his bike before craning around to look at me again. "Seriously. Next time we're around these people, you're going to have to let me kiss you and do it without swooning like it's our first time."

I wrinkled my nose in the face of such cockiness. "I think I can manage not to swoon over a kiss. Even if it is granted by the all-mighty Rhys Morgan."

"Oh, Tinker Bell, you're making my ego swell." He reached for his helmet.

"If it swells any bigger, it'll explode all over your sweet ride."

"You think my ride is sweet?"

"I can't confirm that until I research its emission levels."

I felt his body shake with laughter. "Of course you can't."

And then his helmet was on, the engine started, and the bike purred between my legs as Rhys drove us away from the yacht. With every second, I felt myself relaxing more and more into him as he took me away from a world I'd never fitted into.

SEVEN

Parker

STARING across the bistro table at my little sister, I felt like I was waiting for the other shoe to drop. She would ask me about Rhys because surely Stephen Chancer had told his aunt about meeting the boxer on Fairchild's yacht last week. His aunt would have immediately called my mother to ask me about the relationship and my mother would set Easton on me.

Why else would my little sister come into Boston for the weekend?

I winced inwardly at my own paranoia.

Easton visited me often in Boston, so her appearance wasn't suspicious at all.

All the lying was making me crazy.

"You seem tense." Easton didn't look up from the breakfast menu. We were at one of my favorite little cafés around the corner from my building.

"I'm not tense." I was *so* freaking tense.

My sister sighed and lowered her menu. "I think I'll have the omelet."

"Mmm," I agreed distractedly.

Her dark eyes narrowed. There was no denying Easton and I were related. Although there was a four-year gap between us, we were much alike. We had the same dark eyes, dark hair, olive skin, and petite build. The only difference was Easton had a far more interesting face. Her eyes were slightly more tip-tilted than round, her nose a little sharper and character-filled, her mouth wider.

And while my preferred style was "quirky preppy," Easton almost always looked like she'd just come from the office, in a very stylish, expensive way. Today she wore a red silk blouse, the top buttons opened to reveal a little cleavage, and it was tucked into a gray pencil skirt. Her dark hair was styled in soft waves and the only jewelry that adorned her were a pair of diamond studs in her ears, a classic steel Jaeger watch, and the massive diamond ring on her engagement finger.

"It's because of this, isn't it?" Easton said, waving her left hand with the knuckle-duster on it. "Are Mom and Dad putting pressure on you because of this?"

If you called longing looks thrown my way whenever Easton's engagement came up pressure. "Not really."

"Not really, as in they haven't said anything but there are enough lengthy pauses and meaningful looks to make you feel like you're disappointing them?"

My goodness, my sister knew me, and them, so well. I shrugged. "I'm happy for you. They're happy for you. That's all that matters."

And it was true. Easton had stumbled across a unicorn. Her fiancé, Oliver Bowen, had inherited a wealth borne from the fruits of a cocoa-bean empire. He was a human rights defense lawyer and was involved in so many philanthropic ventures; you couldn't hate the guy if you tried.

There was nothing to hate.

He was a prime example that not all East Coast socialites were prinkles.

Argh, I couldn't even curse in my head!

I frowned. Since when did I want to? Cursing was *blech* and unnecessary. Or was that just my mother talking?

Rhys Morgan, damn you. He was infiltrating my headspace.

"Yes, I'm very lucky," Easton said, dreamy-eyed. I felt a prickle of envy as I remembered how it felt to love someone like she loved Oliver.

"*He's* very lucky."

"Yes, I know." My sister shot me a look. "But I'm allowed to think I'm lucky too."

"Of course, you are. Omelet, you say." I mused over the menu. "I'm thinking bagel."

"You're distracted today. You were distracted last night too."

"Work is all-consuming," I lied.

The truth was I'd been worrying about my parents finding out about Rhys and, at the same time, a little disconcerted to find myself itching to text the man. When he'd dropped me off after the party, I'd told him I'd be in touch when I needed him next.

So far there'd been no need of him.

Hmm.

The waiter arrived and my sister and I studied each other. I was waiting for the Stephen Chancer bomb-drop, and she was waiting for me to admit there was something going on I hadn't told her about.

My cell sounded a musical ditty that announced a text. "I

have to," I said apologetically as I reached for my purse. "It could be work."

It wasn't work.

HotHarley: No hours for me this weekend, Tinker Bell?

I grinned, hearing his Boston accent in my head.

ParkerB: Bored, Morgan?

HotHarley: I don't do bored. Got nothing, then?

ParkerB: Not this weekend. You're free to watch wildlife documentaries. I'll send some tissues.

HotHarley: No need. I have my own. What you up to?

I frowned at the question, even as my stomach fluttered.

ParkerB: I'm spending time with my sister. We're ordering breakfast.

HotHarley: Well, if you weren't so stuck on keeping our deal from your family, I could have made you both my famous frittata.

He cooked?

He rode a hot bike (the emission levels were terrible and my guilt was real over the fact that it had not diminished its appeal nearly enough), he watched wildlife documentaries, and he cooked.

Ugh, I should have stuck with Dean. He was way less complicated.

ParkerB: Is that a euphemism? Or did you just admit to being able to cook?

HotHarley: I just admitted to being able to FUCKING cook. There's a difference.

"Okay, who are you texting that's making you smile like that?" Easton's voice cut through my Rhys bubble.

My head jerked up. I was mortified to realize I'd momentarily forgotten she was there. "Um, my boss." I hedged. "He's a funny guy."

"Single?" Easton asked, hopeful.

I snorted. "No. Even if he was, you're really encouraging me to sleep with my boss?"

"I'm encouraging you to be happy."

"And that requires a man?"

Easton narrowed her eyes. "You know it doesn't. But it does require moving on. It's been thirteen years, Parker. Don't you think it's time?"

"It's not that I don't want to." I shrugged. "However, I know how it's supposed to feel, and I've tried to find it again and failed. Maybe a person is only allowed it once in their lives. Why waste all that energy dating men who don't fit when I can just concentrate on the things that make me happy? Like my job. And helping my little sister plan the wedding of the century."

Now it was Easton's turn to snort. "Helping me plan a wedding is the equivalent to dental torture for you."

"I'm your maid of honor."

"Yes. You are. But I love you and I don't want to torture you, so I officially release you from all maid-of-honor duties. Just turn up for the dress fittings and the wedding events and I'll be happy."

"I love you, you know that, right?"

She grinned. "I'm very lovable."

"You are. But I refuse to relinquish my maid-of-honor duties. My little sister is getting married and I want to be a part of it." Even if my idea of a bachelorette party was a quiz night followed by takeout and hanging out at my apartment with the girls. Somehow, I didn't think that would cut it for Easton. It was going to have to involve a trip somewhere. Vegas or Hawaii.

And she'd want strippers.

Mostly to mortify our mother.

"Fine, but I want strippers on my bachelorette trip," Easton said, pointing a finger at me, her expression determined.

Chuckling to myself, I nodded as I glanced down at my cell.

ParkerB: Do you know any male strippers?

There was no immediate answer.

As I bit into my bagel, I got a text.

HotHarley: I'm gonna have to charge extra for that, Tinker Bell.

I laughed, almost choking on my breakfast.

"Your boss really must be funny, huh?" Easton had a knowing twinkle in her eye.

Oh God, I didn't know what was worse. Worrying about my parents finding out from Stephen Chancer's aunt that I was "dating" Rhys Morgan, or my sister thinking I had a crush on Jackson.

This is what happened when you lied, people.

In the words of Sir Walter Scott, "Oh, what a tangled web we weave, when first we practice to deceive."

"Did you just mutter Shakespeare under your breath?" Easton asked.

Poor Sir Walter Scott. "I'm thinking Hawaii for the bachelorette." I sought to distract her again.

Her eyes lit up. "Ooh, yes. Strippers in loincloths. Mom will die."

I shook my head at her determination to mortify our mother, but deep down, I was a little jealous. Easton wasn't a people-pleaser. She did what she wanted, no matter what. It just so happened most of what she wanted to do with her life fit into my parents' ideas of the perfect career woman/society lady.

Yet Easton didn't fear disappointing our parents. She didn't strive to make them happy above her own happiness, and in fact, she liked to find little ways (like hiring male strippers) to ruffle their feathers.

The truth was, I knew why I so desperately wanted to please the people I loved. It was a grief buried deep down, and although I wished I could let it go, live my life as a grown woman who didn't care about her parents' opinion, I wasn't sure I'd ever be able to.

"And we have to make Mom wear a grass skirt," Easton continued.

"When hell freezes over, Easton. When hell freezes over."

My sister frowned in thought and then nodded. "The strippers will just have to do."

Rhys

PARKER DIDN'T TEXT me again. It shouldn't pluck at my guts, but it did. She'd asked if I knew any male strippers. Seriously? I'd like to think she was joking, but I was fairly certain she wasn't. Which meant, somewhere out there, prissy Parker Brown was hunting down male entertainment.

My fingers twitched, tapping out an agitated rhythm on my desk. Why did she want a stripper? Best guess was a bachelorette party. I couldn't picture it, though. Couldn't see Parker, with her cute little skirts and tops that had floppy bows, getting rowdy with other women, squealing over some naked dude.

A smile tugged on my lips. Or maybe I could. It'd be something to catch a glimpse of her like that, totally free from the stiff confines she normally held herself to. Without thought, I grabbed my phone and looked at her last texts, wanting to talk to her again.

"Idiot," I muttered, tossing the phone on the desk in disgust. One freaking date with the woman—one fake-ass date —and I was acting like an adolescent.

"You're in my seat."

From the doorway, Dean wore his shit-eating grin.

"Deanie, you might be working here for the moment," I said mildly, "but this here seat is mine."

"Yeah, well, it's parked in front of my desk, so ..." He waved a hand toward the door. "Shove off."

"It's amusing the way you think I'm going to listen to you."

Dean strolled into the office. The little shit actually had on a suit. "It's not like you're working. I watched you stare off into space for the past ten minutes."

The knot in my stomach twisted tighter.

"You've been watching me for ten minutes? That's creepy, little bro."

The corner of his mouth lifted. "No, what's creepy is the witless smile you had on your face the whole time. Well, just before you snapped out of it and grimaced like you had indigestion."

Crap. I'd been smiling? God, no. I didn't know what horrified me more—that I'd been making goofy faces or that Dean had caught me. When he kept on silently laughing at my expense, I rubbed my eye with my middle finger.

"Nice." Dean looked me over like he was trying to read my mind. "What's got you loopy-eyed? Could it be a certain preppy heiress?"

This line of conversation had to end. Fast.

I stood and stretched the kink out of my tense neck. "I was

considering all the ways I could make your life a living hell while you're here."

Pocketing my phone with casual ease, because I did *not* want to check for texts, I rounded the desk and clasped Dean's shoulder. "See that pile of papers on the conference table?"

The table in question ran along the far length of the room and could seat fifteen.

"Piles of paper, Rhys. I see piles."

I grinned. "That's the accounting work for Lights Out."

His eyes widened in horror. "You don't have it on the computer?"

I did. But he didn't need to know that. Shrugging, I let his stiff shoulder go. "Guess Dad liked doing things the old-fashioned way, and I haven't had the time to get around to it. I guess it's up to you."

A few ripe curses ripped through the air as Dean stalked over to the table and lifted a folder to thumb through it. "I'll be here all fucking month!"

That was the idea. And he'd never get the chance to see the true mess Dad left behind.

"Then you better start now." I made a show of glancing at my watch. "I'm going to get a coffee. You want one? You'll probably need the caffeine."

"Fuck you, Rhys," he said it without much heat, already slumped down on a conference chair and reaching for more files. "Seriously. Fuck you. This is an embarrassment. And you call me irresponsible. No wonder the gym is on shaky ground." His brows winged up as he looked over his shoulder at me. "How can you possibly run a business this way?"

"Hey, I never said I was a businessman." In truth, I wasn't bad at business. But it was damn near impossible to be in the black when you started off with a mountain of debt. And I damn near shuddered at how my relatively innocent brother would have received that bit of news.

Although I was deliberately messing with him, I couldn't ignore the small twinge of shame at his disappointment. He'd looked up to me all his life. I'd been his idol. Now, he clearly saw me as a has-been and a fuck-up.

I was beginning to think I'd never rid myself of the hot, sticky tar of regret and rage that coated my insides and pulled on my skin. It shouldn't matter what others thought of me. But Dean mattered. I both loved and hated him for it.

Without saying another word, I turned and left the office, the sound of Dean's bitching following me down the hall.

Carlos met up with me in the lobby. "Please tell me Dean working here is one of his jokes."

"It is, but he seems determined to try." I glanced at the office. "How long he'll actually keep at it is anyone's guess."

"He is easily bored."

"Usually." Grimacing, I headed for the lounge. It wasn't in the shape I wanted it to be; we needed something better than yellowing vending machines and two ancient coffee makers. In my mind's eye, I replaced the clunky percolator with a push-button espresso maker, set up a new juice bar on the far side of the room, and changed the cracked tile floors to smooth, wide hardwoods.

Fairchild could make it happen. With his money, I could fix everything; more importantly, I could hire instructors and trainers and get bodies in the door, membership cards in their hands. Admiring my former career wasn't enough, though. I had to figure out how to sell this place to him. I might be an okay businessman, but I definitely wasn't a good salesman.

I poured myself a cup of truly shitty coffee and faced Carlos. He punched in the code for a power drink and bent to retrieve it.

"You aren't worried about Dean getting into the accounting?" Carlos twisted the cap off the bottle and took a long drink.

"I left every bill and financial transaction the gym has had since time began on the conference room table and told him nothing was on the computer."

Carlos choked on his drink. "Damn, man. That's just evil."

"But necessary. Hopefully Dean will give up long before he realizes there are holes in the accounting."

Laughing, Carlos followed me out of the lounge. We headed toward the front stoop. Sadly, the gym smelled like feet —something I couldn't figure out how to get rid of—and the stoop was the only place we could get some fresh air and be certain Dean wouldn't hear us.

The sunshine blinded me as I stepped outside. Yet another reminder of how dark and dank the damn gym was. I glared down into my Styrofoam cup and then tossed the whole thing into the nearby trashcan. I didn't want shitty coffee. I didn't want to be here at all.

Do not think about her.

Was she really hiring a stripper?

"Fuck me."

Carlos raised a brow. "Sorry, bro. There are some things I am unwilling to do. You'll just have to live with disappointment that my extraordinary dick is unattainable."

I snorted. "I guess that dream will have to die." I was about to give him shit when a Land Rover rolled up in front of the gym. A much-needed tide of white-hot rage crashed through my system. I planted my feet and let it ride.

At my side, Carlos stood up, his hands fisting. "*Puñeta.*"

A chauffeur opened the back door, and a tall blond guy got out. Garret.

Ignoring the ribald Spanish curses flowing from Carlos's

mouth, I tried not to glare down at the guy. But he was a persistent fucker.

He nodded at us both as he stopped at the bottom of the stairs. "I wondered if you had time to chat?"

"If it's about buying the gym, then I don't think so," I said.

"I have a new offer for you."

Shit. My gut churned. Part of me wondered if turning this guy away made my choices just as fucked up as my dad's. "The gym is not on the market. It would just be a waste of your time and mine."

Garret sighed and glanced down the street before turning back to me. "I know you're in trouble with the bank."

Heat crawled up my neck, but I kept my voice neutral despite my anger. "Yeah? And how the fuck would you know anything about my finances?"

He shrugged. "I know people."

"Yeah, well, you don't know me, Garret. I'm not selling my gym." I crossed my arms over my chest and spread my legs.

Garret's gaze drifted over me. "I understand pride, Mr. Morgan. But if you'd put yours aside for a minute, you'd realize I'm doing you a favor."

"Yeah, sure."

His smile was thin, half amused, half pissed off. "When the bank takes this place from you, they'll auction it off on the cheap."

Like I didn't know this. I had nightmares about it. They'd auction off my gym and then turn around and suddenly I'd be on stage. Behold the final death of a broke-down boxer's pride. So, yeah, I knew about pride. Sometimes it was all you had.

"Makes me wonder why you're bothering now, instead of waiting."

Garret shrugged. "Maybe I'm just a nice guy."

"Maybe." But he wasn't. In my experience, no one was

when it came to money. No, somewhere in Garret's head, he feared I wouldn't fail and he wanted to snap the gym up now. It bolstered me, and I stared him down.

Finally, he nodded. "You know where I am if you change your mind."

The tension released from my body as he walked back to his fancy SUV.

Carlos's shoulders sagged but his chin remained stubbornly fixed. "You're doing the right thing."

"Am I?"

He nodded. "It's the last resort. We're not there yet."

"All we got is ourselves. And the promise of Parker Brown's connections."

"You better hope your fake sweetheart has some generous ones."

I didn't know what I'd do if Fairchild failed to take the bait. But I'd figure it out when I got there. The gym door squeaked open. Dean frowned down at us. "Who was that?"

"Who?" Carlos parroted, looking around. "I don't see anyone."

Dean rolled his eyes. "The guy in the Land Rover. You know, the one with the chauffeur?"

My jaw clenched. "One of Parker's friends looking for boxing lessons."

Carlos muttered at my side—something about my lying abilities being faster than my jabs.

I headed back up the stairs. "You finished with the files?"

Dean was still peering down the road, a thoughtful look on his face. "Fuck you, Rhys." His blue eyes, the exact color of my mother's, met mine. "I thought you were getting me a coffee."

"I was just about to go. You want to come?"

He got a look on his face as though he couldn't figure out if I was still messing with him. I wasn't. For once, I didn't want to fight with my baby brother. I wanted to remember what it was like when we got along. I wanted to forget this fucking day.

"Naw," he said. "I'll just grab a Coke out of the machine."

He slipped back inside, and I tried not to feel disappointed. Without thought, I pulled out my phone.

RhysThis: Tink, about this stripping gig. Am I going to need a sparkly thong? Or are you down for the full monty?

PARKER DIDN'T ANSWER. And I tried not to feel disappointed about that either.

EIGHT

Parker

I PACED the sitting room in the apartment I shared with Zoe. My mind volleyed between giving up the ruse with Rhys and finding a new job.

Out of my periphery, I could see my roommate's head swinging as she watched me.

"I don't understand why those are your only options," Zoe announced.

I halted mid-pace and stared incredulously at her. "Did you not hear what happened?"

"Yes. And I think you're making way too big a deal out of it." She took a sip of wine, curled up on the opposite couch, casually, and completely immune to my glare. "Honey, you hate lying. You hate lying so much, it's a surprise you haven't broken out into hives. Because of that, you're making what happened today into something it's not."

Slumping down onto the other couch, I put my own glass of wine on the glass coffee table and rethought the events of today.

It was Thursday, almost a week since I'd texted Rhys about the strippers, and I still hadn't seen him. There had been no need. Or so I thought. While I was minding my own business at work that day, Pete from payroll had wandered over to my desk to ask a question. However, our office was small and open plan. The only person who had walls enclosing their office was Jackson. Everyone else... no walls. Which meant conversation *traveled*.

"So," Pete said, eying me speculatively instead of walking away upon my answer to his overtime question, "you and the boxer aren't together anymore."

My heart fluttered unpleasantly. "Excuse me?" I saw heads turn out of the corner of my eye.

"Well, you never talk about him, you're always here so you're clearly not with him, and Evan"—he gestured to our tech guy across the room—"said you two weren't that cozy at Fairchild's yacht party."

And they said women gossiped.

I cut a look at Evan who blushed beet red and slid down on his chair to hide behind his desktop.

Turning my attention back to Pete, I tried not to sneer. I liked all my colleagues at Horus, except for Pete. He was the one who took great glee in telling me it was doubtful Fairchild would allow Jackson to keep me on after the six months was up. There was something sneaky and petty about Pete, and I had to wonder if he was jealous he never got invited to our events with Fairchild.

"Cozy?" I attempted to sound casual.

"No kissing, you barely touched him. You left the party early and then no more Rhys."

"That's not true."

"So why do you never talk about him?" Pete sat on the edge of my desk.

I huffed. "You don't talk about your personal lives. What? Because I'm a woman, I should?"

He scowled. "We refer to our personal lives. Say, when we leave the office at a respectable time, we always mention it's because our partners are waiting for us."

I glared around the room and saw heads jerk back to their computers.

Anxiety filled me.

"Evan said Rhys seemed into you, but it doesn't surprise me that you're not into him. You're from different worlds after all."

Seriously? Who was this guy? And Evan needed to shut up. I narrowed my eyes on Pete, suddenly wondering if his problem with me was more personal than I'd realized. It wouldn't be the first time someone had taken a dislike to me because I came from a privileged background and a well-known family.

Still, Evan, the little gossip, had said Rhys seemed into me but I wasn't into him? All this time I was worried Rhys would let me down and it was me who was screwing up.

A knot tightened in my gut. "I'm just very private," I replied. "Rhys and I are still together."

"Pete, don't you have other things to do?" Jackson's voice cut through the room as he strode out of his office toward us.

Pete jumped off my desk. "Of course, sir." He threw me a look, as if I were the reason he got caught not working, and hurried across to his side of the room that I would now refer to as the Creepy Pete Department.

Jackson wound around the desks and stopped in front of mine. He smiled down at me. "I'm glad to hear you and Rhys are still together because we've booked a paintball tournament. Everyone in the office is going and they're bringing their partners. You should bring Rhys. I have no doubt he'll make things interesting."

Confused, I asked, "Paintball?"

"A team-building exercise. I've done it before, and it works great in bringing a team together. Even when you're on opposite sides." He flashed me a cheeky smile. "A little competition is invigorating and since you're new here, I'd really like to see you there."

"Of course." Paintball. My idea of hell. Yay. But wait! "Is it environmentally friendly?"

Jackson grinned. "The shells and fill are biodegradable, yes."

"Okay." *Damn it.* "I'll be there."

"And Rhys too?"

I nodded. "I'll ask him."

The rest of the day I'd spent worrying instead of focusing on work, and then I'd come home to Zoe, still agitated.

As I told her about Pete, I realized I couldn't keep up the Rhys charade. I was a terrible liar, my colleagues already didn't believe in our relationship, and they were really not going to believe in it if we joined the paintball tournament.

My other option was to give into the inevitable and start looking for a new job.

An ache flared in my chest at the thought.

"The solution is staring you in the face," Zoe said.

"It is?"

"Call Rhys, explain the situation, and tell him you need to arrange a fake date, just the two of you, so you can work on the intimacy thing."

My cheeks flushed at the thought. "What does that mean exactly?"

Of course, my best friend knew about my whole deal with Rhys since she first suggested the app where I met Dean. Zoe

Liu was a lot more outgoing and adventurous than I was. She pushed me out of my comfort zone and had a habit of doing that to most people.

Zoe grew up in Boston with her single mom, Anna Liu. Anna had emigrated from Shenzhen, Guangdong, China, when she was eighteen years old, in search of the American Dream. Instead Anna's life here had only led to motherhood, poverty so extreme she and Zoe had been homeless for a while, and then eventually terminal cancer when Zoe was sixteen. It was a long story but that's when Zoe's wealthy British father was hauled into the picture. She didn't have much of a relationship with him, but he set her up with a trust fund that allowed her to attend Boston University. Zoe was now an assistant producer on an afternoon daily talk show.

Zoe had taken some of her trust fund when she was in college and launched a charity for the homeless called Street Warriors. We met when I volunteered to help raise money,

My best friend was pretty awesome.

And I always listened to her advice. Even when it landed me in the position I now was in.

"Get your mind out of the gutter." She grinned. "I didn't mean that kind of intimacy. Unless you want it to be. I've googled him. I wouldn't blame you."

"Stop." I waved away her comment. I didn't need to know Zoe thought Rhys was hot. "What *did* you mean?"

"I mean you need to practice getting comfortable with each other. Have a chilled-out fake date together and get that first kiss out of the way. Maybe even a second and third kiss. When he reaches out to you and you reach out to him, it has to look natural."

I scowled. "I thought I had been natural. He's a touchy-feely guy, and I let him hold me." It had been nice.

Zoe frowned. "I've never known you to be averse to physical affection so has it occurred to you that Creepy Pete is just trying to mess with your head?"

"Why would he do that? And it was Evan who was gossiping, apparently."

"Yes, but maybe Creepy Pete twisted those words around to suit his purpose. This is the guy who freaked you out about your position at Horus in the first place." Her expression softened with sympathy. "It wouldn't be the first time someone resented you for merely breathing just because of who your family is."

I sighed because she was reiterating my own suspicions about Pete. Both Zoe and I had dealt preconceived notions at college from people who judged us first and thought our parents' money had paved the way for our success.

"But I know you, and it'll put your mind at ease to *practice*. Call Rhys. Do it now. Tell him about paintball, tell him about Pete, and arrange a date. You're paying him a lot of money, Parker. He's not going to say no."

"He did mention the whole kissing thing." I nodded, coming around to the idea. Relief began to move through me as I realized there was still hope. "He said we needed to get a little more affectionate with each other to sell this."

"I bet he did," Zoe muttered.

"Excuse me?"

"Nothing." She beamed. "Go call him."

Little butterflies sprang to life in my belly at the idea of contacting Rhys. It had seemed like ages since we'd talked, and I was a little unsettled by the rush of anticipation I felt as I hurried through the open-plan living space and down the hall to the privacy of my bedroom.

Out of fairness and really a lack of preference, I'd taken the smallest of the bedrooms. It was still a little bare and unlived in because I hadn't had time to put my stamp on it yet.

Settling down onto my bed, those butterflies grew frantic. Heart racing, I hit Rhys's name on my cell before I could talk myself out of it.

It was a Thursday evening, I realized. Maybe he was on a date.

The thought caused an unpleasant lurch in my stomach.

"I was beginning to think I was being ghosted," Rhys answered without preamble.

A stupid smile curled my lips at the sound of his deep voice. "It appears I'm not very good at this fake relationship stuff."

"Yeah, I'm getting that."

Glad to hear amusement in his voice, I continued, "I need your help, Morgan."

"Hit me."

I explained about Pete and Evan's gossiping.

"Fuck, don't these guys have anything better to do?" he huffed.

My thoughts exactly. "Apparently not."

"So, what do you need, Tinker Bell?"

"You and I are invited to a team-building paintball ball tournament next weekend. Are you available?"

"I'll make myself available."

"Great. But I think we need to practice before then."

"Practice?"

"Go on a fake date together. Just you and I practice…being together. Try to create that illusion of intimacy." I felt my cheeks burning but forced out, "Maybe share a practice kiss."

There was silence on the other end of the line.

"Rhys?" Oh my goodness, had he changed his mind? Did he feel like I was trying to prostitute him? "Or not!" I hurried to say. "Whatever you're comfortable with."

A rumbly chuckle down the line created a tingling in my

body I desperately ignored. "Dahlin', I told you this shit at Fairchild's yacht thing. When are you going to start listening to me? I'm very smart."

I grinned. "You are. And I should have listened. Does that mean you're willing to go on a fake date with me?"

"You free tomorrow night?"

My smile widened to almost painful. "Yes."

"Then I'll pick you up at seven."

NINE

Rhys

"WHAT ARE WE DOING?" Parker's arms were wrapped around my waist, her slim, strong thighs clenching mine. It felt so good that I was momentarily distracted.

Didn't stop me from answering. I was good at multitasking. "Honey, if you don't know, there's no helping you."

She laughed, sending a glossy strand of hair fluttering, and then poked my ribs with a bony finger. "Cut it out. And. Tell. Me."

Each word ended with a poke. Violent little pixie. I approved.

"We're going to my place."

Her response was lost to me as the light turned green and I took off down the street. She squeezed me tighter, but I knew she liked speed. Her fingers did this massage thing on my abs when I accelerated, as if she could urge me faster just by touch alone. I knew she wasn't aware she was doing it; Parker was too self-contained and careful when she thought about her actions. Which was why the little touches got me off even more. They were glimpses of the real her, usually buried deep inside.

A bolt of pure heat licked the underside of my dick. Damn. My mind kept jumping to sex, and I needed to cut that shit out. Especially since I was about to "practice" kissing her.

Practice. I wanted to laugh at the sheer ridiculousness of that. Kissing was the last thing I needed to practice. Pretending to be a boyfriend? I had no clue how that was done.

I entered the covered loading dock area at the back of the gym's warehouse and parked. Parker's hair, once pulled back into a smooth, tidy ponytail, was now a mess of flyaway strands when she took off her helmet. She didn't seem to notice but gaped around the grimy, cold space.

"We're at the gym?"

"I live here." With a jerk of my chin, I gestured toward the back door and headed that way.

"You live at the gym?" She followed, still looking around, brown eyes wide and bright.

The woman seemed to have endless curiosity about everything. What would it be like to see the world through her eyes?

Hitting the button that would close the big bay door, I shook my head and then led her to the elevators. "You should see your expression, Tinker Bell. I'm not sleeping on the couch and taking showers in the locker room. My apartment is on the top floor."

Pink swarmed her cheeks as she stood up straight and gave me a repressive glare. "I didn't presume to think ..." She trailed off with a huff, and her lips quirked. "All right, that might have been what I was thinking."

"Gotcha." I barely stopped myself from reaching out and

tweaking her ponytail. That would have pissed her off. What was it about this girl that had me acting like an awkward teen?

The elevator opened straight into my loft, and I held out my hand, making a motion for her to enter first. She hesitated for a second, that pink blush remaining, then carefully stepped out and started slowly walking around, taking it all in.

My loft wasn't one of those high-priced remodels they were selling off for millions. It was the genuine article, old and drafty industrial grid windows, exposed brick and ductwork—not because a designer decided those things looked cool but because that's what was there to begin with. Didn't really matter to me; I loved it anyway.

The place held all that remained of my past life, the things I couldn't let myself sell off or let go. Some of it was essential to living here: the Swedish wood stove I'd picked up while on tour that put off so much heat, I didn't have to worry about drafts and cold in the winter; the butter leather couch and two chairs I relaxed on when not working; Mom's dining room set, and a dozen other odds and ends of hers I'd kept.

Parker's gaze drifted over everything. Her little heels clicked in the echoing silence. The loft was enormous, taking up the entire top of the building. I'd cordoned off a bedroom, bathroom, and personal workout space on the back half, but the main space still dwarfed us.

She stopped and turned to face me. "It's perfect."

I shouldn't give a rat's ass if this woman liked my place. I shouldn't care if anyone did. But something in me eased at her statement. Then I got annoyed all over again.

Grunting, I headed toward the kitchen. It had taken Carlos and I the better part of a summer to put it in, but we'd got the job done. Black cabinets on the bottom, open shelving—which is damn cheaper—along the top. We'd spent two weeks cursing like fiends trying to figure out how to pour a proper concrete countertop, but we figured it out eventually. I glanced at the lumpy end of one counter and swallowed a laugh. Okay, so we'd gone with wood butcher block for the center island after the whole concrete experiment.

"It's home, anyway. Used to have a condo by the harbor." A sleek penthouse with views for miles. "Seemed easier to fix up the loft and live here when I took over the gym." Cheaper. It was cheaper, and I needed the cash. "Saves me commuting time, that's for damn sure."

Babbling like a fool, I stopped at my fridge and pulled out the groceries I'd picked up for tonight. But a thought hit me, and I paused to glance back at Parker. She'd followed me to the kitchen and was standing by the island, her big brown eyes on me.

She'd taken off her jacket and draped it over the back of a barstool. Even so, she appeared far from relaxed.

"You okay with fettuccine carbonara?" Maybe I should have picked something ... lighter. Fish. Chicken. I had no idea what Parker ate.

"It sounds delicious. Can I help?" She edged closer, clearly too aware of every move she made.

We both were. Blowing out a breath, I rooted around for a head of butter lettuce and vegetables. "Yeah, sure. Can you make the salad?"

"I can do that."

Well, this was going...horribly. I'd had easier conversational flow with strangers in elevators. Get Parker and me alone, where no one might interrupt us, and we were stiff as old sticks.

I grinned at the ridiculousness of our reaction, and Parker immediately noticed.

Her nose wrinkled. "We're acting like strangers, aren't we?"

"Yep."

"We're not going to fool anyone, are we?" Worry clouded her eyes.

"Fail?" I placed a hand over my heart in mock horror. "I don't know the meaning of the word."

She rolled her eyes and grabbed the lettuce and salad fixings. "Good. At least one of us doesn't." Before I could respond, she glanced around. "Where are your knives and cutting board?"

I got her what she needed, and then turned on the stove and set a pot of water on the burner. Parker was already cutting up the tomatoes.

"Since you're holding the knife," I said, "I'm warning you now—I'm about to touch you."

She huffed in wry amusement but held herself very still. "Probably a good call to warn me."

"Getting stabbed isn't on my list of activities for tonight." Slowly, like I was approaching a skittish cat, I eased up to Parker, standing right next to her, and then gently placed my hand on the small of her back.

The fine muscles flanking her spine tensed and quivered. She stared down at the cutting board. "Why is it so much...*more* when we're alone?"

The quietly asked question went straight to my dick. I had to let out another slow breath. "Because it feels real."

I hadn't meant to say that.

Her smile slanted when she glanced up and met my eyes. "It's easier to act when there are eyes watching the performance."

She was still twitching against my palm, as though she was fighting the desire to move away. I kept my hand on her, letting her feel my heat, the weight of my touch. "All actors have rehearsals. That's what this is."

With a quick, efficient nod, she reached for the avocados. "You ever do any real acting?"

"Me?" I laughed at the absurd image. "No. Wait—scratch that. There's definitely an element of acting in boxing. Playing it up for the crowd before a bout, promotional crap. The shit you do to psyche out your opponent."

"You mean when you guys go nose to nose and say terrible things to each other?" She seemed amused.

"I keep forgetting you've never watched me fight." My ego was just fine but, without even trying, she was surprisingly good at taking it down a notch. "Yeah, sweetheart, that's what I meant. But," I added, "I hated that bullshit. It used to make me laugh when a guy got in my face and went off on some tangent. Shut up and fight already, man."

The corners of her eyes crinkled. "That's exactly what I think whenever I see one of those clips." Because Parker hated bullshit as much as I did. Which was a bit of a revelation. Her smile grew sly. "Also, I *have* seen you fight. I watched a YouTube video."

Surprise licked down my center. "You did, huh?"

Her nose wrinkled when she grimaced with apparent embarrassment over her confession. "It was...illuminating."

"Illuminating?" I chuckled, but inside I was starting to squirm as much as Parker. What the hell did that mean? Had she been turned off by it? Turned on?

Her fingertip touched the edge of my sleeve where it met my skin. I felt it down to my balls. "You were fierce, relentless. The way you'd take those blows and just keep at it." Her breath hitched. "I don't know how you did it."

I could tell her, but she was standing there all soft and open to me, her eyes holding something that felt strangely close to admiration. I didn't know what to make of that. Didn't really matter because I was growing aware of other things: her smoke and roses scent, the fact that we were standing close enough that our bare arms brushed.

The touch of her warm skin against mine raised the little hairs along my arms. I had to break this hold she had on me. I cleared my throat and copped a cocky tone. "Like I said, it's all for show."

With a wide, fake-ass grin, I swooped down and gave her a quick kiss on the cheek.

She flinched, lips parted with a gasp.

I turned away so I wouldn't be tempted to kiss her again. "Gotta make dinner."

"Are you going to be doing things like that all night?" she asked after a minute.

All night. Jesus, she put the wrong images in my head.

"What? Kiss and touch you?" I glanced over my shoulder to find her leaning against the counter, salad done, her eyes on me once more.

"Yes, that."

So prim. She was wearing slim dark jeans and a sleeveless blouse buttoned up to her neck. Aside from her bare arms, not an inch of skin showed. Before meeting Parker, I had no idea how enticing that could be. It distracted me, made me want to peel off those jeans and see ...

I cleared my throat. "Isn't that why we're doing this? So you could get used to my touch."

A thoughtful look passed over her delicate features, and she made a short, precise nod before pushing off from the counter. Determination radiated from her small body as she stalked forward, and I had the insane notion to back away, run for it.

Ridiculous.

I was over a foot taller than she was. I was an ex-pro boxer. I had no fucking reason to feel nervous.

But when she placed her palm on my lower abs?

I nearly yelped.

She didn't move away but lightly stroked me. Holy hell, what was she trying to do here? Kill me?

"I need to get used to touching you too."

"Uh-huh."

Touch me lower, woman. I'll do anything you ask.

I cleared my throat again, but couldn't think of a word to say. Aside from the sizzle of pancetta in the pan, the room had gone utterly quiet. Her warm hand pressed a little harder into my abs, the tips of her fingers dragging over my shirt. Sweet mother of mercy, the light exploration nearly buckled my knees.

Endless brown eyes stared up at me. "Is this okay?"

Was it hot in here? I sucked in a quick breath. "Yeah, sure, sweetheart. Why wouldn't it be?"

Pink lips curled into a sly smile. "You're blushing."

"I'm not blushing. I don't blush." I gave her a proper warning glare. "I'm cooking. It's hot over here."

"Hmm ..." She didn't break my gaze. "You do feel a tad warm."

Fucking hell.

Get it together, Morgan.

I turned back to the stove, and her hand slipped free. "Don't want the pancetta to burn." *Or my dick to poke its way out of my jeans.* "Hand me that plate?"

Giving her something to do got her away from me. She did as asked, and I started in on the rest of the pasta dish. She remained silent as I finished up.

"You want to eat outside?" I jerked my head toward the terrace at the south side of the building. During the warm months, it was my favorite feature of the loft. Big enough to hold a long L-shaped outdoor couch and a table for twenty, I'd filled the edges with potted trees and plants. Carlos had helped me build a pergola that was now twined with wisteria. "It's a nice night, and I've got a fire pit we can light."

Parker took one look at it and beamed. "Oh, yes, please."

I really had to stop reading sexual things into everything she said. It wasn't healthy.

***

"FIRST TIME I stepped into the ring, I got knocked out."

Parker's dark brows lifted high. "No!"

"Flat on my ass." We'd had dinner, the conversation easier once we'd gotten over our initial awkwardness. We hadn't talked about anything deep but exchanged working information: our favorite movies, foods, preferred drinks for each meal, foods we couldn't stand—all the stuff we'd need to know if we'd been dating for any length of time.

There hadn't been many surprises, other than the fact that Parker's favorite movie was *The Godfather II*. I'd expected something lighter and with a save the world message. But she loved the drama, the layers of meaning—her words, not mine.

She'd been equally stunned to find out my favorite was the first movie in the franchise, *The Godfather*. We had similar reasons, but I liked the original because that's where we got to see Michael succumb to The Family.

Now we were on the outdoor couch, the fire pit flickering and giving off enough heat to keep us warm.

Parker rested her head on her hand and smiled wide. "So, the great Rhys Morgan got knocked out. Who did it? The current champion?"

God, she was cute.

"No. It was a training bout. I was green, full of piss and vinegar and wanting to prove it." I chuckled. "It was my dad."

Her lips parted. "Your dad punched you?"

"He had to. He was my trainer." A pang of loss seared my heart. "Besides, he was teaching me a lesson. Next time, keep your guard up."

In the face of her stunned silence, I shrugged. "It was a good lesson. Never got knocked out again."

The glossy strands of her ponytail swayed as she shook her head. "Boxers are a breed apart."

She said it with admiration. I could almost imagine she was looking at *me* with admiration. But that was probably wishful thinking on my part.

"Yes, we are." I couldn't help but ease closer. All night, we'd been touching. Nothing sexual. Simple light touches. Fingers skimming over hands, fleeting strokes along forearms, and quick press of a hand to a shoulder.

At first, we'd gone at it like the assignment it was, making a concerted effort to remember. But as dinner wore on, it became easier, natural. And while those touches had been completely PG, nothing more than what you'd expect a middle school kid to do, it had been sexy as hell.

Touching Parker while knowing it wouldn't go further than that had gotten me so worked up, I was now aware of the smallest move she made. The woman would inhale and I'd be waiting to hear her exhale.

Firelight and the glow from the loft's windows painted her skin in golds and oranges, highlighting the sweet curve of her cheek, the little pout of her lower lip. I liked her this way, all soft and easy and looking at me as though I was someone she wanted to know.

I touched a strand of her hair with the tip of my finger. "Tell me something."

"Hmm?" She stayed languid, her head resting in her hand.

"You actually looking to hire a stripper or is it just a sexual fantasy you need help acting out?" Because I had to know what the hell that text had been about.

Parker's eyes widened, then she blinked and laughed. I loved the way she laughed—light and carefree, her cheeks plumping and her eyes crinkling deeply at the corners.

"I totally forgot I'd texted you that." Her hand landed softly on my thigh. I doubted she was even aware of doing it. But I was. I so fucking was. She smiled up at me. "My sister is getting married, and I'm in charge of the bachelorette."

"Which of course needs strippers." The thought of Parker and her uptown friends squealing over gym-toned, oiled-up guys gyrating in thongs had me grinning. Part of me couldn't imagine her letting loose like that, but I wanted to see it happen —although preferably with me first.

I pushed lustful thoughts of Parker watching me strip firmly away. But I couldn't stop staring at her. Under the string lights, she was all shadows, curves, and shining eyes.

"Honestly, my mother would probably die of embarrassment if we went through with it. Which is, admittedly, an incentive for my sister." She laughed again, and the sound struck me right in the chest.

"You're beautiful when you laugh." The words came out in a husky rush. I shouldn't have said them. But she stopped and stared, her lips parting as though I'd pleased her, and I couldn't regret what I'd said.

Everything slowed down and the air thickened. My body grew heavy with need. She was so damned pretty. I wanted to touch that smile, run my hands over her golden skin.

Her gaze slid to my mouth, and my lower abs clenched tight. With a hitch to her breath, she spoke. "We should kiss now."

God, yes. Kiss me. Let me kiss you. I'll learn every sweet inch of your mouth. Kiss you till it hurts to stop.

The words nearly left my mouth, when my sex-hazed brain finally cleared and that small, sensible, sane part of me hit the brakes hard and fast.

Kiss her? Shit. Fucking shit. I couldn't kiss this woman. Not when I was so worked up I'd fall on her like a starved man.

Faced with my deer-in-the-headlights silence, Parker frowned. "That is... I mean, I thought we were supposed to..." I didn't need brighter lighting to know she was blushing.

"Hey." I reached out to cup her cheek but stopped halfway, my hand hovering there, making everything worse. My fingers curled into a fist and I dropped it to my thigh. "You're right. We should. We were. Supposed to, that is."

Fuck. I was sweating again.

She sucked in a sharp breath, bracing herself, and her gaze turned steely. "Let's just get it over with."

It wasn't the most flattering statement. Which was good. This was a job. A job. I repeated the fact as I moved closer, wrapping my arm around her shoulder to draw her up against me. Later, I'd be laughing my ass off at myself. I wasn't this guy, freaking out over the prospect of a simple kiss. A fake one at that.

But Parker was right; being alone made it more.

Parker pressed a hand against my chest—to brace herself or hold me at bay, I didn't know. My mind was fuddled, spinning around like I'd taken a solid hit to the chin.

God, she was tiny. Delicate. Fragile. The back of her head fit perfectly in the well of my palm.

For a second, I didn't know what to do. One wrong move, and I'd crush her. I'd been forged to be a fighter. Brutal strength was my weapon. It didn't feel like an advantage at the moment. I felt like a bumbling oaf.

Parker let out a soft breath as her gaze searched my face. She was clearly waiting for me to make the first move.

I can do this. I can do this. It's nothing big. A kiss. Done it plenty of times. I can keep it neutral.

We moved at the same time, Parker lifting her face to mine as I ducked my head. Our lips met in the softest kiss I'd ever had. I felt the plush give of her lips, tasted a whisper of the white wine she'd drank. The sweetness of the way she kissed— so very shy but curious—punched right through my chest and squeezed.

I swear the floor tilted.

But she was pulling back, a furrow of concentration forming between her brows. "There," she said.

There?

My lips throbbed. I stared at her mouth and wanted more. I wanted back there. Now.

Through my haze, I heard her talking in that efficient Little Miss Priss voice. "One more thing crossed off the list."

I blinked, trying to focus. It was difficult; her mouth held all my attention. "Sorry?"

Soft pink lips pursed. "That was good enough, right?"

A laugh tumbled about in my chest. Good enough? Not by half. I shook myself out of the stupid lust fog that had invaded my brain. She stared up at me, looking quite pleased with herself. She really should be; she'd almost wrecked me with one brief kiss.

Damn it. I needed to get my head in the game. Play my part. I needed to feel her mouth again. Oh, how I needed.

"Nope."

Her nose wrinkled as her eyes narrowed. "No? What do you mean no? We kissed, didn't we?"

The way she kept asking questions, I had to smile. It was like she wanted me to argue. I was more than willing to do that.

"That wasn't a kiss, sweetheart."

Hot color licked over her cheeks. "It was so."

"It was a little peck on the lips. I barely felt it." I eyed her in mock suspicion. "Is that how you kiss guys you're with? Because, if so—" I broke off, shaking my head sadly.

She growled. "Look here, you. The men I've kissed have been perfectly satisfied."

I had no doubt about that. But I wasn't about to let that show. "Put your money where your mouth is, Tinker Bell."

Sparks lit her eyes—it might have been the firelight. Didn't matter, she was hopping mad now. "You smug—" With another growl, she reached for me, hauling my head down.

Sweet Mary, she got down to business, sweeping my mouth open with the thrust of her greedy tongue, her lips nipping and caressing. She went at me like she was starved for it. White-hot heat roared through me like wildfire.

With a groan, I let go, kissing her like I wanted, canting my head to get closer, deeper. I licked into her sweet-tart mouth, totally lost to her. Our lips parted and met over and over, each time a little more desperate, a little more hungry.

Parker's hands slid into my hair, grabbing at the strands hard enough to hurt. I wanted it harder. When she arched against me, pressing those firm tits into my chest, I swept her up and set her on my lap.

She keened, whimpering as though she might actively cry if she didn't get closer. She was driving me out of my mind with the way she sucked at my mouth, sliding her tongue over mine.

Cradling her head in my hands, I let her have what she wanted. Shit, I'd give her anything right about now. Our kiss became sloppy, bruising. Parker rocked her hips against my hard dick, and I was the one whimpering.

"Hell yes," I panted against her mouth. "Give it to me."

The second I'd uttered the words she froze. And I knew I'd broken the spell she'd fallen under. Fuck. *No, no, no. Don't stop*. But she was already lurching back, her eyes wide in shock and horror.

I opened my mouth, trying to think of something to make her stay, but she scrambled off my lap as though it were on fire. When she got a few feet from me, she simply stared, panting faintly.

I tried not to look at her breasts trembling under her blouse. They'd felt so good pressed against me. The silence felt like condemnation. What to say? I had no fucking idea. She'd knocked me on my ass.

Parker proved yet again to be the steadier one.

"I'm sorry." She licked those swollen lips. "I... uh...haven't done this before. Faking it. Was, uh, that okay?"

Faking. It.

Right. That's what we'd been doing. She looked at me with a plea in her eyes, and I knew she needed me to make this okay. She didn't want the reality; she needed the lie.

I ran a hand over my mouth, trying to wipe away the feel of her. Jesus, my hand was shaking. "Yeah." I cleared my throat. "Yeah, we're cool."

Parker sagged in relief. And I gave her my standard bullshit smile, letting her know we were back on script. But in my head, the truth rang clear as a bell. We were anything but cool.

TEN

Parker

"OKAY, is everyone happy with the teams?" Jackson asked, glancing between the two groups he'd created with a random generator app on his phone.

I stood at Rhys's side and ignored the smirk Creepy Pete gave me. We were on opposing teams, and he had Jackson on his. And gossipy Evan. Pete was also the only one who had brought his own paintball gun.

"It's more powerful than the guns they supply here," he'd said when Evan asked about it, puffing up his chest as he did so.

"Someone's overcompensating for something, huh?" Rhys had winked at me, and I'd almost choked trying to stifle my laughter.

Now we were ready to play. Ten staff members plus their partners had shown up for paintball. The grounds were a forty-minute drive west of Boston, and to say it had been the most awkward forty-minute ride was an understatement. I'd rented an electric car to take me and Rhys to paintball and those babies were so quiet, they only enhanced the silence between me and my fake boyfriend.

So, I rambled. I rambled the entire way to distract myself from the memory of Rhys's mouth, from his hands on me, and the delicious feel of his strong body against mine.

The kiss on our fake date had gotten out of hand.

Understatement.

My toes curled in my sneakers at the mere memory.

Rhys had offered to give me a ride home after we pretended like our kiss hadn't been explosive and hot and pretty much the best kiss of my life.

Guilt suffused me.

It might have been epic for me, but I had to remind myself that it was probably nothing new to Rhys. He'd most likely had a million kisses with similar physical effect. It was a sexual kiss.

I'd had better *romantic* kisses.

I had.

Struggling to remember a specific one made me feel like hell.

My only recourse was to forget the night in Rhys's awesome loft or die of self-flagellation.

"Let's do this." Jackson grinned at us, buzzing with energy. His fiancée, Camille, stood at his side, somehow still glamorous in her army fatigues. She and Jackson had taken dressing appropriately seriously. They both wore a light khaki T-shirt under a matching camouflage shirt and pants, and Camille had tied her shirt in a knot at her waist.

Except for Pete, who not only wore camouflage but a chest guard too, the rest of us dressed in comfortable green or khaki clothing to help us blend with the woodland. When Rhys and I arrived, we'd changed into our paintball clothes so as not to get paint on the seats of my rental car on our way home.

Upon advice from my colleague Stuart, I wore layers. Despite the nice weather, I had on yoga pants beneath loose-fitting cargo pants, and a long-sleeved T-shirt beneath a button-down shirt.

Rhys had come out of the changing rooms in a long-sleeved Henley and cargo pants, the muscles of his biceps flexing with every movement. He stood among my colleagues like Thor surrounded by fans at a comic book convention.

Our team included me, Rhys, my colleagues Stuart, Michael, Xander, and Ben, plus their respective partners, David, Freda, Laura, and Ben's friend Nick because his wife was pregnant and couldn't play. My colleagues and their partners could not have looked more overjoyed to be on Rhys's team.

It was hard not to roll my eyes.

"Walkie-talkies." Jackson handed me a bag and kept another for himself. "To communicate with your team. And your flag." Ben took the bright red flag from our boss; Jackson held onto a bright yellow one. "First team to capture the other's flag wins. We'll split up. Yellow team goes east, red team west. We'll both choose a team leader and where to hide the flag." He grinned cockily. "May the best team win."

"Yeah!" Yellow team shouted, following it up with light-hearted ribbing that my teammates responded to. Rhys and I stayed silent, although he smirked in amusement, listening to what must've sounded like tame banter compared to the insults he'd exchanged with opponents in the ring.

"Let's go," Rhys instructed our team as the yellow team departed.

We followed him and took off through the woods to the west side of the compound. The paintball face mask and visor were a little uncomfortable, and the gun was a foreign object in my hands.

"I vote Rhys as team leader," Stuart said as we came to a stop. "Any objections?"

Xander chuckled. "None at all."

Rhys assumed the role like it was a foregone conclusion. "Talkies." He took the bag from me and handed one to each of us. "Everyone know how to use 'em?"

We all nodded.

My fake boyfriend suddenly frowned. "These are on a different frequency from the yellow team, right?"

He was so serious and into this.

It was not hot.

Okay, it was mildly warming.

"Yeah, Jackson plays fair," Ben assured him.

Rhys gave a militant nod. "Ben, Nick, you'll hide our flag and take the nearest position to protect it."

Oh, all right, he was more than mildly warming.

"You radio its location to Xander and Laura, who'll take up a secondary position as the first line of defense." He turned to Michael, Freda, Stuart, and David. "You're our offensive teams. The object is to take out as many of the yellow team as possible, while trying to find that flag. Parker and I are the third offensive team. We'll take east, middle, and west respectively of the eastern perimeter. If you find the flag, you radio the other two teams for backup. Sound good?"

I'd been warm in my layers before but now I was *hot*.

As an organized, take-charge kind of woman, I really admired that quality in a man.

"Is this going to hurt?" Freda frowned, biting her lower lip. Genuine anxiety was bright in her eyes, and I wondered why she'd agreed to come if she was afraid to play.

I was participating because I had no choice.

Rhys studied Freda and then turned to Laura and Xander. "How would you feel being offense instead of defense?"

"I'm up for it." Laura shrugged with a cocky smile. She was tall with an athletic figure and a natural energy that would've told me she was into outdoor activities if Xander already hadn't. Her boyfriend nodded in agreement.

"Michael and Freda, you'll be the first line of defense instead. That work?"

They nodded but Freda still looked concerned. Michael threw his arm around her shoulder and hugged her into his side. "We got this, gorgeous."

She smiled gratefully and seemed to relax.

"Ben, Nick, go hide that flag," Rhys ordered.

The guys took off and soon I was hurrying at Rhys's side on high alert. "I would have to end up with you on the offensive side, Morgan," I whispered.

He shot me a look over his shoulder. "I could have put you and Freda on defense, if you're scared, Tinker Bell."

"I am not scared." My eyes felt huge behind my visor as I searched the woods. "But out of intellectual curiosity ... does it hurt?"

"It stings." Rhys grinned at me. "Don't worry, Tink, I got your back."

That's when I realized I wasn't worried. I, one hundred percent, believed Rhys could kick everybody's butt and cover mine at the same time. A lurid image filled my mind suddenly and felt my cheeks heat. Dear God, we should have never kissed at his loft.

"I'd give a million bucks to know what's behind that blush, sweetheart."

Scowling at his cocky grin, I gestured with my paintball gun. "You just concentrate on leading us to victory, Morgan, and if you happen to use up all your paint on Creepy Pete, I won't be upset."

He shook his head, amusement curling the corners of his mouth. "Remind me never to get on your bad side."

We ran from tree to tree for ages before Rhys drew to a halt. He lifted his fist up like they did in the army. A flutter of excitement filled my belly as he crouched down behind a large trunk and signaled me to hide behind him.

"Clearing ahead with a bunker," he whispered. "Most obvious place to hide the flag because you can protect it."

"Jackson wouldn't go for obvious."

Rhys nodded. "Still, let's be cautious. It's a good place to play sniper."

Our walkie-talkies crackled, and Ben's static-filled voice informed us where he'd hid the flag. We scrambled to turn them off, and I cut Rhys a sardonic look. "I've found a drawback to the walkie-talkies."

Smirking, he peered around the tree, the line of his shoulders tense. It was ridiculous how hot his competitiveness was making me. I'd never thought of myself as a competitive person, but I really wanted to wipe that smug smile off Creepy Pete's face by winning with Rhys.

After a few seconds, Rhys looked over his shoulder at me. "There are two man-made mounds acting as a barrier against possible sniper activity from the bunker, but they're on opposite sides of the clearing. It makes more sense for us each to take a barrier, but if you want to stick with me, we can do that."

I straightened my shoulders. "I am perfectly capable of independent combat."

His lips twitched. "You got it, Tink. I'll take west." He gestured with two fingers. "You take east. On three ..."

Even though my rational mind knew it was a game, my heart pounded as I launched out from behind the tree and separated from Rhys. Seconds before I reached the guard barrier, a popping noise filled my ears and yellow paint splattered on the ground near my feet. Adrenaline spiking, I lunged behind the barrier and looked across the clearing at Rhys. He was hunkered low like me behind the man-made mound on his side of the clearing.

"Turn your walkie on!" he yelled.

I fumbled to do so, hearing paint splatter against the barrier near my head. The angle of the shot suggested our attackers weren't in the bunker. Lowering my belly to the ground, I switched on the walkie. "Rhys, they're not in the bunker. Over."

"I know. I missed the tree house behind the bunker. Sneaky bastards. Over."

Trying not laugh at how seriously he was taking this, I asked, "What now?"

"You run toward the bunker while I cover you. Run to your left but don't go in. The outer wall will act as a shield and I'll need you to fire from that left flank position to clear a way for me to get to the bunker. Over."

Despite my trepidation, I felt a thrill go through me that he trusted me to do that. "Got it. Over."

"When I start firing, you move. Over."

"Yes, sir. Over."

"I'm trying to concentrate here, Tinker Bell. Don't make this sexy. Over."

Our eyes met across the clearing and, at his wink, I flipped him off, which only made him laugh. When he slipped his walkie-talkie into his pocket, I did the same and tentatively peered around the barrier to visualize my route to the left of the bunker. Realizing it would be easier to dart out from the opposite end of the barrier, I shuffled backward and let out a little squeal when yellow paint splattered near my hand. Tucking myself back into the guard, I crouched near the opposite end and glanced back toward Rhys. I could just make him out and no more.

"Now!" he yelled, and I lifted my head to watch as red paint balls soared through the air toward the tree house behind the bunker. It was well camouflaged. Red paint splattered against the walls and there was sudden movement as guns disappeared behind windows.

I was clear.

Pushing up off strangely trembling legs, I tore across the clearing toward the bunker as Rhys fired a few more paintballs to keep our attackers down.

As soon as I hid behind the bunker outer wall, he stopped.

I peered up through the trees and saw a flicker of movement as the yellow team prepared to attack again. Not giving them a chance, I aimed my gun and fired.

To my delight, red paint splattered near the window.

Yay! My aim was not too shabby.

Muffled curses filled the air, and I chuckled in devilish delight, taking way more pleasure in firing paintball after paintball at them than I ever thought I would. A touch on my shoulder startled me, and I spun back against the bunker wall to find Rhys crouched beside me, grinning. "You can stop now, Carlos Hathcock."

"Comparing me to arguably the greatest sniper in history is a compliment, Morgan."

An eyebrow rose behind his visor. "You got that reference?"

My answering smile was admittedly a little cocky. "I have a rounded catalogue of knowledge in this old noggin—" Rhys cut me off with a finger against my lips, and I tensed with a renewed awareness of him. He smelled earthy and spicy, his green eyes mesmerizing behind his visor.

In fact, I was so aware of him, it took me a second to realize he'd shut me up for a reason.

"They're coming down the tree house. Bunker." He grabbed my arm and guided me toward the small opening. Inside the bunker was mostly dark except for pools of light that spilled in from a window on either side of the doorway.

"Take a position."

I followed his order and his movements, taking the window farthest away and mirroring how he positioned himself with his gun at the ready by the corner. It meant he was out of sight, but he had a clear shot.

Feeling the rush of another spike of adrenaline, my heart raced.

A boot appeared around the edge of the bunker, then a leg, then a torso—

I fired, red paint hitting Evan all over his chest.

"Fuck!"

I grinned evilly. That would serve him right for talking about my private life to Creepy Pete. Karma was a bitch.

Evan turned around and ripped off his facemask. He threw up his hands in despair. "That's me out."

"Well, don't give my position away, you idiot," a female voice, presumably belonging to his wife Annabelle, snapped from somewhere behind the side of the bunker.

"That's a nice way to talk to your husband."

"I told you we should've stayed in the tree house!"

So engrossed in their amusing argument, I hadn't even noticed Rhys moving, let alone leaving the bunker, until he suddenly appeared at Evan's side and fired his gun toward Annabelle's voice.

"Jesus!" Annabelle yelled. "That stings."

"Now you're both out," Rhys said, chuckling. "Feel like telling me where that flag is?"

Evan scowled. "Just because we're out doesn't mean we don't want our team to win."

"Ugh, I couldn't care less." Annabelle appeared in view, her mask off. "I'm heading back to the club for a beer."

She'd barely walked out of sight when Evan yelled, "Fuck!"

Swiveling my head back to him and Rhys, I watched Evan clutch his knee.

"That's against the rules." Evan gritted his teeth, his face red. "What the hell was that?"

Realizing Rhys had shot him again, I lurched to my feet, about to call him out, when his pissed-off answer stopped me. "That was for gossiping like a little bitch to the dick in payroll about me and my woman."

Shock rooted me to the spot, and while I knew I should be annoyed by his macho antics and illegal shooting, I couldn't help but feel a thrill go through me. Except for Zoe, I couldn't remember the last time someone had my back.

If possible, my colleague turned an even darker shade of red. "Okay, I will let that shot go because you're right. Pete shouldn't have approached Parker in front of everyone. He embarrassed us both and took what I said out of context. I'm sorry."

"Apology accepted."

They shared a wary nod, and Evan followed his wife. I felt terrible that Rhys had embarrassed my colleague, but a darker side of me enjoyed my fake boyfriend's version of justice.

Coming out of the bunker, I found I didn't know what to say as our eyes met.

Turns out I didn't have time to say anything because a ball of yellow paint flew past my ear.

Rhys dove and took me to the ground, covering me as he spun around and fired. "Back into the bunker!" he yelled.

Ignoring the ache in my rump, I shuffled out from under

him and lunged for the doorway. When I didn't hear him behind me, I turned and looked out into the clearing.

Rhys ran across the field, firing his gun, missing hits aimed at him from the woods near the tree house. He jumped over the man-made barriers as if his body were made of air and set up his position there.

Scrambling toward the bunker window, I stationed myself as before and saw Creepy Pete and his friend Alan peeking out behind two trees.

My walkie-talkie crackled. "They could be a second defense team. The flag might be in the fucking tree house. Over."

Before I could answer, Xander's voice crackled down the line. "Where is your position? Over?"

"About five minutes from where we started on the far northwest side of the yellow team's perimeter. We're in a clearing with a bunker and a tree house. We've taken out two yellows but there are two more on our left flank. Come up behind them. Take them out. Over."

"We've taken out a team too. On our way," Xander said. "Over."

There must still be three yellow-team pairs left. We were facing off with one, which meant the other two were probably in our territory looking for our flag.

"Our guys have worked out where you're hiding your flag!" Pete yelled from behind a tree about fifty yards from Rhys's position. "You might as well give up."

My walkie crackled. "That Pete? Over."

Curling my lip in annoyance, I lifted my walkie. I'd explained to Rhys before the kiss on our fake date that I thought perhaps Pete had it in for me because of my background. Rhys thought Pete sounded like a... well, he referred to him as a dick. He wasn't wrong. "That's Creepy Pete. Over."

No answer was forthcoming. Instead, Rhys suddenly tore out from behind the barrier and sped toward Pete's position like a champion sprinter, roaring this deep, terrifying bellow.

There was a shuffle of noise and curses from the trees, but Rhys's tactic to scare the shit out of Pete and his friend Alan worked. I ducked my head out the window to see better and caught sight of Pete, now out from behind the trees, gaping at Rhys in shock, while Alan fumbled with his gun. Rhys skidded to a stop, gun up, and fired continuously until both Pete and Alan were covered in red paint.

Pete looked shell-shocked while Alan cursed in pain.

I laughed so hard, tears leaked out of my eyes.

Rhys lifted his gun and strolled casually over to Pete. He smacked him hard against the upper arm, causing Creepy Pete to wince. "No hard feelings, huh?"

My colleague nodded slowly. "Uh ... sure."

I pulled my gun back and hurried out of the bunker just as Rhys walked toward me. He grinned and gestured toward the tree house. "Go on up, see if the flag is there."

A small part of me hoped the flag wasn't in there so I could watch Rhys go all commando on the rest of the yellow team's butts. Yet, if the flag was there, I could take comfort knowing he'd schooled the two guys in my office who'd upset me that week in a way that wouldn't affect my relationship with them in the office.

It was all part of a team-building exercise after all.

Giddiness filled me as I hurried up the ladder and through the hole in the floor. Sure enough, lying in the corner was the yellow team's flag.

I crawled into the tree house, snatched it, and hurried back down. Rhys waited at the bottom, smiling up at me. I jumped from the third rung with a girlish squeal of delight and he caught me with a bark of laughter. I lifted the flag in victory. "We won!"

Our eyes locked, and suddenly the air expelled out of my lungs as the urge to kiss him became almost impossible to hold back.

"Uh, looks like we aren't needed." Laura's amusement-filled voice drew our heads apart.

Rhys slowly lowered me to the ground, and I avoided his gaze. With a smile less genuine than the one I'd given him, I turned to Xander, Laura, Stuart, and David with the flag. "Rhys kicked their butts."

Stuart grinned at my fake boyfriend. "There's a surprise."

Rhys shrugged while I attempted to tell myself that I didn't find Paintball Rhys sexy as hell.

STANDING in the clearing where our paintball exercise had begun, I grinned at the sight of my colleagues covered in paint. The only teams who remained unscathed were Rhys and I, Jackson and Camille, Xander and Laura, Stuart and David, and Ben and Nick.

Everyone else had been shot.

Jackson grinned at the red team. "Well done."

"We had a great team leader." Xander patted Rhys's shoulder.

"Yeah," Jackson chuckled, "we're all surprised the ex-professional boxer whooped our asses."

Rhys shrugged, a slight smile curling his lips. My eyes zeroed in on his mouth, as Jackson's voice grew muffled.

"Are we all set?"

"Huh?" I asked, dragging my gaze and thoughts off Rhys.

Jackson gave me a knowing look. "I said, now that the team exercise is over, let's just play."

My heart dropped. "As in ... no rules. Just ..."

"Play until we're exhausted? Pretty much. We booked the outdoor grounds for three hours, and Rhys led the red team to victory in thirty minutes. We might as well get our money's worth." Jackson lifted his gun. "You all have ten seconds to get your ugly, khaki, no-good keisters out of here before I cover your cargo pants in paint."

Laughter filled the woods at his *Home Alone* reference as we took off toward the cover of the trees. This time, knowing Rhys was the enemy, I went off on my own.

Pain flared in my shoulder, and I cried out, realizing I'd been hit. Spinning around, I saw Pete aiming at me with his stupid overpowered gun, a calculated look in his eyes. Just as he was about to fire again, red paint splattered all over his visor.

Then just all over him, period.

Glancing around, I found Rhys, standing behind a tree, gun aimed at Pete. His head turned toward me, and he winked.

I grinned. Grateful.

Then I shot him.

Rhys looked down at his chest in apparent shock, and I threw my head back in laughter. It cut off when he lifted his head, eyes narrowed in determination.

Oh dear God, what had I done?

With a yelp of apprehension, I spun around and bolted through the trees. I half expected to feel the sting of shots across my back, but instead I heard racing footsteps.

Oh hell!

A strong arm caught me around the waist, a heavy weight propelling me toward the nearest tree. At the last second I found myself turned and pulled into Rhys's arms as we collided with the trunk. He wasted no time pushing me against the tree as he ripped off his mask. Determined heat filled his beautiful green eyes as he gripped the bottom of my mask and gently took it off.

"What are—"

My words were lost in his kiss.

A deep, thorough, searching kiss that made my toes curl in my sneakers and my fingernails bite into his shoulders. His body pressed deep into mine, and I instinctively spread my legs to accommodate him. Everything faded in the heat of his kiss. Watching him kick butt—no, Rhys kicked *ass* —and defend me was unexpected foreplay.

It wasn't a typically romantic kiss. In fact, it was much like our kiss at his loft—wet, hungry, breathless, needful, passionate, sexy. And I never wanted it to stop.

Rhys's grunt rumbled deliciously down my throat seconds before he broke the kiss with a grimace. "Fuck."

As he glanced over his shoulder, it took me a second to come out of my lusty, lip-swollen haze to realize Jackson, Camille, Laura, and Xander surrounded us. They grinned, and I blushed beet red.

"This is just too easy," Jackson snorted, stepping back to hold up his gun.

He, like the others, was covered in paint.

Rhys stepped back.

Convinced I was blood red from the tip of my toes to the top of my head, I avoided everyone's gaze as Rhys turned to the others. That's when I saw four paint splatters on his back. He'd taken hits while we were kissing, and I hadn't even noticed.

My goodness.

"You've been hit." I stated the obvious in all my fluster.

Rhys looked over his shoulder at me, eyes full of laughter. "It was worth it, sweetheart."

"Yes, thank you for the show," Xander teased.

I lifted my gun in warning, and he chuckled, aiming back at me.

To everyone's surprise, Rhys stepped in front of me, his hands raised in surrender. "How about we let Parker walk out of here unscathed, huh?"

"That's okay." I moved around him, even though I really didn't want to get shot at again. It hurt more than a sting. "I can take it."

In answer, Rhys pulled down the neckline of my shirt to bare my shoulder. His thumb swept the skin. "You've already got a nasty bruise from where Pete hit you."

As lovely as his concern was (and he seemed genuinely worried about my bruise), I covered his hand with mine and guided my shirt back up to cover the skin. "Everyone else has been hit."

Rhys frowned. "Everyone else is not five foot nothing, weighing in at ninety pounds."

"Uh, five foot two and a hundred and ten pounds, thank you very much. Plus, I can take care of myself."

"Fine. Let them take aim."

I nodded, my inner feminist pleased.

However, Rhys crossed his arms over his chest and stared at my colleagues. "Of course, if it were me, I wouldn't really want to risk my mortality by bruising up an ex- heavyweight champion's girlfriend. But that's just me."

Groaning, I watched as the others exchanged knowing looks, and then my boss called time on the game.

Rhys looked at me, his gaze dragging down my body and back up again. His eyes lingered on my mouth for a second too long.

"Why?" I blurted out, referring to the second explosive kiss he'd given me.

He shrugged. "No one will question our relationship now, Tinker Bell."

Disappointment filled me as I realized the kiss had not been a spontaneous response to me shooting him, but a calculated move. A strategic play.

Rhys wanted to earn that money I was paying him, I reminded myself.

Right there and then, I decided for my well-being not to let Rhys Morgan's mouth anywhere near mine ever again.

I left the field with only Pete's yellow paint splatter on my shoulder and a whole bunch of pent-up indignation and sexual frustration in my gut.

ELEVEN

Rhys

My fist slammed into the bag. *Jab. Jab. Cross. Jab. Hook. Cross. Jab.*

Calm settled into my bones even as they felt each impact. Hitting something didn't exactly hurt. Not anymore. But I definitely felt it. Working the bag drew my awareness inward. It clarified things.

I needed clarity. Because I was in very real danger of losing it around Parker. Freaking disturbing. Control wasn't something I lost. Never. I'd spent my life honing it.

I had excellent control.

God, she tasted sweet. Felt even better. Her mouth should be listed as a national treasure. Freaking perfect. And when she wrapped those tight thighs around my waist...

My glove glanced off the edge of the bag. The bag swung back into me, knocking my ribs.

"Shit." Disgusted at myself, I ripped off the gloves and tossed them aside.

"Losing your touch?" Dean lounged at the far side of the sparring room.

Grabbing my bottled water, I took a long drink before answering. "Get in the ring with me for a couple rounds and find out."

"I'm a smart-ass," he said, walking farther into the room. "Not a dumb-ass."

That made me laugh. I set the bottle down and grabbed a towel to wipe the sweat off my face. "What's up, little brother? Bored already?"

"Of course, I am." He shrugged. "Aren't you? Or do you like hanging out in empty gyms on a Friday night?"

Dean might not have been able to box at a pro level but he was an expert at verbal hits. I kept my eyes on the tape I'd started unwinding from my fingers, not wanting to look at the forlorn gym that should have been full of members on this rainy evening. Fact was I often closed early because the bulk of our members used the gym during the day.

Failure never sat well with me, and this place reeked of it. Sometimes, I imagined I stank of it too, that it followed me around like a fug, keeping everyone away.

Snorting, I tossed the tape in the trash and flexed my fingers. Self-pity wasn't my thing either, and I'd be damned if I'd fall into that trap.

"No, I don't like it," I told Dean truthfully. "But I'm stuck here. You, on the other hand, are not."

He'd ditched the suits and was now wearing jeans and a T-shirt. Thank fuck. The sight of Dean in a suit while hanging out here annoyed the shit out of me; he should be in a corner office somewhere changing the world with that big brain of his. He should be hanging with someone like Parker, creating algorithms or having in-depth conversations about chaos theory.

How would it have gone if Dean had been the one to meet up with Parker like she was expecting? Would she have stuck to the whole "business only" thing? She disliked me on sight. Dean, she'd recruited.

A sour taste filled my mouth, and I walked over to the vending machine. A sports drink tumbled down to the open slot in the silence, and I knew Dean was watching me, thinking God knew what.

"Why do you keep this place?" he finally asked.

It was the earnest tone, no longer pissy or trying to piss me off, that had me answering with another truth. "It's all I got."

It hurt to say. Hurt to admit to myself. But I was used to pain. I turned and found him staring at me with sad eyes.

"You had it all." A frown worked its way over his forehead. "Shit, I was so proud of you. My big brother Rhys, kicking ass and taking numbers."

Jesus, this kid. He never needed to use his fists to lay someone flat. He just needed to open his mouth.

"Dean ..." It was a plea but he didn't seem to hear it.

"And for what? This dump?"

My back teeth ground together. "This dump was Dad's dream. Mom's dream. It was responsible for putting food on our table and training me to be the fighter you claim you admired so much."

Dean nodded, clearly unfazed. "Yeah, it was. But now? Rhys, it's falling apart around you. I've seen enough of the accounting to know it's so far in the hole only a miracle can save it."

Parker was that miracle. Or the cute fairy who'd get me one step closer to it.

Dean threw up a hand in irritation. "So, don't tell me that this place makes you happy."

"It doesn't," I snapped, unable to hold back. "All right? It doesn't. Not now. But it could, Dean." I glanced around, imagining it like it was in its heyday. Imagining it *better* than it was. "It's something worth saving."

He fell silent and studied the room with a jaundiced eye, seeing all its flaws. I didn't know if he cared to remember the old days, or if he saw a different version of it than I did. Likely so. This place had been my second home. It had given me a sense of myself that nothing else ever did. I'd become a fighter here. It was part of me. And if it was worthless, what was I?

Dean met my gaze again and his was still troubled. "If you were fighting, you'd bring in enough money to fix all this. In a heartbeat."

"Dean ..."

"Don't 'Dean' me in that way. Jesus, you sound like Ma when you do that."

"I sound like Ma? Somehow I doubt that."

"Well," he said with a slight smile, "your voice is a lot lower and you're ugly to boot, but you have that same repressive 'You're getting out of hand and do I need to put you in time out?' tone."

I laughed again, even though my chest felt tight and heavy.

Dean shook his head in disappointment. "I just don't get it. You said you took time off to look after me. As if I couldn't do that at twenty-two."

"Could you?" I countered, dryly. "Because the way I remember it, you were a fucking wreck, well on your way to becoming a deadbeat drunk."

Annoyance flashed in his eyes, and he sucked in a sharp breath. "Okay, fine. It was ... nice of you to do that."

I snorted. "High praise."

"But I'm out of college, and I don't get drunk anymore. That shit won't fly anymore. You can't hover over my life. Unless you're aiming to become one of those creepy pseudo-helicopter parents? Which, I've gotta say, you're skirting the edge of that already."

"Like hell," I muttered. Shit. I *had* been hovering. Like a fretful parent.

He ignored that, thankfully. "So why not get back into fighting? You're too good for this." He spread his arms out to encompass the gym. "You're too good to be running around town as some fake-ass boyfriend—"

"*You* wanted to be her fake-ass boyfriend." The thought of Dean with Parker rubbed raw on my skin. "So you're saying it was okay for you but not me?"

"Yeah," he countered. "I am. I'm the fuck-up. I don't have a job. You ..." He pointed a finger in my direction. "Were a world-class boxer, a fucking champion. If I had that talent, I wouldn't be wasting my life in this shitty gym."

"Don't call this place shitty."

"Don't prevaricate."

"Using big words on the stupid ox brother?"

"Don't pretend to be stupid. You're smarter than you look!"

We were face-to-face now, yelling at each other with increasing volume.

Dean took another step closer, eyeing me as good as any old opponent would have done. "And don't fucking try to change the subject. You keep saying that Dad's death took the fight out of you. But I can't believe it. Tell me the truth for once. I'm an adult—"

"All evidence to the contrary."

"You clearly aren't in mourning over Dad anymore," he went on as if I hadn't spoken. "So why won't you go back to boxing?"

"None of your fucking business."

"Are you scared?"

I scoffed at his taunt. "Scared? Fuck you."

He didn't blink. "Scared that you will suck? That you'll get your fat ass out there and someone will kick it?"

"The day I'm afraid of someone kicking my ass is the day I lay down and die."

He sneered. "You're already dead. You're just walking around like an animated corpse. A fucking waste."

I grabbed his collar and hauled him close. He didn't resist. My voice came out in a snarl. "You should talk, you little shit—"

"Yeah, yeah." The rage in his eyes was unavoidable. "Tell me another one. Won't change the fact that you're a fucking chicken—"

"Shut up!"

"No. Tell me why! Why, Rhys?" His words hammered into my skull, pushed against my chest. "Why won't you go back? Huh? Why?"

"Because I can't!" I shouted, my voice breaking. My body sagged. "I can't ... Jake. He ... I ..."

Dean's face became a blur, and I let him go, thrusting him away and turning my back on him. Chest heaving, I tried to draw in a breath, looking for that calm, dead place that I lived in now.

Behind me, Dean uttered a soft curse. When he talked, his voice was small and hesitant. "It's because of Jake?"

Bracing my hands low on my hips to hide their shaking, I blinked up at the ceiling. "I saw him die." I swallowed convulsively. "I knew it was going to happen. The second he took that hit ... I knew it was over. The light went out of his eyes. And I knew."

I could still see it. Nausea surged up my gut, and I swallowed again.

Dean appeared at my side. I hadn't heard him move. "That was shitty of me, pushing you. I'm ... I'm sorry, Rhys."

I knew he was apologizing for Jake too. A sound of wry amusement mixed with ugly pain left me, sharp and loud. "Yeah, well, it's what we do."

He didn't smile but moved a bit closer. I felt the brush of his arm against mine, and I swear to God, I wanted to run out of the room. I was too close to breaking. I took a few deep breaths, refusing to move away.

"I can't get in that ring again," I said in a low, tight voice.

"I get it," he said softly.

I nodded, and we both fell silent. After a minute, Dean stirred, clearing his throat. "I used to love coming here. Back when you were training."

I stayed as still as I could, just breathing.

He kept talking, tentative, reaching for a truce. "It was great. And you're right. It could be great again."

"I'm working on that," I bit out, the words costing me. Talking meant acknowledging that I was there. When I wanted to be any place but.

"I know you are. It's a good plan." He glanced over at me, regret painted on every line of his face. He'd never truly understand that I never wanted him to feel regret. I never wanted regret to be his burden.

"I'll help you, Rhys."

Shit. Shit. Shit. It took everything in me to hold onto the fragile thread of calm I'd gained back. "All right."

He nodded, looking pleased. "Any tips you need for handling Parker?"

A rusty laugh broke free. "You think I need help with women? That's cute."

He rolled his eyes. "I meant more along the lines of hanging out with her geeky friends and coworkers."

An evil grin spread as I remembered peppering those gossipy little asshats with paint bullets. That smug weasel Pete had actually squealed. So satisfying. "I got that covered."

"What did you do?" Dean asked with growing amusement.

"Nothing." Showed them just what they faced if they messed with my girl.

She isn't your girl, idiot.

My smile fell, and I rolled my shoulders. "I act like myself and they pretty much run in fear. It works."

"Yeah, I bet it does," he said dryly. "But what about when you eventually meet people she actually likes?"

Hell.

"I'll let you know."

He eyeballed me for a long moment, then shook his head. "We'll work on your manners later."

"Asshole."

His grin was quick and a bit forced. Couldn't blame him for that. Mine was too. But then he damn near killed me when he reached in and gave me a quick half hug, slapping me on the shoulder as he let me go.

"You stink," he said, covering the awkward moment. "Go shower."

He left me before I could get another word in. I was grateful as hell.

The gym fell silent, stinking of sweat and mold. I closed my eyes tight and then shook it off, striding out of the room. Pulling my phone out of my pocket, I stared down at my text messages, my hand shaking. I couldn't stop it.

I couldn't stop myself from texting either.

RhysThis: Hey, Tink. What you up to?

Seconds later, my knees felt weak with relief when little dots formed at the bottom of the screen as she typed in her answer.

AngryTink: Who is this?

A smile pulled at my lips, my chest already feeling lighter.

RhysThis: Rhys. The great and powerful.

AngryTink: I thought that was The Wizard of Oz.

Chuckling, I took the stairs to my loft.

RhysThis: Close enough. You're no longer in Kansas, little girl.

AngryTink: I'm going to ignore the little-girl part. Because it reeks of misogyny.

My steps grew lighter, faster, the smile spreading over me like a wave. I could breathe again.

RhysThis: I thought you were going to ignore it?

AngryTink: Anyway … Why are you texting?

Because I need you. I need your sass. I need you …

I tried to shake the thought away. It was a weakness I couldn't afford. But the thought remained. I needed her.

Shit.

AngryTink: Rhys? You there? Or did you run off the road on that mildly enjoyable bike of yours? Please don't tell me you're texting and driving! That's illegal, you know.

Huffing out a laugh, I answered.

RhysThis: You enjoy my bike, huh?

A pause, and then she replied.

AngryTink: A little. Just a little. And you didn't answer.

RhysThis: Don't worry, sweetheart. I'm at home.

AngryTink: Sweetheart?

She sent an eye-roll emoji and then: **What's up? Is there something you need?**

You. Here. Please.

Shit, I had to get out of this. I didn't know what to say.

AngryTink: Actually, it's good you texted. I need you.

For a hot second, the bottom dropped out of my stomach. She needs me. My heart rate kicked up like I'd just gone ten brutal rounds with a top opponent. *She needs me.* I was about to smile, about to text her back with something like: *Thank Christ. What took you so long?*

Another text dinged.

AngryTink: Argh. That sounded wrong! Sorry. Distracted. I need you for another "date."

I was a damn fool. An idiot. Of course that's what she needed. What the fuck was wrong with me? I was getting soft and stupid on a girl that would never fit in my world. And I'd never fit in hers.

My thumb hit the screen hard as I tapped out my reply.

RhysThis: What is it this time? Croquet with the queen? Watching yuppies row their little crew boats?

It took her a bit to answer. Time enough that I felt remorse for taking a cheap jab.

AngryTink: Not that I don't love a good crew race, but no. It's a garden party on Saturday. Yuppies will be in attendance. Can you handle that? Or do the yuppies scare you too much?

I had to give it to Parker; she was a fierce competitor. She'd block any hit I sent her way and followed through with an excellent counterstrike.

Like that, I was smiling again.

No. No. No.

No more smiling at texts. This is business, you moron. Play your part.

RhysThis: Babe, for the money you're paying me, I can handle anything you throw my way. ;-)

She didn't answer with her usual sass but simply sent me the time I was supposed to pick her up. Completely professional. Exactly what I wanted.

Then why did it feel like yet another defeat?

I was still pissed off at myself when Dean popped in an hour later. "You want to go have a drink?"

Anything beat sitting around trying not to think. I needed to be Rhys again. Have some damn fun for one damn night.

TWELVE

Parker

THE LOW-LEVEL CHATTER escalated in the Irish pub as the bar owner, who'd introduced himself as Bill, announced a ten-minute beer break. I shared a bemused look with my friends. We'd never been to a quiz where there was a beer break for the "quizmaster."

We'd also never been to a quiz night in a bar in Chelsea, but my oldest friend, Ren, was our quiz finder and he took us wherever the questions were. Usually I didn't care where we ended up. Moreover, the prize didn't matter to us. We just loved hanging out, happy to be with fellow nerds, and our bimonthly quiz nights gave us that.

Tonight, the winning team got a crate of beer and a gift card to Yankee Lobster. It wasn't a bad prize. But I couldn't care less. What I did care about was that we were in Chelsea. Not only were we in Chelsea, we were in a bar right around the corner from Lights Out. I hadn't told the guys about Rhys because I couldn't tell them the truth and I couldn't lie to them.

"You're quiet tonight." Ren nudged me with his elbow before sitting back against the wall. He took a swig from his beer, his eyes on me the whole time.

I tried not to squirm under his gaze. Ren and I met at college orientation and had been friends ever since. Zoe thought I was nuts for not exploring something more with Ren. He had been, and still was, one of those guys who made nerdy sexy. He was tall, lean, with a surprising amount of wiry muscle beneath his shirt, and behind his black-framed glasses was the face of a model.

No joke.

Irish American—dark hair, olive skin, angular features, and bright blue eyes— the man was beautiful. He was also devoid of cliché—a great mix of athleticism and intellectualism, a geek and a jock, friends with extroverts and introverts alike. Ren was a hockey player in high school. He was captain of the math and debate teams. Huge nerd. But he was also kind of an alpha, pain in the ass, overprotective big-brother type.

"I'm tired," I lied.

Ren narrowed his eyes. "You're lying."

"I'm not lying."

"I've known you for twelve years, so I know when you're lying."

"Jesus, leave off, man," Elijah ordered with an appeasing smile. "So what if she's lying?" He winked at me. "Parker's allowed her secrets."

"Since when do I have secrets?" As soon as the words were out of my mouth, I had to fight not to flinch. Oops. I absolutely had a secret.

"We all have secrets." He shrugged and turned to Navin. "Isn't that right?"

Elijah was Re
become good frien
Elijah's lab partner
nent fixture in our
Zoe who had, unfort

Navin scowled at

Glad to have the
table and leaned towa

"There's nothing t

"You're among f
dancing with laughter.
from the rooftops."

Ren grinned. "She's not
handle the fact that you
woman. Met someone
likes to handcuff
things."
I choke
coughe

Ooh, now I was intrigued. Shouting what?"

"Yeah, shouting what?" Ren smirked at Navin.

I knew that smirk. "You know what it is," I accused and sat
back with a huff. "Oh, come on, I can't be the only one who
doesn't know."

Navin shot Ren a filthy look. "You're a dick too."

Something occurred to me. "Oh, your parents aren't trying
to arrange another marriage, are they?" Navin's parents lived in
Mumbai, both successful lawyers. Their marriage was also
arranged, and from what I had gathered from my friend over
the years, they'd lucked out and were happy together. Because
of that, whenever Navin was single, they tried to convince him
to go through with an arranged marriage.

Elijah laughed and shook his head.

"Oh, just tell me, then."

With a beleaguered sigh, Navin shrugged. "I met
someone."

Why was that a secret? "Okay...?"

Ren snorted. "Is that what you're calling it?"

Navin curled his lip. "I didn't want to tell Parker this. It's
not for her delicate ears."

virgin, Navin, I think she can
re screwing around with an older
e"—he snorted again—"yeah, one who
you to the bed. Among other kinky, dirty

d on a sip of my beer and felt Ren pat my back as I
d. The knowledge that my friend was into kink was
welcome.

"Okay," I wheezed, waving a hand between me and Navin.
"I didn't need to know that. I was happy not knowing that."

"See?" Navin sat back in his chair, embarrassed. "And
thank you very much for airing my private business in public."

"Parker isn't public." Elijah shared an evil grin with Ren.

"You two are mean." I kicked Elijah under the table and
slapped Ren across the head at the same time. Their curses lit
up our table and put a giant smile on Navin's face.

Before I could say another word, an unexpected shiver
tickled down my spine and a sudden awareness drew my eyes
toward the bar entrance. My breath caught in my throat as my
gaze collided with Rhys Morgan's.

What the hell?

Of course he would come to the bar on the one night I just
happened to be there.

And he wasn't alone.

Dean was there too.

As Rhys strode toward me, his expression unreadable, my
heart raced and my palms grew clammy. It had been five days
since the paintball exercise. Five days of a complete lack of
focus on my part. Not only because I had come to the uncomfortable realization that I had a humongous crush on the guy I
was paying to date me (rookie mistake!), but because Fairchild
had invited us to a garden party tomorrow. Jackson, with

obvious discomfort, had made it clear that my invitation to this party was contingent upon Rhys escorting me.

Rhys had, of course, agreed to come but I couldn't stop thinking about the fact that I'd vowed to keep myself physically and emotionally distant from this man and how impossible it would be to maintain that vow when we had to continue to pretend to be in a relationship in front of all my colleagues.

As Rhys stopped at our table, I let out a shaky exhalation I knew he didn't miss. His eyes narrowed on my mouth before he gave me what might have been a tender smile, if I thought for a second he had tender feelings toward me.

Which I knew he didn't.

He was a very good actor.

Something he'd proven when he kissed the hell out of me at paintball, only to be completely unaffected by it.

My knees were still like jelly when I'd gotten home that night.

The big jerk.

The text he'd sent me this evening was also fresh in my mind. Apparently, he felt the need to remind me he was getting paid to escort me. And kiss me. While I was emotionally and physically discombobulated by his superior kissing talent, he was clearly concerned I might be getting the wrong idea about our "relationship."

Like I needed the reminder I was as far from his type as a woman could be.

Some of my irritation must've registered on my face because he grinned, and it was filled with mischief. "Hey, sweetheart." He bent down and kissed me full on the lips, quick, hard, and pulled back before I could react. "You didn't tell me you were going to be in my part of town tonight."

"Uh ... I didn't know."

"And who are you?" Ren asked belligerently, reminding me we were not alone.

And crap.

I did not want to lie to my friends.

"Rhys Morgan." His expression turned blank as he checked out Ren. "I'm dating Parker. You are?"

Ren's eyebrows drew together, and he cut me a hurt look. Double crap. "Your boyfriend?"

"Well ..." My mouth opened and shut like a guppy. "You see ... I was going ..."

"We haven't been dating long. On that note"—Rhys clamped a hand on his brother's shoulder—"Tink, this is my baby brother, Dean. Dean, this is Parker."

Dean gave me a knowing smirk. The fact that it was sexy was more of an observation on my part, rather than a reaction. Huh. Strange, because Dean Morgan was definitely more my type. Although he and Rhys shared similarities in their features, Dean was blond and clean-cut while Rhys was all dark, rugged masculinity. Dean was in shape, but he was an academic, while Rhys was the ultimate athlete. Dean was all-American handsome; Rhys was ...

Rhys was ... just looking at him caused a delicious ache between my legs, even in the midst of my anxiety over lying to my friends.

How was this possible? How could this mortifying night-mare be happening to me?

Rhys Morgan was so not my type.

Argh!

And I was definitely not his.

Therein lies the problem.

"Nice to meet you, Parker. Heard a lot about you." Dean shook my hand, and I couldn't help but glare at him as I noted the laughter in his eyes. Obviously, he shared his brother's twisted sense of humor.

"Nice to meet you too," I replied politely. I avoided direct eye contact with my friends as I gestured to them. "Elijah, Navin, Ren, this is my ... boyfriend, Rhys, and his brother, Dean. Rhys owns a boxing gym right around the corner. Rhys, these are my college friends. I think I told you about our quiz nights."

"Yeah, I remember."

Before anyone could say another word, Bill the bar owner returned to the stage to continue the quiz.

Rhys bent toward me, his lips near my right ear as Bill's voice quieted the bar. My fake boyfriend's breath caressed my skin, and I hunched up a shoulder to chase away the answering shiver. "We'll just grab a beer and be right over. You want anything?"

Trying to make my smile as natural as possible, all the while cursing my bad luck, I shook my head. "We're good."

"An encomium is a speech or piece of writing that does what?" Bill asked into the mic as Rhys and Dean walked away from the table. Bill looked up from the card in his hand toward the bar. "Jesus fuck, Della, where the fuck did you get these fucking questions?"

The tables of quizzers chortled. It wasn't the first time Bill had stopped in the middle of the quiz to ask Della, whom we'd soon learned was his wife, where she'd found what were truly random, difficult questions.

"It's like an admiration thing, right?" Elijah said, his voice low as he sat forward. "To praise a person."

"Yeah, you're right." Navin nodded. "Write it down."

Ren looked at them like they were crazy. "Are we seriously not going to talk about the fact that Parker is dating an ex-heavyweight boxing champion and didn't tell us?"

I raised an eyebrow. "You know who he is?"

My friend glowered. "Yeah, I know who he is. As soon as you said boxing gym, I remembered why he's so familiar. So, what's going on? Is this why you've been quiet?"

My belly roiled. Oh my goodness, I did not want to lie to Ren. But if I told him I had hired Rhys to be my fake boyfriend, he would probably take a swing at Rhys, assuming I was being taken advantage of, and not caring that the Widowmaker could crush him.

"As you can imagine," I started, trying not to lower my eyes because he'd know I was lying if I did, "I've been somewhat surprised by this turn of events, and I've been attempting to figure things out and ... I honestly didn't even know we were dating until he just said it." I fibbed the last part.

"Do you want to date him?"

Oh boy, wasn't that the question of the century.

"Yes," I said shyly.

Ren studied me a second and then nodded. "Okay, then. Just would've been cool if you'd told us about him."

Elijah tapped the table in front of us. "Uh, this is all very interesting but we're missing the questions."

"Bill asked"—Dean suddenly appeared, sitting down beside me with a beer in hand, forcing me to budge up next to Ren —"'What is nanoscience?' Easy. It's the study of molecules and structures whose size ranges from one to a hundred nanometers."

The guys all looked at him; Rhys drew my attention as he pulled a chair next to the table. "My brother's wicked smart," he said, straddling the chair and sipping his beer.

"We knew the answer," Navin said, his geek pride rearing its competitive head.

Dean shrugged. "Six brains are better than four."

"Six?" Ren shot Rhys an incredulous look, and while Rhys

might have looked through my friend like his words meant nothing, anger suffused me.

I slammed my foot down on Ren's under the table. I was still wearing my heels from work, so that had to hurt.

"Fuck!" Ren bit out. "What the hell was that?"

I gave him my most disappointed look, and he had the grace to appear ashamed. With a grimace and a sigh, he turned his attention toward Bill. His next lot of questions, we answered easily, while Rhys watched on with a bland expression I couldn't decipher. Was he bored? Irritated? Indifferent. He was puzzling and distracting.

Why did I care so much?

"Last question," Bill finally said. "Which animal does not drink water?"

We all looked at each other.

"Camel?" Elijah asked.

"I think they can survive a long time without water, but they still need it," Dean said.

"It's a kangaroo rat," Rhys said, voice quiet so teams nearby wouldn't hear.

"I've never heard of it," Navin said, scowling.

"Probably because it's made up," Ren huffed.

"Write it down," I said.

Ren nudged me. "What? No."

Oh boy, he was really ticking me off. "If Rhys says it's a kangaroo rat, it's a kangaroo rat. Write it down."

"Whatever," my friend muttered.

I practically growled at him. He knew using the word *whatever* in that manner was a pet peeve. It was a word for petulant teenagers, not for adults. It made adults sound like immature morons.

"Okay, you all got your answers done?" Bill asked as he approached our table. "Hand 'em over. Sorry they were so fucking hard. I think Della must've googled a quiz from the fucking MIT website."

Navin handed over the bit of paper and Bill scanned it. "Hey, looks like you guys might win." He frowned down at it. "How the fuck did you know it was a kangaroo rat? I hadn't even heard of that shit."

A smug smile spread across my face as Ren turned to me with a sheepishly apologetic look. I turned to Rhys, who wasn't smiling until he caught my expression. His eyes glittered with amusement as he took a swig of beer; I felt an unwelcome flutter of attraction in my belly.

Elijah pointed to Rhys. "Apparently this guy has."

"Rhys, didn't even see you there." Bill grinned as he came around the table to clap a hand on Rhys's shoulder. "How's it going? You haven't been by in a while."

"Been busy, Bill. How's you and Della?"

I studied Rhys as he talked to Bill, my eyes drawn to the hand resting flat on the table. He had big hands, big knuckles, long, surprisingly graceful fingers. It had never occurred to me that a man could have attractive hands. But Rhys's were. I imagined they must have gotten pretty bruised up when he was fighting professionally, and that made me frown.

Thinking about him getting back in the ring was alarming. I was glad he no longer fought. The idea of him taking a hit made my stomach lurch.

Uh-oh.

I shouldn't care if he fought or not.

But I did.

Oh hell.

"You and my brother seem to be getting along." Dean's voice cut through my thoughts.

I jerked out of my Rhys daze and turned to his younger brother. "Huh?"

Dean grinned mischievously. "What were you staring at?"

"Nothing." I blushed furiously and sought to distract him. "You're working with Rhys at the gym now, right?"

"Yeah. Place is kind of a mess, but Rhys is determined to fix it."

Something about Dean's derisive tone annoyed me. "His dedication to the gym is admirable."

"I know that." Dean dipped his head toward mine. "But my brother is trying to save it because of what it meant to our dad. It shouldn't be his burden. He would be better off walking away."

The idea that Rhys was stuck at the gym out of loyalty to his father's wishes was more troubling than I'd like. My fake boyfriend's happiness shouldn't mean anything to me. "Surely he enjoys running the gym?"

"He likes training young boxers. And he runs junior classes that help keep kids out of trouble."

"It sounds like a worthy job to me." I scowled at him. "Why would he be better off walking away from that?"

"Financially, he would."

"Money isn't everything."

"Says the woman who has money."

"Fair enough." I sighed. "But there are more important things. Like caring about your community."

Dean nudged me with his shoulder like we were old friends. "Why the fuck do you think I'm sticking around?"

"What are you guys talking about?"

Rhys's voice drew our heads up and my eyebrows nearly hit my hairline at his dark expression.

"The gym." Dean shrugged and then looked at Elijah. "You guys go to MIT with Parker?"

And thus began a night that went from awkward to even more awkward. The only people not affected by the epic levels of awkward were Elijah, Navin, and Dean. Eventually, Ren got over the fact that I'd kept Rhys a secret and joined the guys in their conversation.

After Bill came over with our prize, Dean talked easily with my friends. Sometimes they tried to draw Rhys and me into the conversation, but they didn't meet with much success. They asked Rhys a little about his boxing career, but his answers were short and didn't invite further questions. He stared around the bar, merely an arm stretch away from me, but he might as well have been on another planet.

And I didn't like it.

I had no idea what had crawled up his well-formed ass.

"So how did you two meet?" Ren suddenly gestured to me and Rhys. "Because you're not her usual type. And I've seen you on TV with your ring side 'fans'... she's not your usual type either. What gives?"

Rhys's expression didn't change. "Not sure that's your business."

Ren frowned at that. "Parker is my friend, so she is my business."

Looking between them like I was watching a tennis match I became increasingly annoyed. I opened my mouth to tell them the only person who had a right to my business was *me*, but Rhys opened his mouth first.

"You think? Hate to burst your bubble, but the only men in Parker's life who have a right to her business is her dad and the guy in her bed."

"Yeah? I've known Park for twelve years." Ren leaned forward. "I have more right to her business than you. I know her better than anyone. Well, except Theo." He shrugged. "And just a heads-up, no one's getting in there like Theo."

Confusion and fury rooted me to my chair.

"Ren, man, not cool," Navin practically growled.

"Yeah, think it's time we got you home before Parker decides to beat your ass." Elijah pushed back from the table and gave me a sympathetic smile. "Sorry, Parker."

I shook my head, mute with anger.

"Aw, shit." Ren rubbed a hand over his eyes. "Fuck, shit, I'm sorry." He looked at me in horror. "One too many beers and a shitty friend am I. Sorry, Park."

"It's fine." It was *not* fine.

"Let's go." Elijah nodded at Ren as he stood. He turned to Rhys. "Will you see Parker home?"

Rhys's expression remained confusingly blank. "Of course."

"Park, I really am sorry," Ren said again as he stood. "You know sometimes I say shit without thinking. I'm an asshole."

It was true that for a very smart guy, he didn't have a filter between his brain and mouth sometimes. "It's okay," I said, this time meaning it.

He gave me a remorseful smile. "We'll talk later when the memory of my assholery has faded."

This time I did smile. "We'll do that."

Relieved I was no longer pissed, Ren grinned. "See you later."

"I'll see you guys out." Dean stood, carrying the crate of beer that we'd won as he followed the boys out of the bar.

"Let's get you home."

Looking over at Rhys, I sighed. "You don't have to see me home. I can get a cab."

His expression tightened for some reason. "I'll see you home."

As soon as the cool night air hit, I felt a wave of exhaustion rush over me. "Well ... that was fun."

"You know your boy Ren is in love with you, right?"

The idea made me guffaw.

My reaction did not make Rhys happy, or I was misinterpreting the way his jaw muscle ticked as he clenched his teeth.

I rolled my eyes. "I've known Ren since freshman year of college. We're best friends. He has a long-term girlfriend who is lovely and intelligent. Trust me, he's not in love with me. He's more like an overprotective big brother."

"You know, for a smart woman, you're fucking clueless sometimes."

I narrowed my eyes. "What is your problem tonight?"

"Who's Theo?" he asked instead.

My breath stuttered. "Rhys—"

"Ren might be a dick, but he brought up a good point. He knows you better than I do, and if we're really going to sell this, you need to start telling me shit that's real. Like who's Theo?"

"Ren is not a dick."

"Parker."

Hearing the warning in Rhys's voice, I looked at him in surprise. He hadn't used that tone with me since before we signed our contract.

Cursing Ren to hell, I let out a shaky breath. How could I put much-needed distance between me and Rhys if I confided deep, emotional history to him? "It's not relevant."

"I think it is, if your boy is making such a big deal about it. My guess ... Theo is some rich little fucker who screwed you over. Is that why you don't have a man? You don't trust guys 'cause of a first love gone bad?"

The memory of Theo still caused a deep ache in my chest, and Rhys's supposition left a bad taste in my mouth. "He died," I blurted out. "He was my childhood sweetheart. We grew up in the same town, started dating when we were twelve. He was my first everything." I turned toward him as he drew to a halt beside me. "I loved him in a way I thought I would get to for the rest of my life. Until one night when we were seventeen, he walked home from a friend's party, drunk, on a dark country road, and a car hit him. And they left him there to die by the side of the road." Tears burned in my eyes, but I fought them back. "He was my best friend ... and then he was just gone."

"Jesus, fuck ..." Rhys suddenly pulled me into his arms, and I didn't stop to think before I rested my head on his chest and slid my arms around his back. "Tink, I'm so sorry."

We were silent a while, just holding each other in the middle of the street, until I felt his arms tighten. His voice carried softly down to me. "My best friend died too." The words sounded torn from him. "I watched him die in a bout. Jake. We grew up together. He was like a brother to me. And ... there was nothing I could do. One minute he was alive ... and the next, I watched the light go out of his eyes."

He shuddered against me and I dug my fingers into his shoulder blades, wishing I could dig the pain right out of him. I tilted my head back and the agony I saw behind all the cocky charm and humor in his eyes made my heart squeeze.

"Rhys," I whispered, hating to see someone so big, capable, and strong filled with so much grief.

"He left behind a wife and kid. Marcy and Rose. The fucking sport I loved tore away my brother, tore away Marcy's husband, Rose's dad." He shook his head, fighting his emotion. "First time someone called me the Widowmaker after he died ... I threw up."

"Rhys." I pushed deeper into him.

Now I knew. I knew why he couldn't get back in that ring.

"So I get it to a certain extent." He caressed my cheek, his eyes following the trail his fingers made across my skin. "I get how it feels to lose your best friend. To not be able to move on."

And I realized he did. Gently extricating myself from his embrace, I reached for his hand. "I don't think not going back to fighting is an inability to move on, Rhys. It's a choice you made.

A choice you should be proud of." At the abject surprise on his face, I curled my hand around his and gripped it tight. "I can't imagine the expectations people had of you as a champion ... but I can imagine that those expectations weighed heavily on your shoulders. To turn your back on that, to do what was right for *you,* to follow your gut ... Rhys, that takes more courage than putting on those gloves and getting in that ring."

Pain flickered across his features, the muscle in his jaw flexing again, as he stared into my eyes. Then he lowered his gaze to where I held his hand and his grip tightened. When he eventually looked up again, there was something like awe in his expression.

Something sweet.

Something significant.

And something dangerous to my emotions.

When he spoke, his voice was rough, hoarse. "Let me get you home, sweetheart."

Our walk to the gym was silent but Rhys didn't release my hand. When we got to his garage, to his bike, he brushed my hair off my shoulders and carefully put my helmet on for me. Once I got on the bike after he'd straddled it, he took my hands and drew them around his waist so I was pressed as close to him as I could get.

Part of me feared arriving at my place because with the thick tension between us, I half expected Rhys to ask to come up.

And the scary thing?

I wasn't sure I would say no.

However, Rhys didn't ask to come up. He stayed on the bike as I got off. He removed his helmet, waiting patiently as I took off mine. He reached for my hand and jerked me toward him.

My heart jumped into my throat, only to nosedive down again when he placed a brotherly kiss to my forehead.

Huh.

"'Night, Tinker Bell. I'll see you Saturday, yeah?"

I had to clear my throat to speak. "Saturday," I agreed, stepping back.

"Not leaving until you're safe inside, sweetheart."

Confused, disappointed, I nodded numbly and hurried inside my building. It was only when I was inside the elevator that I slumped against it and whispered, "You are seriously, seriously in trouble, Parker Brown."

THIRTEEN

Rhys

I HAVE TO ADMIT, there was something immensely satisfying about rumbling up the guarded gate of some richie's estate in my red 1970 Chevy Chevelle SS 454. My girl announced her presence with a throaty growl, drawing a sneer from the rent-a-cop on duty. My satisfaction multiplied as I handed him the gilded invitation to this trumped-up garden party and he immediately started kissing ass.

"A valet will meet you at the end of the drive, sir. Have a lovely afternoon, sir."

I waved him off and gunned it up the drive. Much to Parker's irritation.

"You're loving this, aren't you?" she muttered. She wasn't a fan of the Chevelle. Well, not outwardly. I swore she got a gleam in her eye earlier when I'd hit the gas on the highway.

She'd covered that little slip of enjoyment by complaining about the amount of gas we were wasting.

I glanced over at her and smiled. "As a matter of fact, I am. Did you see that guy's face? Like he'd sucked a lemon through a straw."

She sniffed and then turned to look over her shoulder at the winding drive.

"What now?" I asked. Ahead, the drive curved and a massive white clapboard house, sprawled out over a carpet of emerald green, came into view. Jesus.

"I was just checking to see if this fossil-fuel dinosaur was leaving behind a cloud of noxious black fumes."

Laughing, I shook my head. "Cute."

I'd taken the Chevelle because I didn't want to subject her to the hour's ride out to Manchester-by-the-Sea on the bike. Some thanks I got.

Parker crossed her arms under her pert breasts and glared straight ahead. "I'm serious. The greenhouse emissions this thing gives off is the stuff of nightmares."

One thing I knew to be true about Parker was that she started in on her favorite subject when she was nervous. When Dean was a kid, he used to rattle off equations for the same reason. Thus, I knew the only thing for it was to offer a distraction.

"Hey, I didn't see you throwing a fit when you told me to throw out those brown bananas at my place the other night."

Her brows winged up and she looked at me as though I'd grown another head. "I'm not following. At all."

Gotcha, babe.

I shrugged as I turned onto a circular drive where valets helped rich people out of their Astons and Jags. "Just that almost 11 percent of greenhouse gas emissions comes from methane created by rotting food. So, if you're going to attack

Ruby, you should probably side-eye all the food you throw out too."

Her mouth opened but nothing came out. I grinned wide. "Guess you're not as up to date on environmental issues as I thought."

Parker growled. "I knew about that!"

"Uh-huh."

Rolling her eyes, she sat back in her seat and huffed. But soon her lips were twitching and she let out a small, self-deprecating laugh. "Fine. You got me."

I couldn't help laughing too. The sky peeked through the leaves overhead, dappling the car in sunlight. It gleamed on Parker's smiling face, and something in my chest flipped over. I had to suck in a quick breath, but I was still left feeling light-headed.

She damn near broke my heart the other night when she told me about Theo. I had no idea what it was like to love someone that way, but I knew about loss. Her pain pierced me, and I never wanted to see her cry again.

Crazy thing was, I damn near cried when she'd looked right at me and said it took courage to quit, that I'd done something right. In that moment, I'd felt seen. I'd felt understood. I'd never had that from anyone. That a whip-smart, small but mighty woman like Parker saw something worthy in me was a gift I didn't know I needed until she gave it to me. A gift like that made a man crave more.

It was a fine line I walked now. Tenderness and the need to protect her nearly overwhelmed me every time I looked her way. But this was business. It did me no good to get attached. Even so, it was nice being with her, laughing because we could.

Still chuckling, I stopped the car.

"Did you really name your car Ruby?" she asked as a valet jogged over to open her door.

"Yep." I patted the gleaming black dash. "My girl here. Her name is Ruby."

Her reply was lost to me as she stepped out of the car.

I handed the valet the keys and followed Parker into the house. "Mansion" was the better word. I was a big guy but standing in that center hall with its soaring ceilings and gilded oil paintings, I felt small. Maybe that was the point. You put your guests in their place the second they walked through the doors. Or maybe the owners just liked a lot of light and air, because, looking around, I kind of wished I could still afford a place like this.

Parker seemed right at home here by the way she moved with ease through the scattered crowd. "Jackson is probably somewhere on the lawn."

The lawn in question was visible through the massive and ornately carved French doors at the far end of the house. The blue of the harbor winked at us in the distance.

"So, this is Fairchild's summer house?" I asked as we stepped outside. Garden terraces flanked either side of a wide flagstone patio. A set of central stairs went down to a pool straight out of *The Great Gatsby*. Well, if Gatsby had women wearing string bikinis. Fairchild definitely liked the whole bikini-model cliché.

"One of them, anyway." Parker didn't look impressed. "I believe this one was his late parents—oh, shoot."

Shoot?

My lips twitched. "You can say 'shit,' sweetheart. Your mom's not gonna pop out of the bushes and point the finger at you."

But Parker wasn't listening. Panic flared in her eyes as she did a half step away from me before whirling back to grab my wrist. "Quick, this way—"

"Parker Brown?" a woman called out, as though surprised.

Parker went stiff as a pipe. "Fiddlesticks," she said under her breath. She plastered on a fake smile—more like a grimace —and moved to greet an elegant older woman with sleek dark hair. They did that kiss-on-the-cheek thing some women liked.

"Vida," Parker said a little less stiff but clearly still pained. "It's nice to see you again."

"And you, sweet girl." Vida drew back and gave Parker an approving look. She was clearly aware of me; I just hadn't been acknowledged. "It's been too long."

"My new job has been keeping me busy."

"Ah, yes, of course." The woman glanced at me, calculation in her dark eyes. "You're working for Franklin."

"Well, in a way, yes," Parker replied. "I didn't realize you knew him."

Vida laughed, her red lips parting to reveal some truly white teeth. "Doesn't everybody?"

Parker's cheeks turned pale, and her slim shoulders hunched. "Seems that way." She gave Vida another plastic smile. "Well, I'll just go say hello to the host ..."

"Aren't you going to introduce me to your friend?" Only then did Vida look my way. Her gaze slid over me with slow appreciation.

I was used to that look. I got it before and after every match. Women wanted to fuck me for the thrill of it, for bragging rights. I made the mistake of accepting a few of those advances, only to have some of their friends contact me afterward, so very certain I'd do them too. After all, I was nothing more than a sexed-up, muscle head.

I should be grateful; I learned what it was to feel cheap and used. That familiar crawling sensation writhed in my gut. Then it occurred to me that Parker hadn't introduced me. I was here to be her arm candy, and she was leaning away from me as though she wanted to be anywhere but here.

That sure as shit didn't sit right.

Parker eyed me, and I saw another flare of reluctance. Shame. Regret.

I felt sick.

"Yes, of course," she said, her voice dull through the buzzing in my ears. "This is Rhys."

That was it. No boyfriend or date. Just Rhys.

My lips went numb as I stood there. A big, dumb ox.

Vida smiled at me, sly as fuck. "And does Rhys have a last name?"

She didn't give a shit about my name. She was digging. We all knew it.

I smiled wide and stuck out my hand. "Rent boy." My smile grew teeth. "It's more of a title."

Parker gasped, and Vida tittered.

"How marvelous, Parker." She sounded truly impressed.

Parker, on the other hand, was bright pink. Good. I rolled my tight shoulders. "If you'll excuse us, I need a beer."

I took hold of Parker's elbow and guided her away as gently as I could. I was pissed, which meant I had to be extra careful with my strength. Yeah, Parker had acted like I was garbage at her side, but I wasn't about to manhandle her.

"Rhys," she hissed, stomping along at my side. "What the heck was that?"

"I could ask you the same thing," I shot back. Several bars were set up on the various terraces. I went to the closest. "Beer. Just give me the bottle."

Parker tried her best to glare a hole through my face, as I grabbed the bottle of offered beer and took a long pull.

"You didn't want that woman to know who I was," I said. "Why?"

Biting her lower lip, she looked away. "She's a friend of my parents."

The words were a kick in the balls. "Ah."

Parker glanced back with eyes that were wide and pensive. "That's it?"

"What's there to say?" I shrugged, gripping the beer tight.

"Well, obviously, there is something to say because you're clearly in a mood."

God, for a smart woman, she was fucking blind sometimes. "Whatever, princess. It's nothing."

Her eyes narrowed. "Very mature."

"About as mature as hiring a fake boyfriend because you can't tell your asshat boss to fuck off with his misogynistic bullshit."

She blinked, pausing for a beat before starting up again. "I'm really angry with you, and truly want to tell you where you can stuff that comment, but I find myself compelled to give you credit for your use of 'misogynistic.'"

God, this girl. I liked her, damn it. I couldn't let myself. A good fighter protected his weak points.

"Five whole syllables in that word too," I said dryly.

With a huff, her eyes narrowed and the fire returned. "I was more impressed by the usage than the length."

Too easy. I tipped my beer bottle toward her in salute. "Sweetheart, with me, you'll get both."

"What ...?" A blush shot across her cheeks. "Oh, you ...you ..."

I leaned in. "Come on, Tink. Say it ... asshole, dickhead... You know you want to really tell me off. Let me have it."

I could almost see the words floating around in her head, dancing on the tip of that sweet tongue. I wanted to suck it off, lick into her mouth and taste her anger. Jesus, I was hard. Fucking turned on, panting. Her mouth would be pillow soft, her rage hard and swift.

When I noticed she was panting too, my arms jerked. I

clenched my fist to keep from reaching for her. But it hurt to hold back.

A sound escaped her. Not a whimper but something close. Needy. Confused.

I'll make it better, honey.

I took a step closer. She smelled so good. Looked so fine.

But we were interrupted again.

"Parker?" A man this time.

Seriously, fuck this party.

If Parker had been panicked before, she appeared down-right appalled now. Her mouth fell open in horror, as we turned in unison toward the man standing a few feet away. Salt-and-pepper hair, steel-rimmed glasses, tailored gray slacks and an ivory silk shirt. He looked like a New Yorker slumming it for the weekend.

Parker had his eyes. I didn't know why I noticed. But I did. And I knew exactly who he was. They shared the same smile too.

Parker's voice came out in a strangled squeak. "Dad."

Here we go ...

PARKER'S DAD SMILED. "PEANUT."

"Peanut?" I whispered to Parker, expecting a glare or maybe an elbow to the gut. She remained stone still.

Her dad leaned in and gave her a kiss on the cheek. "I didn't realize you'd be here."

Parker swallowed audibly. "I was thinking the same thing."

He was a few inches taller than she was, but wiry where Parker was delicate.

Unlike Vida, Parker's dad immediately zeroed in on me and

thrust out a hand to shake. "Charles Brown. No relation to the little bald guy, I'm afraid."

Charles Brown? Realization hit, and I grinned as I shook his hand. "I take it you don't go by Charlie?"

He laughed shortly. "Not if I can help it. Childhood was enough hell for me."

Despite his easy-going manner, power flowed off Charles Brown. Some guys thought they had to be biggest or the tallest guy in the room to be the strongest. That was bullshit. Physical strength rarely mattered as much as mental toughness and confidence.

Brown was the rare sort who knew he didn't have to prove anything to anyone. He was comfortable in his own skin. I admired the hell out of that. And the way he put a protective, affectionate arm around his daughter. Not so much a claiming but letting her know she was loved.

"Rhys Morgan," I filled in when Parker stayed quiet. The lights were on in Parker House but she'd clearly left the building. "I'm a friend of Parker's."

I had no idea what she wanted me to say in this situation. Did we lie to her family?

Parker blinked and then pushed a smile. "Rhys is an ex-boxer. Fairchild is a fan."

Brown nodded, his gaze moving between me and his daughter. "I'm a fan too."

Now that was a surprise.

"That fight with Davis, when you took him out with a KO in the second round? Legendary."

It felt oddly good to know Parker's dad knew of my career and approved.

"People either hate or love that fight." Personally, I loved it. Davis had a big mouth and a glass jaw.

"I suppose it depends on which way you bet." The gleam in

Brown's eyes told me he hadn't lost money.

"That's usually the case."

When we both chuckled, Parker finally found her voice.

"I had no idea you knew about Rhys, Dad."

"Why would you? I don't think we've ever had a discussion that revolved around sports." The tone of his voice and the look in his eyes made it clear he knew Parker wasn't with me because she was a fan. And it was just as clear he wanted to know *why* we were friends—and how close.

Parker averted her gaze but then looked up at me. "Maybe we should let Fairchild know we're here. He's been wanting to show Rhys around," she explained to her father.

I almost rolled my eyes. That's how we were playing it? I was here as Fairchild's guy crush?

She might have gotten away with that, but a pretty older woman with honey-blond hair and a younger woman who shared a startling resemblance to Parker joined us. It didn't take much to guess they were Parker's mother and sister. I swore I heard Parker groan under her breath.

"Mom. Easton." She might as well have been eating nails.

Easton watched me with avid eyes. This one was obviously happy to find Parker with a man in tow. "Well, hello, Parker," she said, not taking her eyes from me.

Like her dad, Parker's mom immediately focused on me. "Hello, I don't believe we've been introduced. I'm Marion Brown."

"Rhys Morgan."

She shook my hand with a firm grip and a steady gaze.

I didn't say anymore because, frankly, this one was on Parker. She shot me a look that read something close to "Save me from family hell." I empathized.

"Morgan!" Fairchild swooped, all eager beaver.

A laugh escaped me. I couldn't help it. It was a pile-on at

this point.

As usual, Fairchild completely ignored Parker. He clasped me on the shoulder as though I were his kid while turning toward the Browns. "Did I mishear or are you two just meeting Parker's boyfriend?"

The word landed like a bomb, leaving behind a stunned silence. Parker looked so miserable, I couldn't stop myself from slipping my hand into hers, giving it a gentle, commiserating squeeze. The action wasn't missed by Marion Brown.

"Boyfriend," Marion repeated. It was difficult to tell if she was upset or surprised.

No, that wasn't right. Parker's entire family appeared shell-shocked. The memory of Parker crying over Theo slid through me, and I knew with cold certainty she hadn't brought a man around them since.

Her hand grew clammy, but she gripped me a bit tighter. "Ah, yes ... that is ..." She glanced at an expectant Fairchild. "We just started dating."

Fairchild nodded with impatience, his hand returning to my shoulder. I really fucking hated when he touched me. My muscles clenched but I held still. Not that he'd noticed. "Rhys, why don't we let Parker catch her parents up? There are some men I want you to meet. They're really interested in investing in the sport."

At this point, I figured it would be a blessing to get out of Parker's hair. She looked one step away from screaming. Fairchild waved to a group of men in the crowd. He then grabbed my arm and tugged like I was a dog on a leash.

Money. I needed sponsors to save the gym.

Parker. I needed to pander to this asshole or she'd be in trouble.

Gritting my teeth, I let him lead me away. This truly was the party from hell.

FOURTEEN

Parker

THERE WERE VERY few moments in my life when I wasn't happy to see my parents. This was one of those rare moments. I watched Fairchild lead Rhys across the lawn toward a tall, blond man, wishing he'd stayed. The comforting feel of his hand clasping mine had been the only thing holding me together when Fairchild announced to my family that Rhys and I were dating.

That I wanted to be comforted by Rhys was a contradiction because he was the reason I dreaded the next few moments. I would have to lie to my parents and my sister.

How had this fake dating business spiraled so completely out of control?

And where was that damn door to the sand-snake dimension so I could throw *myself* through?

Strike that.

I was absolutely shoving Franklin Fairchild through that door if it ever did make a miraculous appearance.

"I didn't know you'd be here," I wheezed out, my chest tight with anxiety. "Or that you knew Franklin Fairchild."

Dad's brows drew together. "Everyone knows Fairchild. Your mother is on several charity boards with Fairchild's wife, Evelyn."

I hadn't known that.

Crap.

"Oh."

"We had breakfast not that long ago and you never mentioned a boyfriend," Easton mused, her tone unhappy. "Especially not one who looks like that."

"Like what?"

She shrugged. "Like one of the strippers we'll hopefully hire in Hawaii."

"Strippers?" my parents said in unison, my dad's eyebrows raised, my mother's mouth open in horror.

Ignoring them both, I scowled at my sister. "Don't objectify him."

Easton grinned unrepentantly. "I wasn't, my darling sister. I was merely making the observation that your *boyfriend* is rather fun to look at, and not at all what we'd expect. So, spill."

Hands clammy, heart racing, I met my family's inquisitive eyes one by one, and hated myself as I blurted out the lie Rhys made up. "We bumped into each other. Literally. I'd met Zoe for drinks. She had to leave for work, but I stayed to finish my drink. When I was leaving, Rhys was coming through the door and he nearly knocked me over. He asked if he could buy me a drink to apologize and ..." I trailed off with a miserable shrug.

"Why do you look like you're in pain?" Easton seemed caught between amusement and concern.

"And why is this the first time we're hearing about this boy?" Mom huffed.

A nervous snort escaped me at my mother referring to Rhys as a *boy*. "Where's Oliver?" I avoided the question, asking after my sister's fiancé.

"Business trip. I decided to tag along with Mom and Dad out of boredom—and wasn't that the best decision I've made in ages."

My cheeks heated, and I glared at her. She smiled sweetly. "Mom asked a question."

"I did ask a question," Mom said, stepping close to touch my arm. "Why are you acting so strangely about your young man?"

"Should we be worried?" Dad already looked worried.

"Oh, 'rentals, leave her alone." Easton shrugged, almost spilling champagne out of her glass with the movement. "Isn't it obvious she's being strange because it's been a while, a *long* while, since she's had a boyfriend? It still doesn't answer Mom's question," she reminded me.

"I can't remember you ever being as helpful as you're being right in this moment." I gave her a toothless smile. "In fact, you're being so helpful, I might have to *repay* you for your help-fulness in the near future."

This time her grin was wicked. "Nonsense. What's family for?"

A growl burrowed up my throat.

"Parker, darling, that noise is very unladylike." Mom shook her head. "Now, you were saying ..."

Was the ground shaking? Or was that just my trembling knees? If my parents found out I was using my trust fund to pay a man to pretend to date me, they'd be mortified. Mortified and so, so disappointed. The air started to feel a little thin. "Is it warm in here?"

Easton's lips trembled. "Outside, on the lawn?"

Oh shit.

I blinked in surprise, realizing I'd cursed in my head.

I couldn't remember the last time I'd cursed in my head.

I waited for my mother's voice to infiltrate, to make me feel guilty for using bad language, but it was replaced with the image of her finding out I'd hired an escort.

Shit!

Rhys was right. That felt good. "Shoot" just didn't alleviate the feelings of frustration the way a curse word did. And let's face it ... I was in deep shit.

Shit, shit, shit, shit, shit, shit.

"Shit."

"Parker Brown," Mom hissed. "Language."

By this point, Easton was giggling so hard, I'd have sworn she was drunk.

Cheeks blooming red, I threw my mother an apologetic look. "Sorry. It's just ..."

"It's just what?" Dad strode forward to cup my cheek.

The concern in his dark eyes made me hate myself even more.

"Peanut, what's going on here?"

Staring into my father's eyes, I curled my hand around his wrist and gave him a tremulous smile. "I just thought I'd have more time to adjust to being in a relationship again before I introduced Rhys to you all." The lie tripped off my tongue, every word making me more and more nauseated.

That feeling was further compounded by the relief I saw on my dad's face. "Peanut, I'm just glad to see you moving on. If you need a little more space, we can do that."

"Of course." Mom squeezed my arm, giving me a small smile. "I don't know how we can give you much space right now since we're all at the same party, but I promise not to push for a family dinner with Rhys just yet. Rhys." She smiled at my father. "That's a solid name, don't you think?"

Dad returned her smile and then focused on me again. He brushed a thumb over my cheek before releasing his hold on me. "All I know is he must be something special to have caught our Parker's eye."

It didn't surprise me that my parents couldn't care less that Rhys wasn't of society. All they cared about was seeing me happy again.

And that was what made lying to them so goddamn awful.

"Parker!"

Feeling exhausted by my mental self-flagellation, I had to paste on a smile as I turned toward Jackson and Camille. My boss strode across the lawn with his fiancée, and they weren't alone. A woman around my height, a little curvier, dressed in a white, conservatively cut summer dress accompanied them. Her shining dark hair was styled into an immaculate bob and when she raised her arm to take a sip of champagne, sunlight dazzled off her diamond tennis bracelet. Her face was strangely ageless, either because of enviable genetics or the best plastic surgery I'd ever seen. She could be anywhere between thirty-five and fifty and you wouldn't know, unless you asked.

However, since her face was also familiar, I knew she was forty-seven years old.

She was Diana Crichton Jones. Billionaire. Her grandfather opened an asset management company in the mid-1940s. Her father then ran it, and when he died, Diana was twenty-three. People scoffed when she stepped up to take his place as CEO.

However, Diana had proven to be the best thing that ever happened to Crichton Investments and Research. They now had over $2 trillion in assets under management. Moreover, she had private investments that took her personal fortune to a staggering number.

I knew all this because she was a very impressive woman and it was difficult to not have heard of her when you grew up in society.

However, I had never met her.

Until now.

Momentarily distracted from the disaster unfolding between me and my family, I shook Diana's hand when Jackson introduced her, and then introduced my family to my boss, his fiancée, and the somewhat awe-inspiring billionaire.

My father, with his usual canny instincts, seemed to sense that Jackson had brought Diana over for a reason. He touched a hand to my mom's lower back. "Why don't we get another drink?"

Mom nodded and gave my boss a little wave as she allowed Dad to lead her away.

"I'm ... with them." Easton threw me another cheeky grin before hurrying after my parents.

Relaxing marginally to be out from under their watchful gazes, I turned to Jackson.

I recognized the light in his eyes as excitement. It was the same light I'd seen when he realized how significant my suggested changes to the forecast model were going to be.

"Parker, I don't know if you know this, but Diana is very interested in the future of renewable energy, and I was telling her what an asset you've been to our team."

There was something emphatic in his tone I didn't quite understand, but I smiled anyway, pleased by his praise. "Thank you, Jackson." I turned to Diana, feeling a little nervous in her presence. She had steely gray eyes that seemed to look right through you. "You're interested in renewable energy?"

"Very much so. I'm interested in anything that's important

to our future." Diana stepped toward me, tilting her head slightly as she inspected me. "So far I haven't come across that many women in your field. Not that there aren't any. It's just very male dominated."

"Engineering tends to be." I shrugged as if to say, "What can you do?"

"True. I was telling Jackson I've been looking to invest with a renewable energy company but I'm very cautious about where I put my money and my own energy." She gave me a cool smile. "I don't like male-dominated companies. I like diversification. I like passion. I like to know that a company hires the best because they are the best and not because they have a dick."

Blinking at her blunt language, I felt a bubble of laughter on my lips as I wished Rhys were over here. He'd like her forthright manner.

This time I blinked because, whoa.

When did Rhys become part of my equations?

"I almost passed over Horus when I saw there were no women on their roster. But then you showed up and not only that, according to Jackson here, you've shown up impressively. There are no other companies using a model like yours. Which is why you're gaining the traction you are abroad."

I nodded, knowing all this but wondering where Diana was going with it.

"I have a real passion for green energy, Parker."

Excited to hear that, my nervousness melted away and I found myself conversing with Diana Crichton Jones about our model, about the urgent need we had as a world, not just a nation, to introduce the right infrastructure to institute electric-only vehicles, about corruption, about the true effectiveness of wind energy, solar panels ... we even talked about my little hybrid bike. She was thinking about buying one.

Diana. Crichton. Jones.

If I could convert one billionaire at a time in this country to go green, I might save the planet.

Okay, that was melodramatic, but this was exciting stuff!

"You were right." Diana smiled at Jackson, whom I'd almost forgotten was there with Camille. "Parker is everything you said she was."

Jackson grinned. "Yes, she is."

Diana sobered. "I'm interested. Leave it with me."

My boss turned serious too. "Excellent." He raised his glass to her.

She nodded at him, then Camille, and then turned to shake my hand. "It was nice to meet you, Parker. We'll hopefully speak again soon."

"Yes." I was suspicious about what had just passed between her and my boss, and those suspicions meant I hoped I'd speak with her again soon too. "I'd like that."

With that, she departed, crossing the lawn to stop at the side of a tall, distinguished-looking gentleman who slid his arm around her waist and leaned down to whisper intimately in her ear. I turned to Jackson.

"What was that?"

Jackson was beaming from ear to ear. "I was glad I hired you when you made those changes to the model. Now, I thank *fuck* I hired you, Parker."

Camille laughed at his side as my eyes widened at his effusive cursing.

"I don't understand."

"Hopefully, you will. Very soon."

Suspicions formed in my head, a little glimmer in the back of my consciousness that clung to the hope that Jackson was working on replacing Fairchild. He could just be attempting to bring in a new investor alongside Fairchild so there was no point getting my hopes up.

But it was hard for a girl not to dream.

JACKSON AND CAMILLE WANDERED OFF, leaving me speculating over our interaction with Diana. I searched the lawn for Rhys. He was no longer out there with Fairchild. Thankfully, I couldn't see my parents either.

Or maybe not so thankfully.

Anxiety ripped through me at the idea they might have hunted Rhys down and were "interrogating" him. Hurrying across the lawn back to the house, relief flooded me when I saw Rhys step outside. I knew he'd been watching for me by the way he strode deliberately toward me.

"I'm so sorry," I said, a little breathlessly. "I got caught up with Diana Crichton Jones, who is a billionaire with a passion for green energy. I think I convinced her to buy a hybrid electric bike. Can you believe that? Diana Crichton Jones on an electric bike."

Rhys's lips twitched as he studied my face. "Converting people to green really gets you going, huh?"

I shrugged, glancing at the party behind me. "It's more fun than talking about terrible nannies, investments, and where I plan to summer." I turned back to him. "FYI, I plan to summer in Boston. And by "summer", I mean working like 99 percent of the rest of the world's population has to do."

He grinned. "Your family doesn't summer?"

"When we were kids, we spent the season in our vacation home in Cape Cod, but my mom and dad only spent two full weeks of that with Easton and me. They both worked. My mom's sister, Aunt Debbie, is a writer, so she would care for us the rest of the time. Mom and Dad would fly to the cape on the weekends and then back to New York for Monday. It was a lot. I didn't realize that then, but they did what they could to be there for us."

"They could've kept you in New York with them."

"They could have. But summer in New York can be miserable, and our cape house is right on the beach." I'd loved our childhood summers in Cape Cod. Until I met Theo and begged my parents to let me stay in New York so I could spend the summer with him. They'd relented.

"Speaking of your family, how'd that go?"

Remembering the lies I'd told my parents, I blanched, looking away. "It went."

There was such heavy silence from Rhys, it drew my gaze to him. A muscle flexed in his jaw and his eyes were flat. "They're pissed you're dating someone like me."

Why would he think that?

Opening my mouth to deny it, I was cut off by, "Rhys! There you are."

Fairchild.

Something dark flickered over Rhys's face before he turned to my boss's boss with a strained smile. My eyes drifted over Fairchild's determined expression, and I shivered at the hardness in his gaze.

Rhys moved into me, sliding his arm around my waist and drawing me to his side.

"Where did you go to?" Fairchild came to a stop in front of us. "One minute you were there, the next, poof." My boss flicked me a look. "There's no doubt who's to blame. You can't seem to keep your hands off this one, Morgan."

I tensed against Rhys and felt him squeeze my hip in reassurance.

"What can I do for you?" Rhys bit out, and there was no hiding his impatience.

Concerned, I looked up at him to gauge his expression, and he was staring blankly at Fairchild.

Fairchild narrowed his eyes at Rhys's tone. "Well, for a start, we can finish our conversation. Now, I'm happy to come look at that gym of yours, but I'd be even happier to do it if you'd just listen to me."

Feeling Rhys's grip on my hip turn bruising, my concern escalated. "Rhys, what's going on?"

"Or perhaps Parker can convince you since she seems to be holding your balls captive."

I sucked in a breath at Fairchild's insult.

Rhys made a step forward in agitation.

I pulled him back, not understanding what was happening here. "Rhys?"

"I'm trying to set up a private fight for your boyfriend, Parker, and it will make him a lot of money." Fairchild looked from me to Rhys and then back to me. "Perhaps you can convince him not to be a fool and accept this invitation."

With that, the slime strode back to the garden party, and I watched in stunned silence before turning to Rhys. Avoiding my gaze, he marched toward the house.

What the ever-loving ...

Hurrying after him, I caught up in the foyer. "Rhys!" I grabbed his wrist, pulling him to a stop. He glared down at me in a way I once would have found intimidating but now just found maddening. "Where are you going? What is going on?"

He flicked a look at a passing server, and then removed my hand from his wrist. He then clasped my hand in his, and I could feel his anger as he pulled me along behind him. We cut down a hall that was clearly off-limits to guests, and Rhys pushed open a door. He guided me in first, and I stumbled into the room, hearing the door close behind him.

We were in what I could only presume was a TV room that faced the front of the house. There were two short steps leading to a lower level, where a massive seven-seater sofa was placed directly in front of a projector screen. On the shelves beside Rhys and I was a modern projector along with shelves and shelves of DVDs.

"Why are we in here?" I turned to face him. "Fairchild—"

"Wants me to fight. Yeah."

"In exchange for helping you with the gym?"

He crossed his arms over his chest, expression dark but removed. He didn't respond.

Suddenly, everything made sense.

"This was your plan? From the moment you met Fairchild?"

"My gym is in trouble. It was an opportunity."

For some reason, that stung. "I see."

"Do you?"

His countenance, although still cloudy, was no longer distant. In fact, his green eyes were burning in a way I recognized. A shiver tickled down my spine.

This one was the good kind.

"Rhys," I whispered, "how far are you willing to go to save your dad's gym?" I stepped toward him and placed a tentative hand on his hard chest. His heart was pounding. "Don't do it. It's not worth what it'll cost you."

Our eyes met and held, a heavy silence falling thick between us. My breathing shallowed as his eyes dipped to my mouth, resting there as he bit out, "What about you? What about what you're willing to do to impress Fairchild and the people who sniff at his ass? Why the fuck do you care what these people think?"

Confused by the subject change, I moved to step back, lowering my hand, but Rhys caught my wrist and pulled me against him. I uttered a little gasp, one hand falling against his abs while he kept the other imprisoned against his chest.

"Rhys?"

"Why?" he growled.

I didn't understand why I was the object of his anger. It wasn't that he was transferring his frustration with Fairchild to me; I realized that Rhys had been visibly annoyed with me almost from the moment we'd arrived. What was more alarming, however, was the current of sexual heat that accompanied that annoyance.

I didn't understand it.

Rhys kept telling me this was just a job to him.

Yet he was looking at me now like he wanted to devour me.

"Rhys?"

"Why?"

My nerves were stretched taut by this point and my patience snapped. "I don't care what these people think!"

"Bullshit!"

My chin jerked back at his vehemence. "Not bullshit."

Rhys's eyes widened marginally at my cursing.

Defiant, aggravated, turned on, confused, I tried to pull away again, but his other arm wrapped around my waist, imprisoning me against him. "Let go."

"Why do you care what these people think?"

"I don't care what they think! I care what my parents think!"

To my utter confusion, Rhys's beautiful eyes darkened with fury. His grip on me tightened, pulling me up onto my tiptoes, and he bent his head so our noses were almost touching. "You're fucking thirty years old," he seethed. "Time to get your head out of your ass and start living for yourself."

"Oh, you hypocrite—"

His mouth crushed down over mine, and he released my wrist. I knew I should push him away, stop a kiss that had nothing to do with our pretense, but I didn't want to. I loved the way he kissed. Demanding and hungry. No one had ever kissed me like Rhys. My skin had been hot from our inexplicable animosity but now it was burning. I clutched at his body, trying to press deeper, and Rhys let out a little growl of frustration that rumbled sexily in my mouth.

Suddenly I was off the ground, Rhys's hands under my armpits, lifting me up as he continued to kiss me. Instinctively I realized it was uncomfortable for him to bend down to me, so I wrapped my arms around his shoulders, my legs around his waist, and felt him stumble back against the door.

One of his hands slid under my dress to cup my ass while his other curled around my nape. Unbelievably, the kiss grew more voracious. Everything disappeared in that moment. Everything but Rhys and how my body could fit to his. I found myself rocking my hips, and Rhys broke the kiss to mutter "Fuck" against my mouth before capturing it again.

I was aware of us moving as we kissed, and a few seconds later, our lips disconnected as something soft hit my back. Rhys came down over me, not giving me a chance to react to the fact that I was now sprawled on the sofa.

His hips fell between mine, and I gasped into his mouth as I felt him nudge between my legs. Oh my God, he was hard. A lick of lightning heat scored down my spine, and my thighs closed around his hips, my fingernails biting into his shoulders to pull him closer.

His lips trailed away from my mouth, whispering hotly across my skin, as he lightly tasted his way down my throat. I whispered his name, tilting my hips, needing to feel more of him, and trembled as his hand glided up my inner thigh.

My eyes flew open as his lips followed a path down my chest, while his fingers slipped beneath my underwear. Two thick fingers suddenly pushed inside me, and I whimpered and arched my back into his touch. His grip on my hip turned bruising, and I heard him murmur hoarsely, "So tight."

Rhys's head came up, and I caught a flash of undiluted desire in his eyes before he crushed his mouth down over mine again. He drank in my moans as his fingers played and pushed me toward climax. I'd never felt anything like it. Such desperate need.

"Oh, Jesus Christ, sorry!"

We froze at the unexpected voice, and Rhys lifted his head to meet my devastated gaze.

No!

I was so close!

The muscle in his jaw flexed as he turned his head toward the doorway. I reluctantly followed suit and saw my sister standing there, lips trembling with laughter, eyes averted.

Oh my God, someone kill me now.

"Uh, your boss and Fairchild are looking for you. I'll tell them"—laughter bubbled in her words—"you'll be out in a few minutes."

The door closed behind her and with it a cold, hard splash of reality.

I saw it on Rhys's face.

"Shit." He pulled away from me in every way, and my body protested at the deeply empty, unfulfilled feeling. "Oh fuck."

Hurt by the raw regret on his face as he got off me, I scrambled to push the hem of my dress down. I lowered my gaze as I swung my legs off the sofa, unable to meet his eyes.

"That shouldn't have happened. I'm sorry. I was pissed at Fairchild and you were acting—"

He cut off when I scowled up at him. "Acting like what?" I said.

Rhys glowered. "Don't pretend like you don't know how you were acting."

"I don't know how I was acting. Enlighten me." I stood and crossed my arms over my chest, feeling the burn of unsatisfied lust heat my temper.

"You know how you were acting." He dragged his gaze down my body and back up again in a way I did not like. "But you certainly forget all about that when I put my hands on you. Fuck, sweetheart, you light up so hot, I was just along for the ride. You like that for your society boys, or does slumming it get you off?"

Pain flared in my chest, an ache so deep I stumbled back from him, ignoring his flinch.

"Parker—"

I held up a trembling hand, glaring at him so hard, it was a wonder his head didn't explode from the power of my angry, angry mind. In fact, I was so furious and so hurt, I couldn't speak. I strode past him, sliding my hands down my dress to smooth it, before turning my attention to combing my hair into some semblance of order.

"Tinker Bell—"

I whirled around just before I got to the door, not caring at the remorse I saw written all over his face. "Go *fuck* yourself, Rhys."

Instead of the surprise I thought I'd see on his face, I saw something else. A glitter of light in his eyes as he moved toward the steps that would lead him up to me. "I think we both know I'd rather fuck you."

Ignoring the thrill that shot through me, I held onto what he'd said, to the derision in his voice just a few seconds ago. "So you can add me to all the notches on your belt? I'm not a challenge. I'm not an opponent. And I—" Stupid tears burned my eyes that I determinedly tried to blink back.

"Tink ..." Rhys made to move toward me.

"Don't." I lowered my gaze so he couldn't see how much he'd hurt me. "This is done. I'll pay you for the month, but this is done." Tears successfully pushed back, I lifted my chin, my expression flat. "No job is worth someone making you feel this badly about yourself."

He scowled. "Yeah, you're right, it isn't. Pot meet fucking kettle."

Confusion momentarily subdued my anger. "What—"

"But we have a deal, and you're not getting out of that deal." He strode toward me, and I braced. Thankfully, he reached past me to pull open the door. "Let's go talk to your bosses, and try not to act like you're dying of embarrassment to have me at your side."

What on earth?

"Rhys—"

Footsteps sounded in the hall outside, and my sister appeared. "Uh, seriously, if you don't hurry up, Fairchild is going to come looking."

Sighing in frustration, feeling like I was missing something with Rhys, I hurried after my sister and heard my fake boyfriend fall into step behind us.

"Is my hair okay?" I whispered to my sister.

She smirked at me. "Your hair is fine."

I was just about to sigh with relief when she continued, "But your mouth is most definitely swollen."

Heat bloomed on my cheeks as I touched my fingers to my lips.

"Morgan, Parker, there you are!" Fairchild's voice carried across the foyer. He gave Rhys a salacious smirk. "Those are private family rooms down there, but I'll let you off since I know you're a man with an appetite. I understand that."

Ugh.

I shivered in revulsion and felt a comforting hand on my lower back. Glancing over my shoulder at Rhys, I wanted to move away. However, the unhappy look on his face stopped me. The man was a contradiction. I was completely discombobulated by him.

No matter what he said, I had to end this deal. My feelings ... well, my feelings were now involved, and after what just happened between us, I knew this man had the power to hurt me.

Deeply.

Nope.

This game had to be over.

"Jackson and I were talking, and I've decided to invite the Horus team and their partners to my lodge in Colorado Springs. I think"—his shrewd gaze landed on Rhys—"it'll be a good way for us to bond as a team. And to make sure *all* team members feel like they're an important cog in the wheel of Horus Renewable Energy. I'll consider any team member who doesn't decide to participate in this event a team member who doesn't want to remain at Horus."

Rhys's hand on my back pressed deeper, and I swallowed a howl of frustration. Fairchild's words from earlier came back to me, words I'd forgotten when things heated up with Rhys.

"Perhaps you can convince him not to be a fool and accept this invitation."

Oh my God. Fairchild was so goddamn determined to get Rhys to fight, he was going to force us to spend the weekend in Colorado so he could persuade him.

My eyes flew to Jackson who did not look pleased about our current discussion.

"Well?" Fairchild's gaze came to me.

I hated him.

I had never hated anyone other than the person who had left Theo on the side of that road, but right then, I hated Franklin Fairchild.

Was my job important enough to push Rhys into doing something I knew would harm him emotionally?

Even after the horrible argument we'd just had, I couldn't do it.

"I don't know if we'll be able—"

"We'll be there," Rhys cut me off.

My gaze flew to his, but he was studiously avoiding it.

"Good." Fairchild clapped Rhys on the shoulder. "I'll give Jackson the details."

The jerk stalked off, happy with his wicked machinations, and as soon as he was out of earshot, my sister said, "Why do I feel like I'm missing something?"

Jackson and I shared a weary look.

We were all just flies caught in Fairchild's net. Trapped by his whims.

My boss turned his attention to Rhys. "It looks like you've made quite an impression on Franklin."

Yes, Jackson knew exactly what this "team-bonding" trip was all about.

"Lucky fucking me," Rhys bit out.

I winced. "Easton, Jackson, I need a word with Rhys."

My sister threw me a concerned look, her earlier amusement gone now that she'd been witness to the tension with Fairchild. However, like Jackson, she murmured her assent and they left us alone in the foyer.

"You don't have to do it," I said. "My job is not worth it."

Rhys's gaze softened. "You are a contradiction, you know that, Tinker Bell?"

Uh, what did he say earlier? Pot meet kettle. "How am *I* the contradiction in this scenario?"

He didn't answer. His expression grew taut. "I shouldn't have acted how I did or said what I said. I'm apologizing. It won't happen again. Now, you're paying me to help you keep this job, so we're going to that lodge. Fairchild can bug me all he wants while we're there about getting in that ring. Doesn't mean I'm going to."

"But—"

"It's cool, okay?" He sighed. Heavily. "Can we get the fuck out of here?"

Yes. Although I did not look forward to the car ride home with Rhys, I really, really wanted to leave. "Let's go."

He frowned. "We're not saying goodbye to your parents?"

I blanched at the thought of having to lie again to their faces. "Uh, no."

And just like that, Rhys's expression shut down. "Right," he muttered, as if he'd tasted something bad.

Confused, I could do nothing but follow him as he marched out of the house to collect his car.

He didn't say a word to me the entire drive back to Boston.

Not one word.

His anger toward me was obvious.

The reason for it, not so much.

My irritation grew as we neared the city.

And when I got out of his car, I slammed the door so hard, his car shuddered. I heard him cursing behind the wheel.

Smirking with a small kind of satisfaction, I hurried into my apartment building. Yet my satisfaction died as soon as I got in the elevator and replayed the last few hours.

Easton's words from earlier rang in my ears.

"Why do I feel like I'm missing something?" I murmured.

FIFTEEN

Rhys

THERE WAS nothing worse than being stuck on a plane next to a woman determined to give you the cold shoulder. Oh, I deserved it. There wasn't any doubt. Yes, I'd been disappointed in Parker's clear horror over her family thinking she was dating me. But instead of shutting down, I'd been a dick in return—a huge, massive dick. I was ashamed of myself.

Thing was, I couldn't actually say what I wanted to say while stuffed into a seat that was about ten sizes too small for my frame and surrounded by dozens of other passengers practically on top of me. I knew Parker well enough to realize she'd be mortified if I talked about her personal life in front of strangers.

So, I waited, all the while acutely aware of Parker at my side. Aware of the way she smelled—like smoky roses and warm vanilla—of the way she made those constant little noises of discontent. Weirdly, they sounded a lot like the noises she made when she kissed me, and I didn't know if that was a good or bad thing. Regardless, the memory gave me wood. Which was uncomfortable as fuck.

We maintained stiff silence all the way to Aspen, and again in the rental SUV. It was unnerving. I didn't *need* to talk to people. I'd always been happy to keep to myself. And yet here I was, needing Parker to talk to me. I missed her spirit. I missed her voice.

"We're almost there," I told her in a sad attempt to start a conversation.

She hummed under her breath—a sound that could mean anything from "Yes, we are" to "Fuck off and die, Rhys."

Twitching in my seat, I drove us down a private road that seemed to stretch on forever. Despite the tension inside the car, the outside scenery was spectacular. Craggy, dark gray mountains with snowcapped peaks stretched toward a clear blue sky. Amidst the evergreens, aspen trees punctured the landscape with their ghost-white trunks and lacy golden leaves. It was all so beautiful, it turned a dumb-ass like me into a poet. I'd smile at that, but there was still the matter of Parker hating me.

We crested a small hill and the house came into view.

"Jesus," I muttered under my breath.

Parker leaned forward. "It's quite impressive."

The first actual sentence she'd uttered in at least three hours. A downright gift. And she wasn't wrong.

Fairchild's lodge was a low-slung modern ranch mix of stone, logs, and peaked roofs. The center house split off into two main wings on either side. Smoke drifted from six chimneys as sunlight glinted off wide picture windows. It was beautiful.

Envy never did anybody any good. And yet, in that moment, I felt it like an acid wash in my gut. I fucking hated that a sleaze like Fairchild owned this place and got to retreat here whenever he wanted. If there was any justice in the world, Fairchild's home would reflect his insides and we'd be staring at a dank and empty cell instead of this grandeur.

I swallowed my bitter hate and envy down and put on my game face.

The drive led straight to a massive front door, where a young guy wearing pressed dark jeans and a collared shirt/sweater combo stood waiting. We'd had to pass three security checkpoints before getting to the main house gate a mile back. Apparently, in places like this, the rich owned whole mountainsides, and they didn't share.

The guy trotted up and held open the door for Parker. Another valet came around to greet me and take my keys. If I didn't know this was a private residence, I'd think we'd arrived at a resort. It was big enough.

"Mr. Morgan, Ms. Brown," said Mr. Sweater. "I'm Andrew, Mr. and Mrs. Fairchild's house concierge."

House concierge? Who knew?

"As guests are still arriving." He smiled, tight as a drum. "I'll see you to your room and get you settled before drinks on the terrace at five. Would you like a mulled-cider cocktail while we walk?"

A waiter in the same sweater-jeans combo—which apparently was some sort of bizarre uniform—appeared with a tray holding two steaming glass mugs. I almost laughed, but I didn't want to hurt their feelings. Jesus, if I had to cater to Fairchild and his friends, I'd want to launch one of those mugs into the nearest face.

At my side, Parker gave what I was now calling her polite public smile. I hated that smile.

"If we could just head to the room, that would be wonderful, thank you."

At least we were on the same page when it came to the drinks.

"Of course," Andrew said. "Right this way."

The house was as beautiful as expected. That is, if you overlooked Fairchild's decorating tastes. We entered a grand hall with a wall of windows overlooking the valley and two massive stone fireplaces on either side of the room. Two suits of armor holding spears flanked the doorway. I refrained from rolling my eyes.

Every wall had weaponry and tapestries, and more suits of armor guarded the halls, as though we were in a castle in England instead of a resort in Colorado.

Andrew yammered on about the lake, the heated indoor and outdoor pools, nature walks, movie room ... I tuned out and watched Parker instead. I couldn't help it. She was wearing jeans, and they hugged her ass like a second skin.

Unbidden thoughts crashed in. Parker's mouth devouring mine. Parker arching her back, her thighs spreading. Parker moaning my name when I slid a finger inside her. God, she'd been so damn tight. Wet. Hot.

Nope. Don't go there. Not now.

Andrew led us to our room. As far as guest rooms went, it was the nicest one I'd ever been in. Like the rest of the house, it was a study of rough stone and dark woods. We had a corner room with two walls of paneled windows and a set of doors that led to a wide stone terrace. A large iron canopy bed dominated the far side. I kept my eyes off it.

I knew Parker dreaded staying here with me. It was evident in every tight and unhappy line in her body. She stood to the side, looking out the windows as Andrew explained about how to work the fireplace, the electric blackout curtains, where the minibar was hidden. When he started in on what kinds of soap our en suite had, I cut him off.

"I think we got the gist. We're good now." I gestured toward the door in an unmistakable sign of "Get the hell out."

"Of course," he said, straightening his sweater—the one with aspen leaves knitted into the threads. Poor guy.

"Thanks, man," I said easier. But as soon as he left, I let my shoulders sag and leaned against the door to look at Parker. She hadn't moved from her spot by the windows.

Remorse cut into my gut with sharp blades.

"Parker—"

"At least it's a king bed." She didn't look at the bed, though. She kept her eyes away from the entire room. "I'd hoped for a little loveseat, but I don't think I can curl up on those armchairs. I'm small but not that small."

There were two chairs set up by the French doors. She'd contemplated sleeping on them. It didn't matter that she was ashamed of me meeting her family; I'd become something petty and small when I'd lashed out and made her feel this way. As for myself, I felt about two inches tall.

"Parker," I said again, this time sitting on the bench at the foot of the bed so we'd be eye to eye. "I'm sorry. All right?"

Her gaze stayed unfocused as she nodded. "It's fine. Things were said ..."

"No." I took her hand and found it cold. Unacceptable. Holding it between both of mine, I softened my voice as best I could. "I was a fuc—a jerk. I shouldn't have said those things, making you feel cheap. It wasn't true and I didn't mean them. It was a dic—It was wrong to do."

Parker's lips wobbled with a smile. "Am I imagining things or are you attempting to refrain from cursing?"

"Yeah, well ..." I rubbed the back of my tense neck but kept hold of her hand with my other one. "It seemed like a good way to show my sincerity and respect for the situation."

Her smile finally bloomed, and I swear it was like the sun coming out of clouds. Hell. I was a fuck—freaking mess.

"Just when I finally start cursing, you've gone and stopped."

It felt good to grin. "Well, that's different." I tugged her a little closer. "You letting go and cursing is sexy as he—heck."

Her laughter sparkled over my skin and lifted a weight off my heart. "As heck, huh?"

"Heck, yeah."

Laughing softly, her gaze clashed with mine. Heat bloomed under my skin, and I drew in an unsteady breath. God, I wanted to hold onto her slim but curvy hips, cup her fine ass and give it a squeeze.

No. I couldn't do that. We had undeniable chemistry, but we'd never work in the real world. Not when she couldn't even introduce me to her family without looking like she was about to throw up.

My smile died, as reality sank like a stone in my gut. We didn't have a future, but we *were* partners, and I'd done her wrong in more ways than one. "I shouldn't have grabbed you like I did. I regret that most of all."

A frown wrinkled between her brows. "Let me see if I have this straight. You regret ... getting physical with me?"

This felt like a trap. My instincts were screaming that it was most definitely a trap. "Yes?"

Her eyes narrowed. "Is that an answer or a question?"

Yep, definitely a trap. Resting my forearms on my thighs, I tried to think of a way to explain myself without digging a deeper hole. "I'm a big guy with a hell of a lot of strength. I didn't ask for permission, didn't handle you with care. I just ... took."

She hummed under her breath. I had no idea what that meant, so I forged on, acutely aware that I was probably stepping in it. "I shouldn't have manhandled you."

Parker turned away and went back to her post by the window. Afternoon light slanted in and colored her skin bronze. I couldn't tell if she was pissed, grateful, disappointed, or something else. She'd shut down completely.

I'd have admired her game face if it wasn't currently being used against me. I stood and rubbed my neck. "It was especially wrong considering we're just ..." I couldn't say it, though. My mouth refused to do it.

Parker glanced back at me, her brows a fierce line. "Just what?"

The memory of her ashen face when she told her parents that I was her boyfriend flashed in my mind, and the words punched out of me. "Business. We're just business partners, Parker."

She made a sound, not quite a snort but close, then tilted her head back to blink up at the ceiling. For a horrible second, I thought she might cry. But then she laughed with a bitterness that surprised me. "You want to hear something funny?"

She sounded so dull and remote, I wasn't sure if she was asking. I didn't get to answer before she looked at me again, those deep brown eyes spearing my chest. "You kissing me, me kissing you, the way you touched me on the couch, that was my favorite part of the whole horrible day."

The floor tipped my feet as heat rushed up my back. "Parker ..."

"I'm attracted to you," she went on, like I hadn't said a word, her tone growing stronger. "Despite everything, I find myself wanting you. I dread sleeping on that bed with you because I find it exceedingly hard to keep my hands to myself."

Holy shit. My knees went weak, my dick hard as a pike.

"Which really just ... sucks," she said, growing a little wild and shrill. "Because you keep throwing the truth in my face. That we're nothing but a deal, a monetary means to an end for both of us. And I feel ..." She looked around wildly as though searching for the word, and then it exploded out of her. "Stupid. *Fucking* stupid!"

God, she was brave. Magnificent. *My brave, beautiful girl.*

I had to hold her. I needed it. I made a move to go to her, but she thrust up a hand. "No. You don't get to touch me *now*." It was a snarl of rage. "Not when you've made it clear how you see me. Not after you've been a total *dickhead*."

She reveled in cursing, like she gained power from it. I loved that. Watching her rail into me should have left me feeling chastised, but it inflamed me. I was the lucky bastard who was getting to see her bloom.

Slowly, I advanced, holding my hands up in surrender. Because I did. I fucking surrendered. I was hers to do with what she willed.

"I'm not gonna touch you," I promised when she went stiff. "But let's clear a few things up. I said that stupid shit about us being nothing more than partners because I thought it's what I was supposed to say. I was trying to be professional and keep myself under control."

I stopped in front of her, letting her see all the emotions I'd tried so damn hard to hide. "But there's nothing controlled about the way I feel about you, Parker. I want you so badly, it hurts." My hands clenched into fists so I wouldn't reach for her. "I think about your mouth more than I should. Everything about you gets to me. You dread that bed? Well, so do I. Because being next to you and not being able to touch you is absolute torture."

Parker swallowed hard and her lips parted. But a small frown worked between her brows. "Is that why you've been shutting down on me? Because it doesn't add up; you were downright angry with me at the party."

For a second, I didn't want to answer. I didn't want to

expose that insecurity. But it was still there like a thorn in my side. And this was never going to work if I wasn't honest with her.

"All right, fine. I was pissed." I held her gaze. "I knew what you thought of me going into this. I was okay with that because it was a job then. But I figured your opinion of me would change when we got to know each other. Mine did. But yours clearly hasn't."

Parker gaped at me as though I'd been speaking in tongues. But then a spark of anger lit her gaze. "How on earth would you come to that conclusion? Because I must say, Rhys, you're pissing me off now."

Seriously? I snorted. "Come off it. You looked like you were going to puke all over your penny loafers when your parents showed up. Before that, even. Hell, you practically ran from your parents' friend too. When it really counts or it's in front of someone you actually care about, you're ashamed to be seen with me."

She didn't back down. I'd give her that. Her hands went to her hips as she squared off. "I wasn't ashamed of you! I couldn't be attracted to someone I didn't respect and like as a person. I was ashamed of lying to my parents, you complete and utter blockhead!"

Nonplussed, I took a step back like she'd landed an uppercut to my jaw. My ears were ringing. "You ... ah ... what?"

My brilliant reply only made her nostrils flare.

"Got nothing to say now, huh?" She shook her head with another snort before going on the attack. "My family means everything to me. Did you honestly believe it was easy for me to lie to their faces?"

"Even with that short meeting, I could tell they want the best for you. Why don't you tell them the truth? You gotta know they'll forgive you." I wanted to say more, but my head was reeling. The fact that I'd gotten it so wrong pulled the rug out from under me.

"Because ..." She lifted her shoulders in a helpless gesture. "Then I'd have to admit that I'd paid a man to be my boyfriend. And it's too mortifying to contemplate. Sorry if that offends your delicate sensibilities."

Delicate?

My lips twitched as tenderness washed through me. "Parker." I reached for her.

"No ..." she said, shaking her head.

"Yes." Gently I tugged her forward and pressed her palms to where my heart beat hard and fast. "Parker, I'm sorry. I was a dickhead. A blockhead."

Her gaze slid sideways and a smile ghosted across her lips. She wasn't pulling away. "You forgot asshole," she said.

"Did you call me that too?" I murmured, warmth spreading outward, need for her building. "I must have missed that one."

"In my head, I did."

I grinned, and after a brief aggrieved sniff, she did too. I leaned down and brushed a kiss across her temple. "I'm sorry I was an asshole, Tinker Bell. My only excuse is that I'm so into you, I've lost all my good sense."

A sigh gusted out of her, and she leaned her forehead against my chest. "Well, as excuses go, I suppose I can accept that."

I rubbed the back of her neck with my thumb, easing the tension there. "You sure? Because I'm willing to do some physical labor as recompense. Offer up a back rub, maybe."

She huffed out a laugh and melted into me. "I'm not going to object to that."

We grew quiet and held onto each other. I had no idea it would feel so good to simply hold a woman. Then Parker stirred.

"I didn't expect this," she said.

"Neither did I. You were supposed to be a snobby, rich woman of loose morals." I laughed when Parker poked my side, and then I snuggled her closer. "Not a gorgeous, quirky environmentalist with excellent taste in motorcycles."

"My taste is excellent in everything," she said. "And you were supposed to be a boorish, money-grabbing jerk."

Aside from the money thing, she wasn't far off. But I wasn't stupid enough to mention that. I nuzzled her hair instead, drawing in her scent. "Just because we didn't plan on this doesn't make it any less real, though, does it?"

"No, it doesn't." Her arms wrapped around my waist and it felt like heaven.

"I'm not taking any money from you," I said into her silky hair.

"Then it's a good thing I never got around to paying you."

Laughing softly, I leaned back enough to see her face. She smiled up at me, a little hesitant but no longer angry. My fingertips traced the line of her jaw. "I won't take the money, but I'm going to help you. We're still partners. Just ones who are into each other."

Warmth bloomed over her face. "All right."

My hand slid to her cheek. "You mean something to me, Parker." Because she had to understand that, and I didn't know how to say it any better. "I want to know you."

Her lids lowered as she leaned into my touch. "Crazy thing is? Right now, you already know me better than almost anyone."

Hell. My heart gave a meaty thump and my throat closed.

"You do too," I rasped, sliding a hand to her nape.

Before, when I'd kissed her, I'd done it in a lust-induced haze or under the guise of practice. Now there was just us. No bullshit. Just need.

My lips caressed Parker's, drinking in her sigh. I explored her with slow strokes, gentle glides. When her lips parted, I slid my tongue in to taste her. The feel of her mouth sent a lick of hot pleasure through me.

Bending down further, I gathered her up and lifted her against me. Parker was tiny, and she was perfect. Our kiss turned deeper, stronger. I felt it everywhere, in the backs of my knees, in my heart that was beating faster. Her kisses made me weak, made me want in a way that was equal parts terrifying and exhilarating.

I staggered back, my ass hitting the bench, Parker sprawled over me. She laughed into my mouth. The sound lit me up. I grinned in return and nipped her lip.

"You're wonderful," I said, hands sliding into her hair.

She laughed at that, a husky sound. She was exploring too, running her palms over my shoulders, down my arms. "You're magnificent. I could touch you for hours."

"I like that plan." My lips trailed down her neck. "Fuck, I love that plan."

I'd never done this—laughed and teased while making out with a woman. It hit me like a sucker punch that I'd never actually made out with a woman at all. We'd always gone straight to the main event. With Parker, I could kiss her all day, suck on the fragrant curve of her neck, and it would still be pure bliss.

Heat washed over me, and I found her mouth again. Our kiss was more this time. A little frantic. A little wild. The world melted away. There was only her. And more. And now. And oh, fuck yes, right there.

It was so good, so hot, that when the whiny sound of a man's voice in the room finally registered, I nearly leapt out of my skin. I wrenched Parker to my side, as though I could shield her, and looked around wildly.

But we were alone.

"Mr. Morgan?" the voice said again. Andrew. "Ms. Brown?"

"There's a house phone," Parker said, pointing to the spot by the minibar set into an alcove. "He's using an intercom."

This fucking place.

My tension eased a touch, but I huffed out an irritated breath. "Little fucker better not be spying," I muttered before standing and, carrying a squeaking Parker with me, stalked over to the phone to hit the talk button. "Yeah?"

"Uh ..." Andrew paused, unsettled, I guess, by my tone. Tough shit. I'd unsettle him a lot more if I found out anyone could overhear us through this system. "Drinks are being served in the living room now."

A summons, then.

"Thanks," I said. "Bye, Andrew."

"Oh—ah ... Goodbye, Mr. Morgan."

As soon as it was silent, Parker snickered, leaning her head into the hollow of my shoulder. I liked her there. "He scared me to death," she said.

A reluctant smile pulled on my lips. "Yeah, me too. I thought he was in the room."

We both chuckled, a release of tension. But then Parker pulled back. "I guess we better get out there before he shows up in person."

"He shows up in person and I'm tossing him out the window." I groaned and buried my face in her neck, idly kissing along the smooth curve—because I could. Because she smelled so damn good and felt even better. "Fuck it. Let's stay here. They can figure out why."

She shivered when I hit a particularly sensitive spot, and I was gratified to find her arching into me. But her hand slid to my shoulder and stayed my progress. "You know Fairchild won't give up that easily."

With a sigh, I set her down and ran a hand over my hair. "Yeah. Fuck, I hate that guy."

Parker fixed her pink cashmere sweater. "I do too. But it is what it is."

"I thought I'd charm him a little, not give him a permanent boxing boner for me."

A choked laugh escaped Parker, and she grinned. "You should be more careful with that charm, Morgan. It's very potent."

Chuckling, I bent my head and kissed her. "I'll save it all for you from now on." When she hummed in satisfaction, I eased back and met her gaze. "I don't know how, but one day, when you're safe from retaliation, I'm going to make sure he gets what's coming to him." Specifically, an ass-kicking.

She smiled wide with a spark of evil glee that I loved. "Just make sure I'm there to witness it."

"Count on it, sweetheart." I kissed the tip of her nose, then held out my hand to her. She took it and something inside me locked into place.

Before we headed out of the room, I paused. The phone system made a pleasing sound when I yanked it out of the wall and cracked it in my hand. Parker squeaked and laughed.

"Rhys!"

"It needed to be done." I tossed the phone aside and grinned. "Let's do this."

SIXTEEN

Parker

FOR THE FIRST TIME, walking into a room with Rhys holding my hand didn't make me feel like a fraud. Or that any minute someone would jump up and point at us and shout, "Aha! Stop right there, you charlatans!"

Not that anyone really talked like that in real life.

Still, despite being trapped in Fairchild's house, I walked with giddiness in my step.

Rhys Morgan and I were now officially a real thing.

I didn't know how it had happened or what would happen between us in the future—I just knew I had to explore it. Our chemistry could not be ignored.

Yes, I was unbelievably attracted to Rhys, more than I'd ever been attracted to anyone, but it was more than that. He was a really good man. I felt like I could trust him.

That was a huge deal for me.

He was the first guy since Theo who made me feel brave enough to take the chance on something real. The idea of walking away hadn't even crossed my mind. I should probably be overanalyzing that and freaking out, but thankfully, there was plenty to distract me from doing so.

As we wandered into the main living room of Franklin Fairchild's house, Rhys's hand tightened reflexively in mine. A few of my colleagues and their partners were gathered, drinks in hand. Fairchild stood in front of the fireplace talking with Jackson.

His house was ... interesting.

A massive Renaissance painting hung above the huge brick fireplace. Situated around the hearth were sofas and chairs where my colleagues sat beneath large, circular wrought iron chandeliers that held electric candles.

These would not have looked out of place in a medieval banquet hall.

A tapestry hung on the opposing wall; suits of armor stood at quiet attention in several corners. All of it distracted guests from the massive picture window perpendicular to the fireplace that captured the stunning snow-covered landscape beyond.

Two smaller windows on either side did just as beautiful a job framing the scenery.

Yet, that view, that amazing view, was lost in the over-the-top decoration that said Franklin Fairchild saw himself as some kind of feudal lord.

As soon as Rhys and I crossed the threshold into the room, a server approached us. "Drinks, sir? Madam?" He gestured to a small bar tucked into the far corner.

"Tink?" Rhys said.

"Uh ... I'll have a beer."

"Make that two."

"Export or import?"

I pressed my lips together to stop my laughter at Rhys's expression. He covered the flash of incredulity and replied, "Whatever you recommend."

"Bottled or draft?"

Rhys looked at me. I shrugged. He turned back to the guy. "Bottled is fine."

The server nodded, moved to the bar where another server waited, and then returned a few seconds later with two opened, chilled bottles of a German beer I'd never heard of.

"Jesus." Rhys took a drink and then glanced down at me. "Ready?"

I wasn't the one Fairchild was intent on annoying the hell out of. "Am I ready? Are you?"

"Morgan, there you are!" Fairchild's voice rang across the room.

Rhys gave me a tight smile. "Ready as I'll ever fucking be."

I squeezed his hand to let him know I had his back, and we both exhaled before turning toward Fairchild.

Smiling hello at my colleagues as we strolled into the center of the room, I wondered why only me, Jackson, Michael, Xander, and Evan and our respective partners had been invited.

Hadn't Fairchild said that attendance by *everyone* in the company was mandatory? No wonder Pete was extra rude toward me that week. Anytime we'd crossed paths, he'd pretended I didn't exist.

Charming, charming man.

As for Fairchild ... ugh, what a liar. He couldn't have made his real agenda any more obvious, and he was completely unconcerned about being obvious. Which was probably why Jackson looked like he was sucking on a lemon.

Poor Jackson. He loved Horus Renewable Energy. It must

have caused him no end of frustration to have to rely on financial investment from someone like Franklin Fairchild.

Fairchild was grinning, a devious twinkle in his eye, that made me suspicious. "Morgan, I have something to show everyone that I think you're going to love." He turned to my colleagues. "Grab your drinks, leave them, whatever you like— there is a bar in the theater. Let us proceed." He strode toward Rhys and slid an arm around his shoulders. "This way, son."

My ... well ... whatever he was now glanced over his shoulder as Fairchild led him across the room. I would've felt guilty for letting go of his hand if Rhys hadn't given me a reassuring nod.

He was a big guy. He could take care of himself.

So why did I feel like I was failing him when I should be trying to protect him from Fairchild?

"Come on, Parker," Jackson said, his voice gentle. I looked up to see him and Camille at my side, twin expressions of concern on their faces. "It'll be all right."

I frowned. "You know what he's attempting to do?"

Jackson cut Camille a look before turning back to me. He lowered his voice as the rest of my colleagues followed the big boss out of the melodramatic living room. "I'm not sure exactly but it's obvious this is all about Rhys."

Nodding, I sighed. "I'm sorry. We both are." I shouldn't have apologized for Rhys, but I knew him well enough to know that he was most likely pissed off that Fairchild had pulled my colleagues into this ridiculousness.

"Why are you apologizing?" Jackson frowned, staring toward the now-empty doorway. "I'm the one who introduced you both to him."

Camille squeezed Jackson's shoulder and whispered, "Honey."

Realizing my observations had been right, that Jackson was

struggling with Fairchild, I wished there was something I could do. However, Rhys had to take priority. Once I was sure I had him out of Fairchild's reach for good, I could turn my concentration to figuring out how to help free Horus Renewable Energy from an egomaniacal billionaire.

One of the servers had to direct us to the theater since we'd lost track of everyone. When we stepped inside, I shouldn't have been surprised to discover it was an *actual* movie theater. There was an expensive, mahogany-topped bar with brass tap handles and rows of glass shelves behind it filled with every alcohol imaginable. At the opposite end of the room was a screen that took up the entire wall, with rows of real cinema chairs situated in front of it. A discreet projector was built into the ceiling.

Rhys stood at the bar with Jackson, and I decided I was done being pushed aside by Fairchild while he attempted to convince Rhys to fight. Striding toward them, I saw my boss's boss narrow his eyes on me, but I remained undeterred.

"Hey," I said softly to Rhys as I nestled into his side and wrapped an arm around his waist.

He gave me a soft look before sliding his arm around my shoulders to draw me even closer.

His familiar scent, earth and spice, made me wish I could just haul him out of that room and back to the guest bedroom. Butterflies tickled my belly at the thought of finally being with him in all the ways I'd tried (and failed) to convince myself I didn't want.

The hard heat of him pressed against me wasn't helping my wayward thoughts.

Forcing myself to concentrate on the task at hand, I met Fairchild's annoyed gaze. "So ... what are we watching?"

"It's a surprise. Come, Rhys, let's take a seat." Fairchild cut me a dismissive look. "Why don't you sit with the others, Ms. Brown?"

Feeling Rhys tense beside me fueled my indignation. Relying on years of practice dealing with unjustifiable snobbery, I kept my voice pleasant. "I'll sit with Rhys, but thank you." Before Fairchild could say anything, I pulled away, taking Rhys with me, and led him to two seats in the back.

"Sit up front." Fairchild stood over us.

"We're good." Rhys didn't even look at him, the muscle in his jaw ticking as he reached for my hand to hold it on his knee.

For a moment, I thought Fairchild would argue because he hovered over us longer than appropriate. Finally, however, he strode away, back toward the bar.

"Fucking psycho," Rhys muttered under his breath.

I squeezed his hand. "What do you think this is about?"

"One guess." He cut me a dark look. "We're about to see a match."

Understanding dawned and anger rippled through me. "One of yours?"

"I'd place money on it."

Ugh! That man! My skin was hot with anger as I sat stiff beside Rhys. "I am so sorry."

I felt a tug and turned to Rhys as he pulled my hand against his chest. "Don't you apologize. I mean it."

Seeing the sincerity on his face, I nodded, but that didn't mean my guilt miraculously disappeared.

"Ladies and gentlemen," Fairchild called from the back of the room, "some of you may know that we are in the presence of one of the finest boxing champions of his generation. Rhys Morgan."

I looked over my shoulder at Fairchild, along with the rest of my colleagues. Rhys stared straight ahead. When Fairchild began to clap, forcing everyone else to join in, I wanted a hole in the floor to open so Rhys and I could disappear from the awkwardness of the moment.

"Jesus fuck," Rhys murmured.

"I agree," I whispered. "Jesus is probably asking himself, 'What the fuck was his Father thinking making this guy a billionaire?' That is ... if you believe in that stuff."

Rhys grinned at me, and a pleasurable ache spread across my chest at the sight of it.

"So, without further ado," Fairchild said, his awful voice ruining the moment, "I have procured footage from Morgan's most memorable fight with Cal Davis. Settle in and enjoy."

The lights went down and the screen flickered to life.

If it weren't for the tension emanating from Rhys, I might have enjoyed watching him fight. However, knowing about his best friend, understanding the soul-deep fear Rhys had of ending someone's life or leaving his brother alone in this world, killed that enjoyment.

Instead, I tried to take Rhys's mind off the fight playing out on the screen, and the man behind us, who was attempting what felt like underhanded mental warfare to get Rhys to do what he wanted.

I leaned into Rhys, my voice low, my lips touching his ear as I whispered, "You are unfairly hot."

He stiffened a little but didn't move away as I continued. "I could ignore it, the hotness, I mean, if you weren't so funny, charming, sweet, kind, and loyal. It takes your hotness to combustible levels. Oh, and the bike. The bike that—" His mouth cut off my words.

I clasped his face in my hands, feeling the bristle of his unshaven cheeks as he kissed me hard and deep in the dark of the theater. The sounds of the fight became background noise as I made out with him in public.

And I didn't care.

As long as I was distracting him from Fairchild's under-handed antics, I remained unconcerned what anyone thought of my actions.

Rhys broke the kiss to whisper, "I ain't sweet, dahlin', but fuck, you definitely are. Taste it too."

The lights suddenly came to life, and we blinked against it. Our colleagues murmured around us and we realized the fight had finished. I could feel their eyes on us, but Rhys and I were engrossed in one another.

He brushed a thumb over my lips. "Thank you."

Understanding, I smiled. "That kind of distraction wasn't really a hardship."

Rhys chuckled, pressed a cute kiss to my nose, and stood, taking me with him. Glancing around, I saw I was right—my colleagues were looking at him, entirely fascinated.

They may have known he was an ex-heavyweight boxing champion, but knowing and seeing were two different things.

"Isn't he something?" Fairchild said to the room as he walked toward us. "Now that our viewing entertainment is over, my guests must be hungry. My staff has laid out a world-class buffet in the dining room. Follow Andrew." He gestured to the exit where Andrew the house concierge waited. "He'll show you the way."

Rhys and I moved toward the door, but Fairchild blocked our path. He held up a hand to stay us and waited until everyone else had left the room before opening his mouth. "Morgan, you and I need to talk." His eyes cut to me and his expression hardened. "I need to speak with Rhys privately. Please follow the others to the dining room, Ms. Brown."

I didn't want to leave Rhys. My tight hold on Rhys's hand told him that. After glaring at Fairchild for a good couple of seconds, Rhys looked down at me. His expression gentled. "Baby, you should go. I'll be there in a minute."

I felt more than a flutter in my belly at the "baby" endearment. That was new. It caught me so off guard, I found myself nodding. "Okay. I'll save you some food."

He grinned, but it didn't reach his eyes. "You do that."

Leaving him there felt like I was abandoning him, my frustration real as I stepped into the hallway. To my surprise, Jackson was waiting on me.

"He's a big guy," he said. "He can handle Fairchild."

Grateful for his perceptiveness, I gave my good boss a tremulous smile and let him lead me toward the dining room.

FRANKLIN FAIRCHILD WAS A SLIMY, inconsiderate, obnoxious bulldozer of a man.

He held Rhys captive for the rest of the night.

When I realized his plan all along had been to get Rhys alone and badger him endlessly, fury filled me. I was terrible company, sitting amongst my colleagues as they talked about work, life, and their plans to ski the next day. They eventually all started to cotton on about Rhys's importance to Fairchild when my boyfriend (if he was that) didn't reappear. I began to worry something had happened to him.

Everyone moved to retire for the night, so I asked one of the servers to put together a plate for Rhys from the cold selection; I was informed that Rhys had already eaten with Mr. Fairchild.

Well, that was something. At least he wasn't attempting to starve him into submission.

More than three hours after I'd been separated from Rhys, I paced our guest bedroom, growing antsier by the second. Unable to deal with this madness any longer, I crossed the room toward the door, intending to search the house for Rhys.

Yanking open the bedroom door, I was brought to a halt.

Rhys.

Thank goodness.

My shoulders slumped in relief, and I stepped aside to let him in.

Looking drained, Rhys moved into the room, but instead of walking by me, he turned into me, his soulful eyes locked with mine. My breath hitched as he curled his hands around my biceps and slowly backed me up against the door until my body weight closed it. He released one arm to lock us in.

My heart raced as anticipation of yummy physical intimacy filled me.

Instead of ravishing me, however, Rhys cupped my face in his big hands, bent down, and pressed the sweetest, softest kiss to my lips. He let out a little exhalation as he released me, his breath tickling my mouth, before he straightened and wrapped his arm around my shoulders.

I moved into him, slid my arms around his waist, and rested my head on his chest.

"Are you okay?"

Rhys was silent so long, I thought he might not answer.

But then, "I think I'm gonna have to fight."

Shock rooted me in place, and I stiffened in his hold. "Rhys, please tell me you did not *agree* to fight?"

"Not yet."

Oh, thank God. I pulled out of his arms and placed my hands on his chest. He looked down at me, curiosity in his expression, and then surprise when I gently pushed him backward.

He let me.

Of course he let me.

Like I could move a man his size without him *letting* me.

I backed him up to the bed. "Sit."

A tired smile quirked his lips. "You got it, boss."

How could he possibly find anything amusing right now after three hours of interrogative warfare that had clearly worked?

I studied him. We'd only just decided to explore what was between us, so pushing him to confide in me was a big risk. Yet, I knew there had to be more going on if he would agree to fight, despite his deep-seated aversion to it.

For his sake, I had to be brave. I couldn't be selfish just because I was afraid he'd turn away from me.

"Okay ... I don't know what he said to you in the three very long hours he held you captive"—Rhys raised an eyebrow at my word choice but I pushed on—"but what is going on? Something has to be going on beyond the financial problems of the gym to make you even contemplate this fight. Did Fairchild threaten you?"

"No, but it was implied that your contract would be made permanent if I fight for him."

I felt my fury boil down deep inside. "I can find another job. He is not manipulating you into this fight."

He looked momentarily stunned.

Realizing what it said about my feelings—that I'd walk away from a job I loved to save Rhys from Fairchild—I blushed.

Rhys studied me intently, his expression warming by the second. "That means a damn lot to me, Parker. But we started this thing together because of how much your job means to *you*. I don't want to see you lose it because of this."

When I opened my mouth to object, he held up a hand. "There's more. The fight is worth a lot of money."

Although I was relieved that Rhys wasn't lingering over what I'd inadvertently revealed about my feelings for him, I was concerned about what fighting would do to him emotionally. "I asked before and I'll ask again—is the gym really worth the toll this will take on you? Or am I missing something here? Rhys ... what am I missing?"

Rhys's expression hardened, and he looked away. "It's nothing, Tink."

"It's not nothing. It's most definitely something. I know you and I are ... new ... but before the kissing and the very hot touching started ... well, Rhys, I'm your *friend*. Talk to me."

His lips twitched. "Hot touching, huh?"

I struggled not to smile. "Don't change the subject."

He stared at me for a long moment and then sighed, deep and heavy. "I'm going to lose the gym if I don't start making payments to the bank. I have a guy interested in buying it, and it's looking more and more likely I'm going to have to sell."

My stomach dropped. I knew how much the gym meant to him. "Rhys ..."

"Before my dad died, he told me the gym was in trouble and that he was behind on his payments for the gym, and that he'd also mishandled my finances. He'd gambled ... almost everything was gone."

Oh my God. All his earnings. Every hit he'd taken in the ring ... all for nothing in the end.

I felt a little off-kilter and stumbled toward the nearest armchair. "Oh God, Rhys."

"I've been hiding it from Dean."

I frowned. "But he's managing the accounts now, I thought?"

He snorted. "I fucked with him, gave him a shit ton of paperwork to go through, and kept the real accounts—digital accounts—to myself." Rhys slumped forward, resting his head in his hands as he stared at his feet. "When I started making real money boxing, Mom got sick with cancer. I didn't want my parents to have that debt, so I paid all her medical bills."

My heart ached. "Rhys ..."

"Dad was renting the building for the gym. I bought it for him. Paid Dean's tuition. But I also left my dad to handle my finances, and I found out too late it was a mistake. He made a lot of bad investments, gambled ... what I had left went to paying Dad's funeral costs when he died, and I paid off a chunk of the debt to the bank by selling my condo. But now we're a few months behind on the mortgage ..."

Nerves fluttered in my stomach. All this time he'd had this hellish pressure on his shoulders. No wonder he'd jumped at the chance to make friends with someone as powerful as Fairchild.

"Does Fairchild know any of this?"

"Not that I'm aware of but I wouldn't put it past him to have done a background check into my finances."

"Manipulative cur. You can't let him persuade you to do this. Seriously... I hope that man gets eaten by sand snakes."

Rhys frowned but there was laughter in his words. "Wait a second ... is that what you muttered when we first met?"

Uh-oh.

"Maybe. You did accost me just as my boss was arriving so I may or may not have wished for a door to another dimension to open, in which you'd fall through into a world of terrifying sand snakes."

"Like *Beetlejuice*?"

I flashed him a quick grin, amazed he could amuse me when I was so goddamn angry at Fairchild. "Yes. But back to the point ...

There was a moment of silence between us while I gathered my thoughts on this new information. Finally, I said, "You need to tell Dean."

"No." Rhys sat back on the bed, his countenance granite. "No fucking way."

"I know you've been protecting him a long time ... but,

Rhys, he deserves to know the truth. He's a grown man now, and keeping this from him, fobbing him off with fake accounting, isn't protecting him. It's making him a chump." I ignored his blistering glare and continued. "Your brother is very smart. Confide in him. Take the pressure off your shoulders. Then maybe the two of you can come up with a plan."

"I have a plan. I'm going to fight."

I stood, anger at Fairchild ripping through me. "You are not fighting for that man." I pointed toward the bedroom door. "He doesn't get that from you, Rhys. If you fight for him, you know that will mess with your head in more ways than one. Please ... before you do anything, please promise that you'll talk to Dean. And I'm here. I can help ... you know I am a problem solver. It's kind of what I do."

When he didn't say anything, I whispered, "Please, Rhys. Trust in Dean. In me. Don't do this alone anymore."

Something warm entered Rhys's gaze until his shoulders slumped. He nodded, his voice hoarse. "Okay, sweetheart. I'll talk to Dean."

That ache, the pleasurable kind I'd felt in my chest earlier, spread through me again. Tenderness filled me. I stood from my seat and walked slowly toward Rhys on the bed.

That warmth in his expression turned to heat as I pushed between his legs to curl my hands around his neck. He reached for me, his fingers flexing on my waist as he pulled me close.

"Had a shitty night, Tink," he said, his voice low. "You interested in making it better?"

A shiver tingled down my spine as I felt a familiar tug of need low in my belly. I brushed my thumbs along the bristle of his cheeks and leaned in to whisper against his mouth, "I'm interested in making it phenomenal."

He grinned, his eyes dancing. He slid a hand under my

shirt, and I trembled a little, undermining my verbal cockiness. "Big talk, sweetheart."

"You don't think I can make your night phenomenal?"

Rhys deftly unclipped my bra and my eyes widened. His grin softened to a sensual smile. "I was exhausted when I walked in this door. But all you have to do"—he slipped his hands out of my shirt to grasp the hem—"is press that gorgeous little body of yours to mine"—he drew the shirt up over my head, and I raised my arms to help him—"and I'm harder ..." Rhys paused as he watched me lower the straps of my bra. Nervousness filled me as I bared myself to him.

I wasn't voluptuous.

Not at all.

I worried for about a millisecond that I wasn't enough. Only a millisecond because Rhys literally growled under his breath as he stared at my breasts. His eyes dragged back up to meet mine as his hands coasted up my sides. "The last time I was this hard, I was a fucking teenager, so my night is already phenomenal, sweetheart."

I gasped as he cupped my small breasts in his big hands, shivering against the delicious rough calluses on his palms, moaning as his thumbs caught my nipples. "Rhys."

Seconds later I was in very real danger of turning into a melted puddle as Rhys tugged me toward him so he could wrap his hot mouth around my left nipple.

Pleasure zinged straight between my legs. I clasped my hand behind his head, writhing against him as he lavished worshipful attention upon my breasts. Swollen, needy, I sighed as he trailed hot kisses up toward my neck. I bent to him, offering my mouth, which he took with a voraciousness that shattered my control.

"Too many clothes," I gasped against his mouth, pushing at his shoulders.

I felt him chuckle against me, and then I let out a squeal of delight as I suddenly found myself on my back on the bed.

Rhys's eyes burned with a desire that rocked me as he reached for the top button on my jeans. "You first," he demanded, gruff with impatience.

Shimmying my hips, I aided him as he yanked my jeans down my legs. Once he'd discarded them, his eyes held mine as he reached for my underwear. My breath caught as his fingers curled around them. Sensing he was waiting for permission, I attempted not to smile at the sweetness of the gesture and nodded. He pulled them slowly down my legs, eyes locked on mine, until I was so beyond ready, a whimper escaped me.

Rhys drank his fill as I laid out on the bed for him. I bit my lip, my nipples tightening as anticipation rippled through me.

"Fuck," Rhys choked out. "Fuck, Parker, how can anyone be so beautiful?"

His tender words caused a burn of emotion in my throat and suddenly, I was no longer concerned about comparing myself to the other women Rhys had been with.

This was so much more than that.

For both of us.

I just knew it.

Something seemed to snap in Rhys as he divested himself of his clothes much faster than he'd divested me of mine. I watched him in awe, studying the light and shade of his beautiful body. I'd never been with anyone like him before. I'd always thought I'd be intimidated because he was so much bigger than me ... but I was excited by the idea of being covered by him, wrapped up in all that sleek hardness. My brutish boxer with his gigantic heart and secretly gentle soul.

My eyes explored him, moving down his roped abs to—

Oh my.

I swallowed hard as I watched him tear open a condom

wrapper. He rolled it on and as he did so, I grew wary over his size.

"Do you think that'll fit?" I blurted out.

Rhys blinked as my words penetrated, and then he grinned through a groan as he moved onto the bed. "We'll make it fit."

"Um ..." My gaze was locked on him, hard and very, very big. Not just long but the girth ... oh my. "Rhys, seriously ... I am very small, and you are very big." He crawled over me and my legs automatically spread to accommodate him. "You can't fit a large object into a tiny immovable hole—it's physically impossible. That's a scientific fact."

Rhys suddenly dropped his face against my neck, his body shaking with laughter.

"Rhys?"

Finally, he lifted his head, amusement mingling with lust in his beautiful eyes. He throbbed between my legs, his heat pushing against mine. "For a start," he said, laughter on his lips, "you're not immovable, sweetheart. In fact, you're about to be so *moved*, you'll feel the earth shake."

My breath caught. "Well ... if you're sure."

He held himself still above me. "It's not about if I'm sure. Are you sure?"

I could feel his muscles trembling, saw the way the muscle in his jaw ticked as he held himself back from what he wanted. His eyes were dark with need but there was a light of affection, maybe even concern there.

It made me melt. "You're right, I'm not immoveable. Things stretch down there. Go for it."

Now he was shaking with laughter. "I love when you talk dirty to me."

My own giggle was cut off as he moved against me, teasing. Desire flooded me. "Rhys, now, please—oh!" I cried out, gripping onto his waist as he drove inside me, a pleasure pain vibrating through me as my body adjusted to the overwhelming fullness.

Rhys was braced over me, his face strained with pleasure. "Fuck," he choked out. "You weren't lying."

I instinctually flexed my hips, needing him to move.

He cupped my left hip, caressing my outer thigh. "Wait." He shook his head, closing his eyes for a second. "I just need a minute."

But I couldn't help it. I tilted my hips again, feeling him move deeper inside me, causing a coil of pleasure within me to tighten.

Rhys shook his head, laughter in his voice. "Patience, baby. I want to do this slow and if you keep doing that, it's not gonna go slow."

Seeing the sincerity in his eyes, realizing he was trying to be tender, emotion flooded me again. I wrapped my legs around his back, drawing him gently into me, our breaths puffing against each other's lips before he kissed me. It too was slow, sweet. At complete odds with his size.

I felt fragile and cared for.

It was beautiful.

But I also wanted something more, something that made me feel like I was more than just a cute, petite woman. I wanted to feel sexy, so sexy, he couldn't help but screw me six ways until Sunday.

"Okay," I agreed breathlessly. "But next time, we get to do it hard and fast."

At that, I felt a shudder move through Rhys. "She's trying to kill me," he muttered against my lips.

Maybe. But goodness, what a way to go.

SEVENTEEN

Rhys

SLOW. I was supposed to go slow. Parker Brown was sprawled out beneath me like a feast. A pocket pixie, delicate and beautiful. I'd never touched skin so fine, smoother than satin, honeygold and sweet. I was half afraid I'd break her. Hell, I'd thrust my dick into her slick tightness, trying to think straight long enough to slow the fuck down.

God, she felt good, though. So damn tight. So damn hot. She chuckled against my mouth and moved her hips in a small circle as I thrust. Pleasure shot down my spine, over my skin. I paused deep within her, my dick throbbing. My body shook with the effort to keep still as Parker wiggled beneath me.

"Rhys."

I nipped her succulent lower lip and took a ragged breath.

"You gonna behave now?" I asked, knowing she liked it when I was bossy.

Her shining brown eyes smiled as she met my gaze. "Yes, Rhys."

Oh, hell. She really was trying to kill me. My nostrils flared as I pulled back and thrust hard. Parker sighed on impact, her sweet little tits jiggling. Fuck. Yes. I did it again. Hard and deep. Slow.

The sounds of our bodies meeting filled the silence. Her breath became a pant, her lids lowering as she watched me fuck into her. Something was taking over; I stopped thinking, stopped worrying. Nothing mattered anymore. Not the gym. Not my brother or bills. Not Fairchild.

There was only this. Only Parker. She lit me up, made me something new—something good. Groaning, I found her mouth and devoured it. My thrusts became frantic. No more finesse, no more control, just this *need* to push into her, get as close as possible to her skin so that maybe she could absorb me.

My thoughts grew jumbled, my breath harsh and dry. I needed more.

Her skin was slippery with sweat as I grabbed her thigh and hauled it up higher, spreading her wider.

"Yes," she rasped, arching up, pressing her breasts against my chest.

Yes. The best word in the English language. Yes. And more. And fuck.

Grunting, I worked her hard, my lips finding the fragrant curve of her neck. I sucked her skin, moved my hips, and fucked her with everything I had.

Parker cried out, her body going tight around me. I could feel her on the edge. Her skin was flushed, her eyes wide on me. "Rhys."

I heard the plea. My voice was a thick rasp. "What do you need, Tink?"

"Grind it," she said, gasping. "My clit."

God. I loved the way she thought. My hips slammed into hers, and I paused there, pushing against her swollen clit. She moaned, her eyes closing, her head tilting back.

It was beautiful. And I was the lucky bastard who got to see this.

"Let go." I thrust again, pausing, working her. "Give it to me, Parker."

Her hands grasped my shoulders. She came with a spectacular wail, her body milking my dick so hard I saw stars. It set me off. I lost all sense of time, of anything but moving inside Parker, kissing her soft mouth.

I groaned into her mouth as I came. Everything drained out of me, and in that moment, I didn't know my own name. Only hers.

I was hers.

"AND THIS LITTLE beauty is an authentic Japanese samurai sword, owned by a World War II Japanese officer." Fairchild lifted the sword off its display mount and held it aloft. "Note the blade. Made by Yoshimichi."

His houseguests attempted to look interested as Fairchild beamed.

"Story goes, when the US occupied Japan at the end of the war, they confiscated the sword and presented it to an officer as a reward for his work in defeating the Japanese. Set me back around thirty thousand, but I was glad to pay the price."

This fucking guy.

I caught Parker's eye. I didn't need to make a face—one glance and it seemed she understood me completely. Just as I knew she was fighting not to wrinkle her nose in disdain.

Fairchild was some piece of work. Not only did he have zero social awareness, he actually gloated over it.

All through the miserable dinner with him, I kept myself sane by imagining the various ways I could punch him in the face—a right cross, an uppercut, a one-two combo. Juvenile, maybe. But definitely satisfying. One day, I promised myself for the thousandth time, I'd see that he got what was coming to him.

There was no way I'd let him get away with being such an utter fuckwank to Parker.

Parker.

Hell. I started to sweat, lust rising like a heat wave.

We'd spent all night in bed. Fucking. Laughing. Fucking again. We'd fall asleep, then one of us would wake, reach for the other, and it would start up all over again.

I'd never had a more perfect night. I'd never laughed like that in bed, just for the joy of it. Parker made me happy. Free in a way I'd never been. She was also the tastiest, most luscious little ...

"You're getting that look again," she murmured at my side.

My fingers threaded through hers, and I stroked her knuckles. "What look?"

Her lids lowered demurely as her lips pursed. I wanted to kiss those lips, lick my way into her hot, sweet mouth. "You know."

Yeah, I knew. It was the "I want to fuck you so bad, I hurt" look. I was pretty sure I'd be wearing that look all the time now. Biting back a grin, I tried to focus on Fairchild, still yammering on about another piece of weaponry.

Don't get me wrong—they were beautiful pieces. And if they were owned by anyone else, I might have been more interested. As it was, though, I just wanted out of there. If I couldn't take Parker to bed, I'd settle for a walk with her and some fresh air.

Anything, as long as we were alone.

"And this," Fairchild said, moving on to a big, glass case filled with sand, "is my newest edition to the collection."

Jackson and his fiancée trailed along, obviously dragging their feet. He shot me a quick, pained look, and I empathized. We were all in hell together. I had no idea what sort of weapon Fairchild would keep in sand, but I obligingly led Parker to the case.

When my eyes finally fell on the object in question, I found myself balking.

"Is that ..." Parker trailed off, her hushed whisper holding a hint of garbled laughter.

I stared at the stripped snake coiled in the case, and my lips twitched. "It's a sand snake."

Fairchild heard me and grinned wide. Now that I had said I'd seriously think about the fight, he'd mellowed. No more hard sells. No more glaring at Parker. Fairchild was king of his castle and loving life. The asshole.

"Technically, it's an American sidewinder rattlesnake," he said. "But don't worry. Shani here is a venomoid—which means his venom has been removed."

As if that was my worry. I wasn't getting anywhere near the thing. Fairchild, on the other hand, seemed to think it was a great idea to lift the lid off the case.

Camille made a noise of distress, then laughed as if she hadn't meant to, but she pressed up against Jackson. Fairchild ate it up, smiling like an ass as he waxed poetic about the majesty of his snake.

Parker snuggled in closer to me, and I wrapped an arm around her shoulders. "You think if we say Beetlejuice three times, he'd show up and eat Fairchild?" I whispered in her ear.

She nudged me in reply, her lips pressed together in a tight line to keep from smiling.

Fairchild began to reach into the case.

"Are you sure you should do that?" Camille said.

He laughed. "The ladies are always nervous around snakes." *Yeah, no shit, dude, they saw your act coming a mile away.* "Don't you worry, honey, Shani and I are great friends."

I rolled my eyes and kept a good hold on Parker. It wasn't that the snake scared me—much—but I had a healthy appreciation for predators, and venom or not, a rattler wasn't something I'd fuck around with.

Shani the snake had been napping in the sand, but Fairchild had woken him up. His diamond-shaped head lifted, and he tracked the movement of Fairchild's hand with small, unblinking black eyes.

"Shani loves rats," Fairchild explained. "Especially big ones—ah!"

His scream made us all jump. Shani had moved so quickly, there wasn't time to react. His fangs sank into the fat of Fairchild's hand, once, twice. Fairchild screamed again and whipped his hand back.

Cursing, I shot forward and slammed the lid onto the case before the snake could get out. All hell broke loose as Fairchild howled about his hand and staff came running.

As Fairchild moaned and slumped to the ground, clutching his wounded hand, I caught Parker's eyes. God, it wasn't funny a man getting bitten by a snake.

It wasn't.

It couldn't be.

My lips twitched.

Her eyes lit up, her nostrils flaring on a sharply drawn breath.

All around us, people shouted and hustled to help Fairchild. Shani coiled himself back in the sand. *In the sand.*

Parker's gaze held mine. I could see the words in her head: bitten by a sand snake.

Laughter bubbled up my throat, pressed hard against my closed lips, wanting out. A gurgle escaped Parker, and I knew she was about to lose it. It took me two steps to get to her, wrap my arms around her.

"She's afraid of snakes," I told the room. I didn't think anyone heard.

Practically running, we escaped the room. Our laughter held on by a thread until we got outside, and then it burst free. Parker doubled over, tears running down her face as she snorted and laughed. I was right with her, leaning against the house as I choked on my laughter.

"Oh god." She wiped at her eyes. "I'm going to hell! But his face. Did you see his face when the snake struck?"

"The *sand* snake?"

Her eyes were two triangles of glee. "A sand snake!"

"Shani loves rats," I intoned, laughing harder.

Parker's gaze collided with mine, mirth gleaming in her eyes.

"Especially big ones," we said in unison, and lost it all over again.

Weakly, I pulled her into my arms and held her as we wore ourselves out. Parker finally sighed, a happy, drained sound. Her brown eyes were glossy with tears of humor and her hair had gotten mussed. She was gorgeous. My hand cupped her smooth cheek as I leaned down and kissed her.

She melted into me. Perfect. A fucking gift in the middle of chaos. I kissed her and the world slipped away. Kissed her until our lips were swollen and my body grew tight with need.

Parker made a greedy little noise in the back of her throat and wrapped her arms around my neck.

"I want you again," I said inside of a kiss.

"Then have me again," she said with a lusty little sigh.

I was so completely gone on this woman it was scary.

Cupping her ass, I hauled her up, and she wrapped her legs around me. When I began to walk her back to the room, she grinned wide. "You think this means dinner for tonight is off?"

"Doesn't matter." I gave her lower lip a quick nip. "I slipped Andrew a hundred bucks to make sure we get room service."

Her brown eyes widened. "And he agreed?"

I loved that it clearly made her happy. "Guess so, since dinner arrives at seven."

Parker kissed me hard and fast before leaning in to nibble on my ear. "I love the way you think, Rhys Morgan."

"Yeah? Because I've been thinking a lot about what I want to do to you when we get back to the room. Want to hear?"

She did. And I told her. In detail.

Happiness wasn't something I was used to. I felt it then, so strong it almost seemed like a dream. Maybe it was. Nothing about this place or being with Parker here seemed real. I pushed away the fear that it would change when we got back to the real world. Nothing would change. It couldn't.

After all we'd been through, Parker and I deserved our happiness.

And yet even when I finally slid into her again and she made that sound of utter satisfaction, I still couldn't shake the feeling that being with Parker was something that could shatter with one wrong move.

EIGHTEEN

Parker

It shocked me how much I didn't want to say goodbye when Rhys dropped me off at my apartment.

I'd clung to him as he kissed me, wishing he would drive us back to his place. Spending the weekend with him had spoiled me. It had also surprised me. And not just because of the tremendously fantastic sex.

Although it was worth noting that I was having the best sex anyone could have possibly ever had.

I hadn't even known sex could be that intoxicating.

My appetite for Rhys Morgan was ... *unexpected*, shall we say.

"Yet it's about more than just the sex," I told Zoe as I stood at our kitchen counter with a glass of wine in hand.

I'd just gotten done telling her about the weekend with Fairchild. How Rhys and I had decided to explore the very real chemistry between us. Then that horrible billionaire's machinations. How it had led to a phenomenal night of sex and laughter. The hilarity (it was wrong to be amused, it really was) of Fairchild *literally* getting bitten by a sand snake, and how that led to more excellent sex. In fact, we'd stayed holed up in our room all night.

I was pretty exhausted.

However, it was the very best kind of exhaustion.

Fairchild hadn't shown his face the next day. Andrew had been there at breakfast to see us out, and then we all got into our cars and drove to the airport. On the plane, I slept with my head on Rhys's shoulder, content beyond any time I could remember.

Zoe sat on a stool at the counter opposite me, her chin resting in her palm. Her expression was contemplative. "Are you sure it's not just sex? Because the sex you just described would convince any woman she was emotionally involved."

I rolled my eyes. "I think I can separate my sexual feelings from my emotional ones. But that's the thing. I can't with Rhys. The sex isn't just fantastic because the man is beautiful and athletic and very, very generous. It's fantastic because there's a connection between us. I feel it. We make each other laugh, and he has this wonderful ability to make me feel completely safe, even though when we're together it's like we're free-falling. Scary and exciting ... but I trust him."

My best friend's eyes glistened. "Oh, Park. Honey, I'm so happy for you."

"Don't get all emotional on me, you dork," I teased, because if I didn't tease, she'd make me cry.

"I know. I just ... for years you've pushed guys away. Some very nice guys. Guys who wanted to be the one to pick up the pieces that shattered when you lost Theo."

"It was too soon back then."

"It's been too soon for thirteen years, until Rhys," she pointed out.

I bit my lip, trying to stop my dopey smile, and failing. "I want to spend all my time with him, which is extremely out of character. You know me. I've always needed my space from potential romantic interests." I grinned now. "I don't want space with Rhys. Space is officially unappealing."

Zoe smirked. "You've got it bad."

Avoiding the topic of just how bad I might have it, I continued, "You and Dean are the only people who know our relationship started out fake. I'm asking you, and hoping Dean will agree, to keep that quiet. No one needs to know it wasn't real from the beginning."

"Agreed. My lips are sealed." Zoe tilted her head to the side in thought. "Can I ask ... does Rhys know about Theo?"

"Yes. I told him."

"It's not weird for him that you haven't been able to move on from the love of your life?"

Irritation rippled through me, even though I knew she didn't mean to offend. "I am moving on. And Theo was my first love, Zoe, he always will be. But I don't know if he was the love of my life."

Her eyes widened. "Oh, Park. You *have* got it bad. Should I be worried?"

I blushed. "I'm not saying *Rhys* is the love of my life. We're not there yet. I'm just saying ... what I had with Theo was different. It was sweet and lovely. It was first love. It was the love between two fumbling kids." I smiled now, amazed at the way it didn't hurt so much anymore. "I think I held onto what I had with him for so long because I was afraid to get hurt again. To lose like that again. This, with Rhys ... it isn't a choice to move on, to take that risk again." I shrugged. "I just can't *not*. I want him more than I'm afraid of losing him."

There was a moment of heavy silence between us, and then Zoe threw back the rest of her wine and announced, "I need to buy that man a big goddamn present because I've never seen you this happy, and it makes me ecstatic. I love you, Park."

This time, tears did thicken my words. "Love you too, Zo."

"But just saying"—she leaned over the counter, her eyes hardening—"he hurts you in any way and I will *personally* see to his physical, financial, and emotional evisceration."

I laughed. "Good to know."

"Speaking of, is he really going to fight?"

The thought of Rhys fighting against his will made me sick to my stomach. "I hope not. He's talking to Dean tomorrow about the gym's finances. He asked me to come over just after. He didn't say it, but I think he needs some moral support."

"Of course, he does."

"I hope I'm right to trust Dean to help Rhys out with this."

"Hopefully, honey."

I exhaled heavily and then waved a hand between us. "Enough about me. What's new with you?"

"Not much." She lowered her gaze, a little frown line between her brows. "I agreed to go on a blind date set up by my producer last Friday."

"And?"

Her beautiful dark eyes finally met mine. "He researched me. All he did was talk about Richard."

Zoe never referred to Richard Bancroft as her father.

"In what sense?"

"He was fangirling." She curled her lip. "The guy is a fan of the money."

It baffled me that someone as kind and funny and drop-dead gorgeous as Zoe Liu was single. Unfortunately, the men she dated either ended up being intimidated by her inherited wealth or were too obvious about their *interest* in her inherited wealth. There had been a few who seemed to genuinely be into Zoe, but then they'd destroyed it by cheating on her or getting annoyed by the hours she worked on the talk show.

Her lack of romantic entanglement was not for want of trying, and part of my reticence to date over the last few years had been from watching my amazing best friend try and fail over and over.

I was exhausted for her.

But I had faith there was someone great out there for her. Someone who would challenge her and excite her the way Rhys challenged and excited me.

"Then he's not worth another thought," I said, referring to her blind date.

She gave me a weary smile. "Hey, maybe Rhys has a friend."

Oh, I'd seen the handsome guys who worked out at Rhys's gym, and they'd fall on their knees to get within breathing distance of Zoe Liu. I grinned at the thought. "Maybe."

"Or there's his brother."

I frowned at the thought of Dean. "The jury is still out on Dean Morgan. Rhys may think his brother has nothing to prove, but I don't agree. Rhys has done a lot for him. I just hope Dean sees that and steps up. But until then, no Dean Morgan for you. In fact, maybe never. Truthfully, it's going to be diffi-cult to find a guy worthy of you."

Zoe laughed. "Okay, then, *Mom*."

"Oh, please. You love it that I think the sun shines out of your ass."

My best friend's eyes widened. "Did you just curse?"

My lips twitched. "Possibly."

She threw her head back in laughter. "Oh man, I'm defi-nitely buying that boy another Harley."

Rhys

"YOU SLEPT WITH HER, didn't you?"

Dean's voice cut through my fog. He leaned over me from where I lay sprawled on the couch. A stupid grin lit up his face.

"What?" I hedged, then gave up and shook my head with a laugh. "How the fuck did you come to that conclusion?"

Dean rounded the couch and slumped down on the armchair next to it. "By virtue of that dopey-ass grin you're wearing and the fact that I called your name three times without you even blinking."

"Shit." A grin pulled at my mouth. Because, yeah, I had a lot to grin about.

"Fuck," Dean muttered. "You totally got laid. Asshole."

"Why am I the asshole?" Brothers. You'd think Dean would be happy for me. I'd be happy for him if he found a good woman who rocked his world. Hell, I'd be ecstatic; maybe he'd focus on his future, then.

"Because it could have been me," he said with a wink.

I lurched up with a snarl. Dean wisely scrambled from his chair and danced out of reach.

"I'm joking." He lifted his hands in apparent innocence.

"Yeah? Well, tell a better joke because I'm not laughing."

His lips twitched. "Not even a little?"

"Still not funny, shithead."

It was unsettling how much his "joke" bothered me. I couldn't shove it aside. If I hadn't locked Dean in my office, it *would* have been him. Dean would have been the one going on dates with Parker. Dean, who was smart in the same way

Parker was smart. And while I might have ended up being the better choice to woo her boss, Dean definitely fit in better with her true friends—with her life.

A twist of something deeper than jealousy hit me low in the gut. If I hadn't locked Dean in the closet, would Parker have ended up with Dean instead? Would she have kissed him? Invited him into her body?

I couldn't stand that I didn't know for certain. I wanted to tell my stupid-ass insecurity to shut it. Parker liked me for me. That should be enough. But she'd been in love with a guy like Dean—lighter, sweeter. Not a big bruiser with a foul mouth. Maybe I was simply Mr. Good for Right Now, not Mr. Right.

God, I couldn't believe I actually thought that. I sounded like a *Cosmo* article.

Dean's goofy smile fell. "Hey, you know I didn't mean that, right? It's obvious that she's really into you, Rhys."

"I don't want to have this conversation." I glared at him. "When was it obvious?"

Damn it, I sounded needy as fuck.

Thankfully, my brother didn't point that out. "At the bar. She couldn't keep her eyes off you. I knew then you two would get together."

Sighing, I sat back on the couch and pinched the bridge of my nose. "She's great. I like her. A lot. But ..."

"She has scabies?"

I dropped my hand and shot him a look. "Do you even know what that means?"

"It's a condition that—"

"Forget I asked. She doesn't have scabies. She has a dead first love."

His eyes glinted. "Let me guess—she killed him and now you fear for your life."

It was perverse that I wanted to laugh. I glared instead.

"Would you cut it out? No, Deanie, he died. Hit and run. She hasn't dated anyone since."

Dean went pale and flopped back on his seat. "Jesus. That's ... harsh. And a lot for you to live up to, huh?"

"No kidding." I shook my head. "How do I compete with someone she's obviously built into a perfect paragon of young love?"

"Well, I mean, good sex has to help." He narrowed his eyes on me. "You rocked her world, right? Left her good and satisfied?"

"What do you take me for? I'm not a chump." I kind of loved Parker using that word earlier and felt a smile forming at the thought of her. "My woman was definitely satisfied."

Because she was my woman. At least for now. I wasn't about to give her up to a ghost. If Parker eventually grew bored with me or wanted to move on, there was nothing I could do about it. But I was damn sure going to enjoy what I had with her right now.

"You left her limping, then?" Dean asked.

I threw a couch pillow at him.

Laughing, he batted it away. "Thought so."

"Keep it up and I'm putting you in a headlock." It was my greatest threat when we were younger, and Mom would freak out if I got too rough with Dean.

The thought of my mother was sobering. Parker had said I was making Dean a chump by keeping him in the dark. She was right, I'd had all but become a hovering, interfering parent to my brother. Shit, but I hated talking about this.

My stomach curdled as I searched for a good way to get it all out.

"I've been lying to you." Okay, not the best way to start.

Dean frowned. "You didn't rock Parker's world? Because I have tips—"

This kid.

"Jesus." I huffed out a laugh. I loved my brother something fierce. "No. Not that. Dean ... shit. It's about Dad and the way he left things."

"You mean with the gym about to be repossessed by the bank?"

"What?" I blinked. "How ..."

His smile was slanted and more than a bit annoyed. "Yeah, I don't know if you truly understand this, but I'm not a total dumb-ass. And your method of hiding shit from me sucks balls, bro."

Well, hell.

I sighed again. "There's more to it than just that ..." I told him the whole sordid tale, Mom's medical bills, Dad's stupid gambling mistakes, how he'd made a shit ton of bad investments with my earnings. I ended with Kyle Garret's offer to buy the gym, and Fairchild's attempts to push me into another bout.

He swallowed several times before speaking. "Why did you ... fuck, I know *why* you kept it from me." He glared as though he was mentally punching my face. "It's insulting as fuck, you know, treating me as if I'm a kid."

"I know." I rubbed my aching chest. "I'm sorry. I just got in the habit of looking out for you and I didn't want you to worry."

His tight nod was his only answer.

"I shouldn't have done that," I added.

"No, you shouldn't have. But you told me now, so I guess that's something." He blew out a long breath and shook his head as if to clear it. "You quit boxing because of Jake."

The pain in my chest grew. "Yes."

Dean's blue eyes, the exact shade of our mother's, met mine. Sorrow and worry rested in his. "This guy will own a piece of your soul if you do this."

"Yes," I said again, because I knew that too. It's what pissed me off the most.

"Then don't fucking do it."

"We need that money, Dean. I either fight or I sell the gym."

"There are always ways to get money. I'll get a job." He leaned in. "A real job. No more messing around. I'll find something good."

I gave him a weak smile. "It won't be enough. Not with the limited time we have left."

Dean moved to speak, but I lifted a hand. "It's no longer just the money. That asshole has it in his head to see me fight. This isn't just about money with Fairchild. The fucker has a psychotic inability to take no for an answer. And he's made it clear he'll mess with me if I don't do this."

Dean leapt to his feet and paced. "Son of a bitch. There's gotta be a way around this."

I sighed and watched Dean pace.

"That ... that ..."

"Fuck?" I supplied wryly.

Dean grinned wide. "Yeah." His smile dropped. "He's treating you like a freaking zoo exhibit. Pay a ticket and watch the great Rhys Morgan step back into the ring. Fucking hell."

Something sparked and rippled through my mind. "Wait. Stop."

Dean halted mid stride and faced me. "What?"

That something danced around, growing bigger. "A zoo exhibit, you said."

"Yeah, uh, what?" He huffed out a laugh. "I'm not following."

I stood and picked up where he left off pacing. "It struck a chord. What if I did an exhibition fight?"

"Isn't that what Fairchild wants?"

"Yeah—no. I mean, what if we"—I gestured between us —"organized a fight? An exhibition fight, for charity."

Dean chewed his lip as he watched me. "For charity? But how does that help us?"

"I don't know …" I kept pacing. "It might not work. But if I put on a fight, I pull the rug out from under those fuckwads. If we make it for charity, maybe somehow we can find a sponsor for the gym. Find a way to help not just ourselves, but the community too."

Slowly Dean's expression lightened. "It could work." He paced the other way, both of us wearing a groove in the floorboards. His stride grew quicker as he mulled over what I'd said.

"It *could* work, Rhys." He sounded excited now. "But I have no clue how to get something like that started. Do you?"

I stopped next to the kitchen counter. In my mind, I could still see Parker standing there, pretty as a sunrise, her eyes alight as she watched me get ready to cook. I'd been falling for her from the first. She gave me hope, made me want to reach further, raise my head a little higher.

I didn't know shit about organizing a fundraiser, but I was fairly certain she did. I met my brother's eyes and smiled. "We need Parker."

I needed her. That was the truth. I needed her in more ways than one.

I grabbed my phone and called her, filled with satisfaction that I could do that. Shit, I missed her already. I wanted her. I wanted her so bad, I felt like I was missing something when she was gone.

She answered with a breathless voice. "Hey, you."

A goofy smile pulled at my mouth as my head went hazy with lust. "Hey, Tink. What are you up to?"

"Thinking about you."

Jesus. I was so gone on this girl.

"Good answer." I grinned, then told myself to focus. "Can you come over? I need you."

"It's like that, is it?" She sounded cheeky, and sexy as hell.

I laughed. "It's always like that where you're concerned, babe."

At my back, Dean gagged. And I shot him a look before focusing on Parker. "Ahem. I need that too. But Dean's here right now."

"You told him, didn't you?" Pride filled her voice. Pride for me.

"Yeah. And we got to talking about the fight. I have a plan. Want to help me with it?"

She didn't hesitate. "I'll be right over."

Because she was my girl. My right-now girl. And, right now, it was enough for me.

NINETEEN

Parker

ZOE WAS A TERRIBLE LIAR.

I watched her warily as we walked up the front steps of Rhys's gym. Her dark, intelligent gaze took in the building, her frown deepening as we walked through the doors.

Under the guise that she wanted to be in on the meeting between Rhys and the event manager, Fiona, for Zoe's charity Street Warriors, she was tagging along to Lights Out.

Considering Zoe let Fiona have free rein as event manager, we both knew Zoe was really using this as an excuse to meet Rhys. However, since Ren and the guys had already met my boyfriend (yes, I was calling him that in my head now), I wasn't going to quibble with my best friend over this.

That didn't mean I wasn't nervous as heck to see what she'd think of Rhys, and I didn't want him feeling any pressure either. He already had enough stress in his life.

Two weeks ago, he'd called me to his place after his discussion with his brother. Not surprisingly, Dean had learned about the loan when he dug into the gym's finances. Upon finding out the extent of the debt and whom it was owed to, Dean proved himself to be a good brother. He immediately began brainstorming with Rhys and they'd come up with the idea of a charity fight.

I hated that it meant Rhys would still have to fight, but he seemed content with the idea since it would be on his terms. They required my help so I went into full battle-plan mode.

Rhys had already held a meeting with Fiona at Street Warriors; this was their second meeting to finalize details. Since we didn't have a lot of time, I'd called in Easton to help, as well as my mother. With both my sister and my mom's knowledge of society, we picked a date in the social calendar that we knew most people would be able to attend. The event would be held at Rhys's gym. The idea had been to bring the gym the exposure it needed in the hopes of gaining sponsorship from some of the more exalted guests, but to our delight a few of my parents' friends involved in community development programs had already visited the gym with my mom to offer sponsorship.

The fight hadn't even occurred and already a lot of the pressure was off for Rhys.

To lure people to the event, Rhys had called in a favor and had gotten ex-heavyweight world champion Jarrod "The Thunder" Johnson to fight him. Jarrod was a little older than Rhys, and although they were friends, they'd never fought each other. Which meant this exhibition fight was a huge draw for sports fans amongst the elite. We'd already secured ticket sales from Diana Crichton Jones—the billionaire I'd met at Fairchild's garden party—and her fiancé, as well as Adriana Bellington, the owner of Sportsbox.

She wanted to air the charity fight on her network, and we were donating the rights payment to Street Warriors. The free promotion would only help us out by gaining more of those sponsorships.

Easton and my mother were the best at organizing receptions, so I'd put them in charge of organizing catering for an after-fight party on the gym's second level. My quick-talking mom had convinced a caterer and party planner to donate their time and work with us as a tax write-off, so we didn't have to pay for that either.

Fiona was in charge of ticket sales, so she was meeting with Rhys today to give him an update on where we were at with those. The fight was in three weeks. Although Rhys and I spent time with one another the past few weekends, I hadn't seen him as much as I'd like because he was in training mode.

"This place is sad," Zoe murmured as we walked across the glass-fronted atrium and through the double doors to the public gym. There were only a few people working out. "A redecoration overhaul is definitely needed."

"Hence the charity fight," I reminded her. "This way."

Since dating Rhys for real, I'd visited the gym a few times and knew my way around. I led Zoe to the back stairwell that would take us directly to the second-floor corridor that housed Rhys's office.

At my knock, Rhys called, "Come in."

His voice sent a thrill through me, and I reached to push open the door.

Zoe's groan halted my action.

"What?" I frowned.

"You are sickeningly in love," she whispered, smirking.

My heart lurched at the word. "Take that back."

"Nah." She shook her head, pushing Rhys's door open. "I only speak the truth."

Attempting to squash the heat her words caused in my cheeks, my eyes darted to Rhys who was standing by his desk with Fiona at his side. Dean and Carlos were also in the room. My gaze flickered from them back to Rhys whose face split into a wide grin.

"Hey, Tink."

Ignoring Zoe's disturbing last words, I crossed the room with a small smile and went up on my tiptoes as Rhys bent down to kiss me. Everything about him—his smile, the contented expression in his eyes when he looked at me, his cologne, the feel of him under my hands—caused a score of pleasure pain across my chest. His arm moved around my waist, drawing me to his side.

"Hey."

He grinned at me for a long moment and then looked up. "Aren't you going to introduce us?"

Oh, dammit.

I looked over at my best friend and blushed at the expression on her face.

It clearly said, "You just made my point for me."

"Right. Rhys, this is my best friend and roommate, Zoe. Zoe, this is Rhys. You already know Fiona, of course." I smiled at the blond grad student who had more energy than anyone had a right to. My gaze moved past her to Carlos and Dean who were both staring way too intently at my best friend. "This is Dean, Rhys's brother, and Carlos, Rhys's friend. He also works here."

"Hey." Rhys gave her a chin lift. "Nice to meet you."

"Yes, you too. I've heard a lot about you."

"I'm gonna go ahead and assume it was all good."

"You do that."

I kept my gaze on Rhys during this exchange. It took me a

moment to realize I was studying his reaction to Zoe. My friend was a knockout, but I didn't want Rhys to notice.

Of course he'd notice; she was beautiful inside and out.

I was proud Zoe was my friend.

I just wanted Rhys's attention for myself while we were in our Honeymoon phase.

And it irritated me that I could be so insecure and possessive.

Rhys's expression was pleasant enough greeting my friend, but there wasn't any hint of discernible interest beyond that.

Unlike Dean and Carlos, who both stepped forward at the same time to shake Zoe's hand.

Dean glared at Carlos and nudged him out of the way. "I'm the brother."

My friend took Dean's proffered hand. "I'm the roommate."

"And I'm Carlos." He pressed a palm to Dean's chest and shoved him back like he was a little kid. "Zoe, bonita, it's a pleasure to finally meet you. Thanks for helping my boy out with this event."

Eyes dancing under the flirtatious bedroom eyes of Carlos, Zoe shook his hand. "Well, it's mutually beneficial."

Carlos grinned, his dangerous dimples popping in each cheek. "Well, if mutual benefits are something you're interested in, you and I should definitely talk some more."

My friend laughed and withdrew her hand. "Oh, I'm not really into sharing benefits with someone whose pool of sexual companions is probably so big, it qualifies as a population."

I tried to contain my snort at Carlos's baffled expression. Clearly, he was used to women falling at the first sight of those dimples.

"Let's get back on track." Rhys squeezed my shoulder as he turned to Fiona. "Tell them about the ticket sales."

Fiona beamed at us all. "We've sold out."

Whoops filled the room and soon, failed flirtations went out the window as we discussed what had been done and what still needed to be done to make the event a success.

About an hour later, Fiona departed and Zoe sighed as the door closed on her. "I need to get back too." She gestured to me. "You coming, or going?"

I shook my head. I was on the desk facing Rhys, who was sitting in his chair, his fingers chasing the goosebumps created as he caressed the back of my left calf.

She grinned knowingly. "Right. I'll see you later, then." Her gaze moved between me and Rhys. "Also, not that it matters, but I approve."

I heard Rhys grunt as I beamed at my best friend.

It did matter to me what she thought of Rhys. Not enough I'd stop dating him, but still, I was glad she could see how happy he made me.

"I'll walk you out," Carlos offered.

"Oh, you don't—"

"It's my pleasure." He opened the door and gestured for her to walk ahead.

As soon as the door closed behind them, I turned to Rhys. "You might want to tell him he's got no chance. Zoe can spot a player a mile away and she has no interest in them." I glanced over my shoulder at Dean. "That goes for you too."

"No worries." Dean curled his lip in thought. "She's gorgeous but I like my women commitment-phobic. Shame. I would *not* tire of looking at her."

"She's more than a pretty face, you know."

"Yeah, her ass and legs are fucking fantastic too." Dean laughed at my grimace and stood. "I'm kidding, Parker. Guess I better leave you lovebirds alone. But you"—he pointed at his brother—"got training this afternoon."

I felt Rhys's hand slide farther up my leg. "I'll get my workout in, don't you worry."

Shivering at the promise in his voice, I couldn't even laugh at Dean's disgusted expression. "I understand innuendo, fuckface."

Rhys chuckled. "You leaving or what?"

"I got shit to do, so yeah."

"I hope that shit has something to do with finding a decent job."

"Hey, who is the smartest person in this room?"

"Parker."

I laughed as Dean rolled his eyes. "I meant out of us two."

But Rhys wasn't laughing. "I mean it, Dean. Time to get serious."

"I already told you I am." He left before Rhys could say another word.

I frowned. "You're still worried about him?"

"I'll keep worrying about him until he nails down a good job and starts to settle. Now, can we stop talking about my little brother and go up to the loft?"

Before I could answer, he placed his hands under my ass and lifted me up so I had no choice but to wrap myself around him like a monkey.

"That was a rhetorical question." His lids lowered over his eyes as he stared at my mouth. "If I don't get inside you in the next five minutes, I'm gonna lose my mind."

I would've chided him for such melodrama if his phone hadn't vibrated on the desk.

He glanced over my shoulder and scowled.

"What is it?" I twisted to have a look down at his phone screen. "Who is Colonel Dipshit?"

"Fairchild."

I snorted and grinned at him. "Colorful."

Rhys didn't laugh. "It's the third time he's called since yesterday."

"He's heard about the fight," I surmised, feeling a trickle of trepidation run through me. "Answer it. Just get it over with."

The muscle in his jaw flexed. "I'm kind of in the middle of something."

"I won't be able to concentrate until we know what he has to say."

Rhys sighed heavily and gently lowered me to the ground. His phone stopped vibrating for a second and then immediately started again. "Colonel Dipshit was too kind," he muttered under his breath as he reached for the phone.

I pressed into his side, one palm on his lower back, the other on his abs, my physical support a show of my emotional support. Rhys curled his arm around my shoulders and answered, putting the phone on speaker. "Fairchild."

"Morgan," Mr. Fairchild answered tersely. "You do realize this goddamn charity fight you're putting together has affected the level of interest in my fight?"

"Well, it doesn't really matter because I never agreed to do your fight."

There was silence. Then, "You sneaky little fuck."

I stiffened at the same time Rhys did, a growl burrowing up my throat.

Hearing it, Rhys rubbed my shoulder and shook his head at me. "I don't give two shits who you are, Fairchild. Nobody talks to me like that."

"Oh, you'll care, son, when I'm done with you. Did you think you could get one over on me and survive that?"

"You threatening me?"

"Not in the way you think. There are other ways to destroy a man's life without touching a single hair on his head. Now, here's what you're going to do. You'll continue with this asinine charity fight, but you're still going to fight for me."

"Or what?"

"Or I start with that little bitch who, according to my staff, really likes getting fucked." Rhys's fingers bit into my shoulder, and his expression turned dark. "Well," Fairchild continued, "I'm going to fuck her too, just in a different way. I'll start with that job of hers. Not only will I make sure she never works for Horus again, I'll make sure she never works in Boston again, and I'll go even further than that and make sure she never works in renewable energy. Every move she makes to further her career, I'll be there to fuck with her."

My heart pounded in my chest, nausea roiling in my gut because I knew Fairchild was capable of doing exactly that.

"And if that isn't enough to make you see things my way, I'll move on to your brother. It would be a shame if someone as intelligent as Dean, with such a bright future ahead of him, were to find himself unemployable."

Rhys shuddered against me and I held on tighter, as if I could contain his fury. He opened and shut his mouth. Seeing his struggle, I caressed his cheek, drawing his gaze to mine.

I shook my head at him and mouthed, "We can fight him."

His eyes asked, "How?"

I thought of all the connections my family had to powerful people in society and although it made me uncomfortable thinking about using those connections, I would to help us out of this. Fairchild thought he was untouchable, but for myself, for Rhys, and for Dean, I'd do anything to prove him wrong.

"I see I have your attention," Fairchild said, sounding smug. "Good. I'll be in touch about my fight, Morgan, so next time I call, answer the fucking phone." He hung up.

Rhys's fingers curled around his cell and seeing his knuckles turn white, I quickly extricated the phone before he threw it across the room. I set it on the desk and turned to him. "We can fight him. My parents have a lot of powerful friends and, although I've never thought about them in that way, Charles and Marion Brown are not people you mess with."

"I thought the reason you wanted a fake relationship was to keep your troubles away from your parents?"

I stiffened. "Well, I'm not happy about the idea of going to them either, but I don't think we should just allow this man to steamroll us. It's better to ask for help from people who care about us than to let Colonel Dipshit blackmail us."

Rhys's eyes searched mine for what felt like eternity. Then he exhaled slowly. "Parker, you came to me—well, technically, Dean, but let's not think about that—for help. This job means so much to you, you were willing to pay a guy to pretend to date you to keep it. I can't let you jeopardize all that."

I slid my hand up his chest, resting my palm over his fiercely pounding heart. "I don't want to jeopardize it either. It scares me. A lot. But the idea of Fairchild using you, what that'll do to you and Dean—that scares me too. Let's just get through the charity fight. We don't know what's going to come of that. Once we know what cards we're holding, we can deal with Fairchild. For now, we'll just find ways to hold him off."

Rhys continued to frown. "I don't want you choosing me and Dean over your job. You've worked your ass off for that job. It's important to you."

"You're important to me too, Rhys."

Quite abruptly, Rhys wrapped his hand around my nape and hauled me up his body for a hard kiss. I whimpered in surprise, and he lifted his head briefly to growl, "You really have no idea, do you, Tink?"

Before I could respond, he lifted me back up into his arms and kissed me with a breath-stealing desperation. His mouth never left mine as he tried to walk us out of there. We bumped into a wall, or two—our laughter and groans, his grunts and my moans, filled the corridor as he took us to the elevator that led to his loft.

Once those doors closed, he started grinding into me, kissing me until I could barely breathe with the anticipation. My whole body was on fire.

"You wet?" He kissed my neck below my ear.

"You know it," I gasped, clutching at him as he thrust against me again. "Rhys!"

"You want me to fuck you, you gotta say it, Tinker Bell."

Trembling with need, I turned my head and whispered in his ear, "I want you to fuck me, Rhys."

He shuddered beneath my hands and just as soon as those doors opened, Rhys stumbled into the loft and set me down on the nearest bit of furniture—his dining room table.

His beautiful green eyes blazed with desire as he slid his hands up my dress to pull my underwear down my legs. I leaned back on my hands, my inner thighs trembling as I watched him hurriedly take a condom out of his wallet, undo his jeans, and push them and his boxer briefs down just enough to free himself.

Once the condom was on, Rhys grabbed my hips and pulled me to the edge of the table so I could wrap my legs around his waist. Without further ado, he drove inside me with a deep-seated groan of satisfaction. Holding onto his left shoulder with one hand and the tabletop with the other, I braced against his vigorous thrusts, gasping as the tension he'd built in me just by grinding in the elevator grew to the breaking point.

I loved when he was tender ... but my goodness, I loved when he lost a little of that control and took me like he'd die if he didn't.

Knowing me already, understanding what I needed, Rhys reached between my legs and rolled his thumb over my clit.

The intense tension broke, my cry of pleasure filling the loft as Rhys pounded into me, wave after wave of my voluptuous orgasm driving him closer to his. Finally, he tensed, his face taut, his fingers biting on my outer thighs. And then his hips jerked uncontrollably as his hoarse cry of release joined the echoes of my own.

He slumped, still flexing slowly in and out of me as he rested his forehead on my shoulder.

Holding Rhys to me, I slid my arms around his back, caressing him over his shirt and wishing we were naked. He turned his head and nuzzled my neck, making my legs instinctively tighten around his waist.

"You know," I said, my voice soft, quiet, "there are some people who believe an athlete should abstain from sex. That the frustration boosts aggression and energy for a game or a fight."

Rhys lifted his head, his expression relaxed except for his eyes. "Where you going with this, Tink?"

"I just wanted to confirm that I'm not interfering with your training."

He raised an eyebrow. "You know what my answer to that is?"

I shook my head.

Rhys gripped my waist and pulled out of me. I immediately wanted him back. "We're going to clean up. You first, then me. By the time I get out of the bathroom, you're going to be naked on my bed waiting for my mouth. Then you're going to give me your mouth because I've been dreaming about it wrapped around my cock since we first met. And you're not leaving my bed until both of us are fucking exhausted from coming our brains out."

Renewed heat shot straight to my core. "That is a very, very good answer."

He grinned, and then I squealed in delight as he hauled me off the table and carried me to his bathroom.

Then we spent the rest of the afternoon coming our brains out.

And it was spectacular.

Until afterward, as I lay sated and sweaty in his bed, my legs tangled with his. I reached for him, caressing the backs of my fingers down his chest that was now damp with perspiration. "We need to come up with a game plan for Fairchild."

Rhys's sigh was one of pure exasperation. "I don't want to talk about him when we're in bed. It's almost enough to turn me off for the rest of the day."

I sighed with my own frustration. "He's a problem that's not going away anytime soon."

"Yeah, and I'm making him *my* problem. No way is he going to fuck with you, and that means I don't want you worrying about this shit." Rhys sat up, swinging his legs off the bed.

"He's *our* problem and where are you going?"

He stood but then put a knee on the bed to bend over and press a quick kiss to my lips. "Gotta train, Tinker Bell. Up to you if want to hang around. Would shower with you but we both know where that'll lead so better I don't."

A flutter of nerves flickered to life in my belly as he strode into his bathroom and shut the door. It bothered me he didn't want to talk about Fairchild when we talked about other stuff that was just as important and personal.

And suddenly, it bothered me that instead of talking about Fairchild and the fight, he'd used sex to release his frustration. Okay, the sex obviously didn't bother me, but ... well, now I felt like I'd just been dismissed.

The sudden wall he'd put up between us was confusing.

Ugh. Was it even a wall?

Was I overthinking this?

The shower turned on, and as I sat on Rhys's bed, waiting to use his shower after him, I did what I always did and spent way too much time in my own head.

TWENTY

Rhys

Life was strange. One aspect of it could be going great while other parts gave you hell. For the first time in years, I felt happy. It was weird. She made me truly happy in a way I didn't know how to deal with; I'd never been like this with a woman. I went about my day like a giddy goof, smiling continuously, my insides flipping and twitching with anticipation of seeing her again. Once I had my hands on her, it was bliss. Pure, freaking bliss.

Parker was fun. She made me laugh. And she made me horny as hell. I'd turned into a horny-ass poet. Dean was amused at my "transformation."

I took his ribbings with good humor—as I said, I was too happy to care.

And then there was the rest of my life. I had a plan. I'd stick to the plan. But I wasn't exactly what you'd call happy with it. It was too close to the past.

Every time I stepped into the ring to spar, I was hit with a bold elation, a sense of utter rightness and confidence. And, at the same time, I'd feel vaguely sick. The scent of sweat and blood and the rank stench of boxing boots brought it all back. I'd instantly remember Jake's expression, the blankness in his eyes, the fucking shock of it all.

I'd had broken ribs, broken nose, busted-up knuckles, and had two concussions. Pain is life. The true horror of death was the sheer nothingness of it. Nothing was bringing Jake back. He was gone.

It was a refrain as I jumped rope, going faster and faster.

He's gone.

He's gone.

"Double time, Morgan!" Jimmy's growl snapped me back into the moment. His craggy face twisted into a glare. "You're not here to daydream."

"I'll do that on my own time, boss," I replied with a smile. I'd trained with Jimmy since going pro. When I'd asked him about doing a charity match, the old man had gotten a tear in his eye. Apparently, he'd been waiting years for me to come back.

Guilt was a bitch.

"If you're going to dream," he said, "then dream about moving that fat, lazy arse of yours. Jaysus, did you not keep in shape at all?"

Jimmy was a funny fucking guy.

"Apparently not, boss."

Not to his standards, anyway. I'd thought I'd been in pretty good shape. Nothing like getting back to the sport to remind a man how badly he'd deluded himself.

"If you can smile like that," Jimmy said, "then you can sing the song while you're at it."

Horror lit through me. Oh fuck.

"Come on, Jimmy," I pleaded. Yes, *pleaded*. "Have a heart."

His beady black eyes gleamed under the gray hedges of his brows. "Sing. It."

Fuck.

With a sigh, I started. "'I am the very model of a modern major general, I've information vegetable, animal, and mineral...'"

The sadistic bastard waved his hands around like a damn conductor as I skipped rope and sang the Major General's song from *The Pirates of Penzance*.

Sweat poured down my spine and my legs felt like noodles. But my chest was clear, my blood pumped strong, and my voice stayed loud. "'I'm very well acquainted too, with matters mathematical, I understand equations both the simple and quadratical...'"

I actually had no idea how to do equations that were quadratical. Maybe I did in high school. Parker would know.

God, Parker. If she saw me now, she'd laugh and laugh. Her pretty face would light up with glee. Those pink lips would curl into a smile.

God, those lips. They had, in fact, been wrapped around my cock the other day. She had this technique, a little quick flicker of her tongue along the tip when she drew back on my cock that was mind-blowing. I'd almost proclaimed my undying devotion when she'd done that.

Thoughts of Parker sucking me off pulled me through the song and the warm-up. But Jimmy, evil man that he was, knew perfectly well my mind had been elsewhere.

"You've lost your focus," he grumped later when he was

taping up my hands. I could do it myself, but he insisted on getting it just right. "It won't serve you well in the ring."

I stared down at my hands. They were softer now, not as battered. "I know. I can't ..." I shrugged, not wanting to admit it but trusting Jimmy enough to know that I had to. "I'm trying. But it's difficult."

He paused and peered at me. Small as a gnome and just as bent, Jimmy had always made me think he was part magic. Every guy he trained seemed to be that much better than the others. I was damn lucky to have him on my side.

"Your heart's not into it."

"Not like it was. I lost something when Jake ..." I trailed off with a shake of my head.

Jimmy finished taping up my hands. "Saw the light die in your eyes that night too. Knew it was it for you." He sat back on his heels and rubbed the salt-and-pepper stubble on his chin. "Look, lad, what you're doing is a good thing. And if it gets you out from under the bank and that billionaire arsehole, then even better."

I knew all this. I'd *told* Jimmy this. Strangely, it still felt good to hear. I nodded and flexed my hands, testing the tape. There was something comforting about being taped up, good and familiar.

I made two fists and stood.

Jimmy followed. His head came up to the bottom of my sternum. I felt oddly protective of the old guy, like maybe he too would someday be gone if I didn't look out for him.

"So your heart's not into it," he said succinctly. "That's a problem."

"I know." I just didn't know what to do about this. The idea of losing chafed; I was too much of a competitor for it not to. The idea of losing in front of Parker was a humiliation I really couldn't stomach. I wanted her to see the best of me, not some washed-up version. I wanted her to see what I could do.

Jimmy nodded as though he knew my thoughts. "You find something to fight for, be it your girl or your gym. Whatever it is, dig down and hold onto it, yeah?"

Something to fight for. Damn it, that was the thing that got to me. I'd fight for Parker, but she was mine. I felt it in my bones. Win or lose, she wouldn't hold it against me. Sure, it'd be a disappointment if I lost but I wouldn't *lose* her. That internal knowledge made it difficult for me to find the proper motivation there.

Fight for my gym? I'd been doing that all along. Why, then, was it so hard to get my blood up when it came to this match? Maybe because when I'd fought in the past, I'd fought for the joy of it, the thrill of the win. That had been enough for me. Now the joy was a pale copy of what it used to be.

Something to fight for. Fuck, I needed to figure this out.

Rolling my neck to work out the kinks, I managed to give Jimmy what I hoped was a reassuring look. "I'll think about it."

He snorted and muttered under his breath about bone-headed boxers. I smiled.

Jimmy glared around the gym. "Where's Carlos?" He was my sparring partner. We were evenly matched for power, but I was faster. Carlos, however, was a tricky bastard who had a way of making me keep my head in the game or risk taking a hard hit to the face.

"Probably watching porn in the office," I said, throwing Carlos under the bus.

Jimmy muttered more choice words and stomped off to get him. I didn't say a word; I wasn't fool enough to get between Jimmy and a tongue-lashing.

Snickering, I went to the small bag and worked it to keep warmed up.

Something to fight for?

I had the gym.

I had Dean.

And ... Parker. I had Parker.

I should feel good about all that. Ecstatic, even. But there was still something off, something riding me. I needed ... absolution. I needed to get all this weight of guilt and anxiety fully off my chest.

Sex with Parker had relieved a lot of tension. Being with her made me feel whole. But Parker couldn't help with this particular brand of atonement. I couldn't work this out by losing myself in her arms.

I needed someone else for this. For a hot second, I thought about telling Parker, confessing. But I couldn't. I had to do this or I'd never be able to fight well. She'd understand that. She'd get it, even if she thought less of me.

She had to. Because I couldn't do this fight any other way.

TWENTY-ONE

Parker

IT WAS nice to escape the office for lunch. With only a week to go until the charity fight, I was preoccupied. However, not preoccupied enough to not be worried by how quiet Jackson had been lately. He was spending a lot of time going to meetings that he never explained and talking on the phone with his office door closed.

Moreover, I still had to deal with Creepy Pete and his petulant attitude. He no longer crossed the office to speak with me when he had a payroll question about my overtime. I received an email. And whenever there was a discussion amongst our colleagues, he deliberately acted like I didn't exist.

The man was like a five-year-old.

That morning he'd asked a mathematical question that I'd answered.

His response was to keep searching the room. "Anyone?"

My patience finally snapped. "I just answered your question, Pete." I glowered at him. "I'm getting a little tired of your attitude toward me, the only *female* member of staff in this office. If it doesn't stop, I'm going to consider this a problem I'll have to report."

Pete's shocked expression was almost funny. "No need, there's no problem here." He held up his hands in a surrender gesture and returned to his desk.

Xander shot me a proud look but the tension in the office was awful after that. Deciding to use the extra hours I'd accumulated with overtime to take a long lunch, I departed the office with a relieved sigh. Leaving the building, I tried to call Rhys but got his voicemail. I sent him a text just before I got on my bike.

ParkerB: I'm on a long lunch. Do you have time to join me?

Rhys's training had only escalated and the times I did see him, we mostly spent in bed. As far as I was aware, there had been nothing from Fairchild yet and Rhys was completely focused on the upcoming fight.

This meant we didn't discuss much. He asked about my day, of course, and seemed interested in what I had to say, but anytime I turned the conversation on him, it felt like he immediately initiated sex.

And I had absolutely no willpower because the sex was amazing.

My phone beeped a few seconds later as I turned down Spring Lane off Devonshire Street. I drew to a halt on my bike to pull my phone out of my purse.

HotHarley: Sorry, can't, Tink. In the middle of something. We'll talk later?

Disappointment filled me but I texted back.

ParkerB: Of course. Talk to you soon xx

I turned around and decided it was such a nice day, I'd hit Boston Common Coffee Company for a takeout lunch and then ride to the Common to eat it.

Once I had food in my basket and the great weather lifting my mood, I rode down the pedestrian area of Summer Street toward the Common. As I glanced to my right, however, a familiar head and pair of shoulders caught my gaze and I slowed.

Seated at the tables outside Café Nero was a broad-shouldered guy with long legs, sitting close to a gorgeous blond. His head was bowed toward her, his hand on top of hers, and she was looking at him with utter tenderness on her lovely face.

I slowed to a halt, my heart racing. I watched as he turned his head, and I caught his profile.

Confusion and pain scored across my chest as the familiarity that had caused me to pause revealed itself.

Rhys.

Who was in the middle of "something."

With a beautiful blond whose impressive cleavage was visible in her tight camisole. She had lots of hair and her makeup, although heavy, was done to perfection. She was tan and her long, bare legs were resting against Rhys's beneath the table.

She was everything I'd always assumed Rhys would want in a woman.

Feeling sick, I shook myself a little.

There was an explanation. Obviously.

There had to be.

But then she pushed her chair even closer to his and wrapped her arms around him, her head resting on his chest.

And he pressed an affectionate kiss to her forehead, holding onto her like he'd done it a million times.

That was it for me.

My chest tight, the pain almost blinding, I turned my bike around, not wanting him to spot me, and used the electric motor to get me the heck out of there.

I couldn't even remember the ride back to the office. The next thing I knew, my hands were shaking as I chained up my bike in the underground parking area.

Rhys wouldn't cheat. Right?

And what I saw wasn't cheating.

Yet, he didn't tell me he was going to meet some gorgeous blond for lunch today.

You told your girlfriend that kind of thing, right?

Feeling sick, I slumped against the cold concrete wall. We'd never talked about the status of our relationship since that night at Fairchild's lodge. Obviously, somewhere down the line I'd started to think we were more than we were.

But that didn't seem right either.

Even Rhys had admitted there was a connection.

Oh God.

Maybe he'd realized that connection was just physical after all and the blond was more his speed.

If that was true, I had to believe Rhys would be up-front with me about it, right? That's the kind of guy he was.

Or so I'd thought.

My phone suddenly beeped in my purse. Fingers trembling, I fumbled for it.

HotHarley: Hey, Tink. Do you want to meet up tonight?

I stared at Rhys's text, confused as hell. Was he going to meet me to tell me it was over? Or would we meet and he wouldn't say a word about the gorgeous blond?

Whatever was going on with us, I wasn't sure I was ready to face him. I texted back:

ParkerB: Sorry. They need me to stay late at the office.

I'd been investing myself emotionally into this relationship, but analyzing the last few weeks, I realized I had been doing that while Rhys had been locking me out emotionally, even if he was not pushing me away physically.

I was going to get my heart broken.

I knew it.

The only way to soften that blow was to put some distance between me and Rhys Morgan.

Tears burning my eyes, I stayed hidden in the corner of the parking lot until I was sure I could return to the office without crying.

Rhys

"THANKS FOR INVITING me over for dinner. This lasagna is delicious. Did you make this, Rosie?"

"It's Rose." Big eyes, the exact light brown of Jake's, stared back at me with a clear warning. I had to grin. God, she had his sass too.

"Apologies, Rose."

She gave a small sniff as if to reluctantly accept my gaffe and then tipped her tiny chin in acknowledgment. Jake had done that exact chin tip countless times. For a moment, it hurt to breathe. It hurt so bad, my eyes burned.

How could a person be missed so much, it was painful? I didn't like it. Didn't want this pain. It never fully went away. Some days it would dull, but then moments like this brought it all back. Part of me wanted to jump up and get my ass out of the house.

I kept said ass in the chair and ate the damn lasagna.

"So," I prompted when I could speak without sobbing like a baby, "did you make it?"

Rose's nose wrinkled. "Mommy did. I don't like cooking."

Given that she was five going on fifty, I had to admire her bluntness and gave her a chin tip of my own.

From the other side of the small kitchen table, Marcy laughed, genuine love and happiness lighting her eyes. "She doesn't like cleaning her room or doing her homework either. Big surprise, huh?"

"She has homework?" I blinked in shock. "She's frick—uh, she's five."

"I'm not a baby," Rose pointed out in that very Jake-like "screw you" way. "Big kids have homework."

Marcy grinned, toying with her wineglass stem. "They have worksheets for math and reading assignments."

Personally, I was happy my kindergarten class focused on *Reading Rainbow* and sharing time. I told them so and got a scowl from Rose and a laugh from Marcy.

"Amen to that," Marcy said, raising her glass.

I clinked mine to hers, and though I still felt the pain of Jake's absence, there was something good about being here. They were a family, these two precious females. There was love in this house that Jake and I had restored years ago. Contentment.

Coming here had been the right thing to do; I'd been away for too long. I had wanted to ask Parker to join us, but she'd been distant and busy when I'd texted.

"What's that frown about?" Marcy's question pulled me back to the present.

"Was I frowning?" I reached for the bowl of salad. Since

training had resumed, I was hungry all the time. All the freaking time. Hungry for food. Hungry for sex.

No. Don't think about sex at the table. Bad idea, Morgan.

Marcy tipped her head and examined me. "Well, I'd have called it pouting, but I didn't think you'd appreciate that."

I laughed. "No, I wouldn't have." With a sigh, I sat back. "I've got a lot on my mind is all." I glanced at Rose, then shut my mouth.

Marcy followed the action. "Rose," she said to her child, who was basically stabbing her food with a fork but no longer eating. "If you're done, you can put your plate in the sink and go play."

Rose immediately jumped up, nearly knocking over her milk in the process. While I righted the glass, she grabbed her plate and turned to go, but then paused. "When you're done talking to Mommy, do you want to play *Minecraft* with me?"

Warmth spread through my chest. "Sure. But you gotta promise that you'll protect me from those blockhead zombie things."

Her nose wrinkled as she smiled. "You're a weirdo."

"Takes one to know one, kid."

We made faces at each other, and then she scampered off, heading for the family room.

"God," I said. "She's just ..."

"Like Jake?" Marcy supplied with a tinge of sadness. But her eyes were lit with love. "I know. I see it more every day."

A lump filled my throat, and I swallowed hard. Earlier, when I'd met Marcy for coffee, I'd planned to tell her everything but found I couldn't do it. The words got stuck in my mouth, filling it up like cotton. All I could do was reminisce about Jake and hug her when it became too hard for both of us.

But this? It's another level. I would rather be punched in the face, frankly. Yet here I was, ready to confess.

"So," she asked. "What's up?"

"I met someone." Okay, so I wasn't ready to confess about the fight.

"You?" Marcy's brows lifted high.

"Yeah, me. What's with the face?" But I knew. Marcy, Jake, and I had grown up together. She was the sister I'd never had; Marcy could read me like a well-worn book.

She laughed, the sound uncomfortable yet hopeful. "It's just ... It's you, Rhys. You've never been involved with a woman." She paused and peered at me. "We are talking about a woman, right? You're not yanking my chain and it turns out you really meant you met a good accountant and want to recommend him, right?"

"Jesus, Marse." I rubbed my tight neck with a laugh. "You're that skeptical I'd commit to someone? And, yes, I'm talking about a woman."

She shrugged then grinned wide. "So, the mighty Rhys has fallen."

This time, when I smiled, it felt hopeful too. "I guess I have."

"Tell me about her." Marcy followed this command with a pinch to my arm that had me yelping.

"Easy, woman." I rubbed my arm but was unable to keep the smile off my face. "What to say...?" I tapped my chin, stalling, but when Marcy made a move to pinch me again, I held up my hands in surrender. "Okay, okay. Her name is Parker. She's ... different."

"Different," Marcy repeated.

"She's quirky. Cute. She wears these preppy dresses that cover her from neck to knee." But turned me on like nothing had before; I kept that part to myself. "She's wicked smart. Like Harvard smart. Technically, MIT smart. She gives me shit for everything but only recently started to cuss. Can you believe it? The woman wouldn't so much as say damn."

I laughed at the memories of Parker struggling not to curse when ticked off. "She's an environmentalist. Recycles everything. Hates my car, though I'm pretty sure she's faking that. But she can't hide her love for my bike. She does this thing when she laughs. Her nose wrinkles and her cheeks plump up like a chipmunk's ..."

Damn, it was cute when Parker full-out laughed. Especially when she was in my bed. Shit, I missed her.

"Oh my god." Marcy put a hand to her chest and gaped at me. "You're in love!"

"What?" My entire body twitched. "No. I... we've just started. It's ... I care about her, sure, but—"

"But nothing," Marcy cut in with glee. "Look at you. You're going on about her chipmunk smile and her clothes. Her *clothes*, Rhys. And not in a 'she wears sexy clothes that make me hot' kind of dude-bro way."

"Dude-bro?" I huffed. "And her clothes *are* sexy."

Marcy spread her arms as if to say she rested her case. "Guys don't notice stuff like that unless they're totally gone on a girl."

I leveled her a long look but then folded like a card tower. "Fine. I'm into her, yeah? I really like this girl. But love?" No. No. No. Love was ... pain. It was loss. Your parents. Your best friend.

Jesus. The mere thought of Dean dying on me made my breath grow thin and fast.

I couldn't love Parker. I could enjoy my time with her. But love? No. Because one day, I might be like Marcy, sitting alone at my kitchen table, wishing Parker was with me with all my heart and ...

Fuck.

I rubbed my chest and swallowed convulsively. A soft hand on my free one had me turning to face Marcy. Understanding lit her eyes.

"It's good that you found someone to care about, Rhys." I didn't miss the emphasis on care. She was throwing me a bone. I caught it and nodded like my heart wasn't trying to tear itself out of my chest.

"How did you meet?"

Right there. That was my limit on evasion. "Funny thing ..." I took a deep breath and started to tell Marcy the whole story. Her eyes got bigger as I explained.

"You're going to lose the gym?"

"Either that or I have to sell it. Neither option appeals to me."

"But ... how? You're so responsible with everything."

I looked away. From the other room came the puffs and clangs of Rose's video game. I could see a slice of the couch and her small legs swinging back and forth as she played. She moved like a kid who hadn't a care in the world. But I knew she suffered nightmares now and then. She'd scream out for her daddy, even though she'd only been two when he died. When Marcy told me that, it just about killed me.

I rubbed my chest again. "My dad. He ..." I forced myself to meet her worried gaze. "You know he liked to gamble."

Understanding dawned. "Oh God. Rhys. It was when he gambled on Jake, wasn't it?"

She might as well have kicked me in the chest. I flinched, the air rushing out of me. "You knew about that?"

I felt sick. Pushing my empty plate back, I rested my face in my hands and tried to breathe.

Her gentle voice broke through the darkness. "Your dad visited me before he died. He confessed what he'd done and apologized."

"Fuck." I rubbed my aching jaw and looked up. "I'm sorry, Marse. I didn't want you to deal with that."

"But why?" She looked genuinely confused. "It wasn't your mistake."

"Jake was my friend. My dad took advantage of him. I don't ..." I blew out a harsh breath. "It feels like my mistake too."

Suddenly, Marcy was at my side, wrapping her slim arm around me. "No, Rhys. No, it wasn't."

"I should have seen how bad Dad was getting."

"He was your dad," Marcy insisted. "You weren't responsible for him."

I grabbed her hands and held them in mine. "Marcy, you don't understand. Jake, he knew Dad had bet on him that night. He knew that Dad had everything riding on him." My vision blurred, and I blinked hard. "He knew, and I think it distracted him."

Marcy blew out a breath and rested her forehead on mine. "Rhys. It was a bad hit. It could have happened to anyone. Please," she whispered. "Please, for me. Don't put this on yourself. Let it go."

After all she'd been through, I couldn't deny her anything. But letting it go wasn't easy. My guilt wanted to remain sitting on my shoulders. It had been years, and the burden had become a beast of its own. Marcy wanted me free of it. Dean wanted me free. Parker wanted me free. I could do that for them, for myself.

I closed my eyes and felt it melt away. Lightness expanded in my chest and lifted my shoulders. I squeezed Marcy's hand, so damn grateful that I had people like her in my life. Not for the first time, I wished Parker were here to meet her. I had a feeling they'd become fast friends.

We sat like that for a while until she eased away and met my gaze. "If you need money ..."

I lurched back. "No, absolutely not."

Her mouth firmed. "I have some left from the life insurance."

"No!" I stood and paced, trying to calm my voice. "No, Marcy. I appreciate the offer, but I'm never taking money from you. And I don't need it." When she started to protest, I told her the rest of the story, including the fight and the sponsors that had come from it. "That's why I came here," I said. "To let you know that I was boxing again. To ... I don't know ..."

I looked down at my feet, suddenly feeling foolish.

"To get my permission?" she asked with a small smile. "You know you don't need that."

"It just felt wrong, doing this, getting back into the ring without talking to you. I don't have Jake anymore. You're like his representative or something."

She laughed lightly. "You're kind of adorable, Rhys Morgan."

I shot her a glare, but she only smiled wider.

"You are. You care so much, with your whole heart." Marcy hugged me. I stood there, wooden and unable to move. But she didn't seem to mind. She only hugged me tighter. "You give everything to protect the people you love. But you have no idea how to protect this, do you?" She pressed her hand to my thudding heart.

I could only stare down at her and shake my head dully.

Marcy searched my face. "What's really bothering you about this, Rhys?"

"I'm afraid." The words tore out of me without permission. I winced, humiliated at the truth.

"Afraid of what?" she asked softly.

My mouth just kept spewing. "Afraid of getting hit like Jake, leaving Dean behind, and now Parker ..." I bit my lip to shut myself up and turned my head away from Marcy's knowing gaze. Boxers weren't supposed to fear. It was an anathema to the sport.

"So," she said thoughtfully, "you came here tonight to see how Rose and I were getting on without Jake, didn't you? To see if we were suffering as much as you feared."

Blood rushed in my ears as I nodded, still unable to face her.

"We're okay, Rhys. Yes, we miss Jake. But death is a part of life." Her fingers found my chin and gently guided my face back. Her blue eyes were glassy as she peered up at me. "It happens to all of us at some point. But if you don't let anyone in, you're never going to fully enjoy *living*."

I exhaled, battered inside, but couldn't speak.

"What do you want out of life, Rhys?"

"What Jake had. A family. A home."

I wanted to tend to my gym, teach kids the art of boxing, then come home and make dinner for the brilliant girl with the biggest, prettiest brown eyes I'd ever seen.

The realization stuck in my throat and pushed at my chest until I made a sound of distress. Marcy gave me a sympathetic squeeze. "Then go get it, Morgan."

***

BY THE TIME I left Marcy's house, I felt pulled thin as rice paper. One wrong move and I'd tear. Ordinarily, when I got like this, I ran, no matter the time or the weather. I'd run through my problems, push my body to the limits of exhaustion, and then fall into a deep sleep, dead to the world.

But I didn't want that now. I wanted to see Parker.

Problem was, she wasn't answering her phone. Or texts.

Doubt began to niggle at the pit of my aching stomach. She always answered. Always. My doubt turned to fear when I thought of who I'd been antagonizing lately. Would that fuck Fairchild actually harm her? Ice coated my gut as I hopped on my bike and drove to Parker's condo.

It was pouring rain, and I was thoroughly soaked by the time I got there. I rubbed the rain out of my eyes to clear my vision and headed for the stairs, forgoing the elevator, needing to run, needing to get to her as fast as I could. No one answered when I banged on the door. My fear turned to dread.

"Parker!" I shouted. "Are you there? Open up!" My shouts rang through the hallway, sounding more than a little desperate. "Parker! Don't scare me like this. I need to know you're okay."

Movement sounded on the other side of the door, and finally—finally—she opened the door. My body sagged in relief, and I stormed in, hauling her close and hugging her tight.

"Jesus, Tink," I rasped. "You scared the hell out of me. Why didn't you answer your phone? Or the door?" She felt stiff in my arms, and I realized I was probably freezing her. I stepped back but kept a hold of her upper arms. "Were you sleeping?"

Her eyes were puffy and her face blotched. But she shook her head and stood like a plank of wood staring at me as though she'd never seen me before. "I was ... distracted," she finally said.

Distracted? The uncomfortable pinch of doubt returned to my gut.

"I'm getting your floor all wet," I said.

Water dripped from the ends of my hair and ran over my face. But I didn't let go of Parker. I feared if I did, she'd somehow be lost to me. A ridiculous idea, but I couldn't shake it. Not with the cold and withdrawn way she stared back at me.

"Why are you here, Rhys?" Her voice was thick and stilted.

"What do you mean, why? You're my girl." My throat felt

constricted. This whole night was off, filled with too much emotion that I didn't want to face. "I needed to see you."

When she pulled away, I let her go, never wanting to use my strength against her. But my hands flexed with the need to hold her again.

"It's a bad night," she said dully.

As if to punctuate her point, lightning flashed and thunder boomed.

I rubbed the water from my face. "I know. But today was ... hard." I didn't want to admit the weakness in me. I didn't. But I couldn't stop myself from exposing it. "I need you, Parker."

That was apparently the wrong thing to say. Parker sucked in a sharp breath, and her listless expression snapped into focus. "For sex? Is that what you need?"

I didn't know what to make of her response. Nothing about this night felt normal. "Yes. No," I amended when her eyes narrowed. "Jesus, Tink. I'm not good at this."

"This?"

"Communicating," I said.

One delicate brow lifted. "Oh, I think you do fairly well communicating what you need."

Her disdain hit me like a lash. "Not if this is your reaction, sweetheart. I had a rough night, Parker. And all I wanted to do is to get to you, to be with you. It isn't just sex."

She stood unmovable, but her lower lip trembled once before she bit it hard. "You're right. You could get sex anywhere. A relationship has to be about more than sex, doesn't it?"

I stepped forward, balling my hands to keep from reaching for her. "What the hell is going on, Tink? You're obviously pissed but I'm stumped as to why."

Her expression suddenly turned cold and remote again. I

fought off a shiver. "Our time together was ... enjoyable. But I think we want different things."

Shock prickled my skin as I gaped at her. I'd been sucker punched in the ring and it hurt less. Was she breaking up with me? "Enjoyable? Different things?"

"Would you please stop repeating everything I say."

"I have to." I bit back a shout. "Because everything you're saying makes no fucking sense."

When her eyes narrowed in warning, I took a deep breath. "You want to explain why yesterday we were good and now you're looking at me like I'm a stranger? Because I don't get it." I stretched my arms wide, imploring. "Talk to me, honey. I'm right here."

Parker exhaled, squaring her shoulders, but a shimmer of tears in her eyes betrayed her. "I want something more, okay?"

Flinching, I stepped back, rubbed my face with a shaking hand. It suddenly hit me what this was about. While I'd been sorting my head out, Parker had been spending too much time in hers. I felt dizzy, the floor beneath me tilting. "Yeah, I fucking get it. I'm not *him*. Never will be."

"You think this is about Theo?"

I didn't want to hate the sound of his name on her lips. But I did. God help me, I did. "You're in love with a ghost. I can't compete with that."

Her laugh was thin, and she closed her eyes as if reaching for patience. Well, join the fucking club, honey.

When she opened her eyes, they were shining with irritation. "This isn't about Theo. Yes, I loved him. But he's gone. I'm not pining for him."

I wanted to feel relief. But I didn't. Something was standing between us, but I was damned if I knew what. "Then what the hell? You give me this bullshit line about us wanting different things, that it's over, then you should have the guts to tell me why."

"Are you calling me a coward?"

"If the shoe fits, sweetheart."

Her teeth met with an audible snap. "Don't you dare play that card. Not when you duck your head any time things get too emotional."

The force of her words punched past my defenses, and I blinked, my stance sagging. "You're right. That was a low blow. I'm sorry, all right. But, shit, Parker, I'm lost here."

"I saw you with that blond today," she said abruptly, her eyes big and round with hurt. "At lunch. You were hugging her."

Realization hit. Fuck. She had the wrong idea. "You think I'm cheating?"

"No." She laughed hollowly. "Not when I took a minute to think about it. That's not your style. I know it here." She tapped her temple. "You wouldn't cheat. You're too honorable. But when I saw you hug another woman, it wasn't my head that was leading me. It was my heart. It was my *heart* that broke."

Her pain hit me like a lash, and I reached for her. But she held up a hand, forestalling me. "No. Don't... let me say this."

"All right," I rasped, my throat closing up on me.

"I've only had one other relationship before you—"

"That makes one more than I've had," I cut in, unable to help myself.

Parker nodded. "I get that. But even you must know that a relationship can't thrive solely on sex."

I felt pinned, unable to breathe. I'd been doing her wrong and hadn't noticed. I didn't have a clue what I was doing. Maybe she was right. Maybe I wasn't for her. But even as I thought it, my mind—my fucking *heart*—rebelled.

"It isn't just sex," I repeated through my clenched teeth.

Parker stared at me with those eyes that cut to the bone. "That's the point, Rhys. How am I supposed to know when every time I've attempted to talk to you about how you're feeling these past few weeks you've distracted me and opted for sex instead? Don't get me wrong, I'm not complaining about the sex—I can barely keep my hands off you either." A soft, lopsided smile pulled at her lips but didn't reach her eyes. "But we haven't had a real conversation since we left Fairchild's lodge. We were closer then but now... you have a tendency to withdraw and keep everything to yourself when it comes to emotional support. And it ... hurts."

Fuck. "Parker—"

"Today, I saw you with another woman ... and it hurt so much. It reminded me how painful it is when you lose someone you care about." She nodded, tears spilling down her pretty cheeks. "You... you have power over me, and I don't think," she swallowed hard, "I don't think this is going to work if one of us feels more than the other."

I couldn't stand it any longer. "Why the fuck would you think you feel more for me than I feel for you? It's not true. You have power over me too."

"Rhys, I don't—"

I reached out, hooking an arm around her waist and easily drew her up against me. She gasped at the sudden movement. "You're right; I'm not good at letting people get close, or letting them help me. But I have with you. I told you all my shit and you convinced me to talk to Dean. I asked you to help organize the exhibition fight and you stepped up... if I've been distant since then, I'm sorry. I didn't mean it. But Parker, you're all that I think about. You are the only purely good and clean thing in my life that's just for me. I promise to try harder at talking to you about shit instead of burying it, if you promise to stop having entire conversations between us in your head."

She pressed a hand to my heart, surely able to feel it racing. But she pursed her lips wryly. "I do not have entire conversations between us in my head."

My smile was tremulous—because, fuck, she'd scared the hell out of me with her talk of letting go. I held her closer. "Yeah? Don't you think it might better to talk to me before deciding you and I aren't right for each other?"

Parker sighed and rested her head on my shoulder with a thud. "This *was* the talk to see if we're right for each other, Rhys."

"Ah." I cleared my throat. "Like I said, I'm not really any good at conversations like this. But I'll try, Parker. I swear, I'll try."

"I know you will," she whispered. "If you tell me you'll do something, you always do it." Slowly, she wrapped her arms around my neck, and I squeezed my eyes shut, not realizing how much I needed that simple touch too.

We stood together for a minute, getting used to each other again. I'd never had an argument with a woman where the outcome had the potential to ruin me. That right there told me all I needed to know about how much I was invested in Parker.

She needed me to communicate more. So I'd communicate more. I'd let her all the way in. My hand slid down her slim back, stroking, soothing. "You're not even gonna ask who she was?"

Parker stiffened, but she let out a breath and met my eyes. "I kind of forgot to in the heat of the moment."

My eyes crinkled, even though I still felt bruised and battered as though I'd gone twelve rounds. "It was Marcy. That's who you saw me with."

Her body jolted as if pinched and she turned her head slightly, the tips of her fingers digging into my neck. "Marcy?"

"Yes, Marcy. Jake's wife. We grew up together. She's like a

sister to me. I've been looking out for her ever since Jake ..." I shook my head and exhaled hard. "That hug you saw? I was trying to comfort her because she still misses him."

Silence filled the air broken only by the crash of thunder. Parker blinked at me as if she were confused. Then her head tipped forward, the silky strands of her hair falling into her face. "Well, shit. I feel like an ass."

Her curse made me chuckle. But then I grew serious. "Don't. If I saw you hugging some guy, I'd have lost it."

Parker hummed, then pressed her lips to the sensitive curve of my neck. "You won't have to worry about that happening. I'm a one man only kind of girl."

Thank Christ for that.

"You're a good friend," she said, drawing me back.

I kissed her temple and found it damp. My heart gave a hard thump. "Tonight, I had dinner with Marcy. She asked me what I wanted out of life. And all I could think was that I wanted you."

A sob broke from her and she melted into my embrace, clinging tight. I pressed my lips to her hair. "I want you," I said again. "I want to be with you, to come home to you, to see you smile, to make you mad. Parker, I want it all."

Her slim frame shook and she burrowed in closer. "I want that too."

For a long moment, I simply held her and listened to the rain. But then she drew back and took my hand. "Come with me."

I followed because I wasn't a fool. But I felt compelled to make her understand. "We don't have to do anything tonight. I don't want you to think all I need from you is sex."

She shot a smile over her shoulder and then led me into her bedroom and straight to her bath. I stood compliant and silent as she slowly stripped the wet clothes from my body. No one in my adult life had ever taken care of me. I hadn't realized I craved her care until she stood there, easing the shirt from my head with a tender expression. My heart contracted, and I sucked in a sharp breath.

"Sit." She pointed to a small stool by the dressing table. When I did, she dried my hair with a towel, then tossed it aside and straddled me. She had on too many clothes. I needed her naked, to feel her silky skin moving against mine.

Her expression was serious as she held my cheeks in her slim, cool hands. "Forgive me for living in my own head? I don't have a lot of experience with feeling this way about someone and I got scared."

I cupped her pert ass and pulled her closer. "Do you forgive me for thinking you were still in love with Theo?"

There. I could say his name without flinching. In truth, I couldn't even hate him. Parker had given him her love, which meant he couldn't have been half bad.

Her smile was tremulous. "He'll always be in my heart. But I'm kind of crazy about someone else now."

"Yeah?" I asked, dipping my head to nuzzle the curve of her neck where I knew she was extra sensitive. "Is he worthy of you?"

"Oh, yes," she said with a sigh of pleasure, arching into my touch. "He's the best man I know."

I'd been kissing my way along her neck but stopped and lifted my head at that. She had no idea what those words did to me, how they tore me apart and put me back together. With her, I felt like something new, something better. "I'm so fucking crazy about you, Parker Brown. You have no idea."

Her smile was the sun.

"I might have some idea." She touched my jaw. "Kiss me."

So I did, putting everything into it, every emotion I couldn't say but wanted her to feel. I licked into her mouth, reveling in her taste. Then I stood and carried her to bed to strip each item of clothing from her with care.

She was warmth and soft curves, tender caresses and breathy sighs. I explored her body as though it were new to me, taking my time, kissing every inch. And when I finally entered her slick heat, we both stopped and fought for breath. I stared down at those brown eyes I wanted to see every damn day of my life, and my chest hitched.

Words formed on my lips, words I'd never said to anyone. But it was too much. Too good. I dipped my head and kissed her deep, hungry. Always hungry for her. And she moaned into it as I moved. My hands slid into her hair as I thrust slow and sure. She was utterly precious to me, utterly beautiful.

For the first time in my life, I was making love. And it was so damn perfect. I never wanted it to end. Never wanted to let her go.

And when I finally found my voice, I could only say one thing.

"Parker."

TWENTY-TWO

Rhys

"Rhys." Parkers fingers, threaded through mine, gripped harder with her plea.

Sweat trickled down my back. I moved inside her with a steady rhythm, slow and deep and oh, so good. "You can take it."

She groaned, turning her head to the side of the pillow. Glossy brown strands of damp hair clung to her flushed cheeks. Her lips parted as she panted. Beautiful. I ducked my head and captured that sweet mouth, felt her heat, tasted her need.

Pleasure licked over my skin, and I shivered. God, I wasn't going to last. We'd been at this for hours, fucking and kissing and drinking each other in under the hazy heat of the afternoon sun. But boxers were supposed to have stamina.

Parker moaned into my mouth, craning her head to prolong the kiss with a greediness that had my breath catching. With another moan, she came around my cock, her inner muscles squeezing me so hard, my mind blanked.

"Shit," I rasped. My careful control broke with a thrust, and another. I couldn't get close enough. I needed in, and in, and in. Parker wrapped her strong legs around my waist and pulled me closer.

"Parker."

Her fingers slid through my hair. "Give it to me."

Let go.

I didn't know how. Not in life. I never knew how. But here, with her, I could.

She held me, cradled in her arms, as I poured myself into her with a helpless shout. Weak and panting, I laid wrapped up in her, our sweaty skin sticking. Then I groaned and rolled to my side, pulling her with me.

Parker rested her head on my chest with a sigh. I hauled her closer, holding on, unable to release her. My body hadn't stopped shivering. I was supposed to be blowing her mind, rocking her damn world, but she'd flipped the script.

"You okay there, big guy?" she asked softly.

No. Yes.

"Give me a minute."

She simply petted me, taking it in stride that I was wrecked. I leaned into her soothing touch. After all, she was the one who'd wrecked me. Our breaths evened out, and the sunlight slanting through the loft windows warmed our skin.

Pressing my lips to the crown of Parker's head, I closed my eyes and started to doze. Then my phone rang. Grunting, I grabbed it, intent on turning the damn thing off but then saw it was Dean. He'd texted too: **Answer me, asshole.**

Since I knew his next step would be coming up to the loft, I caved.

"What's the problem?" My voice was shredded.

"That Garret guy is here."

"So tell him to piss off."

He huffed out a laugh. "He isn't in the gym. He's walking around outside with some guy."

I rubbed a hand over my face and tried to focus. "We don't own the sidewalk, Dean." Unfortunately.

"I don't know why I bother..." A long-suffering sigh gusted. "They appear to be surveying the building."

The fuck?

"I thought you might want to know," Dean said. "But, by all means, go back to doing whatever it is your doing."

His tone made it clear he knew exactly what I'd been doing.

With a grunt, I eased away from Parker and sat up. "I'm coming down."

Dean grumbled something unintelligible under his breath and hung up.

Tossing the phone on the bed, I explained the situation to Parker. "I'm going to see what the hell is going on," I said.

She sat up as well, pulling her knees to her chest. "The gym is safe now. You have the sponsors. Why would he keep at this?"

"Some people don't like the word no." I reached for my sweats and stopped. "Shit, I have to shower."

Her smile was sly. "That probably would be a good idea. Not that I mind you smelling like me."

My heart gave a funny little squeeze, and I leaned over to kiss her. "Territorial. I like it." Then I backed away from the temptation that was Parker Brown and took the quickest shower in history.

Garret was still there by the time I got downstairs. He smiled wide and easy as though he wasn't scoping out my property.

"Mr. Morgan. Nice to see you again."

"Wish I could say the same, Garret." I eyed the guy next to him who had a big iPad in hand and appeared to be consulting blueprints. "Doesn't look like you're here to see me, though, does it?"

Garret shrugged. "Just doing a little research."

Research my ass. This was a reminder that the second I fell, he'd be there to profit off my failure.

Before I'd ever thrown I punch, I'd been a fighter. My natural inclination in any situation was to act first, think later. Most people assumed that's what boxing was all about as well—rabid aggression and hard strikes.

They couldn't be more wrong. Boxing taught me a lesson: to win, you had to strategize. I'd stepped away from the sport and forgotten that. Being with Parker—who never let me get away with shit—these past weeks had reminded me.

Tucking my hands into my pockets, I leaned against the sun-warmed brick of my gym. "I've been researching too, Mr. Garret. Why don't you come in and we can talk."

His surprise was evident, but he brushed it off with another oily smile. "Sounds good." He turned to his lackey. "Wait for me here, Kevin."

I wasn't going to fight Garret, but I didn't have to like the guy, and my jaw was tight as I lead him past the studios where high school kids were doing stamina drills before stepping into the sparring ring. Carlos was shouting out encouragement—if you call "stop dragging your feet and move your lazy asses" encouragement.

"We're offering beginners lessons for adults on Sundays, if you're interested," I told Garret.

He turned his attention away from the kids and back to me. "What makes you think I'm a novice?"

"You're not?" I slowed by one of the mats currently unoccupied. "Want to give it a go then?"

Garret gave me a reluctant grin. "No thank you. I like my face as it is."

Laughing, I headed for the office. Parker stepped out of the elevator at the same time. I greeted her with a kiss to the cheek. "This is Parker Brown," I said to Garret as I opened my office door.

He held out a hand. "Kyle Garret. A pleasure."

Parker gave him a polite smile and shook his hand. But she refrained from returning the sentiment. I bit back a grin.

"We're going to have a quick meeting," I told her. "Want to join us?"

The corners of her eyes crinkled as she searched my face. I knew she was wondering what I was up to. "I don't know that I'd have anything to add to the conversation."

"Stay anyway." I wanted her to hear this. More importantly, I wanted her as part of my life. Taking her hand, I led us into the office.

"You've bought every property on this block," I said to Garret as soon as everyone was settled.

"It's public knowledge," Garret replied with a causal shrug.

Humming in agreement, I rested my hands on my abs. "I'm doing a match for charity in a few weeks."

"So I've heard."

"The event has secured me enough sponsors to pay off the bills and keep this place in the green."

Garret's eyes narrowed. "Sure. But for how long?"

"For as long as it takes." I leaned forward and set my forearms on Dad's old desk. "I'm not going to sell to you, Garret. Not ever."

His chin took on a mulish angle, and I held up a hand to forestall whatever he had to say.

"I get it. My gym is an eyesore and smack in the middle of your plan. You're trying to gentrify this community and make a buck. There isn't anything I can do about that. Just like you can't do anything about me being here."

Garret grunted. "What's your point, Morgan?"

"You can either be pissed about it and lurk around on sidewalks, or you can do something constructive." I held his gaze. "You can sponsor this place."

At my side, Parker stirred, but she kept quiet.

Garret, on the other hand, snorted long and loud. "You've got brass, I'll give you that. Why the hell would I help you when I want you to sell?"

"Because it will pretty this place up. You can use it as an enticement for all those young professionals you sell to. A world class boxing gym with pro instructors right in the heart of your safe but 'urban' community."

The chair beneath Garret squeaked as he leaned back and steepled his fingers. He stared at me for a moment, then a slow smile spread. "And I suppose the added benefit of you reaping in all those new memberships is, what?"

"A symbiotic relationship in which we both win."

"I'd win a lot more if I owned the gym outright."

I simply stared, waiting him out. Parker remained silent, but I could feel her there, my loadstone.

Finally, Garret grinned. "Definite brass." He stood, and I did as well, accepting his outstretched hand to shake. "Send your proposal over to my office. I'll have my lawyers look it over."

He nodded to Parker. "Ms. Brown."

As soon as he was gone, Parker turned to me. Her smile glowed. "Would it be patronizing if I told you how very proud I am of you right now?"

For years, all I had was my own sense of pride. I never knew how good it would feel to be the recipient of it.

I opened my arms, and she stepped into them. "Just don't stop being proud of me, all right?"

I could handle anything as long as she was in my corner.

Parker

ONE OF THE reasons I grew to love science and engineering so much was how theories could be proven and knowledge could be gained in this tangible way, uncomplicated by emotion or contradiction.

Life outside of science was messy and definitely contradictory. After Theo died, I wanted nothing but to avoid it.

Yet, if we're honest, there are contradictions in science too. Take the moon, for example. Using uranium-lead dating, geologists dated fragments of the moon and determined it was 4.51 billion years old. But if you calculate the rate at which it is moving away from the earth and then reverse it, the moon would have been sitting on top of the earth only 1.55 billion years ago. A direct contradiction to the big bang cosmology.

So there were contradictions in life everywhere. Even in my beloved world of academia. I just hadn't wanted to admit it. I wanted it to be safe from that. Yet, you can't hide from *life*. It was messy and convoluted and emotional, and I was done cowering behind excuses.

Which was why I cycled to work the day after I confronted Rhys about Marcy with a dreamy expression on my face but an ache of guilt in my chest.

Since then Rhys and I did more than just have hot sex. Sometimes he made love to me. I knew it, lying beneath him as he gazed into my eyes and moved inside me. It was magical and stunning and stole my breath. So, of course, every time I thought about those moments, I couldn't help my goofy goddamn grin.

However, I'd also every now and then get an image of the hurt on his face when I told him we were from different worlds. My guilt was real. I shouldn't have had an entire conversation in my head about our relationship without him out of fear, and I'd spent the last few weeks since that night trying to show him that I wasn't afraid to throw myself into this relationship.

As Rhys's training intensified, there wasn't a lot of time to revel in our newfound certainty in each other this past week, but I was there to show support—like I did when he so cleverly made his proposal to developer Kyle Garret—and to help with any last-minute details for the charity event.

Which was now upon us.

Tomorrow was the big fight, and I had prehistoric-sized butterflies in my belly about it.

Rhys had been avoiding Fairchild for the last few weeks and so far, the billionaire had not made any moves toward killing my career. There had been some coverage about him in the news lately that he was under possible investigation for tax evasion. Rumor had it, there was more to it than just that. The word "fraud" was being tossed around. My hope was that Fairchild would stay too preoccupied by his troubles to bother us.

However, I was still sick with worry about it and attempted to hide that concern from Rhys. He had enough on his plate. Somehow, he knew anyway, assuring me every now and then that me losing my job was the last thing he'd allow to happen.

But Fairchild using Rhys and making him feel worthless was the last thing I'd allow to happen either.

It was messy.

Complicated.

And waiting for that ax to fall was not fun.

My headspace was full as I rode my bike into the underground parking beneath the office that morning. It was so full, it took me a second to feel the prickle of unease on my neck. I locked my bike to the rack and straightened, unnerved by the sensation of being watched.

Turning, I scanned the space. My heart turned over in my chest.

Franklin Fairchild.

He stood near a black sedan, a driver visible inside the car.

Heart pounding, I could do nothing but wait as he slowly walked toward me. Sweat gathered under my arms as I forced myself to meet his cold gaze.

I shivered at the look in his eyes, and I knew he was here to do more threatening.

Just like that, I went from afraid to majorly pissed off.

I was worried about Rhys. My insides churned not only with that concern but with the fact that this man held my career in his tiny hands. I was sick and tired of being out of control of my own goddamn destiny.

I did not need to be approached by this giant bully only to take more of his intimidation.

The thought of what he could still do to me, Dean, and Rhys no longer frightened me. It enraged me. As Fairchild walked closer, I pulled my phone out of my purse and quickly brought up the app I wanted.

By the time Fairchild drew to a stop, my attention was off my phone, my gaze locked to his.

"A bit late to call for help." Fairchild smirked.

My spine stiffened. "And why would I need help, Mr. Fairchild?"

His grin widened but it never reached his eyes. They remained unsettlingly emotionless. "Perhaps because you realize what a tenuous position you're in."

Gut roiling, I pushed through the sensation. "I'm not afraid of you."

"Showing a little spunk might feel good but it is not advised."

Eyes narrowed, I curled my lip into a sneer I was kind of proud of. "Is getting your way really this important? I mean, it seems ridiculous the lengths you're going to for one boxing match."

"Here's a lesson in business, Parker: the first person you allow to get one over on you is the beginning of your downfall."

Oh my God. This man was a megalomaniac for sure. "You know what I think? I think you're a spoiled misogynist who is right now ten seconds from throwing his pacifier out of his stroller because he didn't get his way. Rhys will never cave in to your blackmail, and you know it."

Fairchild took a step closer. "I'd be very careful what you say to me."

"Oh? Why?"

He stared like he felt sorry for me. "Rhys will fight for me, and he'll make me a lot of money doing so."

"And if he won't?" I pushed.

"Then not only will I make sure he loses his shithole gym, I'll blacklist his brother from every industry on the East Coast. And as for you, Rhys's precious little girlfriend whom I'm sure he'll bore of fucking within the month, I'll start making my way through your family. You might not care about your career, but you do care about your family. The Browns' finances are tied up in some investments that are in my power to shit all over.

Convince Rhys to fight, Parker, or I'll come after your family too."

His threats, so casual, no menace, just throwing them out there like we were discussing the weather, made me sick to my stomach. But thankfully, I remembered Rhys talking about his time in the ring. How boxing was all about learning how to anticipate your opponent's next move. I'd been around Fairchild long enough to know the man was so sure of his own invincibility, he said whatever the hell he liked, certain there would be no consequences. And I'd just used that against him.

I held up the phone I'd kept in my hand between us and clicked stop, save, and then emailed the recording to myself.

"What are you doing?" His tone had changed from casual superiority to irritated and suspicious.

I pressed play on my phone. Our conversation echoed around the underground lot.

Color flooded his face, and his hand came up as if to snatch the phone out of my hand.

I pulled it out of his reach, and, despite my fear, I grinned. "I've already emailed the recording to a safe location. It's out of your hands."

"You little bitch." He stepped toward me. "You think you—"

"Problem here?" a voice called. I turned to see Xander getting out of his car, a white box in hand I knew was filled with doughnuts. He came to a stop beside me and Fairchild, a frown marring his brow.

As if he'd just realized where we were, Fairchild stepped back and tugged on his lapels. "You'll regret that," he promised, like a cartoonish villain.

"I don't think so. Because if *anything* happens to *anyone* I care about, I'm going straight to the police with this recording. And in case that doesn't scare you, I'll take the recording to the media too. See, sometimes the world and all the powerful people in it care if someone is proven to be untrustworthy, dishonorable, a blackmailer, a misogynist, and generally a giant turd. In that scenario, life will get that little bit harder, even for a billionaire turd.

"Then again, sometimes the world doesn't care, or they don't care for very long. But I'm not sure you're willing to risk finding out how the world would treat you." I smiled sweetly. "And, according to the *Tribune*, you have enough troubles to deal with, without adding a charge of blackmail into the mix."

His fury was palpable. "And what you're doing isn't blackmail?"

"Hmm, I guess it's all in your perspective? Somehow, I think, since it's *you*, I'll sleep just fine."

Casting me one last hateful look, Fairchild spun on his heel and marched toward his car.

Xander turned into me. "Okay, what did I just miss?"

"Me finally standing up for myself." It had felt good. Even if my insides were rattling with nerves and I was very close to upchucking. At Xander's frown, I blew out a shaky exhalation. "Do you think Jackson will fire me?"

"I think Jackson is more concerned with the fact that the guy financing his company is under investigation. But, hey, way to stick up for yourself. Very impressive."

I *had* just stood up to Franklin Fairchild.

Holy shit.

Xander saw my expression pale and held up the white box he carried. "Doughnut?"

I winced at the thought of food.

"Let's head up. We should tell Jackson and add another worry onto his shoulders."

For a smart girl, sometimes I was way too distracted by my personal life to put two and two together. "Oh my God, is the company in trouble? With Fairchild being investigated, I mean?"

"Jackson asked me to bring doughnuts. He's called a meeting first thing." Concern washed over Xander's expression. "I guess we're about to find out the answer to your question."

As soon as Xander and I walked into the room, Jackson came out of his private office, nodded at my colleague, and announced to the staff. "Meeting room, five minutes. I want everyone there."

One by one, we made our way into the meeting room. It was big enough that we all got a seat at the table. There was a lot of intrigued murmuring.

Evan slipped into the seat next to me. "You know what's going on?" he asked quietly.

I shook my head, probably looking like a ball of nerves because of my altercation with Fairchild. I couldn't stop bouncing my right knee and my fingers tapped impatiently against the desk. "You?"

"Nope. God, I hope it isn't staff cuts. We just bought a house."

My stomach roiled. Staff cuts? Perhaps staff cuts were best-case scenario. If we no longer had financing, we were screwed six ways until Sunday.

Oh hell.

I tensed in my seat as Jackson strode into the room with Ben at his back. Ben was head of sales and marketing. He was the face of Horus Renewable Energy and privy to whatever Jackson knew.

They stood in front of the long meeting table, and Jackson broke into a grin. "I see a lot of worried faces. Don't be worried. I know some of you are concerned about the allegations made against Mr. Fairchild in the *Tribune*. Don't be. It's not a concern for us. On that note, I have good news, but this news means that there will be some changes within the company."

"Changes, as in job losses?" Evan asked.

Jackson shook his head. "The opposite. It won't happen right away, but we'll be expanding, which means more staff and a new office. And the reason is because we're no longer heavily financed by Franklin Fairchild, which means he's no longer on the board as CEO of the company. He's no longer on the board, period."

My breath caught in my throat.

What?

"The board is now headed by Diana Crichton Jones of Crichton Investments and Research. She bought out Fairchild." Jackson's gaze zeroed in on me. "Ms. Crichton Jones was very impressed with our model, our staff, and our diversity, and she has a real passion for renewable energy."

Relief moved through me. The garden party—my conversation with Diana, how pleased Jackson seemed with me.

I'd helped secure her interest in Horus.

And she was ... well, she was even more powerful than Fairchild.

Which meant I was free of him. And it was most likely the reason he'd approached me this morning, because he knew I was about to find out he couldn't touch my career.

So he'd threatened my family instead.

Festering miscreant.

I could *so* live with blackmailing Colonel Dipshit.

I slumped in my chair with absolute relief.

"It will mean changes, and having a board means we're not autonomous here. But they want to make this company a success and they're as dedicated as we are to making the world green. I'll keep you all posted with any changes that I feel you need to be informed of, but I just wanted you all to know—trust me, this is definitely the best move forward for us all."

"No more yacht and garden parties?" Xander dared to ask.

There was some snickering as Jackson tried not to smirk. "Nothing mandatory anymore." My boss looked at me again. "For any of you."

A grateful smile bloomed on my face. Jackson knew the hold Fairchild had on me because of Rhys. He knew Fairchild had no interest in renewable energy and that he was a dangerous, big, spoiled baby of a billionaire, and Horus and its staff needed to be free of him.

God, I loved my boss.

"Right, if you have any questions going forward, do not hesitate to ask. You know where I am. For now, everyone back to work. Except Parker."

My colleagues shot me curious looks but left the office without a second glance, caught up in the news that Fairchild was gone.

Once the door closed behind them, I was left in the room with Jackson and Ben.

"This is good news." My smile wilted a little. "Right?"

Jackson grinned. "Even better for you. I wanted to make your contract permanent from the moment you inputted those changes to our model. However, I needed approval from Fairchild, who as the main investor made his investment contingent on being named CEO of Horus. All big decisions, including staff employment, had to go through him. Usually, he gave his approval, no questions asked. After he met Rhys, for reasons unknown to me, and we don't need to get into it, he held off giving me the authority to make you a permanent member of staff."

"That's illegal, Jackson."

"Which is why he's no longer an issue. Between him being

under investigation and Diana wanting to invest, the board were more than happy to shove him out. And that's why you'll be receiving a new *permanent* contract by the end of the day."

Relief, excitement, joy flooded me, and I knew I was grinning like a big nerd. "Really?"

Ben and Jackson shared amused looks and my boss nodded. "Really. Welcome to the Horus family, Parker."

I HURRIED up the steps and into Rhys's gym, my heart pounding with my news. I'd waited all day and night to tell him about Fairchild, deciding I wanted to tell him face-to-face. His trainer, Jimmy, this gruff older man I liked despite his bluntness because he clearly cared about Rhys, had cock-blocked Rhys.

No sex before the big fight.

Apparently, those articles I'd read about athletes and sexual frustration and aggression were true. Or at least Jimmy was hoping so.

This meant I'd been banned from visiting the gym the night before because Jimmy said Rhys couldn't keep his hands off me. No willpower.

I was definitely not complaining about that.

That time, however, had allowed me to think and remember that Fairchild's removal from Horus didn't mean we were out of the woods entirely. On that note, I realized even Fairchild wasn't stupid enough to turn down an obviously lucrative buyout just to hold Rhys on a string.

Besides, he still had something on Rhys. Fairchild had also threatened Dean and he could follow through on that

Yet, this *was* a win for us and it couldn't have come at a better time, right before the big fight.

The breath left me as I walked into the gym and saw how

the place had been transformed for the fight. Although the first-floor gymnasium was left relatively untouched, the interior decorator had laid a red carpet and golden ropes that led to the second-floor staircase. Huge pots of ferns sat here and there; she'd also hung massive black-and-white canvas photographs of famous fighters, including a beautiful shot of Rhys when he'd just won the heavyweight championship belt.

I gazed around the first floor, watching catering staff wander up to elegantly dressed guests who were taking their time walking along the carpet to stare at the photographs. From here I could see Diana Crichton Jones and her fiancé, and I had a sudden urge to run like a little girl across the gym and throw myself into her arms in gratitude.

Thankfully, I refrained.

"Parker."

I spun around, the short skirt of my dark green dress fluttering around my thighs. Carlos stood in front of me, looking incredibly handsome in a tailored suit. "You look great."

His dark eyes dragged down my body and back up again. "So do you. Maybe too good. Rhys told me to bring you to him before the fight but seeing you in that dress, I'm not sure it's a good idea."

I glanced down at my dress, wondering what was wrong with it. It was by Self-Portrait, a lovely forest green with a pleated skirt, sweetheart neckline, short sleeves, and black lace cutout detail on the waist and upper chest. It was demure as far as I could tell, except for my black platform-heeled, peep-toe sandals. Those were a little sexy.

"Pfft." I waved off Carlos's comment. "I want to see him."

"Okay." He gently took my elbow, and I heard him mutter, "Dios mio, Jimmy is going to kill me."

We took the back elevator to the second floor. It seemed to take forever. I found myself tapping my foot.

"You nervous?"

I glanced over at Rhys's best friend, a denial forming on my lips. However, it didn't come out. The truth was, I was beyond nervous for Rhys to fight. I hadn't slept a wink the night before worrying about it.

Not just because I was concerned about some guy punching the hell out of him, or vice versa, but because I was still anxious about what this fight might do to him. I knew now Rhys had gone to see Marcy because he needed closure with her before he could step back in the ring. Her permission, which from the story he'd told me, she'd given with grace and compassion.

She sounded like a lovely person and someone I wanted to meet. She was important to Rhys, and anything important to him was important to me.

I froze against the elevator doors as they opened.

After all these years, all the running away, I'd finally found someone I wanted to love. Someone I wanted to love me back.

Not wanted.

No ... I *loved* him.

The feeling crashed over me, and I suddenly felt annoyed with myself for not having said it to him. Sure, I'd told him I was crazy about him and I'd alluded to it... but I hadn't said those actual words. I loved him. I couldn't sleep for worrying about him. That's why the prehistoric butterflies in my belly hadn't disappeared even after I got news of Fairchild's demise from Horus.

I loved Rhys.

And he needed to know that. Not tomorrow or the next day... but now.

"Hey, you okay?" Carlos's face appeared in front of mine.

No, I was not okay.

I was in love.

People were a million things when they were in love but "okay" was surely not one of them.

Pushing a strained smile, I nodded. "Yeah."

Carlos didn't look like he believed me, but he didn't badger me. Instead he led me out of the elevator and down the hall to Rhys's office. He knocked and opened the door, sticking only his head around the jamb. "Got a delivery in a very cute fucking package out here."

"How about you not notice that shit from now on?" I heard Rhys say. "Jimmy, give us a minute. Let my girl in."

"No funny business," I heard Jimmy warn just before the door opened fully to reveal the trainer. His eyes dropped down my body, and he rolled his eyes. "For fuck's sake." He cut me a look. "That goes for you too. Jesus."

He strode away, taking a chuckling Carlos with him. When I turned back from watching them go, I found Rhys sitting on the edge of his rosewood desk. He wore long boxing shorts and boxing boots in black and gold. His ripped torso drew my attention for a second because, well, it was magnificent, until my eyes were drawn to his hands all wrapped up.

My stomach somersaulted.

I could not lose him to this fight. Emotionally or otherwise.

"You coming in or not, Tinker Bell?"

Swallowing hard, I strode inside.

Rhys's gaze drifted down my body, and his hands curled around the edge of the desk. When his eyes met mine, they were full of heat. "Did you wear that dress just to torture me?"

I smoothed a nervous hand down the pleated skirt. "It's just a dress."

He cocked his head. "You worried about this fight?"

It was somewhat disconcerting how perceptive he could be. "I know you'll do great."

"But you're still worried. That why you're still standing all the way over there?" He pushed up off the desk, and I crossed the distance between us.

As I slid my arms around his waist and rested my head on his warm, hard chest, Rhys wrapped his arms around me and kissed the top of my head. "I'll be fine, Tink."

"I know." I squeezed him and then lifted my head from his chest. "I have good news."

Rhys gave me an affectionate smile. "Yeah, what's that?"

I told him about my confrontation with Fairchild and about the board buying him out of Horus. "Jackson gave me a permanent contract. Fairchild can't touch my job. And I have leverage on him now. I think ... I think we might be out of those particular woods."

His smile widened and this time he squeezed me. "Baby, that's not good news, that's fantastic news."

My own smile fell. "I blackmailed him."

Sobering, Rhys nodded. "And I know how you probably feel about that. But I think you're pretty fucking brave. Thank you. Not just for me and Dean, but for doing it for yourself. Proud of you."

My breath caught. "Really?"

His hands coasted down my back as he studied me. "Yeah, *really*."

Gazing up into his too-handsome face and those beautiful, warm eyes, emotion welled inside me with such force, I couldn't have stopped it even if I'd wanted to. "I love you," I blurted.

Rhys's eyes widened, his nostrils flaring, his lips parting and he—

"Right, time's up, lovebirds," Jimmy burst into the room.

My boyfriend's arms tensed around me as I attempted to retreat. "Jimmy—"

"Nope, nearly time and Parker here needs to take her seat. Go on, darlin'." He gestured toward the door with his hand.

"It's okay," I reassured Rhys, even though I was trembling with the magnitude of what I'd just confessed. "Uh, well ... break a leg." I frowned and shot a worried look at Jimmy. "No, that's not right. What do you say to a boxer for good luck before a fight?"

The trainer's lips twitched. "*Good luck.*" He threw Rhys a teasing look. "I thought you said she was smart?"

Rhys apparently wasn't in the mood to be teased. His tender gaze fell on me. "She's the smartest fucking person I know. But thankfully, she's got a big blind spot when it comes to me."

Grinning, I shook my head. "Not true. I see you clearer than anyone."

Something big flickered across Rhys's expression, and that was when I found myself being gently guided toward the exit and summarily dismissed by Jimmy. "Enough. I need him juiced, not fucking sweet on his girl."

"Parker," Rhys called my name.

Jimmy let me go, and I glanced over my shoulder at my boyfriend.

"You're the first person I want to see after this fight. Yeah?"

Nodding, I let out a nervous sigh. "Yes. Good luck. And Rhys?"

"Yeah, baby?"

"I'm proud of you too." As soon as the words left my mouth, I took off before I could throw myself at him and ruin the words by asking him not to fight. On shaking legs, I hurried down the hall toward the doors that led out into the main room of the second floor.

As soon as I burst into the space, I halted. Laid out before the main ring were rows and rows of folding chairs. Catering staff moved up and down the aisles with canapés and champagne, offering them to the high society guests who had dressed up in their finery.

"Parker, darling." A soft voice somehow cut through the loud murmur and the music blaring through the PA system. My gaze followed the familiar voice—my mom. She stood by the front-row seats where my father, Easton, and her fiancé Oliver were sitting. She waved me over, and I hurried to take the seat next to her after stopping to kiss everyone's cheeks.

My mom took my hand in hers. "Are you nervous?"

"Am I that obvious?"

She patted my hand. "A mother always knows."

"No need to be nervous, Peanut." Dad's head popped into sight around my mom's. "Your guy is some fighter."

"Yes, that might be true, Charles, but a woman in love doesn't particularly rejoice in seeing another man smash his fists into her boyfriend's face."

My gaze flew to my mom's at the mention of love. "Am I that obvious?" I repeated.

She smiled, her eyes bright with affection. "Like I said, a mother always knows."

Relaxing deeper into her side, my fingers tightening around hers, I thought about how easily my family had accepted Rhys in my life. How happy they were to see me moving on. We had our differences, and I'd spent a great deal of my life worried I'd failed them, but I had a great family. "A good mom."

"What, darling?"

"A *good* mom always knows." I took a deep, shuddering sigh, impulsively deciding to be honest. Rhys and I had talked about coming clean to my family regarding how we really met— we knew we should, but we hadn't discussed when. Needing a distraction from my worry over Rhys, I turned in my seat and said, "You knew there was something between us probably before we did."

Mom frowned at my shaky tone and Dad leaned closer at her side. "Peanut?"

Just say it.

Get it over with.

And hope they don't disown you.

"My old boss wasn't going to give me a permanent contract because he's horrible and he was only interested in married employees or employees who had shown some kind of commitment in their personal lives. Say, having a long-term relationship, a mortgage, or kids."

"That's illegal," Mom snapped, her eyes glittering with outrage.

"I know. But it was Franklin Fairchild. He's a little difficult to dissuade."

My father's features grew taut, but I continued before he could express his own anger.

"I hired Rhys to pretend to be my boyfriend. Well, technically, I hired his younger brother, Dean, but Rhys found out and came to confront me at a dinner with my boss and Fairchild. However, when he realized there might be an opportunity with Fairchild to sponsor his gym, Rhys and I agreed he'd take Dean's place and pretend to be my boyfriend instead."

"What?" Easton slid forward in her seat, surprising me. I hadn't realized she was listening. "You did what?"

I winced. "I know it was shameful—"

"It was genius," Easton said, waving off my comment. "And obviously you and Rhys are really together now, right?"

My parents' eyes bored into me with expectation. "Yes, it turned into something very real between us." I waited as my parents exchanged a look I didn't understand. "Well ... do you forgive me for lying?"

"Did Rhys take any money from you?" Dad asked.

I shook my head. "No. I was supposed to pay him at the end of the first month, but we already knew by then that this wasn't fake anymore."

When they gave me nothing but silence in return, I squirmed in my seat. "Well?"

"Well, what?" Mom gave a delicate shrug. "I'm not happy you did this, but I'm also somewhat impressed by your ambition and tenacity. Moreover, if you two care about each other, that's all that matters."

"Is it?" Dad cut her a look before his eyes returned to mine. "If I find out this man is only after your money, Peanut, I will not stand idly by."

My heart squeezed in my chest. I didn't want Dad being suspicious of Rhys. Feeling defensive, I frowned. "As soon as you get to know him, you'll realize Rhys isn't like that. He's the most honorable man I've ever met." My gaze flew to the ring. "And he's about to let some stranger smash their fists into his face."

Mom suddenly squeezed my hand. "He'll be fine. Just you see."

I didn't know if that meant Mom was on board with our relationship or not. I knew Easton was by the huge grin she kept shooting my way. Dad stared broodingly at the ring so I knew he wasn't going to come around easily to my revelation. I'd suspected as much.

Yet, I had to hope it wouldn't take him long to realize what Rhys and I had was real. That he'd see Rhys for the good man he was. That he made me happy.

He'll be fine. Just you see.

God, I hoped so.

And I hoped I could watch the entire fight without looking away. My nervous energy increased by the second, my foot tapping against the floor as we waited for the fight to commence. So much for the confession acting as a distraction.

I was grateful when Dean, Zoe, Ren, Elijah, and Navin arrived to take the seats next to me, their joking and excitement somewhat diverting.

"I'd like another champagne," Mom said, drawing my attention from my friends. She gazed over her shoulder, obviously in search of a passing waiter.

Needing something to do, I offered to get her one, and strode down the aisle toward the back of the room where I saw catering staff working the guests who hadn't taken their seats yet.

I'd almost cleared the chairs when a familiar blond suddenly popped up from a seat near the aisle. "Parker?"

Almost stumbling to a halt, I gazed up at the gorgeous woman in front of me. Even in my heels, I had to look up. She must have stood six feet in her high-heeled sandals. She wore a red dress that clung to every amazing curve on her body.

Marcy.

The widow of Rhys's best friend.

She beamed at me. "I made Rhys show me a photo of you, I hope you don't mind. Wow, you're even more gorgeous in real life."

Me?

This glamazon thought I was gorgeous? I blushed. "Uh, thank you. You are too. Marcy, right?"

Her grin widened. "Yeah, that's me." She gestured behind me to the ring. "I had to be here. I wanted Rhys to know I absolutely support him."

God, she was so nice. I stepped toward her. "He appreciates that more than you know. But ..." I was afraid to ask in case it wasn't my place.

"But?"

"Are ... are you okay? Being here?"

Her eyes grew a little bright as her expression softened. "I guess we both need to do this. Face our fears. You know." She shrugged a little helplessly.

Without thinking, I reached out to squeeze her elbow. "Why don't you come sit with me and my family and friends?"

Marcy smiled again, her eyes moving over my face as if she was searching for something. "You're exactly how he described."

"How—"

"But I'm here with a few friends." She gestured to the seats beside her and I only then noticed two more glamazons, a brunette and a redhead, watching our interaction. By the narrowing of their eyes and their intense study, they seemed ready to jump to their feet to defend Marcy if need be. "They've got my back."

I nodded. I could see that. "Well, we'll catch up after the fight?" Now that we'd met, I wanted to know more about her. Attending this fight, despite her own grief, said a lot about what kind of friend she was. I admired her already, and any insecurities I'd had seemed silly in comparison to what she'd been through losing the father of her child.

"Oh, definitely. I just wanted to say a quick 'hey' while you were passing." She gave me a little wave and slipped gracefully back into her seat.

I was still smiling about Marcy as I grabbed two glasses of champagne from a waiter and hurried back to my seat. Mom took her glass and sipped it elegantly.

I threw the contents of mine back and ignored my mother

tutting under her breath. For once, I didn't care about being ladylike. I was too nervous to care about anything but Rhys.

My heart skipped a beat as the popular Boston sports anchor Mitch Underwood entered the ring in his finely cut tuxedo. Zoe had used her contacts at work to get Mitch to agree to emcee the fight.

Handsome, charismatic, fair but blunt, Mitch was a hit with male and female sports fans alike. He grinned out toward us. "Good evening, ladies and gentlemen! I'm Mitch Underwood, and it's my great pleasure this evening to welcome you all to this once-in-a-lifetime event. As you know, proceeds from tonight's fight will be donated to the charity Street Warriors, a worthy cause that aims to feed, clothe, and shelter the many homeless souls that share our streets right here in Boston." He paused to allow applause.

Once the clapping petered out, he continued. "Without further ado, in the red corner!" His voice rose as he gestured toward his right side, "Weighing in at two hundred and ten pounds, all the way from New Orleans, Louisiana, will you please welcome two-time heavyweight champion, Jarrod 'The Thunder' Johnson!"

Cheers filled the room, and my heart began to pound impossibly hard as I clapped and watched Jarrod Johnson climb into the ring. He wore similar attire to Rhys but in red and white.

Rhys had told me Jarrod wasn't in the same shape now that he was retired and how that was a good thing because he'd have taken Rhys out easily. He was two inches taller than Rhys and his optimum fighting weight used to be two hundred and thirty-five pounds. It wasn't that any longer but looking at the guy and his extremely fit physique and long legs, I was not reassured as he pumped his hands in the air, drawing more cheers from the audience.

"And in the black corner!" Mitch continued. My breath caught as he gestured to the left. "Weighing in at two hundred and fifteen pounds, homegrown right here in Boston, Massachusetts, please welcome heavyweight champion, Rhys 'The Widowmaker' Morgan!"

I winced, my hand flexing in my mom's.

"It's okay, darling." She patted my hand.

But it wasn't.

We'd forgotten to ask Mitch to not use that moniker.

If it bothered Rhys, he wasn't showing it as he hooked a long leg over the ropes and ducked under, only to bounce up on his tiptoes and roll his shoulders. The cheers were even wilder, East Coast society clearly on their homegrown export's side.

I got to my feet with my family and cheered for my boyfriend, reminding myself this was a charity fight and it was what Rhys wanted.

His gaze fell on me from the ring, and he gave me a cocky wink.

For him, I grinned through my nerves, reminded myself that whatever happened, Rhys and I had each other, and cupped my hands around my mouth and whooped right along with the rest of my friends and family. That was my guy up there.

Like penicillin, the X-ray, the pacemaker, and superglue, Rhys and I were an accidental discovery.

Unlike those aforementioned discoveries, no one but Rhys and I, and those in our inner circle, cared much about ours. Yet that seemed inconceivable as I stared up at the man I loved.

Because what I'd found in Rhys Morgan felt like a discovery for the ages.

TWENTY-THREE

Rhys

A LOT of people think boxers are thugs who just want to hit each other. That a boxing match was nothing more than two people exchanging blows. Bullshit. Boxing was a chess match, the sweet science. You needed to have a plan, to understand your opponent, timing, pacing—everything.

Boxing wasn't simply physical; it was mental as well. Because getting hit? That shit hurt. Worse? There would be seconds after a solid blow when the world would cease to exist. You'd forget your own name, your mind blanking out. And in those crucial seconds, a boxer needed to rely on muscle memory and pure animal instinct.

Parker had landed a solid, mind-altering hit when she told me she loved me.

She loved me.

Me, Rhys "the Widowmaker" Morgan. That smart, kind,

beautiful, perfect woman loved me. I was dazed, my body humming and numb, my head spinning. It was muscle memory that had me walking out of the locker room and toward the ring.

Jimmy was muttering vile curses and ranting about pretty ladies with shit timing. I might have agreed; it was never good for a boxer to lose focus seconds before a match. Then again, she fucking *loved* me.

Around me catcalls rang out, shouts and cheers. The announcer was yapping away. Humid air lay thick in the room. They were chanting my name like a prayer. I caught sight of Johnson. He was pumped, muscles gleaming and twitching, eyes sharp with focus. I should have felt the flutter of prematch nerves, especially given that this was a pseudo-comeback match. Instead? I felt elated. Fucking invincible.

I was loved. Not for what I could do for someone, but for me. Without even knowing it, I'd been waiting my whole life for that, for *her*. Parker. She was the reason I was here now. It was because of her that I was able to save my gym, that my brother and I were in a better place together, that I had a new direction in life.

I felt the shift inside me. The return of joy. It was clean and true once more. I loved this sport, loved what my body could do within the confines of those ropes.

A grin spread over my face as I met Johnson's gaze. His brows hitched. The action was fleeting, less than a second, but he might as well have blinked. I knew I'd caught him off guard and had him wondering what the fuck my smile was about.

Dean met me in my designated corner. "Hey. You all right? You got this strange look."

"Parker loves me." Yeah, I was grinning again.

"That'll do it." Gripping my shoulder, he gave it a squeeze. "Not that I can compete with that, but I wanted you to know, I love you too." A shadow passed his eyes and he blinked. "I mean it, Rhys. You're a pain in my ass but you're a great fucking brother. Always have been."

Emotion clogged my throat. "Shit, Dean. You trying to make me cry?"

Before he could answer with something smarmy, I hauled him to me and gave him a hug, then cuffed him on the back of the head with my glove. "Love you too, kid. We'll be all right, yeah?"

He pulled back. "I'm hot and single, you got a sweetheart like Parker to love you, and we've lined up enough sponsors to save the gym. Yeah, I guess we're not doing half bad."

We chuckled before he grew serious. "I've seen every fight you've been in, bro. Keep your head in it and you'll win. Remember?" His eyes gleamed. "Quick feet and ..."

"Fast hands," I finished. It was what we'd say to each other every time I'd get into the ring, be it for training, sparring, or an actual match.

Like that, I locked into place. I was ready.

Johnson was a friend, and we were both doing this for charity. That didn't mean he'd go easy on me or didn't want to win as much as I did. We faced off with a hard stare. And then it was on. The world around me faded.

Johnson was slightly bigger than me. He tended toward a more aggressive style, talking smack, swinging as soon as the bell rang. I used that to my advantage, dancing around him, not engaging. It drew him out, made him think I was afraid. Especially since I was known for power strikes.

He came for me, trying to daze and confuse with a jab. I dance away from one. Another, guarding my flank—body hits hurt like a motherfucker—and my face. But then, when he truly thought I was plunking out, I tap blocked him and followed with a hard jab of my own, getting him on the cheek.

He went on the offensive again, and I moved away, circling,

taking advantage and working to further disorient him. Quick feet. Move, draw him in, wear him down.

Johnson went for a right cross. I deflected, threw a flurry of jabs, danced back. My body was humming now, an instrument finely tuned. I saw an opening and surprised him by ducking in with a straight left that slammed into his face. He rocked back, sweat spraying in a wide arc, the scent of it mingling with blood.

His brow had split.

First blood. Johnson's eyes narrowed, and he finally got his head in the game.

From then on, it was grueling work. Hard. Painful. I shut down the pain and let my body do what it was trained for. This was a mind game, and I kept playing.

At some point, Jimmy poured water over my face and blotted the sweat out of my eyes. "Keep at the brow. You got him reaching, which is good. He's weaker in the left corner. Get him there."

"Yep." It was all I could say.

"He's also two seconds slower to recover when you get a hit on his right side."

Knew that. But I just blinked in acknowledgment. "Gonna switch it up now," I said to him.

Jimmy nodded with a gleam. We'd planned and trained for this.

Johnson was expecting the same pattern of play—that I'd try to draw him in by evading. The bell rang this time, and I flew out. Quick feet. Fast hands. I laid into him with a brutality I'd been storing within. Relentless jabs, crosses, and uppercuts.

I'd been known as the Widowmaker for a reason. I gave him cause to remember it. And when Johnson tried to spin off the ropes, hoping on momentum to carry him, I saw the opening. Most people would miss it if they blinked, I hit so fast. But, for me, the moment went slowly.

My left hook rippled up from the heels of my feet, firmly planted on the mat, over my torso, down my arm. I connected with the force of a freight train. Johnson toppled like a felled tree, flopping onto the mat. Knockout.

The crowd roared. But I stood there, chest heaving, body vibrating. Some boxers love the idea of a knockout. I used to. Nothing quite like ending a fight with a well-timed, perfect hit. It could be a high that took hours to come down from. That was before Jake.

Now, gore rose to my throat as Johnson's trainer and the doctors rushed in to check him out. The world tilted sickly.

Get up. Get up. Get up.

But he was out. I knew that. I could barely see him though the group of working docs, just his legs, stretched out, boxing boots pointing away from each other.

Someone grabbed my arm. Jimmy. "Great hit, kid!"

My ears were ringing. I couldn't breathe.

Get up. Get up.

Dean came to my other side, his voice tight but firm. "He'll be all right. Just a hard hit."

Hard hit. To the head. Why'd I do it?

Johnson's dark brown legs changed in my mind to pale ones. His red and white shorts became blue. Jake lying there, gone.

I was going to be sick. The crowd jostled. A camera pushed in my face.

Get up.

But then another touch, soft on my lower belly, a gentle stroke. I blinked and looked down. Parker stared up at me with wide brown eyes. "Rhys. It's okay."

Was it? I couldn't answer her.

She leaned into my side, heedless of the sweat. "Just breathe, baby."

Breathe. Was Johnson breathing?

But then ... movement. Johnson stirred, and I swear my legs nearly gave out. Slowly, they helped him sit up. He was dazed, his bell clearly rung. But he was alive. My breath finally came, exploding from me in silent sob.

I didn't fucking care what impression I made. I stalked forward and crouched down. His gaze was unfocused, and I put an arm on his shoulder to steady him. "Hey, man. You all right?"

It took him a second, but he answered slowly. "Good hit. Fucked me up."

A laugh, broken and weak, left me. "Yeah. Good match."

His gaze was still bleary, and I doubted he'd remember this. But he huffed, "Next time."

I knew what he meant. He'd return the favor next match. But this was it for me. As much as I loved the sport, I was officially done.

I had a new life now. For the first time in years, I couldn't wait for it to get started.

———

"I KNOW I shouldn't talk about it," Parker said the next day as she curled up next to me on my bed. Sunlight streamed in through the wall of windows and turned her skin a deep, glowing honey. "But watching you fight was sexy as ..." She bit her pink bottom lip.

"As fuck?" I supplied with a brow wiggle.

Her cheeks plumped on a grin, and she spread her hand over my abs. "Well, yes."

I chuckled but stopped as a shard of pain shot up my side. "Shit, don't make me laugh."

"Poor baby," she murmured, leaning in to kiss my chest. I was covered in bruises and had been in and out of ice baths to mitigate the pain. But her kisses were by far the best medicine. She'd taken me to bed and spent hours petting and stroking me. As much as my dick wanted to play, I wasn't up for that just yet and remained content just to be with her.

Stroking her silky hair, I laid back and sighed as she kissed her way over my chest and then stopped to press a soft one right on top of my heart. She pulled back with a small, pleased smile, like the simple act of being able to touch me was all that she needed. My breath hitched, warmth radiating outward from where she'd kissed me.

"I love you." My husky words pulsed between us, and Parker's eyes widened. With a shaking, battered hand, I cupped her cheek. "I forgot to tell you that."

I'd been sidelined by the knockout and the aftermath when everyone wanted a piece of me. But here and now, I could no longer contain it. I didn't want to.

Parker licked her lips quickly. "You don't have to say it just because I did—"

My thumb touched her bottom lip. "I said it because I meant it. With all of my heart, Parker." I pulled her near. "I love you. So fucking much, it scares me. So much, it fills me up and makes me think of nothing else. Loving you is like breathing. It's impossible not to do."

Her smile blossomed, and she leaned into my touch. "I love you too."

"Sometimes, I still can't believe it," I said softly.

"Why?"

I shrugged. "No one ever has."

"Then they never knew the real you."

This woman.

"I never bothered to show anyone until you."

Parker hummed, her fingers skimming over my jaw, avoiding the bruises. "Maybe you were just waiting for me."

I liked that idea and grinned. "Maybe I was." I kissed her, a simple meeting of lips, then drew back. "I think I knew you were it for me the second you 'shooed' me at the bar."

"Ha!" Her nose wrinkled with humor. "You couldn't stand me then."

"Not true. I thought you were hot and had a smart mouth." I kissed said mouth again. "A perfect combination. I have a good poker face, is all."

"It's a good face." Grinning, she attacked my face with butterfly kisses. "I love this face. I love you."

I'd never get over hearing that. My fingers slid into her hair as I cupped her head and looked into her eyes. "It's going to be so good, Parker. The two of us."

"I know," she said, the excitement in her smile matching what I felt coursing through me. "Because we already are."

EPILOGUE

Rhys

"Stop lowering your guard. Keep your fists up and your chin down, Tink."

Parker stopped in the center of the mat and put her hands on her hips with a huff. "If I do that, I can't see past these big gloves!"

She'd been at me to teach her to box, and I'd finally relented. But I knew she'd give me shit. I'd been anticipating it.

"That's because you keep pressing your gloves right up against your face," I said. "Which is a good way to get that pretty little nose busted."

"You bust my nose, Morgan, and I'm busting your nuts."

Laughing, I swung her up and cradled her against my chest. She was so tiny compared to me but fit just right. And though she glared, she was also smiling as she wrapped her arms around my neck. "Brute," she said.

"I'm the brute? You're the one threatening my nuts."

Her nose wrinkled. "That was a tactical error on my part, I agree. I need your bits in good working order."

I dipped my head and nuzzled her neck. "Maybe we should do an equipment check just to make sure."

She snorted but her lids lowered in that way that told me she'd be ready for me. "I never actually hit your nuts, Rhys."

"I won't tell if you don't." My hands slid to her pert ass, under her shorts where her skin was hot and silky. "You wet for me, Parker?"

She hummed, wrapping her legs around my waist to rock into me. "You're the one who wanted to do an equipment check —why don't you see for yourself?"

Growling, I was prepared to do just that when my brother's voice cut through my lust-filled fog like a chain saw.

"My eyes," he said dramatically. "Would you two have some care for the youth around here?"

I stopped, not putting Parker down, and turned to glare at him. "We're in my apartment."

Since the gym was in the middle of a remodel, there was too much dust and paint fumes downstairs, so we'd taken to working out in my loft's small home gym. Parker had been spending most of her time here over the past few months, and I was planning on asking her to move in.

A year ago, I might have thought moving in with a woman was too much of a commitment. Now, I couldn't wait. I wanted my things mingled with hers, to wake up to her face every morning and to kiss it good night for all the rest of mine.

"Consider this an educational moment," Parker added, clinging to me like a monkey.

I laughed. "Yeah, always remember to knock before entering."

Dean shook his head. "You're both hilarious. Really."

I finally let Parker down. "There a reason you're invading our privacy, Dean?"

His eyes crinkled at the corners, reminding me yet again of our mother. "Brought you some light reading." He tossed a folded-up copy of the *Boston Globe* my way.

I caught it midair and unfolded it. At my side, Parker gasped as she caught sight of the headline and picture of Franklin Fairchild.

A grin spread over my mouth. "So, the weaselly little fuck got indicted for fraud, huh?"

Parker grabbed the flopping edge of the paper and read over my arm. "Not just that. Sixteen counts, including embezzlement, tax evasion, and money laundering."

"I shouldn't gloat over someone else's misery but ..." I trailed off with a shrug. Because fuck that guy.

Parker's gaze was alight with mischief. "Bet he'd rather deal with sand snakes now, eh?"

When we both started laughing, Dean frowned. "You two are weird, you know that? You're morphing into a hive mind."

My arm wrapped around Parker's slim shoulders, and I drew her close. "You should be so lucky, little bro."

He scowled as though he'd sucked a lemon.

"He's making a face," Parker said *sotto voce*. "But one day it will happen to him, and we'll be there to remind him."

"Never," Dean vowed with the confidence of the ignorant.

I tossed down the paper. "For now, why don't we go out for a drink and celebrate?" Without waiting, I leaned down and slung Parker over my shoulder. She squealed loudly and slapped my ass.

But I knew she loved it when I carried her around—mainly because she told me, repeatedly. I lightly tapped her sweet ass in return and strode out of the room.

Dean followed with a sigh. "Okay, but tone it down when we're in public. People aren't supposed to be this happy."

That's where he was wrong. Being in love—being happy as fuck about it—was something we all deserved. I just didn't know it until I had it. And now that I had, I was never letting it go.

ACKNOWLEDGMENTS

While publishing isn't a solitary endeavor, for the most part writing always has been, so it's been a fantastic experience to have someone to share the process with. As fans of each other's books we found ourselves discussing co-writing together, which turned to excitement for the challenge and the decision to go for it. That shared respect and admiration for each other's work, and understanding of each other's process, made writing OUTMATCHED a pure joy. We hope you see that and smiled your way through the pages!

We want to thank our editor Jennifer Sommersby Young for diving into this collaboration with us to help make sure Rhys and Parker's story is its best self. On that note, a huge thanks to Tammy Blackwell and Kati Brown for beta reading and providing us with invaluable notes. Moreover, thank you to Melinda Utendorf for proofreading and helping to make the story as polished as it can be.

A thank you must be given to Dan Eager, who not only allowed us to use his PhD and career as that of Parker's, but who is an all-round fantastic human being making a difference in the world. Thank you, Dan!

The life of a writer doesn't stop with the book. Our job expands beyond the written word to marketing, advertising, graphic design, social media management and more. Help from those in the know goes a long way. Thank you to every single blogger, instagrammer and book lover who has helped spread the word about our books. You all are appreciated so much! On that note, a massive thank you to Nina Grinstead at Social Butterfly PR for agreeing to jump into this new venture with us. You're fantastic!

To our family and friends, for always encouraging and supporting us.

Also to Hang Le, for creating an adorable cover we love. You're so talented!

As always, thank you to our agents Lauren Abramo and Kimberly Brower for coming together to help us with this collaboration, and for making it possible for readers all over the world to find our words. We're so grateful to you.

And finally, the biggest thank you of all, to you our readers. Thank you for coming on this new adventure with us. We couldn't do it without you.

ABOUT THE AUTHORS

Kristen Callihan is an author because there's nothing else she'd rather be. She is a *New York Times*, *Wall Street Journal*, and *USA Today* best seller. Her novels have garnered starred reviews from *Publishers Weekly* and *Library Journal*. Her debut book, *Firelight*, received *RT* magazine's Seal of Excellence and was named a best book of the year by *Library Journal*, best book of spring 2012 by *Publishers Weekly*, and best romance book of 2012 by ALA RUSA. When she's not writing, she's reading.

Visit Kristen Callihan online
www.kristencallihan.com
Kristen.Callihan@aol.com
Twitter @Kris10Callihan
Instagram@kristen_callihan
Facebook Kristen Callihan

Samantha Young is a *New York Times*, *USA Today* and *Wall Street Journal* bestselling author from Scotland. She's been nominated for the Goodreads Choice Award for Best Author and Best Romance for her international bestseller *On Dublin Street*. *On Dublin Street* is Samantha's debut adult contemporary romance series and has sold in thirty countries.

Visit Samantha Young online
www.authorsamanthayoung.com
Twitter @AuthorSamYoung
Facebook Author Samantha Young
Instagram @AuthorSamanthaYoung

***

CPSIA information can be obtained
at www.ICGtesting.com
Printed in the USA
BVHW030553030820
585313BV00001B/24